GLYCOSIS

(glī-kō′sĭs)

D0233714

GLYCOSIS

(glī-kō′sĭs)

A NOVEL BY

LAURENCE D. CHALEM

LOVE IN A HOSTILE, SUGAR-COATED WORLD

GLYCOSIS

ISBN: 1463511310
ISBN-13: 978-1463511319
Library of Congress Control Number: 2011909083

SUGARLESS BOOKS
San Jose, California

Printed in the United States of America
10 9 8 7 6 5 4 3 2 1

...hugest whole creation may be less
incalculable than a single kiss

—E. E. CUMMINGS
October, 1962

Psychosis (sī-kō′sǐs) *noun;* **Psychotic** (sī-kŏt′ǐk) *adjective*
(1) Abnormal condition of the mind.
(2) A severe mental disorder, with or without organic damage, characterized by derangement of personality and loss of contact with reality causing deterioration of normal social functioning.

Psycho (sī′kō) *noun*
A slang word for a person who is psychotic.

Glycosis (glī-kō′sǐs) *noun;* **Glycotic** (glī-kŏt′ǐk) *adjective*
(1) Abnormal condition of sugar in the body.
(2) A physical disorder comprised of too much glucose in the blood (BG). Although low BG is acutely more serious, high BG can lead to complications such as extreme hunger and thirst, fat, muscle or bone loss, frequent urination, depression, dementia, agitation, lethargy, loss of vision, loss of sensation, immune suppression, renal failure, liver and cardiovascular disease, gangrene, coma and death.
(3) Quantifiable maladaptation to carbohydrate(s). Example: if a species that uses glucose as its sole energy source is forced to consume a different carbohydrate instead, the survival rate would serve as the measure of adaptation or maladaptation to that fare. The lower the survival rate, the more the species as a whole is maladapted, the higher the glycosis. In omnivores, glycosis manifests as various afflictions.

Glyco (glī′kō) *noun*
(1) The chemical prefix for sweetness or sugar.
(2) A slang word for a person who is glycotic.

CONTENTS

Prologue

A moment of blinding flash later, picture travelling out from the Sun as Louis Armstrong's 1968 recording of "What a Wonderful World" begins.

"I see trees of green...red roses too...
I see them bloom...for me and you...
And I think to myself...what a wonderful world.

I see skies of blue...clouds of white...
The bright blessed day...the dark say good night...
And I think to myself...what a wonderful world."

Quickly we approach the bright rocky planet of Mercury, a stark landscape peppered with craters. Regions of smooth plains are visible and the Caloris Basin, a crater larger than France comes into view. Just as soon as we became acquainted, we turn slightly and pass, moving toward another sphere in the far distance.

"I hear babies cryin'...I watch them grow...
They'll learn much more...than I'll ever know...
And I think to myself...what a wonderful world...
Yes, I think to myself...what a wonderful world..."

As with Mercury, Venus is in a counter-clockwise, elliptical orbit of the Sun with an average distance of sixty-seven million miles, which means we've travelled an additional thirty-one million miles. Unlike Mercury, this planet spins clockwise and is smothered in sulphuric acid clouds. Venus's surface is hotter than Mercury's despite being nearly twice as far from the Sun. Noteworthy for sure; but, we move on...

"The colors of a rainbow...so pretty in the sky...
Are there on the faces...of people going by...
I see friends shaking hands...saying how do you do...
They're really sayin'...I love you...

I hear babies cry...I watch them grow...
You know they're gonna learn...
A whole lot more than I'll ever know...
And I think to myself...what a wonderful world..."

Twenty-five million miles more or so and we reach Earth's Moon. There's a giant crater on the South Pole — the Aitken Basin — some fourteen-hundred miles in diameter and eight miles deep, the largest known crater in the Solar System.

And then, slightly more than a quarter million miles away, about a second later, Earth. From the Sun's perspective, it's a second, albeit cooler Venus, spinning counter-clockwise on its axis, in counter-clockwise, elliptical orbit around the Sun, replete with a dense, tidally-locked satellite, which in turn orbits it, counter-clockwise.

"Yes I think to myself...what a wonderful world."

See now in your mind's eye being just inside Earth's atmosphere, looking down on the brightly-lighted Western-most portion of the United States at night. Had we moved at the speed of light from the Sun, it would have taken us about 8 ½ minutes. We traversed the distance in about 2 ½ minutes, almost 3 ½ times the speed of light. Impossible; save, perhaps, for a healthy imagination.

The lights go out quickly in sections from the middle-left at land's end, toward the east.

Our Heroine

Your continued imagination is needed to set the scene; it will be called upon later as well. For now, visualize slowly descending from the sky. Just below the clouds, accompanied by crescendos and decrescendos of wind, is an ocean on the left, land mass to the right.

"Another beautiful day in San Diego," a radio disc-jockey began. You could nearly hear the wide smile on his face as he continued, "Seventy-two degrees, sunny, a little more humid than normal, with a cool, gentle breeze coming in from the Pacific Ocean, just like yesterday."

San Diego, with its top four industries of manufacturing, defense, tourism, and agriculture now fill the frame. As we descend, deep canyons and hills separating *mesas* — elevated areas of land with flat tops and steep cliffs for sides — can be seen. They look like large, solid, naturally shaped tables; apt because that's what the Spanish word means.

"Yeah, not even a power-failure could put the kibosh on that," said the second announcer, a female.

Near the top of our view is what looks like most of a nuclear accelerator, a backwards "C," no doubt serving also as the headquarters of some corporate behemoth. Slightly to the left and lower, there is a full-size running track, then, a soccer field. In the middle, underneath a large swath of dark vegetation with trails, we see a large, concrete square, buttressed by vegetation on all sides, with some sort of octagonal edifice in the middle; below that, single buildings, groups of buildings, and winding roads.

A number of unique habitats are visible. One such habitat in San Diego are drought-resistant shrubs called *chaparral* along the coast, though they used to occupy the majority of the area. The endangered Torrey pine, named after botanist John Torrey, has most of its three-thousand remaining individuals in a stretch of that protected *chaparral*.

It looks as though we're going to land in the center of the frame, near an octagonal looking structure. Only, as we descend closer, it's not octagonal. It looks more like a lantern.

"What in the world happened last night?"

"Well, it wasn't from this world, Bob," said the female host, Denise, adding sound effects of a few people saying "Oooo," and "Oh."

She continued, "And our guest this morning is going to tell us about it. We ére joined in the studio with Dr. Sabeena Chandrasekhar, a cosmologist with Skripps Observatory. Hi Sabeena, welcome to the program." She added a track of modest applause.

"Hi Denise, hi Bob," responded a sultry, deep-voiced female that sounded perfectly natural on radio.

"So tell us Dr. Chandrasekhar, is this another reason to have the power industry more tightly regulated?"

We have reached ground. Think of us now repositioning our view from vertical to horizontal, temporarily fixed near a concrete and glass apparition nestled in a canyon surrounded by distant Torrey pines. This dense, concrete wraith, a massive, six-story lantern, a diamond-stepped fortress, dramatically opened up to the sky, stabbed on the sides by strips of windows, is an imposing work of architecture.

Cradling the cantilevered tower are sixteen huge, angled, thick concrete columns sprouting from the base. The fortification is known as Geisel Library and was named in honor of Audrey S. and Theodor Seuss Geisel, the creator of the Dr. Seuss children's book series and his wife, for the couple's contributions to the library and their efforts to combat illiteracy. It was designed by William Leonard Pereira in the late sixties.

The first group of people to come into focus are students, judging from their garb of sweats, jeans and unique, wrinkled t-shirts, right near a Cat-in-the-Hat® sculpture. They have formed a circle around a thin female with stringy, blond hair, carrying a sign and speaking. A little closer in and at a better angle, we see that her sign is one of those anti-abortion signs with a real-life color picture of a terminated fetus, the blood in bright red. The sign's caption read: "This is what you support when you support abortion." For students there, it is entertaining; several of them are eating an early candy dinner, and different kinds of potato chips are visible in different students' hands. Frito-Lay® Lay's® Original Potato Chips here, Proctor & Gamble Cheddar Cheese Pringles® over there, still another student eating a cherry Hostess® Fruit Pie®. The one holding the sign wasn't eating anything; she was speaking.

Fortunately, we can't hear her. We only hear the radio of one of the two older, distinguished men sitting near the scene, taking their afternoon break from work or study.

"No, not at all," Dr. Chandrasekhar began. What we had last night was a typical coronal mass ejection."

"So that's what it was," the male announcer said. "Can you explain what that is?"

"It would be my pleasure," said Dr. Chandrasekhar. "A coronal mass ejection is a burst of solar wind being released into space. Coronal mass ejections release huge quantities of matter, magnetic fields and electromagnetic radiation into space above the Sun's surface, near the corona, farther into the planet system or beyond. And in this case it went well beyond."

"It sure did," replied the female host. She added some sound effects similar to a bike horn, as radio announcers often do, then said, "Please do tell us more."

Dr. Chandrasekhar continued, "When the ejection is directed toward the Earth, the shock wave of the traveling mass of solar energetic particles — which may contain small quantities of elements such as helium, oxygen, and iron — causes a geomagnetic storm that may disrupt the Earth's magnetosphere, compressing it on the day side and extending the night-side magnetic tail. When the magnetosphere reconnects on the night-side, it releases power on the order of terawatt scale, which is directed back toward the Earth's upper atmosphere."

"Uh, okay," replied the male host, Bob. He added some of his own sound effects, reminiscent of bells and applause.

Said the female host, Denise, "Yes, fascinating, please tell us more Sabeena." She did not add sound effects.

"Sure," Dr. Chandrasekhar said. "This process can cause particularly strong auroras in large regions around Earth's magnetic poles. These are also known as the northern lights — *aurora borealis* — in the northern hemisphere, and the southern lights — *aurora australis* — in the southern hemisphere.

Bob interjected here, "Yeah, thanks Dr. Chandrasekhar, I always get those confused. Just like stalactites and stalagmites, I never remember which are pointed up from the ground and which are formed from above hanging down."

Sabeena laughed. "Well, Bob, just remember, anything with the prefix 'australo' or something similar means southern, so the *auroura australis* are the southern lights, and, well, stalagmites and stalactites, well, uh, that's something altogether different. Those are named after the word 'drip,' and are formed in caves from leakage of water and calcite, the predominant mineral in limestone. The ones hanging down from the ceiling are spelled with a 'C' and a 'T' as in stalactite, and the ones formed from them on the ground are spelled with a 'G' and an 'M' as in stalagmite. When they connect over time, they are then collectively called a column. Anyway, think 'C' for ceiling and I think you've got it."

Bob hit the applause sound effect button and simply said, "Thanks Sabeena." He was astounded.

"I think you've given Bob, and our listening audience quite an education on that one, Sabeena, thank you," Denise said as she hit the applause button.

Sabeena laughed and said, "You know, coronal mass ejections originating from active regions on the Sun's surface, such as groupings of sunspots associated with frequent flares, along with solar flares of other origin, can disrupt radio transmissions and cause damage to satellites and electrical transmission line facilities, resulting in potentially massive and long-lasting power outages. Humans in space or at high altitudes, for example, in airplanes, risk exposure to intense radiation. Short-term damage might include skin irritation. Long-term consequences might include an increased risk of developing skin cancer."

"So they really can harm us folks on the ground, huh," Bob added.

"Well, yes they can," Sabeena began again, "but they're not deadly. There are far worse things out there, like gamma rays, black holes, or getting hit by an asteroid big enough to increase or decrease our orbit around the Sun, or, perhaps stop the Earth from spinning. If that happened, and forgetting for the moment the eleven-hundred plus mile per hour winds that would be formed when the Earth stopped spinning, our day and night cycle would be the same as the year. There would be two seasons: bad, and worse. I'm not sure what it would take to accomplish that, but to kill us quickly, we'd need an asteroid bigger than Mars. Something like Venus would do the trick."

Neither host uttered a word.

Sabeena attempted to reassure her hosts, "Don't worry, though, nothing like that is expected to happen in the next few billion years or so."

Denise hit the applause button and said, "Thank God for people like you Sabeena."

"Yes, Sabeena, thanks for coming out to the studio today," Bob said. "Please come again; but, don't wait for the next interplanetary coronal mass ejection."

"It was my pleasure. Thanks for having me."

"Okay," Bob began, "that was Dr. Sabeena Chandrasekhar, a cosmologist with Skripps Observatory educating us about coronal mass ejections, like the one — the interplanetary one — we had last night."

Denise interjected, "And do you remember the difference between a stalactite and a stalagmite, Bob?"

"Well, of course I do, Denise," Bob said, then paused.

"I didn't think so," retorted Denise.

Just a moment after she hit the laughter track, Bob began his queued teaser, "Coming up after the break, a species of ant native to South America has been found in Southern California. The Leafcutter ant, otherwise known as the agricultural ant because it maintains and feeds fungus in its colony for its eventual use as food, may be making a new home for itself in San Diego due to the availability of the fungus and our marvelous — though unseasonably humid — weather." He paused for just a second and added, "Well, if it isn't Earth's destruction by black holes, asteroids, or gamma rays, it's world domination by ants."

Denise laughed briefly and added, "We'll be right back with more news and the best music in Southern California right after the break."

We panned the area during the broadcast from the left of the library counter-clockwise, taking in the sights on the tree-lined, concrete covered ground: a pro-life demonstrator and the group surrounding — probably heckling — her, trees, small buildings, parking spaces, dormitories, some lecture halls, bike and walking paths and back again. We saw several differently sized groups, individuals, then, near where we started, just one thin, unassuming, black-haired young woman.

Dressed in black jeans and a non-descript long-sleeve black cotton shirt, blue sandals without socks, her toenails polished and multi-colored with sparkles, she was squatting, smoking a slim, white, filtered cigarette. Her large Louis Vuitton purse was leaning up against her left side like an old friend. It was Friday, the end to the first week of her freshman year.

In the background, the man with the radio turned it off, got up, and, together with another similarly dressed man, left the scene, probably to another campus building.

Our heroine is not Jane Crofut, from the Crofut Farm, Grover's Corners, Sutton County, New Hampshire, United States of America, Continent of North America, Western Hemisphere, the Earth, the Solar System, the Universe, the Mind of God. It is Chun Hei Park, "Michelle" as she liked to be known in America, a good Korean daughter somewhat trying to fit in to the culture, yet not really sure if the US was really where she wanted to spend the rest of her life. As she liked to live her life, her name means "justice and grace."

That's Chun Hei "Michelle" Park, student, from the University of California, San Diego, San Diego County, California, USA, Continent of North America, Western Hemisphere, the Earth, the Solar System—which, interestingly, *is* the name of our solar system—the Milky Way Galaxy, the Local Group, the Virgo Super Cluster, the Universe, perhaps within the Multiverse.

Michelle was born and raised in Busan, located on the coast of the southeastern tip of the South Korean peninsula. It is the fifth largest port in the world based on container traffic, after Singapore, Shanghai, Hong Kong, and Shenzhen. With a population slightly less than four million, Busan is the second largest metropolis in South Korea after Seoul.

Michelle hailed from a famous, wealthy and traditional residential area called *Dongnae-gu*—a *gu* is equivalent to a district—a few miles inland, close to a natural spa area with many public baths, tourist hotels, restaurants, clubs, and shopping. Much like Los Angeles, Santa Monica, and Beverly Hills, California, all combined, it is the summer capital of Korea since it attracts tourists from all over the country to its six beaches and carnival style boardwalk.

Before coming to the US to study English and literature, she loved to watch and listen to the Wonder Girls, an all-girl

Korean pop musical and dance group. She was the best singer in her circle of friends, though you wouldn't know that meeting her. Yes, she was shy in public.

Toward the end of high school Michelle wanted to be different. Sick of the same-old-same-old, she would dye her hair blond, pink, brown, or whatever color she, her hairdresser or friends would have on hand. She dreamed of going to the States to study something impractical or rebellious like English. Anything but accounting or law like her mother and father studied and now practiced. She certainly had the grades, having scoring well on math, physics, and chemistry classes in high school, and the wherewithal to do it. The trust fund that her parents set up for her had matured, as had their daughter, and at the ripe old age of eighteen, both fund and daughter were ready to go their separate ways. And there was nothing her parents could do to stop her. Secretly, they were happy for her and wished her the best. To her face, however, it was another story.

Mixed emotions is what she felt, exacerbated by her brother, whom she remembered telling her that she should be quiet among guys that she wanted to date, perhaps even giggle a little bit. Yes, men liked to feel smarter than women in her country, and it is still common. That men aren't smarter — or dumber — she implicitly knew; but, she always harbored the dream to meet a smart, American guy that would support her pursuits and be happy for her successes. Whether she would act on that dream, or wind up like her mother raising kids and taking care of the house — still a noble endeavor — was something that she never resolved. But she was going to try.

UCSD was another world, diverse to say the least. Michelle was now immersed in nearly every culture under the Sun. Well, maybe she wasn't so much immersed as she was simply near. While wanting to meet new people, she was just too shy initially to introduce herself to them. Apart from orientation and short, instructor-led introductions on the first day of classes, she felt compelled to be reserved the rest of the time, as happens to most people. Nevertheless, being here was what she wanted, and, if she could have heard what was in her mother's head before she made the decision to matriculate, she would have heard "be careful what you wish for."

It's Friday. Michelle had finished her first week of classes, and she was waiting for her friends to go have some dinner, sing along to some K-Pop, go to a bar, and then get some sleep. Saturday will be her first day studying without having to attend class, and she wanted to get a good night's sleep. Of course, that's what she thought going in to most Friday nights, however, she knew that she will probably sleep in.

She drew somewhat belligerently from her cigarette, still squatting, as the density of passing students increased during the class transition period. Two boys walked by her, staring, and one of the boys said, "Hi there." She didn't smile, didn't even look their way.

A larger group of fraternity boys passed by, all eyes on her, and each of them went from dumbfounded, to excited, to trying to say something, to stumbling with lines such as, "Hiya," and "Wow," and "Hey, uh, what's your name." She again didn't even acknowledge their presence. It's situation normal. Yup, they think she's "hot," and she doesn't much think so. She got the same crap—being objectified—in Korea and thought the US would be different. Nope. Wouldn't some nice guy like her for her? Weren't there any smart guys that wanted to get to know her first, without looking then judging her based on her looks, body or butt? Nope. Are all guys the same? Well, yes, maybe they are, she thought. Women and men everywhere must certainly appreciate kindness and intelligence; maybe women might add wealth and status to the list. Men, she thought, seem to add beauty and youth to the list. Or maybe they start by thinking about beauty and youth, and then add kindness and intelligence. Maybe, maybe not.

A couple of wolf whistles later, Michelle's smiling, sweet, black-haired friends approached. She happily acknowledged them as she dropped her cigarette, smothering it with a graceful squish and twist beneath her petite right foot.

"*Ahn young,*" Michelle said smiling.

"*Ahn young,*" the taller girl, Kimmy, said first, echoed by Shirley. They were both also originally from South Korea. Shirley's real name was Sang Hee Lee, meaning "sunlight," and Kimmy's name was Eu-Ju Kim, Korean for "golden pearl." Both were pretty, wore little, if any, make-up, and were dressed in jeans with pastel-colored t-shirts. Naturally, both were thin, yet Shirley appeared particularly delicate.

"Let's go," Michelle happily blurted out.

"It's Miller time!" Shirley said, though it sounded more like "mirror time," an inside joke that frequented their conversations. You see, they often played upon the concept of Engrish, which refers to incorrect English originating in East Asian countries. The term itself satirizes the frequent habit of people from Japan to confuse the English phonemes "R" with "L," since the Japanese language has one alveolar consonant in place of both. The three young women's humor derived from the fact they were each from Korea, where there is no confusion between Rs and Ls, yet some people they met from America made fun of them because some Americans thought that all Asian-looking people confuse the consonants.

There is, of course, a great difference between Japanese and English. Japanese word order, the frequent omission of subjects in Japanese, the absence of articles such as "the" and "a," as well as difficulties in distinguishing "L" and "R" all contribute to substantial problems of native Japanese speakers utilizing English effectively. But that was irrelevant to Michelle, Shirley, and Kimmy, and all other Koreans living in the US. Thus, while they made jokes about it together in private, they were insulted when having to deal with it in public, taking it just like any other individual from any other group responds to a stereotypical comment.

The three musketeers began walking toward Kimmy's car.

"Mung's or Lek's?" Shirley asked.

"Rrrek's! Definitely Rrrek's," Michelle said excitedly, knowing full-well that she pronounced it with an "R." They all giggled.

"Cleaner bathrooms," Kimmy added.

Shirley and Michelle stopped walking, looked at each other, then both at Kimmy, also now stopped, then again at each other. They all smiled as if they knew what each other were thinking, and then said together, "Boys."

Giggling, strolling away, intermittently leaning against each other, they began their night's adventure. It would be dinner, karaoke, and, apparently, Lek's.

A few hours later, Kimmy, Shirley and Michelle got out of Kimmy's compact car—her mom had promised it to her if she got into a good college in the States—and together, they walked down Bower Drive, having had to park about a block away. Two large buildings on each side of the street came sharply into view. On the right-hand side was a newer-looking two story building and on the left, an older, similar sized building. Although it had ivy covering most of it, the soot was noticeable from afar. The large building signage on the right displayed Lek's logo, a full-frontal view of a big, beautifully colored, Indian blue peacock displaying its entire train; which, by the way, is made up of very elongated upper-tail, covert feathers, and is not really a tail.

Mung's logo, on the left, displayed a huge, fierce, yellow-spotted millipede, standing upright, with three-quarters of its body raised in the air, somewhat in an S-shape, ready to take on the world.

Michelle, Kimmy and Shirley walked toward Lek's front door. Two bouncers standing side-by-side scanned the three girls, smiled at each other, and then each opened their door.

Dark, quiet, and a little eerie, the three girls walked in while the music changed and the lights dimmed. An electric guitar was then heard playing a slow melody. It was the introduction to the song "Party," by the rock group Boston. The twenty-second introduction ended and then the singer began up-tempo and highly energized. Lights flashed with special effects, and the crowd yelled along with the music.

"Oh yeah!
Well you know I don't get off on workin' day after day
I wanna have some fun while I'm here
I play the game when it's goin' my way
And there's nothin' like a party when it's kickin' into gear."

Now, Lek's was unique among bars in the area, and bars in general. Within a square building, it was made up of a large, open, two-story square space, built around a huge, sunken, circular dance floor, with long, wooden, independent bars at three sides on the first floor — the entrance, sandwiched between a rather large gift shop and waiting area made up the fourth side — with tables on the first and second floor overlooking the dance floor. A ten-foot hallway with men's and women's restrooms on the left side, leading to swinging double-doors hiding the kitchen in the back, and a raised disc jockey booth to the right, looking in from the entrance, completed the interior.

Hung from the second floor, surrounding the entire dance floor, and at each bar, were rows of plasma TVs, each tuned to a different sports channel: football, baseball, basketball, college and pro, hockey, car racing, horse racing, and others. On each of the screens was a large sign with the specific game being broadcast and its approximate broadcast time. Thus, the bar positively reinforced coming early to grant each patron the opportunity to sit within viewing range of the particular sport and game they wanted to see. And games could be seen from the dance floor.

In general, the bar attracted guys and the guys attracted girls. While it's common among males to think they have the pick of the females, the more realistic interpretation is that girls have the pick of the guys. At Lek's, females tended to choose males after seeing them dance; a girl has to know what the goods looked like up close and in action as compared to other males, whether any one particular suitor has a neat, thin behind, unique moves, was clean and even-tempered, and more. Although the bar looked like fun and games, food and good times, it was really struggle and contestation amongst the guys for at least temporary possession of a desirable female. Beer, food, videos, music and the many sportscasts served as some compensation for those males that left empty handed.

Michelle, Shirley and Kimmy looked around for a couple seconds, listening to the music and raucous crowd.

"I'm getting' ready for a party tonight
Yes I'm getting' ready to cruise
And if you've got somethin' for me
I've got somethin' for you."

The three musketeers began their walk around the bar, looking for a table to sit down at to have a drink or two and maybe nibble on something more American while the music blared. As they walked in the nearly packed bar, with other people looking for a table, and still more folks coming in behind them, a mixture of beer, cheese, onion rings, French fries, and ketchup piqued their appetite again, even though they had been eating while singing karaoke not an hour earlier.

"Baby
It's a party and nobody cares
What we're doin' there
Baby, it's a party as long as you're there
It's a party, party, party!"

As they walked around, they couldn't help but stare at the huge portions on the tables with food. The two guys at the very first table had a pitcher of beer and a humungous plate of chips covered with beef, chicken, salsa, guacamole, tomatoes, and who knows what else. And lots of napkins. The dish, as our three musketeers would later find out, was called "the World."

"I can't believe it when some people say
That it's a sin that way we live to die
You know, there's never been a more natural thing
Yea there's a brand new story, but it's the same old lie."

They made their way toward a table in the back that they saw still had some dishes, but was probably open. While they looked at the tables, the food on those tables, and the guys sitting and eating there, those guys were looking at them. And as they passed each table of mostly guys, stares followed them. At first the gazes landed upon their faces, then, as they passed, nearly every guy at every table looked at them from behind. Strike that. They looked *at* their behinds, and made mostly lewd comments not intended for them to hear, and, given the music's volume, shouldn't have heard. But they did.

"Nice legs," from the table just passed. "Hey baby," they heard from the next, "Ooooooo, mama," and "Hey, come back here," they heard from just further back. "I'd like to get in there," some guy said from another direction. They each just kept their eyes on the prize and headed toward the open table. So, it was guys, food, and more guys, more food. No one was dancing yet; it was too early for that. In the vernacular, it was a dude ranch: mostly guys. They were almost at the open table.

"So come on
Get ready for the time of your life
'cause I'm getting' right in the groove
And if you've got somethin' for me
I've got somethin' for you

Baby
It's a party and nobody cares
What we're doin' there
Baby, it's a party as long as you're there
It's a party, party, party!
So come on."

"We made it!" Shirley said in perfect English, so happy to have found a table. They all spoke near-perfect English, actually, though they did get confused from time to time regarding some idiomatic expressions. Oh, and double entendres too, especially those with the sexual innuendos and connotations. Kimmy sat next to Shirley, and then Michelle sat down across from the other two in that fine, beer smelling, table freshly wiped with a soapy, though still bacteria infested, wet, dish rag. They were happy to have a table.

"Yea yea yea yea get down and party if you need a cue
You're sure to find one in the crowd
Just meet some friends and have a toke or two
In a place where they can never play the music too loud."

A server came to their table right after they sat down. She said, "Hi girls. You want something to drink? Oh, I love your t-shirt, it's so pretty, and I like your shoes, so you!"

"Thanks," smiled Michelle. "How about a pitcher of, uh, some light beer, we don't care which."

"Okay hun, give me a couple minutes." The server, a slightly heavy girl that could have been a college student, but wasn't, noticeably prepared herself for the next table—all guys—by taking a deep breath and focusing. She forced a smile upon her face and walked to their table, asking them, "What's up guys. Can I get you anything else?"

"Another pitcher of beer and can I get an order of phone number," one of the guys said. The waitress just laughed and went to get them their beer.

"I love this place," Kimmy shouted.

"Well, it only gets better when the dancing starts. Which reminds me, when does it start?" Shirley asked.

"I guess when most of the games end," Michelle added.

"Get ready for a party tonight
'cause I'm getting' right in the groove
And if you've got somethin' for me
I've got somethin' for you
You know what I'm talkin' about."

She was referring to the plasma screens which were each telecasting different games from different sports: college and professional basketball, baseball, soccer, and even a girls' volleyball game. Yes, the bar had not only spent a great deal on the audio-visual system, but also had every imaginable sports channel via cable, Dish Network and the like. In any case, all possible ESPN channels were being broadcasted on the plasmas, and then some.

"Baby
It's a party and nobody cares
What we're doin' there
Baby, it's a party as long as you're there
It's a party, party, party!"

"You know a man doesn't live on bread alone
He's got to have some lovin' each and every night
And a woman's got to have it if the truth be known
Let's get together honey, it's alright (repeated twice)
Oh, get down, get down and party."

The lights came down immediately after the song and the Deejay began his opening remarks, "Okay, sports fans, it's time to get this party started. We have a long mix of tunes coming your way kickin' it off with Katy Perry and Snoop Dogg in "California Gurls" [sic]. So come on down to the dance floor!"

All the plasma screens went black for a moment, then a pink, white and blue box with what looked like the mirror image of the word "Candyland" spelled backwards in all caps on the top right — it actually spelled out "Candyfornia" — amid a similar background of pink, white and blue clouds. This brief scene wiped to Snoop Dogg seated at a table of pastries, dressed in a colorful, pastel suit with a pink tie, who introduced the song by saying, "Greetings loved ones, let's take a cherry."

Here, Katy Perry, dressed in a skimpy skirt with white hosiery on her legs, started singing, *"I know a place, where the grass is really greener..."*

The video was compelling. It featured candy and skimpily clad women in every scene, with intermittent rap by Snoop Dogg and singing by, well, Katy Perry. Everyone seemed to like it, though not many people got up to dance; instead, nearly everyone watched the video and ate the various snacks, appetizers, and dinner on their tables. Of course, the full bar of patrons were drinking beer and other mixed drinks too.

The three musketeers enjoyed the music and the scantily clad women didn't faze them. In fact, they liked it. They watched some of the people get on the dance floor.

It wasn't long before the waitress came to their table with two pitchers of beer and some big, red, plastic cups.

"Here you go girls," the waitress said, as she placed both pitchers of beer and red plastic cups on the table.

"Did you want to start a tab?" she asked.

"No, that's okay," Kimmy said, handing her a twenty. The waitress took the twenty dollar bill, reached into her apron pocket to take out some change, and handed it to Kimmy. Kimmy gave her a couple bucks.

"Thanks ladies," the waitress said, "can I get you anything else right now, snacks or something?" She picked up the other pitcher of beer that was destined for the thirsty, rowdy group of male college students at the next table.

"That's okay," Michelle said. "Just come back and check on us in a while." The waitress smiled as she walked away.

No sooner had the waitress left than Shirley grabbed the pitcher and poured some beer into her new cup. When she was done, she started pouring some into the other cups, passing them to her friends as she filled them.

"Boys," she said, raising her cup and making a toast.

"Boys," Michelle said, tapping her cup to Shirley's, spilling some of each of their beers. Kimmy knocked her cup to their cups too, spilling more from each. They each laughed then took a sip. Of course, they were all still a little buzzed from dinner, having had some beer with their meal, K-Pop videos, and karaoke at the Korean restaurant they went to earlier. They watched and listened to the music video, as they drank.

The next tune to come up on both plasma screens and speakers was "Amazing," by the female performer Inna. It fit San Diego and this bar nicely given the scenes of surfers, surf, and beach-goers.

The girls watched the beginning of the song on the plasmas, drinking their beer, intermittently looking around at the people, the food, and the folks on the dance floor, which wasn't full, but growing. The song didn't so much motivate them to dance, but they knew eventually something would come on that would.

After about three minutes, the video ended and "Hey Baby," by Pitbull, featuring T-Pain, came on.

The three girls looked at each other, seemingly telepathing "let's dance." They each slowly raised their eyebrows a couple times and smiled. Apparently their telepathy was in working order; they got up at nearly the same time and headed to the dance floor. Shirley stayed at the edge of the bench for a moment, grabbed her beer and chugged it down before catching up to the other two.

They joined the several people that were now dancing on the floor and got down to business, not really moving very fast, just kind of making it their introductory dance. More patrons joined them on the dance floor as time passed.

Several guys around the perimeter were checking them out; the girls returned the favor by checking them out at the same time. It was all fairly innocent.

The three or so minutes of the song went by pretty fast, when it was broken up by the deejay's own mix of trance-like electronic drum beats, which would serve as an extended link to the next song.

It was here that an older guy walked into the bar. *He* didn't look like any student: clean cut, slacks, belt, tight shirt — kind of like a turtle neck, only thinner and more stylish — they could see the outline of *his* buff, eight-pack abs right behind *his* tight, clinging sweater. If the pullover-shirt-sweater had a name for when this guy wore it, it would be called "Washboard." And it wasn't just the three of them that noticed *him*. It seemed from all the turned heads of the other women that were there, that all the gals knew *he* was there. *He* looked for his spot; apparently *he* was a regular.

"*Wah! Chal sang gyuh dah!*" meaning "Whoa! He's hot," Shirley said loud enough over the music for the others to hear.

"*Mah juh! Chal sang gyuh dah!*" for "Yes! He's hot," Michelle replied.

"*Jinh cha dah!*," Kimmy added, which meant "Seriously!"

They continued to dance to the extended trance link, all the while changing between looking at each other dance, closing their eyes in their own erotic world of dancing, and looking at *him*. They did look good dancing and probably knew it.

Tight sweater guy didn't walk around long, *he* just walked up through the dance floor, and right to the head table on the right-hand side. A waitress was there waiting for *him* and took *his* order. Almost immediately a group of girls joined *him*.

The tune "Single Ladies (Put a Ring on It)," by Beyoncé came up next. Instantly recognizable, many more people moved toward then on the dance floor; it was filling up quickly.

This video featured Beyoncé and two other girls wearing tight, revealing black outfits, in high heels, singing and strutting about. All the girls on the floor loved it, and so too did our three musketeers. Most tried to imitate the moves on the video; Shirley, Michelle and Kimmy did too for a while, but eventually they performed some individualized strutting of their own.

This action did not go unnoticed by other guys, and, yes, eight-pack abs man. *He* chugged his drink down and headed to the dance floor.

Kimmy leaned over to Shirley and said fairly loudly, "*He's* coming." Michelle looked at the two of them, then to that guy who was getting closer, looked at Shirley and Kimmy, and knew exactly what Kimmy had said.

That guy was trailed by three beauties of his own. They started dancing on the edge of the dance floor; but, as the song developed, they moved closer and closer to the middle. The rest of the folks on the floor let *him* move there, as if that was *his* rightful place.

"Single Ladies" doesn't last very long—about three minutes—and, after a very short electric drum and base line link provided by the deejay, a somewhat unknown song came on. It had a relatively fast, driving beat to it.

They had never heard this song before, but it had a good, fast rhythm to it, so they kept dancing. A little crass for some, the song's name is an immediately accessible double entendre, for native speakers, anyway, which probably, for the moment, escaped our girls' current idiomatic understanding. Titled "Bumpy Ride," and performed by Mohombi, the video shows different people on different four-wheeled ATV vehicles, driving off and on the road. Certainly the phrase "bumpy ride" can mean something completely different; but, you wouldn't know it from the ATVs in the video. Okay, who are we kidding; nearly anyone viewing the video could have plainly seen that the looks given to and from the different actors in the video were clearly hinting at one particular meaning.

While the song played, they noticed some of the other dancers getting a little down and dirty. Some couples were holding each other close, moving back and forth at the mid-section. Some couples were grinding up against each other.

Our girls looked at *him*; *he* had three young women now surrounding *him*, one at either side, and one in front. One girl after the other grinded up against his leg, test driving, as it was.

With most of the couples on the dance floor bumping up against each other, Michelle, Kimmy and Shirley soon figured it out. When it clicked in their heads, they all laughed together. Shirley kept laughing the longest while they danced.

Most dance songs last three to four minutes, and "Bumpy Ride" was no exception. The Deejay once again audibly inserted an electronic drum and base line with added synthesizer sounds linking this song to the next.

Positioned to be a new crowd pleaser, the next song was "Club Can't Handle Me," performed by Flo Rida, featuring David Guetta. The video started off with a couple Lamborghinis pulling up to the side of a club, their drivers opening the gullwing doors and throwing money into the air. The music became a steady, driving beat, and the video showed several scenes of people jumping, dancing and watching the star performer as if in concert.

The dance floor was still packed, and everyone there essentially imitated the jumping and dancing in the video, though certainly not all of it. Some of the dancing in the video consisted of highly athletic street dancing, or break-dancing, moves usually reserved for the most nimble and athletic. Spinning on your head isn't something the average bar patron can do. But the video had it in it, and the customers liked the music, as did the three musketeers.

Meanwhile, the tight-shirted, eight-pack abs man was having the time of *his* life dancing with *his* new girls. Yes, a different set of girls were now surrounding *him*. Funny, some of them stopped dancing with the people they came with just to check this guy out. No harm, it's just dancing, the now temporarily single men hopefully thought.

He was getting awfully close to our three musketeers. Kimmy and Shirley nudged ever so slowly toward *him*, bringing Michelle along for the ride toward the middle of the dance floor. And *he* was happy to indulge them. *He* noticed that as *he* got closer to Michelle and the gang, they responded by getting closer, inches at a time, to *him*. *He* may have been thinking what they were thinking. Finally, the current girls surrounding *him* dispersed somewhat, allowing *him* to make his way to the middle of Shirley, Kimmy and Michelle.

Now, this was by no means a slow song. It was much livelier. Jumping, touching, bumping, they danced happily, with a little rubbing up besides each other. The girls each took their turn rubbing up next to *him*, innocently. Tight-sweater man grew fond of these girls—you could say *he* had each of them in *his* sights—and wanted to meet them. But it was the end of the song now—four minutes goes by quickly on the dance floor—and the deejay slowed it down, and cleaned it up a bit too, with his next selection.

"Nothing on You," by B.o.B., featuring Bruno Mars, came up on video and audio next, and it showed a guy singing to different girls on video about how beautiful they were. In short, it looked as if he was telling a particular girl that other girls had nothing on her, that she was the best. But it showed many girls and he was saying the same thing to each of them, making them all think they were special. Apparently, few people pay too much attention to the words being sung; it certainly went unnoticed by the folks dancing, especially the girls, who were at that particular bar to feel special.

Although staying on the dance floor with *him* was an entertaining idea, the song just didn't do it for our girls. They looked and telepathed to each other "Let's get back to the beer," and headed back to the table without an exchanged word. *He* watched them leave, heading to the bar himself to get another drink, immediately accompanied by a couple female tailgaters, preventing *him* to make a move on our heroine or her friends.

"*He's* so hot," Kimmy said as she followed Michelle into the booth and took her seat.

"Yeah, and *we're* out of beer," Shirley added. Michelle looked at both of them and laughed. Kimmy and Shirley joined in on the laughter

"Yo, waitress," Shirley said to nobody in particular, just trying to fake Kimmy and Michelle out. Noticing that that's what she did, they laughed some more.

Shirley tried again, this time catching their waitress's attention with a wave of her left hand. Shirley grabbed the empty pitcher, and signaled to the waitress by lifting it, hoping she would make the connection between the empty pitcher and their need for a refill. The waitress clearly understood by giving Shirley the universal okay sign and a wink.

"I've never seen this video before," Michelle said, "it's so hip."

"It ain't no Yunho," Shirley said, referring to one of the singers in the K-Pop boy band Mirotic.

"*I got yoooooo oooh, under my skin,*" Shirley sang, imitating a very popular song performed by the group in Korea.

"That song gives me goose bumps," Kimmy said.

"Yunho gives me the goose bumps," Shirley said.

"*That* guy kinda gives me goose bumps," Michelle said, referring not to Yunho, but to *him*, motioning with her head and eyes to eight-pack abs man. Looking at *him*, the girls each let out a devilish laugh.

"Did someone say more beer?" the waitress interrupted with a full pitcher of beer.

"Nice!" Shirley said, immediately taking it from her hand. Kimmy gave her a ten dollar bill and said, "Keep the change."

"Thanks hun. Anything else?" the waitress asked.

"We're good," Michelle said. Shirley poured everyone a fresh beer and raised her cup.

"*Him* under my skin," she said. The girls, giggling and little embarrassed, though fully agreeing with her, raised their cups, knocked it into each others' cups, and took a long swig.

Here the music changed once again to something a little slower, a little more romantic, and in Spanish. It was Juanes — a contraction of his full name Juan Esteban Aristizábal Vásquez — superstar in Spain, and the song was "Es Por Ti," which was number one in Spain in 2002, and made the top five in both US Latin Songs and US Latin Pop Songs that same year.

"Oh, I know this song. It's so nice!" Kimmy said.

"So romantic," Michelle said. Shirley smiled.

The three musketeers sat there for the duration of the song, singing along every time Juanes sang the lovely chorus "Es por ti," which he and they did several times.

So there they were, in a great bar, having a great time, listening and singing along to Juanes, watching his video, having listened to the other diverse music, watching those videos, and drinking beer. It should have been a late night of more of the same fun, dancing, drinking and perhaps a little romance. But it wasn't meant to be.

The wolves in the next table had been looking at the three musketeers from time they sat down, while the girls were dancing, and now that they had returned. Apparently, one of them got the courage to walk over to their table, egged on by his friends. Maybe he thought he was going to be funny, maybe not. Sometimes guys do stupid things trying to meet girls, similar to that grade school ritual when a boy pulls a girl's hair.

Anyway, this guy walked over to the girls' table and, eyes squinted, hands clasped, bowing, said in a terribly offensive, stereotypical way, "Ah so, how was the colonar mass erection rast night?" He started cracking up, as did his wolf pack.

Now, normally when in a situation like this—yes, it happened often, though with different verbiage—the girls would smile, perhaps even mimic the actions of the offender and then just let it go. But they were having such a great time, and it came as such a shock—their minds were adrift in "Es Por Ti," singing along—that Michelle started crying. Not just tearing; but, full face-contorted crying. She put her hands on her face and turned toward the wall to hide.

Kimmy tried to console her. Shirley, on the other hand, like a pit bull, got right up into the guy's face, and in a similarly offensive voice said, "So solly, cholly, ancient Chinese plahvub says: ritter boy flom tayruh pock should stay in tayruh pock."

Kimmy started laughing. Shirley was laughing in the guy's face, pointing at him. Realizing his stupidity, quickly becoming embarrassed, he turned around and walked in shame toward the bathroom, passing his friends—whose laughter also quieted into embarrassed silence—along the way. When Shirley sat back down, Kimmy gave her a high-five.

That didn't do much for Michelle. Still visibly shaken, she wasn't in the mood for staying in the bar.

"Let's go home, you guys," she said, frowning, but no longer crying. With that, she got up, motioned for Kimmy to get out of her way, and started walking toward the door. The other two musketeers followed her.

Unbeknownst to them, the dashing, eight-pack abs man pursued. Finally within reach, *he* tried to say hello; alas, they were out the door, Michelle sprinting to the car. *He* gave up chase and headed back to his bevy of adoring peahens.

The girls caught up to Michelle at the car and, without saying anything, Kimmy unlocked the doors and they all got in.

"Take me back to campus," Michelle said from the backseat, hiding her face in her hands as she cried again.

Kimmy and Shirley looked at each other, both grimacing. Kimmy started the car, pulled out of the parking space and began the drive back to campus, past the huge, yellow Hummer in front, the Lamborghini and Ferrari too, on to the main road, and, eventually, the highway. Michelle laid down in the backseat and nearly cried herself to sleep. Kimmy and Shirley didn't say a word.

Our Hero

"I can walk from here," Michelle said, "let me out."

Kimmy stopped the car right in front of the dark but still inviting Paris Green.

"We're really sorry Michelle," Kimmy said. "Hope you feel better."

"I'll be okay," Michelle replied. "Will you be online later?

"Of course," Shirley blurted out. "We're always online, remember?"

Michelle sort of smiled and absent-mindedly said, "Oh, yeah."

"Are you sure you'll be okay, Michelle?" Kimmy asked.

"I think so. I just need to be alone, take a walk. My dorm's only a little ways from here," Michelle said, no trace of crying remaining on her.

"*Ahn young hee ju mu seyo,*" Michelle said in Korean, the English translation being "goodnight."

"*Ahn young hee ju mu seyo,*" Kimmy said. "Feel better Michelle."

"Byeeeee Michelleeeee," Shirley said.

"Bye Kimmy, bye Shirley," Michelle said, closing the car door. She stood there for a moment, waving to Kimmy and Shirley as they drove off.

She was safe. Looking around, and seeing nobody, she walked along the perimeter of the Paris Green, planning to cut eventually onto a trail which would lead to her dorm. She wasn't really familiar with the medical campus, but knew that if she eventually turned left she would wind up where she needed to be. She walked a couple of blocks, then, when she came up to the Pharmacological Sciences Building across the street on her right, she turned left onto a sidewalk that cut between the Biology Annex on her now left and a smaller, two story, red brick building on her right that she had never seen before, just past a small statue of a column with some sort of angelic figure on the top. She couldn't really make it out in the darkness.

There were numerous lights on up on the second floor of the building to her right. Curious, she went up to the door to see what this building was all about.

Most buildings on campus closed by ten o'clock at night, and, although it was then just past eleven, the hallway lights were still on, and the building was unlocked. She walked in.

She was actually in one of the old music school buildings, though the first floor currently housed medical school administrator offices and, as she was to learn shortly, a lecture hall. The University had built a full music and theater campus several blocks away, but the transition hadn't yet been completed. She was greeted by a stone statue of Mary Smith, the first benefactor of the music department as she entered.

She walked up to the padded double-doors just past the grand foyer and tried pulling and pushing on each of the large brass handles; but, both doors were locked. Michelle peered in through the square, thick window in the door on the left, and, although it was dark inside, she could see that there were many rows of seats facing a raised stage. Michelle could sense that although the room was now being used for lectures, many intimate classical concerts and recitals were performed here in the past. And she was right.

Hallways enclosed the auditorium on all sides, with individual offices on the perimeter; it didn't look like anyone was around, so she walked up and down the four sides. When she came back to where she started, noticeably much calmer, she walked over to the stairway to sit down for a second and think about what had happened earlier, and, hopefully, some new and better things.

As she sat, she could hear music coming from the second floor, which captured her attention, and then her imagination.

She looked up, and, pausing for a moment, tentatively began standing. After a brief pause listening to the sounds, she began a slow climb up the stairs.

Greeting her on the second floor was a large, heavy wood door with a small security window in the middle at eye-level—you know the kind, it has meshed wiring resembling graph paper—and she glanced inside. Paralleling the hallways on the first floor was a hallway on the second floor that undoubtedly went down, across, and back up again, with rooms on either side. She recognized these rooms from the hallway as practice rooms. Yes, these were practice rooms; the drab look of the floor, lack of decorations and fixtures on the light bulbs, the austerity of place, and, of course, the music emanating from each gave it away. She'd seen them before as she used to practice at a college in Korea when she was younger. It was the dream of many parents in middle-class families to have their children escape their plight by performing and delighting the masses, providing a brief respite from the ordinariness or vicissitudes of life. As she thought more about it, trying to make out specific musical phrases, she opened the door.

A massive wall of sound made up of distinct, individual piano music rushed to her ears as that door opened. It was at once a relief, an empathetic rapture combining good memories with new and wonderful thoughts of opportunity. The very first room, closed like all the others, had a familiar sound. It was Mozart, the first movement from his Piano Sonata Number 15 in C Major that everyone could play. Well, anyone that practiced anyway. She played it when a child; played it first as a matter of fact because her mom told her it didn't have many black notes. "Those black notes are evil, don't you know," she remembered her mom having said many years ago. It was a funny flashback to have here and she giggled to herself. Uninterested in listening to this simple piece, she turned to the door on the other side. A more complex piece of music was nearing its end in that room. It was clearly something that she had heard before, but never attempted to play. It was Ravel.

Short, fat, not particularly easy on the eyes, Maurice Ravel described through his music that which he yearned for but never obtained. Ah, unrequited love, the inspiration for many impressive accomplishments.

The particular work emanating from this room was probably the third movement from Ravel's *Gaspard de la Nuit*. Ravel chose three poems in 1908 from Bertrand's *Gaspard de la Nuit (Devil of the Night)*, a dark book of poetry published in 1842 dealing with the language of horror, and set them to musical imagery, producing highly virtuosic piano compositions. The three poems he chose depict the evil seduction of a water spirit, the grotesque world surrounding a hanging corpse, and the terror induced by a menacing gremlin.

Listening to whoever was in that room playing reminded Michelle of another work by Ravel. And so we are whisked out of the Music Building and into Michelle's mind for a bit of a nighttime daydream.

Her mom and dad brought her to many concerts when she was much younger; but, the one that made the biggest impression on her, the one that created a lasting memory, was the one celebrating the new millennium in Seoul, Korea, at the gorgeous, all glass KBS Hall. The finale was Ravel's Piano Concerto for the Left Hand in D Major. She remembered reading through the program notes and to this day recalled that it premiered on November 27, 1931, in Vienna, and was composed for Ravel's friend, a pianist named Paul Wittgenstein who lost his right arm during World War I. The piece was no doubt chosen for its "Chinese sounding" first movement, as it contained the pentatonic scale. Listening to the piece now in her head, she remembered that it transcended the left-handedness of its title. It was pure, expressive music, building from an ambiguous use of double-basses softly playing the notes of their open strings, creating the illusion at the start that the orchestra is warming up, culminating in the fanfare of the whole orchestra. Although Paul Wittgenstein commissioned other notable composers to write pieces for him, Paul eventually learned to love the work by Ravel; she loved it on her first hearing. Even to this day, it was her favorite orchestral piece, especially how the last few minutes build to such an unforgettable, climactic, emotional ending.

As the applause from her daydream subsided, she found herself back on the second floor of the Music Building, being led by sounds from the next room. There, a slower, more melodic work was being started.

"Chopin! It must be Chopin," she thought. Yes, it was the famously romantic Nocturne in E-Flat Major, Opus 9, No. 2.

But that music started to be drowned out by someone in the adjacent room banging away at what first sounded like scales, but then grew into something she was completely unfamiliar with. Again, it sounded like scales, going up, then back down, then up again, and again, like they were just banging away at random notes. It must be something from the twentieth century art music repertoire she thought.

Well, yes, it was. It was *L'escalier du Diable*" French for "Devil's Staircase," from *Etudes, Book 2*, composed in 1993, by György Sándor Ligeti, who lived from 1923 to 2006, and whose music has been featured in many movies including *2001: A Space Odyssey*, *The Shining*, *Eyes Wide Shut*, and *Hitchhiker's Guide to the Galaxy* to name a few. She listened for just a few moments, wanting to hear something a little more lyrical.

She didn't have to move too far to hear just that, as more Chopin was being played in the next room. Here, the student was practicing Chopin's Etude 25, No. 11, the "Winter Wind," though she could still hear that incessant pounding in the room behind her. She tried to concentrate on the Chopin; but, the Ligeti was too loud, so she moved further down the hall.

In the next room, someone was playing a very fast, intricate ragtime that she had never heard before. It was the "Finger Buster," by Jelly Roll Morton.

Just as the "Finger Buster" ended, she moved to the next room and immediately recognized the finale from Edvard Grieg's Piano Concerto, unnumbered, because he only wrote one. She smiled as she listened and envisioned Albert Einstein in his later years, Grieg's look-alike.

She eavesdropped on whoever was playing the Grieg until they stopped, then walked over to the next room, stood there for a moment, heard a cough, and then the beginning of some of the most exquisite notes ever penned to paper. Every time she heard it, it sent her to another world. It was Sergei Rachmaninoff's Rhapsody on a Theme of Paganini, a work for piano based upon twenty-four variations of Niccolo Paganini's Caprices for solo violin.

Rachmaninoff's work is normally performed in one stretch without breaks, but can be divided into three sections, corresponding to the three movements of a concerto. Variations one through eleven became the first movement, twelve though eighteen are the equivalent of the slow, second movement, and the remaining six variations make up the finale. It is the slow eighteenth variation that is by far the most well-known, and is often played on the radio without the rest of the work. Analysis notwithstanding, it is one of the most sumptuous pieces in the classical music repertoire, and she wished whoever was practicing it would play it again. Denied by default for not asking, however, she moved to the next room, captivated by what sounded like Chopin.

It was, of course, Chopin: his Scherzo No. 2, Op. 31. Fast, terribly difficult to master—aren't they all—and she liked it. It was the third section, which, technically, probably serves more as a link to the first section; but, she was still haunted by the music from the previous room. Torn by the thought of which room she should eavesdrop, she was pulled to the next room by still another haunting melodic line. She recognized it from an American-made horror movie dubbed in Korean she had watched at her friend's slumber party when she was much younger, though it was performed on an organ. It was the Toccata and Fugue in D Minor, a piece of organ music believed to have been composed by Johann Sebastian Bach sometime between 1703 and 1707. It is one of the most famous works in the organ repertoire, and has been used in a variety of popular media ranging from film, to video games, rock music, and even cell phone ringtones. She stayed and listened to both parts.

The person in the next room was also playing Chopin, this time it was his Fantasie-Impromptu, Opus 66. She got to the room right as the pianist started the second, slow and exquisite section. She stayed there listening to him or her for a minute or so until the pianist began repeating to the first section. She tried to leave but stayed because she like it so much, leaving when the second section repeated.

Funny, the person in the next room was also playing Bach. Actually, when it comes to piano performance, most students work on a repertoire that a general audience wants to hear. Thus, the common, though difficult pieces to learn are made up of works from only a handful of composers: Bach, Mozart, Beethoven, Chopin, Rachmaninoff, and perhaps Brahms. This time, it was a more involved piece, difficult at times because of the different voices; the left hand is not simply accompanying the right hand, it is playing a different melody, also known as a voice. She knew this piece because she had seen old videos of Glenn Gould performing it on YouTube, and thought how wonderfully strange it looked when seeing him — and hearing him — grunting aloud while playing it. He was probably singing an unwritten harmony at times in addition to singing along with one of the musical lines. It was the Bach Goldberg Variations, from numbers one through seven.

Now, the Goldberg Variations comprised an aria and thirty variations published in 1741. Although probably more myth than truth, these were written for the former Russian Ambassador to the electoral court of Saxony, Count Kaiserling, to delight him while he couldn't sleep; apparently, he was an insomniac. The work is considered to be one of the most important examples of variation form, named after Johann Gottlieb Goldberg, who may have been the first performer.

A spectacular piece was in its final throes in the next room, while another was beginning just across the hall. The one beginning was Rachmaninoff's Prelude in C Sharp Minor, Opus 3, No. 2, and the one ending was Tchaikovsky's Piano Concerto No. 1, from the third movement. The juxtaposition of each piece made quite an impact on Michelle, as the beginning of Rachmaninoff's includes big chords spaced out in time, whereas Tchaikovsky's ending to the third movement is flurry after flurry. As Tchaikovsky's piece concluded, the one by Rachmaninoff was just getting to its second section, about two minutes in, culminating in a flurry of its own. Such a wonderful contrast she thought.

As the Rachmaninoff piece ended, she quickly became bored and walked a little further down the hall where she heard someone playing a familiar classical piece by Liszt, one of his Hungarian Rhapsodies. This kept her interested for a couple minutes until she walked away to one of the last few rooms left.

In the fifth room from the end — there were three rooms left on one side of the hall, and two rooms left on the other — and by the way, it was amazing to her that nearly every room was full on a Friday night — someone was playing another piece of Chopin. Although unfamiliar to her — it was Ballade No. 1 in G Minor, Opus 23 — she came to this room right in the middle of the piece. Well, actually it was about six minutes in, right as the tempo picks up a bit, and she wandered off to see if anyone was in any of the remaining rooms after a couple minutes, about the time that the piece quietly began to restate the original theme.

She put her head to the next room; no, not a sound. She turned half-way around, stepped over a Nestlé® Butterfinger®

candy bar wrapper to listen if someone was in the next room: nothing. The next two rooms were empty as well. She walked slowly but deliberately to the last room remaining, and, if she had wished for her favorite classical music to be played there and now, it would have come true. For in this room, though about four minutes in, someone was playing the third movement to Beethoven's Moonlight Sonata, that is, Sonata Number 14 in C-Sharp Minor, Opus 27, No. 2.

What a glorious work of art she thought. And listen to how this person played it! Fast, furious, she wondered if it was Beethoven himself resurrected from the dead playing. Perhaps one *can* make a deal with the devil. She always wanted to play the whole sonata, not just the first and second movements, but the whole sonata. And she never could. She didn't even try the third movement, just always assumed she couldn't do it.

She listened to whoever was in the room playing intently, and, as the final, two-handed, downward c-sharp minor arpeggios came to a finish, she was unable to contain herself, and she began to clap aloud. To wit, she heard that scrape-squeak noise made by the legs of a piano bench being pushed back on a linoleum floor, followed by light footsteps. The door opened to her applause.

Greeting her at the door was our hero, J. David Bennett. He was a graduate student in biology, though he often practiced in this building as he took piano lessons privately nearly his whole life. He was somewhat tall, unkempt, with intense brown eyes that he would keep wide open, while awake anyway. And he was fat. Not obese; but, obviously a little fat.

Michelle didn't notice his height, looks or weight, simply saying in appreciation, "That was wonderful."

"Oh, well, uh, thanks," the young man said.

"I always wanted to play that piece, I mean, play the whole piece. I could play the first two movements, but never really tried to play the third."

"It's not that hard, you just have to practice it slowly with the right fingering. Speed comes in time."

"It's too hard. I'm so impressed that such a handsome guy can play it so well."

"Handsome? Funny, you must have been drinking. And I've never seen you here, are you a new student, are you studying music?"

She laughed, adding, "Yes, I'm new here. I come from Korea," she paused, then added, "South Korea."

"Yeah," he said chuckling, "I figured that if you're here form Korea, it would be South Korea. I read a great deal about the Koreas when the North sank a South Korean naval ship, then, months later shelled..."

"They ssshell..." She had trouble pronouncing the word.

"Shelled," David said, helping her.

"They shelled Yeonpyeong Island; people were killed."

"Yes, that's what I read," David added. "I don't think anyone on either side of the thirty-eighth parallel understand what's going on there." Michelle was a little stunned that David knew that.

"How can one people have two different destinies," David said. Michelle was speechless; she opened her dainty eyes wide, surprised and happy that she had met someone that understands what people in her country thought.

"That's right, David," she said. "That's exactly right!"

"Well, if you think about it, it goes much further."

"What do you mean?" Michelle wondered.

"If you take that to its logical conclusion, we are all cousins. All of us are descended from archaic humans, which share a common ancestor with the chimpanzees, which share a common ancestor with the apes before them, which all share a common ancestor that lived in Africa, East Africa at that."

"We're all Africans?" Michelle asked inquisitively.

"Yes, we are," David quickly and proudly answered. "Same genome, and same genes, with only slight differences; in fact, the difference between the average person from Southeast Asia and the average person from any other population is less than the differences within each population. And much less than any two unrelated chimpanzees."

Michelle smiled and said, "We're all the same, huh."

"Yes, we are," David said, "with only slight, superficial differences. Like your eyes, let's say. People from Asia are said to have almond-shaped eyes. Technically, that small web of extra tissue overlapping the corner of the eye closest to the nose," he said while getting closer to her and pointing near the corner of her eye, "is called an epicanthic fold. It's not a true epicanthic fold, though. There's a genetic disease called Down syndrome, where the person has three chromosome number twenty-ones instead of the normal two. They have a true epicanthic fold that goes across the whole eye."

"So, my eyes are a mutation?" Michelle asked innocently.

David thought about his answer for a second as he didn't want to scare her by saying she had a mutation. "It's probably an adaptation developed over thousands of years in very bright, sunlit habitats. The narrowing of the eyes probably helped somehow in sight in the very bright climate. And it's really pretty too. We're all the same; but, my, you're so pretty."

Michelle smiled and blushed. "You think I'm pretty?"

"I sure do," David said confidently. He liked the vibes he was getting being in her presence.

"Are you studying music, Michelle?" David asked, changing the subject, as he didn't want to come on too heavy.

"No, I haven't decided what to study, but I really wanted to come to your country to learn English, meet Americans, and hopefully get a good job someday."

"Your English is perfect," he said. Michelle smiled, touched by the positive reinforcement.

There was a brief pause, not an uncomfortable silence, just a pause. They both wanted the conversation to continue.

"Well," David said, "I'm not in the pool of mucous either."

Michelle looked confused. "The pool of mucous?"

"Oh, that's a play on words," David said with a slight laugh in his voice. "Pool is close to the word school, and mucous; well, it's kind of like music."

"Pool of mucous," Michelle raised her hand to her mouth and giggled through it. "Oh!"

"That's okay, not everyone gets my humor immediately," he admitted.

She smiled and added, "I get it. I'll try that one sometime."

"So," he said, "I'm Dave Bennett. I'm a graduate student in evolutionary biology, though most of my coursework is done. I'm just now trying to figure out what to write my thesis on. I spend most of my time now thinking about my thesis, doing research, and get by with a teaching assistantship in human evolution; I teach the discussion class under a great professor who presents the main lecture. I come here to practice sometimes at night and on the weekends."

He paused briefly, looked at Michelle contemplatively, smiled and added, "I love music and can't imagine not continuing, though I don't study it as intensely as I do biology. I couldn't imagine a life in which I was not surrounded by music. It shelters you from the world, protects you, and keeps you at a certain distance from the world. Biology then brings me back."

"Oh, I see," she said almost blushing. Now she understood how David knew so much about apes, chimpanzees, and archaic humans. "There's so much to know, and I just don't know where to start."

"Yes, there is a lot to know, Michelle," David said empathetically.

"Like, take boys. I just don't understand them," she said in a somewhat agitated voice, with a facial expression to match.

David let out a short laugh and said, "What are you trying to understand?" Again, he really wanted to know as he might just have the answer.

"Well, for starters," she began, "I just don't understand why they're so mean to me."

"They're mean to you?"

"Yes, well, some are. And eventually even the ones that are nice get mean. Those are the ones that for some reason get sick of me; but, the ones I'm talking about are the ones that are mean right away. They say mean things when they don't even know me. They whistle at me, or call me "hottie," or say "hey baby," or, uh, worse."

"Oh, that kind of stuff," he began. "Well, most of it is explained from a biological perspective."

"Really?"

"Yes," David replied. "But, do you mind if I talk about sex, about the reproductive organs? I'll have to start there."

Michelle smiled and said, "No, not at all. I like the truth."

"Okay, then, it's pretty simple and straight-forward," he began. He'd told this story before, and knew that it would "click" in the mind of the person hearing it once they had time to think about it. He cared deeply about the subject matter and liked to watch the face of the person he's telling the story to, to watch it change from doubt or perplexity to understanding.

David began, "It's all about the relative size and quantity of our individual, uh, contributions. Men produce about a million sperm an hour from the time they're able up until the end of their average life expectancy. Women ovulate — produce one egg — each month from the time they are able until; well, until the time they're not. Since health professionals advocate that past the age of about fifty-five the risk to females is high for complications during pregnancy, we'll say they can realistically produce about five-hundred eggs in her lifetime. That's one million per hour versus five-hundred per lifetime. For the men, it comes out to a million, times twenty-four, times three-hundred-sixty-five, times sixty — I use sixty because their life expectancy is about seventy-three minus their post-pubescent age of thirteen — which," he looked like he was starting to do the math in his head, but he had calculated it before and said after a couple seconds of fake calculating, "is about five-hundred-billion, with a 'b,' sperm per lifetime, versus five-hundred eggs from the ladies."

Michelle's mouth was open. She wasn't as much interested in him—for now—as much as in what he was saying and how he was saying it. She thought he had a talent for explaining and was patient, nice, caring, calm, and, well, nice.

She smiled, tilted her head to the right and said, "That's a big difference."

"It sure is," David quickly replied. A billion times—not a billion more, but a billion *times* more—difference. That's more than ten times the distance in miles between the Earth and the Sun. Measured in time, a billion days ago is about 2.7 million years ago, corresponding nicely to when one of our ancestors from the genus *Australopithecus* roamed the African savannas."

He had thought of other analogies, but Michelle was pretty quick to interject an example of her own, "I understand the difference, David," she began with a captivating smile. "Build a cube out of one-thousand similarly-sized smaller cubes, then another from one-thousand of those, then still another from one-thousand of those, and you have a cube a billion times the size of the original."

David was at first shocked then pleased by her answer. "Yes," he said, "that's exactly right." Michelle smiled knowing that he appreciated her comment.

"So now let's think about that," David began again. "You have a ridiculously large five-hundred-billion versus a terribly scarce five-hundred; one billion times the amount of the fewer by the greater. What does that say about our natures?"

Michelle deliberated hard on that. She crinkled her nose, moved her head a little and raised her eyebrows.

He concluded, "It basically explains how men tend to be more prone to risk-taking, trying to spread their seeds, so to speak, and women toward being risk-averse, on the whole, judging carefully who will have access to their eggs."

He paused for a moment to take in Michelle's inevitable "aha" moment. And here it came:

"Guys just want to...," she said, "...to get in there?" she questioned, remembering what one of the boys had remarked within earshot of her at the bar.

"Uh, yeah, that's certainly one way to look at it, albeit crassly. But you want to know about the ones that are mean."

"Yes," she quietly replied with a beaming smile.

"Well, men are more aggressive, on average, than females, typically competing, more battling with rivals for access to the desirable females. It is true that both men and women compete for each other; but, in nature, it is more often than not the males that compete more furiously for the females than vice-versa. It does happen; but, for the most part, most males would mate with most females, but most females prefer to mate with less of the available males, the ones that meet their requirements."

"I see, and the reason that some guys are mean to me is because, uh, they are more aggressive?" she asked, crinkling her nose again, not sure of that fact.

Thinking that she was so cute when she crinkled her nose like that, David answered, "Michelle, the reason some are mean is because they probably think that they won't be able to win you — win you over the competition, that is. Far more men probably give up before they even try to win your heart; but, those that are noticeably mean, knowing that they can't beat out a taller, nicer-looking, talented, smarter, or perhaps even employed man, figure they have nothing to lose by just trying to take you for their own. They can't beat out a stronger competitor, but they might think that they can beat you. In other words, some may think that might is right."

"They try to take me because they're bigger than me?"

"Yes," David replied. "Because they think they can."

Michelle understood but struggled to accept this fact. She shrugged, saying, "That's the way it is, I guess."

"Ah, but the story doesn't end there Michelle," David added. Michelle looked intrigued.

"There are many ways to earn the admiration of, to charm a female," David said with a calm, confidant smile.

Said Michelle, "There's more than one way to skin a cat."

"Exactly. If you look to the rest of the animal world, although there are exceptions, females respond to tall, thin, clean males; but, also to those males that sing prettiest, loudest, uniquely, move gracefully, flash brilliantly, touch the females nicely, bring them gifts, build them houses, and on and on."

"Play piano?" she innocently asked.

David laughed and said, "Yes, even play piano."

Michelle smiled. "David, I really enjoyed listening to you play, and really liked talking to you." She shrugged, as if to say "I could stay here all night talking to you," then said, "I'm tired and need to go to bed."

"Yeah, I'm going to go home soon too."

"Let's get together again."

"I'd like that very much," David replied, not giving it any thought whatsoever.

"Say, David, what do you like to do when you're not teaching or studying or playing the piano?"

"I like to stare at Martians."

"Martians?"

"Martians," David stated confidently. They both looked deeply into each other's eyes. "You know, those strange animals you see at SeaWorld, like octopuses, manta rays, seahorses, eels..."

"Oh, those Martians!" Michelle exclaimed before David could give more examples. "I love that place; but, it's kind of expensive," she stated honestly.

"Oh, we can go to Birch Aquarium instead; it's just down the road a couple of miles or so. It's certainly not as big, and it doesn't have any dolphins or those performing killer whales that everyone likes to see, but it does have leafy sea dragons," he said hoping she would like to see what he wants to see.

"Leafy sea dragons," she said wondering, "I've never heard of those. Sure, let's go there. Then I'll take you to dinner at my favorite place."

Again, he didn't take long nor think much about it to answer, "Sounds good. Friday or Saturday?"

"Friday night is best, because I plan to make it a habit of spending Saturday's talking to my family and studying and such," she said, reminding herself of her responsibilities.

"Okay, Friday afternoon and night it is. I teach a class until two o'clock; we can meet in the Darwin Institute Building next door or in front on the Paris Green.

"Can I go to your class and watch you?" Michelle asked while kind of blushing.

"Sure, why not," David replied, positive this was a dream.

"Okay, see you then," she said as she got up from the piano bench and headed to the door. David got up too and followed her to the door.

Michelle was out of the door and already walking down the hallway. David walked out of the door and watched as Michelle looked over her shoulder with a big smile and said, "See you next week."

"See you next week, Michelle," David replied.

"Martians," Michelle said happily, walking backwards looking at David. She turned a hundred and eighty degrees while walking, quite gracefully, and said a little louder to overcome the mass of piano sounds, "I can't wait."

"Martians," David replied. And he couldn't wait either.

Second Date

One week later

He began the lecture on a simple note.

"I'm Dave Bennett, TA for Bio 301, Human Evolution. If this isn't the class you signed up for, you're in the wrong place at the right time." Nearly everyone in the classroom gave a short, nervous giggle.

"Okay, since I don't see anyone getting ready to leave, I'll assume you're all in the right place. Let's dive in, shall we?"

"How do we begin to focus on this subject? I think the best place to start is with geologic time." He sat down to his laptop at the front of the relatively small lecture class, and projected a partially hidden slide on the screen behind him that he would uncover as he went over the material.

He continued, "In geologic time, there are supereons, eons, eras, and periods. Since the Earth is roughly 4.5 billion years old, formed by accretion discs orbiting the sun, the time from 4.5 billion years ago, until about five-hundred million years ago, is referred to as the 'Precambrian supereon.' What do you suppose is the name of the supereon that brings us from five-hundred million years ago to today?"

"Cambrian?" a girl in the first row stated, as she unwrapped a piece of Hershey's® Bubble Yum® Original flavor gum and with her thumb and middle finger placed it into her mouth.

"Exactly," he said. The girl smiled then began chewing almost as if it were a reward for getting the answer correct.

"That's pretty much all we're going to say about supereons in this class. Everything we'll discuss from today until Christmas happens in the Cambrian supereon. So let's divvy it up into its eons, eras, and epochs."

"There is only one eon in the Cambrian supereon, and that is the Phanerozoic. And it lasted how many years?"

"Five-hundred million years," a different student, a chubby though average sized male in a nondescript sweater and jeans said after a brief pause.

"Good. We are off to a great start."

That same student then reached in his backpack, which was on the floor, and brought out a four count, single serve Nabisco® Chips Ahoy® Chocolate Chip package, opened it somewhat quietly, grabbed one, and just like the other student, savored the first bite as reinforcement for his answer; though, obviously, he was going to eat them anyway.

David continued, "The Phanerozoic eon is divided into only three eras: the Paleozoic, Mesozoic, and Cenozoic, which is where we find ourselves today. The Paleozoic era is further divided into six relatively equal periods: the Cambrian, Ordovician, Silurian, Devonian, Carboniferous, and Permian. The Paleozoic era lasts from about five-hundred million years ago until about two-hundred-and-fifty million year ago. Three periods make up the Mesozoic which lasts until the dinosaurs, not including the birds, went extinct sixty-five million years ago: the Triassic, Jurassic and Cretaceous periods. And last, which as I stated, we will concern ourselves over the course of this semester, is the Cenozoic era. The three periods of the Cenozoic are the Paleogene, Neogene, and Quaternary."

"Of course, we can further speak about individual epochs in each of these periods; the Paleogene period contains three epochs, the Paleocene, Eocene, and Oligocene, which collectively last until about twenty-two million years ago; the Neogene period contains the Miocene and Pliocene epochs which last until 2.5 million years ago; and the Quaternary period contains two, the majority Pleistocene and Holocene, only twelve-thousand years old. Moreover, each of these can be further broken down, but this will serve fine as the introduction. Again, our class will focus on this last era, the

Cenozoic, and we will cover those species of archaic humans that lived, and currently live, in this time zone."

As he was going over this information, he took a piece of flimsy cardboard off of the slide that it was hiding on the overhead projector so that everyone could see the whole page.

"This should look familiar to all of you, as geology was one of the prerequisites." He paused for a moment. "Does anyone remember the mnemonic for the periods in the Paleozoic era?" He looked around at the sleepy students.

"Uh, I remember," the thin young woman in the second row said without raising her hand. "Campbell's ordinary soup does make Peter pale. You just have to remember that the Carboniferous period is split into the Mississippian and Pennsylvanian."

"That's right. Good." David noticed that this particular student did not reach for any food.

"So, now let's take a look at the overview of what we will be discussing this semester." He didn't take much of a break between discussions and went right to the next slide. "Here is the big picture; remember that it all takes place mostly in the last two periods of the Cenozoic era discussed previously, the Neogene and Quaternary."

He placed another, more complex slide on the screen and continued, "Note that on the first slide we saw that the Neogene period began around twenty-three million years ago, yet from this slide we see that the superfamily 'Hominoidea' speciated around twenty-five million years ago. Again, let me point out that this class is 'Human Evolution,' so, as advertised, we're not going to focus on material much past this level," David said, pointing to the word 'Homo' four levels below, "however, you will be responsible for understanding and being able to name the distinctions for the full twenty-five million years." There was a noticeable sigh from the students.

Thirty minutes later, David's lecture was near its end.

"Most of the interesting topics we're going to discuss in this class happen between the time of *Homo sapiens* and *Homo habilus*," he said, pointing to the space between the two species on the slide with his pen, "but you *will* be responsible for the other material." Several students sighed.

And then Michelle walked into the room. She didn't want to attract attention, but most of the boys stared at her as she gracefully walked over to one of the open seats in the front row. Some of the girls in the class noticed too, wondering why some men seemed to gravitate to Asian women. Michelle didn't seem to care; she was looking and smiling at David.

A smiling, confident David continued, "By the end of this class, you will be able to write and speak in detail about each of these species." He put up a slide listing all the extinct species pre-dating *Homo sapiens*.

There were more than twenty-five names in all, starting with *Sahelanthropus tchadensis and* then *Orrorin tugenensis*, which had the words "Millennium Ancestor" in parenthesis right next to it. Next were a couple with the first name—the genus— *Ardipithicus*, then several named *Australopithicus*, three with the first name *Paranthropus*, and then ten or so with the similar first name of *Homo*, including *habilis, erectus, neanderthalensis,* and *heidelbergensis*.

"You will be able to list these species, state where they were found, what tools, if any, they used, their comparative anatomy, and how long each of them lived."

"Let me end our first discussion class with a taste of what is to come. As for the Lucies and Robusts, if they prove to be a single lineage that is separate from the South African Man-apes, an effectively certain conclusion, both must relinquish the name *Australopithicus* because this name was first applied to the South African Man-ape *A. africanus*. In these circumstances, Lucies either keep their first name of *Praeanthropus*, or the entire lineage becomes *Paranthropus*, the earliest name for a Robust. And all this emphasizes the extreme subjectivity of current classifications — reminding us, again, that names are inadequate artifacts for such an incompletely understood yet dynamic field as the study of human evolution. Until just a few years ago, a line was drawn between *Homo habilus* and *Australopithicus africanus*, their possible immediate forebears. This line was justified by marginally larger brains and initially uncertain tool associations. However arbitrary or provisional, that boundary takes us away from an exclusively southern African focus."

"And then we'll talk briefly about modern humans. I'll just cut to the chase. Is the obvious geographic variation in modern *Homo sapiens* a sign of initial speciation? Not in the least. The most important thing about human variation is that patterns in one characteristic, say, skin color, are not congruent with those in another, say, nose width. If you map variation in those characteristics, the patterns of change in one do not correspond with those in others, as shown on maps in your assigned readings."

"Geographic variations in various characteristics in our species are not strongly correlated with one another, nor are geographic variations of different attributes within other organisms that have been thoroughly studied. That's exactly why Harvard University evolutionist Edward O. Wilson, of sociobiology fame, and the late Cornell University taxonomist William L. Brown long ago pointed out that subspecies, which are taxonomic subdivisions of a species based on the geographic pattern of a few characteristics, often are not biological entities."

"Widespread species thus can be divided into any number of different sets of subspecies simply by selecting different characteristics on which to base them. Races in people are arbitrarily defined entities; individuals from different geographic regions are capable of mating and producing fully fertile offspring. Indeed, they are often eager to interbreed, as has been seen throughout history in the reproductive consequences of armies occupying new territories. Attempts to treat divisions of humanity based primarily on skin color as natural evolutionary units have always been, and still are, nonsensical."

"In your assigned reading you'll see that anthropologists summarized a key point that makes the designation of such groups nonsensical, that the prime 'racial' characteristic of skin pigmentation can respond quite rapidly to selection pressures as human populations migrate. Because of its high degree of responsiveness to environmental conditions, skin pigmentation is of no value in assessing the phylogenetic relationships between human groups."

"A recent article in *Science* magazine summed it up nicely: 'The possibility that human history has been characterized by genetically relatively homogeneous groups, so-called 'races,' distinguished by major biological differences, is not consistent with genetic evidence.'"

David paused, looked around at the class, half of which looked like zombies, about a quarter a combination of sharp, bright, attentive students, and the other quarter tired from a mid-afternoon meal of snacks, and added, "But it is consistent with the end of our lecture."

The tension was relieved by another sigh from the class. David continued, "Good luck everyone. I'll see you in Dr. Ross's lecture Monday morning, and again in our discussion section next Friday at the Natural History Museum, where we'll look at some of these specimens. Be sure to prepare by reading the first three chapters in the textbook, in which you'll see further reading where I drew generously from in constructing today's lecture. Have a great weekend."

With that, the students started slowly filing out.

As the last student left the small lecture room, Michelle, smile on her face — and a smile was clearly visible on David's face as Michelle approached; he really couldn't believe she liked him — got close to him and said, "*Ahn young* David."

"Hi Michelle," he said almost comfortably. He was excited to see her and fidgeted a little, gathering up his slides to cover whatever nervousness he felt. Those feelings soon passed.

"You're so smart. And everyone listens to everything you say. How long did it take you to learn all this?"

"Well, the information builds upon itself. You learn this one year, and that the next, and before you know it, perhaps with a little review, you know this, that, and the other thing." He was happy with his explanation.

"Oh, I see," Michelle said after a quick giggle. David was enthralled with her giggle. Yes, she was listening to everything he said, and, more importantly, processing it all.

"It all depends upon interest," David began. "After a while, if you keep at it, you could do or be anything you want."

Michelle got a little excited and said, "You think I can do anything? Thanks!"

"Our minds are the architects of our reality," he said. "Yes, given time and focus, all of us can know what it is we want to know and then apply that knowledge in our lives. Time, focus, and practice."

"Like the piano," stated Michelle humbly.

"Like the piano," David concurred. He gathered his papers and a couple books, put them in his backpack, and, looking again at Michelle, didn't say anything. They were on the same page; both were ready for the afternoon's adventure.

"Martians?" David asked.

"Martians!" Michelle responded. She was surely excited. Yes, she had been to an aquarium before; but, somehow, this was different. It wasn't a school field trip, it was a date. A date with someone she looked up to; a guide perhaps, and yet, at the same time, someone she so far liked to be with and could do just about anything. They walked to the door. David let Michelle go first through first, and, following, took hold of the hand that Michelle offered as she led the way.

Creation

As they walked through the hallway to the front entrance, there were numerous other students, faculty, and staff that passed the other way, as if going to class, and some that were headed toward the exit with them. The first to pass in the other direction were two slightly obese girls, one with a large tube of jalapeno flavored Proctor & Gamble Pringles® that she had just reached into, and in pulling a few out, started chomping on them. The other was enjoying the middle of a Hershey's® Whatchamacallit® bar, which she held in her left hand, while her right hand held onto the strap of her backpack on the upper portion of her right front shoulder. That backpack placement was the predominant fashion at college: single strapping was cool, double strappers were not.

As they neared the front entrance of the Darwin Institute Building, where a group of five students stood in a small circle making plans for the evening—each of them, two thin males and three females in slightly different phases of fatness—and were each snacking on something different. One of the girls had just handed the other two pieces of Wrigley's® Doublemint® gum; she immediately opened both and popped them in her mouth and started chewing. The third girl—a double strapper—held a large can of Hershey's® Whoppers® in her left hand, a handful of them in her right hand, and talked while chewing those that were in her mouth. The two boys were sharing a large bag of nacho cheese flavored Frito-Lay® Doritos®; their backpacks were on the floor. Each had a Coca-Cola® or Pepsi® in their right hand or on the floor.

Michelle and David neared the front entrance when a tall, thin, distinguished man exited the main auditorium and began walking down the stairs, also headed out for the weekend. Gray-whiskered, he had a permanent, subtle smile plastered on his face and bore a striking resemblance to the American actor Morgan Freeman. Yes, he was African-American, his face generously freckled.

"David," he called out.

"Professor Ross!" David replied. David stopped, straightened up, and waited as he came down the stairs.

"Getting ready for the weekend, David?"

"You bet."

"Who is this lovely creature?" Professor Ross said with a charm only an older, distinguished gentleman can convey.

"This is my friend Michelle," David replied proudly.

"Hi Professor," Michelle said with a sincere smile. David couldn't help but notice her perfectly straight, white teeth.

"Very nice to meet you," he said sincerely, taking her hand. "I'm Alphonse Ross. Alphonse Laveran Ross."

"Professor Ross is the lecturer for that discussion class that I'm teaching," David said to Michelle proudly.

"Very nice to meet you too professor," she said excitedly, though with some anxiety. She had never really met a professor one-on-one before, and, although she was comfortable and confident, there was a hint of "I'm not worthy" noticeable on her face. And on David's face too.

For, as is probably true of other professors, people hung on every word of his, yet he was a man of few words. Often at social gatherings, a whisper would go around the room: "Alphonse is here." You could sense from people's reactions, like that of David and Michelle, the presence of greatness. He had done no memorable experiments and had made no startling discovery. Yet he was the progenitor of a revolution in evolutionary biology almost as profound as Darwin's, and had written a book twenty years earlier entitled *Adaptation and Natural Selection*, that still towered over biology like a Himalayan peak. It did for biology what Adam Smith had done for economics: it explained how collective effects could flow from the actions of self-interested individuals.

"How did your first discussion class go today, David," Professor Ross asked.

"It went well, sir," he replied humbly.

"He was great," Michelle added. David started to blush.

"Oh," Professor Ross laughed, "great huh? David, you have an admirer here; I knew there was a reason I chose you."

Michelle said, "I had some biology in high school, though never studied human evolution. David showed all those different apes in class today, and I had no idea we had so many, uh, ancestors." She felt pretty good about her comment.

"Yes," Professor Ross began, "I wish we could teach everyone about how we came to be here now. You know, most people think our species is only a few thousand years old; but, this class gives some insight into what happened over a time span of millions of years."

"Did all of those people teach that class here?" Michelle asked naively, looking at the row of portraits on the left side of the base of the stairs.

"No," Professor Ross said with his contagious, subtle laugh through his smile. "No, they are all long dead. Here, do you have a minute? Let's take a closer look."

"Sure," Michelle said happy for the attention from such a mentor. The three walked in between passersby—which included a small, fat, dark-haired, double-strapping boy walking to class, breaking off a single wafer of a Nestlé® Kit Kat® bar and sticking it into his mouth like a cigarette—and made their way to the left-hand side of portraits.

"All of these people made a major contribution to our continuing gain in knowledge about our true nature, and that of evolution. The first person on our wall of fame is someone you've heard about, and his full name is Leonardo di sir Piero da Vinci." The portrait, as with all the others, had dates listed on the bottom of the frame; in this case it was 1452-1519. "Of course he's considered to be one of the greatest painters of all time and perhaps the most diversely talented person of all time.

In addition to painting, he was a sculptor, painter, architect, musician, scientist, mathematician, engineer, inventor, anatomist, botanist, writer and more. But he was also a geologist and quite prophetic for his time when he said, '…if a fossil looks in every detail like a modern shell or bone, then it must clearly be the remains of some ancient organism related to the modern forms.' Thankfully, he wasn't the first to be murdered — he wasn't murdered — for that view. No, we'll get to the first person to fall victim to that horrible fate after this next one."

Michelle was captivated. So too was David.

"Conrad Gesner," Professor Ross began again. On the bottom of the frame were the dates 1516-1565. "He was the next major historical figure. On July 28, 1565, Conrad Gesner, the greatest naturalist of his century, completed his book *On Fossil Objects*. Fossils in Gesner's day meant anything 'dug up,' including fossils as we know of them today, but it also included mineral ores, natural crystals, and rocks; the distinction between them, at the time, didn't exist. Gesner intended his small book on fossils to be no more than a preliminary essay, to be followed at a later date by a full-scale work on the subject. The larger work was never written; only a few months after completing that preliminary book he died at his home in Zurich in an outbreak of plague, leaving behind him a mass of unpublished materials. We know he would have contributed greatly to the field because he had published *History of Animals* about fifteen years earlier which included three innovations: (1) the use of illustrations, (2) the establishment of collections of specimens, and (3) the formation of a scholarly community cooperating by correspondence."

Moving to the next portrait, Professor Ross looked down, paused for a couple of seconds, then simply stated the name and date, "Lucilio Vanini, 1585 to February 9, 1619." He said it slowly but with deliberation; pausing again for a couple seconds. He continued, "It was his second book written in 1615 that did him in. *De Admirandis Naturae Reginae Deaeque Mortalium Arcanis*, roughly translated it means *Of the Admirable Qualities are Mortal and Goddesses of the Queen of the Arcana*, and it was reckless and truth-loving enough to suggest that humankind might have evolved from apes. This book was written 243 years before Darwin's *On the Origin of Species*. The pope ordered his tongue be cut out so he couldn't speak another word about his heretical ideas, and in 1619 he was killed at the stake and burned. His ashes were cast to the wind and another freethinker casually disappeared from the historical record." He paused as he contemplated the ramifications; for himself no doubt, and for his students that he hoped would eventually pursue a teaching career. "Let's move on, shall we?" he said, his comforting voice returning.

Again, he started off with a name and date, but kept going this time. "William Hunter, 1718-1783, was a prestigious Scottish anatomist and physician, who had the Queen as one of his patients, and is quoted as saying, 'Though we may as philosophers regret it, as men we cannot but thank heaven that its whole generation is probably extinct.' He was referring to a jawbone of what would be later known as a mastodon, which didn't look anything like the elephants of his day." There was no pause and he didn't take a step, though turned to look at the next portrait. Both Michelle and David had to adjust to get a good look at the next one.

"Jean-Baptiste Lamarck," said the professor. Jean-Baptiste Pierre Antoine de Monet, Chevalier de la Marck, 1744-1829, was written on the portrait's frame. "He was the first important proponent of evolution, and he stated in *Philosophie Zoologique ou Exposition des Considérations Relatives à L'Histoire Naturelle des Animaux*," he paused, turned directly to Michelle, and said, "which, translated in English, is *Zoological Philosophy: Exposition with Regard to the Natural History of Animals*," he then turned back to looking and admiring the portrait while continuing his soliloquy, "that heritable changes in habits, or behavior, could be brought about by the environment, and that the use and disuse of parts could lead to the production of new organs and the modification of old ones."

Michelle was captivated by his knowledge, and, now his French, and his presentation.

The professor took a step to the next portrait, stood by its left side, turned to both David and Michelle, raised his left arm with palm facing his two-person audience as if presenting a wonder of the world, and continued, "I could talk for hours about Georges Cuvier." The name and date on the portrait was Jean Léopold Nicolas Frédéric Cuvier, 1769-1832. "In hindsight, he was a contradiction in terms; but, at the time, he was highly influential. He proved the concept of extinction, yet was thoroughly opposed to the idea of evolution as he knew it at the time; he supported the idea of a fixed number of species, yet argued that the distribution of fossils in the rock record proves fossils occur in the chronological order of creation: fish, amphibians, reptiles and mammals." He moved to the next picture.

"Like most of the other notable figures up on this wall, it's difficult to just say a few things. Entire books can and have been written. Case in point: Richard Owen, 1804 to 1892. He's probably best known for coining the word 'Dinosauria,' which means terrible lizard. An English biologist, anatomist, and paleontologist, he was one of the chief and outspoken critics of Darwin. And he was also a plagiarist."

"Plagiarist?" Michelle inquired, still hanging on every word of his.

"Yes, a plagiarist. He would near-routinely take the discoveries of other people and make them his own by publishing it. Examples include crediting himself with the discovery of the Iguanodon, completely excluding credit for the original discoverer, Gideon Mantell, whose portrait is not up on this wall. Owen was eventually dismissed from the Royal Society's Zoological Council for…"

Before finishing the sentence he turned to look at Michelle, who was nodding her head as she finished his sentence, "plagiarism."

"That's right. Good. Just out of curiosity, what are you majoring in, Michelle?"

"I haven't really decided," she answered. "It seems so difficult to decide when we're constantly bombarded with messaging that says the world is coming to an end."

Professor Ross, who was listening intently to her, smiled, and said, "What a brilliant response. I think there's a lesson in there somewhere."

"Stop listening to other people, find something interesting and bigger than you, and pursue it?"

"Why, yes, exactly!"

"It's not so easy, not so simple. There are pressures: family, friends, society."

"Yes, the environment does shape our behavior. That's okay, you have time."

Michelle looked at David, reading in his eyes the same thing she was thinking: "it's Friday, this is all interesting; but, let's go have some fun." She raised her eyebrows at him—he shook his head yes—and walked a little to the right to try to move the conversation—the lecture—to an end.

"Professor, who is that?" Michelle asked, skipping over the mostly nineteenth century portraits of James Parkinson, William Smith, Johann Gotthelf Fischer von Waldheim, William Buckland, Adam Sedgwick, Jacques Boucher de Perthes, and Roderick Impey Murchison.

"Oh her," he began, "I can see how you'd be interested in hearing about Mary." He made eye contact with Michelle again and was sincerely interested in being supportive. Michelle sensed his warm, personal connection to her.

He continued, "Mary Anning, 1799 to 1847, was a British fossil collector, dealer and paleontologist who became known around the world for having made a number of important finds.

She discovered the fossilized remains of an ichthyosaur, a giant marine reptile that resembled fish and dolphins, and the world's first Plesiosaur skeleton."

"Taken together, Anning's discoveries became key pieces of evidence for extinction. Remember that Georges Cuvier had argued for the reality of extinction in the late 1790s based on his analysis of fossils such as mammoths. Nevertheless, until the early 1820s it was still believed by many scholars that animals did not become extinct, in part because they felt that extinction would imply that God's creation had been imperfect. Any oddities found were explained away as belonging to animals still living somewhere in an unexplored region of the Earth. Mary Anning found some fossils so unlike any known living creature, that she struck a major blow against that idea."

"Anning's sex and social class, however, prevented her from fully participating in the scientific community of nineteenth century Britain. She struggled financially for much of her life and her father, a cabinetmaker, died when she was eleven. Although she became well known in geological circles in Britain, Europe and America, she was not eligible to join the Geological Society of London because she was a woman, and did not always receive full credit for her contributions; indeed she wrote in a letter, 'The world has used me so unkindly, I fear it has made me suspicious of everyone.'"

"A panel of experts invited by the Royal Society just recently included Anning in a list of the ten British women who have most influenced the history of science, and, indeed, her picture is also up on our wall." Professor Ross paused for a moment to let Michelle take it all in. Michelle was enthralled.

He continued, "She was even the basis of the tongue twister 'She sells seashells.'"

"She sells seashells?" Michelle asked.

"Yes, that's the one. I don't remember it, and I probably couldn't say it correctly even if I did."

"Don't look at me," David joked. They all smiled.

"So, what happened to her?" Michelle inquired.

"Well," Professor Ross said as he thought. "She passed away before she reached the age of fifty, from, uh…" he paused, then, trying to be as tactful as possible, said, "breast cancer."

Michelle grimaced as she noticeably exhaled. "Breast cancer," she sighed.

"Don't you two have anything better to do on a Friday than to hang around with an old academic?" Professor Ross said, trying to raise their spirits.

Michelle and David smiled. David was probably more relieved, as he had heard this all before, and, in fact, gave other folks the same tour.

"David's going to take me to see Martians and then I'm going to take him to dinner."

"Martians!?" Professor Ross asked and exclaimed.

David looked at Professor Ross and said, "Echinodermata, molusca and such."

"Oh, those!" Professor said with his signature laugh. "Well, that sounds much more promising than hanging around with dead scientists."

"William Whewell!" David blurted out.

"Huh?" Michelle chimed.

Professor Ross started to explain, "Oh, William Whewell was one of the tutors at the University of Cambridge who Darwin met during his education there. It was William who coined the term 'scientist' in…"

David cut him off, "In 1834."

"Yes, good, 1834," Professor Ross said, adding credible, positive reinforcement. Michelle was amused and could see that the two boys had a connection.

"We can talk about the others whenever you want Michelle," Professor Ross said as they started walking toward the door. "There's so much more to talk about: Charles Lyell, Alfred Russell Wallace, T. H. Huxley, and let's not forget Darwin."

"David has already given me an intro to Darwin last weekend," Michelle said.

"Oh he has, has he?" Professor Ross said with that subtle laugh and peaceful, humble smile.

"I'll be studying evolution in no time, professor," Michelle said giggling. Professor Ross was amused. The three walked past Darwin's portrait, stopped to look, then proceeded to and out the door.

As they walked out the door of the Darwin Institute and on to the Biomedical Quadrangle, a well-kept, safe, beautifully green, grassy knoll adjacent to the Paris Green, as it was commonly known by students, they couldn't help but notice a small but growing mass of students surrounding a tall, thin, dirt-blond-haired woman, with a noticeably long nose, even from a distance. They walked toward the excitement and could hear her voice that grew louder as they approached.

It might help here to describe this landscape. Imagine a square divided into four smaller, equal squares, each about the size of a small city block. The bottom left square consisted of the Paris Green, which, as stated above, was the student-friendly open space, the grass worn heavily in spots from daily treading. Above that was a group of five four-story buildings — three on the left and two on the right — collectively known as the Biomedical Buildings, numbers one through five. To the right of the Biomedical Buildings was the Darwin Institute, the tallest of the buildings on that site at six stories. It was set at the back of the block; in front of it was the Biomedical Quadrangle — "the Quad," as it was known — which was where David, Michelle and Professor Ross were headed.

In front of the Quad, on the bottom right of the last square, was another biomedical building, number six, which connected to the thin Biology Annex on the right, which in turn connected upward to the Darwin Institute. Besides classrooms on the second floor, the Biology Annex contained a hallway on the first floor which had long, secure, sliding glass doors on both sides, allowing students with security badges to enter from either side after hours.

The entire square made up of the four smaller squares was collectively known as the Biomedical Campus; to the left was the main road, just a couple blocks from the Pacific Ocean. To the right was a small open space with a statue in the middle followed by the Music Building, currently masked as a medical school building, on its own little quadrangle. The top was true north, just a few blocks from Geisel Library, and the bottom led south to the Pharmacological Sciences Building across the street, and, eventually, miles away, to San Diego and La Jolla.

The tree-lined area just described wasn't perfectly square; it looked more like a map of the United States with Florida's peninsula cut off. But the textual picture will have to do as we get back to story with Michelle, David and Professor Ross exiting the Darwin Institute, noticing a small but growing mass of students surrounding a tall, long-dirt-blond-haired woman. They walked toward the excitement and could hear her voice growing louder as they approached.

While the three of them initially walked together out of the building, Professor Ross was struck by a near-two-lane highway of teeny, tiny, reddish-blackish ants marching to and from the east of the entrance to the Darwin Institute Building. He trailed David and Michelle—who were already a few feet ahead and walking toward the event, not noticing his observations behind them—somewhat transfixed on the ants. He vacillated between walking forward with his head turned to the left while looking at the ants, and stopping in fascination. He also walked slowly backwards toward David, Michelle and the action, alternating again between stopping, walking backwards, and walking near-forward with his head turned. "Hello ladies," he said under his breath, realizing that they were, no, not leafcutter ants; but, most likely Argentine ants, an invasive species native to, well, Argentina, amongst other countries.

Professor Ross knew that they were introduced to countries including America by humans transporting commodities such as coffee in the late nineteenth century, and probably before. These ants have been extraordinarily successful, he thought, in part, because different nests of the introduced Argentine ants rarely compete with each other — they are so genetically similar — unlike most other species of ant. Thus, in most of their introduced range they form supercolonies. But his thinking about the ants was overcome by the human commotion now before him.

"Sodom and Gomorrah were infamous hotbeds of homosexuality," the lady in the center of the commotion said. "From Genesis 19:5-8: 'and they called to Lot and said to him, "Where are the men who came to you tonight? Bring them out to us that we may have relations with them." But Lot went out to them at the doorway, and shut the door behind him, and said, "Please, my brothers, do not act wickedly.'" Apart from the fact the city was clearly destroyed by God because of homosexuality in the narrative of Genesis 19, even the New Testament clearly states exactly the same thing in Jude 1:7: 'Just as Sodom and Gomorrah and the cities around them, since they in the same way as these indulged in gross immorality and went after strange flesh, are exhibited as an example, in undergoing the punishment of eternal fire.' Any sinner should always remember that the God who commands us to love our neighbor is the same God who will cast any and all unrepentant sinners into the eternal fire."

Professor Ross caught up to David after staying back a few moments to observe the ants and said, "Looks like we have a new friend lecturing today."

"Yeah, I haven't seen her before," David replied. "But it sounds like the same old same old."

"You'd think they'd come up with something a little more witty after a century and a half," Professor Ross said to David.

Michelle didn't know what they were talking about; but, was interested in hearing more from them and even some more from the fair-skinned beauty speaking. She actually was intrigued at the idea of being lost in a crowd of Americans and participating in some sort of group activity, though this probably wasn't the kind of event she anticipated.

The three of them reached the assemblage as the preacher continued, "My cherished Bible has this to say about homosexuality: from Leviticus 18:22-23: 'You shall not lie with a male as one lies with a female; it is an abomination.'" She paused, looked around at the audience, and continued.

"From Leviticus 20:13: 'If there is a man who lies with a male as those who lie with a woman, both of them have committed a detestable act; they shall surely be put to death.'" She paused again, just looking up at the first person she saw, making eye contact, then turning her head to continue, "From First Corinthians 6:9: 'Or do you not know that the unrighteous shall not inherit the kingdom of God? Do not be deceived; neither fornicators, nor idolaters, nor adulterers, nor effeminate, nor homosexuals.'"

Before she finished this quote, she reached into her back pocket, pulled out her Bible, and opened it to the page that she was about to quote, "From First Timothy 1:9-10: 'Realizing the fact that civil law is not made for a righteous man, but for those who are lawless and rebellious, for the ungodly and sinners, for the unholy and profane, for those who kill their fathers or mothers, for murderers and immoral men and homosexuals and kidnappers and liars and perjurers.'" Again, she paged though her Bible to the next passage she was going to read from before finishing this quotation.

"And from Romans 1:26-27: 'For this reason God gave them over to degrading passions; for their women exchanged the natural function for that which is unnatural, and in the same way also the men abandoned the natural function of the woman and burned in their desire toward one another, men with men committing indecent acts and receiving in their own persons the due penalty of their error.'" She returned the Bible quite gracefully to her back pocket and was pleased to present her summary, as she probably has done many times before, at many different venues, probably mostly college campuses.

"Homosexuality is clearly condemned by the Bible. It goes against the created order of God. He created Adam and then made a woman. This is what God has ordained and it is what is right. Unlike other sins, homosexuality has a severe judgment administered by God Himself. This judgment is simple: they are given over to their passions. That means that their hearts are allowed to be hardened by their sins. As a result, they can no longer see the error of what they are doing. Without an awareness of their sinfulness, there will be no repentance and trusting in Jesus. Without Jesus, they will have no forgiveness. Without forgiveness, there is no salvation."

Yearning for applause, she was met with the crowd's indifference and ridicule. The young man directly in front of her blew a rather large bubble—almost as big as his head—with his mouthful of Wrigley's® Hubba Bubba® bubble gum that he was previously, and annoyingly chewing. A guy toward the far left hand side of the crowd shouted, "Lady, the most anti-gay politicians and preachers that shout the loudest are always the ones looking to keep people from knowing the truth that they themselves are gay and are scared to death of being outed from the closet."

Most in the crowd laughed and few yelled things like "Yeah!" and "That's right!" and "In your face."

All the preacher could retort with was, "Fornicators beware, the devil also has you in his power and nothing good will come of it. Repent."

As the preacher and crowd took some time to reload, our three friends had a private discussion.

"I think I've seen her before. What's she doing?" Michelle asked.

"She's proselytizing," Professor Ross answered.

"Huh?" wondered Michelle. She knew he didn't say she's prostituting, but hadn't heard that word before.

Professor Ross could see that Michelle didn't know what he meant and wanted to provide as objective an answer as possible. He explained in his mentoring style, "Proselytizing," he began, briefly pausing and starting again. "Many Christians consider it their obligation to follow what is often termed the Great Commission of Jesus, recorded in the final verses of the Gospel of Matthew: 'Go ye therefore, and teach all nations, baptizing them in the name of the Father, and of the Son, and of the Holy Ghost, teaching them to observe all things whatsoever I have commanded you: and, lo, I am with you always, even unto the end of the world. Amen.'"

David and Michelle couldn't believe he knew that and their facial expressions showed it.

"Oh," Michelle said after a brief, incredulous pause. "So she's trying to convert everyone to her religion. That's illegal in my country; uh, well, at least nobody does it. Okay, maybe some people do it, but I've never seen it."

"I think it happens on nearly every college campus," said David.

"At least where there's a biology curriculum," Professor Ross added. David nodded his head in agreement.

Michelle was somewhat captivated by the scene and asked, "Can we listen some more or will we be too late to look at the Martians if we do that?"

"Well," David began, "she's as good a Martian as the ones they have on display in any aquarium."

Professor Ross humbly laughed and said, "Amen to that."

David looked back at Michelle and said, "We have plenty of time for more Martians," which helped Michelle feel secure.

The three were now at the outer rim of the semi-circle of students that now totaled about thirty. They each looked around and listened. The woman was situated more so at the focus of a parabola than in the middle of a circle. Funny how mathematics realizes itself in nature, and vice-versa.

So there were about thirty mostly students in the audience, and a couple young men were heckling her, "Preach on sister," one said while munching on a cherry Hostess® Fruit Pie®. "I'm a fornicator, and proud of it," said another through his large wad of chewing gum.

"You will all burn in hell unless you repent," she uttered without hesitation. After a slight pause in which she again gathered her thoughts, she continued, "Do you know why nations are on the brink of catastrophe and churches are overrun with unbelief and rebellion, their walls crumbling by moral decay and sin? The answer is in the Bible, if you really want to know," she said to the audience, turning and looking to just about everyone there as she spoke.

The guy to Michelle's left reached into his backpack and took out a two-pack of Hostess® Snoballs®, opened it, took one out with his right hand and began to eat it as he shouted with a mouthful, "Tell us more!"

She continued her tirade, "Do you know that many people who think they are Christians are deceived, for many ministers and teachers today teach partial truth? Do you know that salvation and good works cannot be separated? Do you know that if you do not obey God, you are not even saved?"

Someone from the audience, which was still growing, yelled out, "No, tell us!"

She continued without acknowledging him, "Do you know that if you do not walk in the light, the blood of Jesus does not cleanse you from sin? Do you know that if you claim to know Jesus and do not keep His commandments, God says you are a liar? Do you know that no liar will go to heaven?"

Another person, this time a girl, asked, "Did you get permission from the University to preach your silliness here?" Laughter came from the crowd. Michelle looked at David, David looked at her and then to Professor Ross who just rolled his eyes. David looked back to Michelle to see if she was enjoying the spectacle. She kind of was and started walking to the front to get a better look. David and Professor Ross followed, both engrossed in the entertainment yet wanting to protect Michelle.

Preacher girl didn't acknowledge the other girl's comment and simply continued, "Do you know that the things Paul wrote in the New Testament are the commandments of God? Do you know that if you are involved in a divorce and second marriage while your first companion is still living, you are living in adultery? Do you know that no adulterer or adulteress will be allowed into heaven? Do you know that God commands men and women to dress modestly? Do you know that there are many other commandments in the New Testament, and that the pastors who say you are all right without obeying them are lying to you, meaning that both you and they will be lost unless you repent? Do you know that to believe in God but not obey Him is death? Do you know that your final judgment will be based on what you did and how you obeyed what you knew?"

While she was pleased with her performance, instead of being greeted with applause, one of the boys near the middle shouted out, "You're a hypocrite. You stand there and preach to us, yet we know not what you do in your spare time, unless this is all you do." The crowd liked that comment and three different folks yelled "Nice," and "Good for you," and "Yes!"

"I keep the Sabbath, I do not murder innocent babies, I go to church and pray, pray for all of you, and will stay chaste until married," she passionately said.

"Yeah, right," said the guy who had just finished eating his Hostess® Snoball® in the back.

Someone else shouted, "Who in their right mind would marry you," which enlisted scattered laughter from the crowd.

The first to shout from the back added, "Explain what type of offense could possibly justify eternal, unbearable torture in hell, and while you're at it, what is hell like and where the hell is it? After all, we have telescopes now that see far beyond Earth and we have never seen anything resembling a place called heaven or a place called hell."

The crowd supported him with laughter and someone was heard to say, "Hell yeah."

She was noticeably distressed and looked around for a scapegoat to help her gain control of the dialogue again. She walked right up to Professor Ross, as he stood out from the rest of the crowd and, composing herself, in a sincere voice, asked, "Sir, all the beautiful things in the world, the hummingbirds, whales, sunrises, sunsets, sunflowers, orchids, roses, all these things that were created by an all knowing, all-loving, all-caring God. Do you believe in God?"

She chose the wrong person.

Professor Ross began to answer her, "You talk about God creating every individual species as a separate act, hummingbirds, orchids, sunflowers and other beautiful things. But I tend to think instead of a Loa loa parasitic worm that is boring through the eye of a boy sitting on the bank of a river in West Africa, a worm that's going to make him blind. Are you telling me that the God you believe in, who you also say is an all-merciful God, who cares for each one of us individually, are you saying that God created this worm that can live in no other way than in an innocent child's eyeball? Because that doesn't seem to me to coincide with a God who's full of mercy."

The preacher was momentarily speechless.

Professor Ross was ready with another strong, witty response from a fellow evolutionary biologist that he had a couple years before committed to memory. He said with a little more passion, "The God of the Old Testament is arguably the most unpleasant character in all fiction: jealous and proud of it; a petty, unjust, unforgiving control-freak; a vindictive, bloodthirsty ethnic cleanser; a misogynistic, homophobic, racist, infanticidal, genocidal, filicidal, pestilential, megalomaniacal, sadomasochistic, capriciously malevolent bully. No ma'am, I do not believe in this type of God." The crowd cheered.

After the audience quieted down, and the few people eating potato chips stopped their munching, the preacher replied, "You mock me. Just like Jesus Christ, I get mocked. I am doing the work of God, and so my annoyance of heathens and other unbelievers is well-justified. I may or may not be in for the brownie points; my primary objective here is to give you a chance to save yourselves from the burning cauldron of hell, and eternity is a heck of a long time to burn. You see, my dear Atheist, I was once one of you. But now I believe in God. I am no longer living a depraved, wasted life like you are living in now. Your life rings hollow, because you do not believe in an Almighty God. It takes more faith to be an atheist than to believe in God, therefore you have to exercise a significantly higher level of faith than me. Atheists invariably vote along similar party lines, hence they are simply following the herd, so to speak. You truly are descended from an ape."

David couldn't contain himself and retorted, "I would rather be descended from an ape than from your God, your parents, or you who prostitutes the gifts of culture and eloquence in the service of falsehood." The crowd went crazy with applause.

As the laughter and other noise subsided, Professor Ross turned to David and said, "Well, there's an original comeback," in his uniquely comforting smile. David smiled. Michelle was so happy being with the both of them and was learning much. She now looked upon them both highly.

"David," Professor Ross began, "I have to leave. Michelle, it was a pleasure to meet you and I wish you great success here."

Other people noticed him saying goodbye, and remained silent. The preacher also noticed the goodbyes, and didn't interfere.

"Yes, very nice to meet you professor," Michelle stated respectfully, as she shook his offered hand.

"Take good care of my number one graduate student, and try to keep him out of trouble," Professor Ross said to Michelle.

"I will, thanks," she replied, smiling.

"Have a great weekend, chief," David said to him as he turned toward the other direction to make for his car. The gathered students cleared a path for him to leave, and bid the Morgan Freeman look-alike a respectful, quiet leave.

As soon as he was out of earshot, the preacher changed gears and gave it another try, "Evolution is a theory, and a theory in crisis at that. It has been taught as fact for years and there is actually no real proof. There isn't one missing link, there are literally thousands of missing links. Let me give you two examples of where science reached the wrong conclusion about cave men, only to be shamed and proven wrong years later. For many years, scientists had two pieces of a skull. They were presented as the skull of a cave man that were found together. For years, this is how this skull was presented. Then the truth came out: the top of the skull had been found miles and miles away from the bottom of the skull. And as far as the two pieces going together, they were actually the top of a monkey skull and the bottom of a man's skull. Then there was the entire cave man family that was built around a tooth that turned out to be the tooth of a pig. Please don't tell me it can be proven, I don't trust science because they reach conclusions and state them as fact every day only to be proven wrong later on."

No one shouted when she finished that statement, which clearly pleased her. She continued, "I believe that God created us. That's my problem with teaching only evolution and not discussing intelligent design. All the alleged scientific proof will never change my belief that I am here because God put me here. I've seen way too many times that science has had to back-pedal because they claimed something to be fact when it was ultimately wrong. God has never back-pedaled."

"I don't believe that it's possible that we have just come out of nothing. If we did by some small margin of chance, then it is because God made it happen. Why is it so hard to believe that there is a God who created us in His own image? Why are so many people working so hard to try and prove He doesn't exist? I'd rather believe in Him now and find out in death that I was wrong, than not believe in Him now and find out in death that I was wrong." She was looking now directly at David.

Apparently David had inherited the group's spokesperson position. He was ready for the chance and began his response.

"First, your comments about gay people are repugnant, not to mention simplistic. Part of the difficulty lies in a definition of the word 'gay.' All you seem to think is that being gay is when two people of the same sex have sex, but the reality is much more complex. Homosexual behavior also includes courtship, affection, pair bonding, or parenting among same sex animals. Such behavior exists frequently in nature such as female-female albatross pairs, female-female rubbing in bonobos, male garter snakes that mimic the pheromones given off by females and thus get other males to mate with them, allowing them the opportunity to mate with females, and the list goes on and on, including scores of mammals such as the African elephant, Brown Bear, domestic cat, cheetah, and dolphin; birds, like the domestic chicken, emu, and king penguin; fish, such as some salmon species, sticklebacks, and whitefish; reptiles, such as the desert tortoise, speckled, red diamond and western rattlesnakes; amphibians, such as a couple salamanders and toads, and even invertebrates like the monarch butterfly, ants, house fly, crickets, dragonflies, spiders, wasps, some cockroaches, and, uh, the screw worm fly."

Some people in the crowd, captivated by David's speech, nonetheless giggled at that comment.

He continued, "No species has been found in which homosexual behavior has *not* been shown to exist, with the exception of species that never have sex at all, such as sea urchins and aphids. Moreover, a part of the animal kingdom is hermaphroditic, truly bisexual. For them, there cannot be any such thing homosexuality. How can you respond to this?" He paused for a moment, and, seeing that she was a little confused, returned to his own speech.

"I didn't think so," he said referring to her inability to explain how a hermaphroditic animal cannot be homosexual.

"Next, and more importantly, the word 'theory' in science does not mean the same thing as 'theory' in the ordinary use of the word. 'Theory' as used in science means that it best explains or models the natural world and can be used to make predictions. A 'fact' just means that something can be deemed true or not. Evolution is both a theory and a fact, because it best explains the natural world and hasn't yet been proven false. For specific evidence you could see Lenski's experiments with bacteria, showing how a specific strain altered both its phenotype and genotype over time when given a new food source. Yes, it adapted."

The crowd was clearly on his side.

"Let me continue," he said, not so much wanting to put her in her place as much as sincerely wanting to teach her the truth. He stepped back a little and, although he was directing his words toward the preacher, he was cognizant of the larger group of people, and spoke loud enough that they too could hear him.

"The mechanism of evolution as first proposed by Wallace and Darwin includes natural, artificial, and sexual selection. There are many good, recent, accessible books on the subject that show the evidence, yet, there is so much evidence that no one book presents it all. For example, if all the fossils were to suddenly disappear, we could study DNA of extant — currently living — species and see the similarities that exist between species, for example, us and chimpanzees, and see that we are more than 98.5 percent similar to them. Regarding fruit flies, although we have other similarities, look up 'Hox genes' to see how chance alone or separate, distinct creation events does not and cannot make any sense in explaining how different species can have similar genes doing similar things, unless there is a God — an invisible invertebrate — that set out to deceive us. And isn't that the ultimate statement of creationism, that the present universe came about as the result of the action or actions of a divine creator, which is most certainly outside the abilities of science to test. Among the two theories presented to date, Creationism, also realized as Intelligent Design, and Evolution, only Evolution stands as the most parsimonious theory to explain the natural world."

He took a breath and continued, "True, science classes at one time taught about Piltdown man — that's the name of the fictional person whose skeleton was connected to the skull you mentioned — but when it was found out to be a hoax, it was no longer taught. Science is about observing the natural world, formulating hypotheses, testing those hypotheses and then either finding that any single hypothesis is false and letting it go, or finding some basis for acceptance, in which case keeping it active. 'Germs cause disease' is an active theory because it has been tested and verified, not rejected, and is taught in science class."

David was pleased that the arguments in his brain were flowing nicely through his mouth. Michelle had been, and was continuing to hang on his every word, much like she did with the professor, only she was becoming enamored with him, thinking that he was the smartest, bravest, most talented guy she had met since coming to the states. Cute too. David couldn't help thinking what on Earth she saw in him.

David continued leaning into the preacher, "Regarding the perceived meaning of Darwin's origin of species, Darwin never proposed a mechanism for the origin of life; that field is young and is called abiogenesis. There are currently many thoughts, but no one theory or tested hypothesis stands out as of yet. The mechanism for speciation, however, which is the term that reflects Darwin's books, includes natural, artificial, and sexual selection. Each one of those mechanisms has never been proven false, yet, admittedly, should continually be tested. The theory of how things evolve, like the germ theory of disease, the heliocentric theory—that the planets orbit the Sun and not the Earth—the standard model, the theory of relativity, and others, cannot be considered proven facts in the sense of absolute certainty, however, they best model the natural world and have not been falsified."

David took a breath, and before the tall preacher could respond, he kept at her, "I'm not sure that even if we woke up tomorrow with the moon in the center of the Solar System— we've been wrong for four-hundred years, it's a lunar system— and all germs were discovered to not get people sick, and mass was no longer related to energy in any way, no, that would not necessarily mean that there is a God. In other words, if evolution is not true, then that doesn't mean that God created it all. The existence of a God presents its own problems, like what came before it, and how was it created. In short, it cannot be tested; thus, it does not belong in science. Again, in religious school, philosophy, and perhaps even literature classes, yes, by all means, feel free to read and talk about God. Science, however, is only about that which can be tested, then falsified or verified. Religions tell children they might go to hell and they must believe while science tells children they came from the stars and presents reasoning they can believe."

Happy he made it this far without getting tongue-tied— most likely because he was in the presence of such a pretty, smart girl who inspired in him the confidence that was, in turn, the quality that she liked in him—he tried to put it all together to end the discussion on a positive note. He did so for Michelle, to make a difference to the preacher who wasn't listening but was thinking of a response, and for the thirty or so spectators that had found their natural leader.

David began his closing remark, "In summary, *On the Origin of Species* was a groundbreaking presentation of the evidence, and inspiration for further refinement, such as the discovery of DNA. Now, *nothing* in biology makes sense except in the light of evolution. It was also the start of looking at the evidence for a mechanism of speciation and radiation that includes natural selection, which would include geographic isolation, artificial selection, which, by the way is best exampled by dogs—dogs are one species and radiated due to human intervention, which is also known as selective breeding—and sexual selection, vividly explained by watching the behavior of peahens and peacocks in their natural setting."

"The discovery of new evolutionary facts, and validations of old, where science is a verb and not a noun, continues today and no example has been found to contradict evolution. Evolution never intended, nor does it intend, to explain the mechanism for the origin of life; that is abiogenesis. God does not explain any natural process, as it cannot be tested and either falsified or verified by a third party. Religion is not a material science. And this seems to me to be the only fair and legitimate manner of considering the whole question, by trying whether it explains several large and independent classes of facts such as the geological succession of organic beings, their distribution in past and present times, and their mutual affinities and homologies. If the principal of natural selection does explain these and other large bodies of facts, it ought to be received."

Taking a big breath, doing his best to empathize, he continued, "I understand your point that you believe that God created us. No problems here with that, and, although I don't speak for all scientists and educators, I don't think they have a problem with that either. It's a free country. Now, if you want to teach that in science class in public school, or any science class in any school, scientists would have a problem with it because it isn't science. You might want to look up the word 'belief' and you will probably not like what you see, as it means 'a false thought.'"

"If you can devise a way to operationally define and then test the hypothesis that God has not back-pedaled, and then not find it false, it should be taught in science class. You can, though, currently teach creationism in religious school, where it is, in fact, currently being taught. You can also teach it as a philosophy in, uh, philosophy class, and you can read some of the wonderful parables of the Bible in literature class."

As he delivered that last sentence, and thought back about what he had just accomplished, he realized that he hadn't done something like that before, performing on the fly and responding to a public preacher. He was pleased. He looked at Michelle who gave him her complete, personal attention, looking deeply into his eyes. She took his hand and held it tight as if to say "nice job," then said, "That was amazing."

"Thanks," he said humbly. But before they could leave to finally start the weekend, the preacher started to speak again.

"If you knew a woman who was pregnant, who had eight kids already, three who were deaf, two who were blind, one mentally retarded, and she had tuberculosis, would you recommend that she have an abortion? Yes? Then you just killed Beethoven!"

Michelle looked at David, and, having spent some time with him in the Music Building, knew that he would have a great response. Michelle then looked at the preacher and said, "You picked the wrong guy to say that to." With that, Michelle looked into David's eyes, and, again without saying a word, David took her look to mean "go get her." And that's exactly what she meant. And he did.

"What absolute garbage," David began. "Though Ludwig van Beethoven's parents had seven children, Ludwig was not the youngest. He was the second born child to his parents on December 17, 1770. The first born was named Ludwig Maria.

Ludwig Maria did die six days after his birth, but there is no knowledge that he was born blind, deaf or mentally retarded."

"Also, his mother did contract tuberculosis, but not until Beethoven was nearly twenty years old. Beethoven's parents had five children after him: Casper Anton Carl, Nikolaus Johann, Anna-Maria Franziska, Franz Georg, and Maria Margareth Josepha. Anna-Maria and Franz died days after their birth. None of the children were known to be blind, deaf or mentally retarded. And none were ever institutionalized."

"There are a lot of versions to this lie," David said to the crowd, gazing at various people there. "Some claim that Beethoven was deaf at birth and became a great composer despite this disability. This is also false information. Beethoven suffered hearing loss which was caused by, most likely, scarlet fever, not genetics. He was already an accomplished composer by the time he started to lose his hearing. But Beethoven's loss of hearing did cause him to go into a deep depression."

Speaking now directly to the preacher, he said, "Lady, your supposed facts of the case, while made up for maximum emotional affect, aren't really relevant anyway. The logical conclusion we are meant to draw is that abortion is wrong and, by inference, it follows that any missed opportunity for conception is also wrong. If an abortion may rob us of a Beethoven then so too may any missed opportunity for a woman to get pregnant. Indeed, taken to its logical extreme no woman should ever be allowed to have a period. Even a rape should not be objectionable or resisted because the outcome may be a remarkably talented musician."

David thought carefully before concluding, "You are a twisted, stupid, desperate, valueless parasite, robbing us all of our time, patience, and energy. We have better things to do, and, I here and now say goodbye."

With that, Michelle gave him a kiss on the cheek, took his hand, and led him away from the pack, who were applauding David and yelling all sorts of put downs and obscenities at the preacher. Michelle and David walked toward the main road, the same way that Professor Ross had traversed earlier, where they intended to wait for a campus shuttle to pick them up and deliver them to the Birch Aquarium, a couple miles away.

They were still within ear shot of the preacher and she tried to give a parting shot, "Fornicators beware, the devil has you in his power and nothing good will come of it. Repent."

Michelle stopped, looked at David who sort of bumped into her, looked at the preacher, then back to David, smiled and said loud enough for the preacher to hear, "I just met him; but, he might get lucky. You never know."

David fully opened his eyes, smiled and let out a little laugh. In like Flynn, he thought. They looked at each other and smiled some more; Michelle once again took the lead and they walked into the sunset together.

That's just a figure of speech, of course, as they were walking nearly in the opposite direction of the Pacific Ocean, to wait for the shuttle.

"Do you think we still have time for Martians?"

"Skripps is right down that way a couple miles; we'll be fine if there's a shuttle," he said with a positive tone in his voice, pointing southwest. "They're open 'till five."

"Martians!" Michelle excitedly proclaimed.

"Martians," confirmed David.

At the Aquarium

David and Michelle exited the shuttle-bus with big bright smiles on their faces. The first thing they saw was a fountain of sorts: two whales standing straight out of the fountain on the left, and one whale tail coming out of the smaller second.

Although they should have walked straight over to the ticket counter, a sign caught Michelle's attention. She walked over to it, and David followed. David watched and heard Michelle read the words of the sign, "Be aware of snakes. Rattlesnakes may be found in this area. They are important members of the natural community. They will not attack, but if disturbed or cornered they will defend themselves. Stay on sidewalk."

"Rattlesnakes!?" Michelle asked, warned and exclaimed to David, her eyes wide open.

"Yup. They're more active in the afternoon when it's warmer, but sometimes, in the morning, they just lie in the Sun to warm up. I'd hate to step on one accidentally, but it happens," he said, empathetic to both snake and human.

"That reminds me," David said after a brief pause. Do you know the purpose of a rattlesnake's rattle?"

"Sure," Michelle started with confidence. "Just like some brightly colored poisonous animals, the rattle is there to warn predators that the snake is poisonous."

"Yes," David began, "that's the popular belief. Unfortunately, it's not the complete one."

Michelle was taken aback. "You mean it doesn't warn other animals to stay away?"

"Well," David began, "rattlesnakes don't purposely use their rattles to warn their potential predators, rivals, or enemies *per se*, though it is an effect. Animals once bitten would tend to stay away from this creature in the future, assuming they survive the bite. No, the real purpose of the rattle is to serve as a decoy."

"A decoy?" Michelle inquired. Suddenly, listening and learning from David became more engrossing than, well, anything else, Martians included.

"Yup, a decoy." David paused to ready his brief lecture. "Most animals, those without natural anti-toxins anyway, that are gutsy enough to try to eat or attack a rattlesnake, will go after the rattle. The rattle must be the head, right? When they do, the snake then bites the attacking animal. You can observe this with wolves or dogs. They go after the rattle nearly every time. When they do—zap—the rattlesnake bites 'em. Pain becomes the only inevitability; the lucky escape with their lives. Needless to say, they never attack a rattlesnake again."

David was pleased with his short explanation and Michelle was happy to hear the story. They walked to the ticket booth where David asked for and purchased two student-priced tickets. It was time to see Martians.

Since David had been here many times before, and had visited other aquariums as well, such as the John G. Shedd Aquarium in Chicago, Illinois, the Monterey Bay Aquarium in Monterey, California, and SeaWorld, the one in San Diego, California, he loved to bring along a radio and headphones to listen to his favorite music while daydreaming through the Martian landscape and staring at the various creatures. Actually, at the first aquarium he visited, the John G. Shedd Aquarium, he remembered wearing a Sony Walkman® that his father had bought for him at Christmas in Chicago, where he spent his childhood. He thought fondly of his father who told him how he worked hard to get into then graduate law school, had a successful career as an attorney, then launched and published *Eloquence Magazine* in print for many years before selling it at the peak of the internet boom. His father had always wanted to study biology, and, instead, happily settled on living vicariously through David who expressed an early interest in the field then excelled in it. He remembered his dad telling him how he named him "J. David." His father was named John, and didn't want to name him John Bennett, Jr., yet he still wanted to continue the legacy. The "J." thus didn't stand for anything, though it did refer to his father. Anyway, these days, David stored much more music on his Apple iPad®, given to him by his father at last year's Christmas, to replace the Sony Discman® then Sony Walkman® MP3 player that his father had given him as Christmas presents at years between the other two.

Walking to the Birch Aquarium's right side entrance, David imagined them being accompanied by, who else, Beethoven. He picked one of Beethoven's late string quartets for their entrance. So, for starters, David and Michelle enter the Martians' domicile to the Third Movement of Beethoven's String Quartet No. 15 in A Minor, Opus 132. He thought it best to start from about eight minutes into the movement, about the time the faster, much happier, joyous section has its reprieve.

He thought "joyful" because this particular movement was entitled "*Heiliger Dankgesang eines Genesenen an die Gottheit, in der Lydischen Tonart,*" which, translated from German to English, means "Holy song of Thanksgiving by a convalescent to the Divinity, in the Lydian Mode." The joy is for living, especially after overcoming a serious illness, as Beethoven did in 1825, in two ways. He did it by, first, listening to his doctors, doing without wine, coffee, or spices of any kind; and, second, by working on this string quartet, eloquently summarized by Beethoven himself when he said, "Notes will help him who is in need," a personal twist on a quote by playwright and poet William Congreve, who, more than a hundred and twenty-five years earlier, created a character named Almeria in his play *The Mourning Bride*, who said, "Music hath charms to soothe a savage breast, to soften rocks, or bend a knotted oak."

And so David and Michelle walked into the Birch Aquarium, Scripps Institution of Oceanography, University of

California, San Diego, accompanied by the thanks and joy of Beethoven, to observe Martians.

There were two sides from which to choose from as they walked into the main entranceway. To the left, sharks, and, to the right, pretty much everything else. They chose the sharks.

As aquariums go, it wasn't a very large shark tank; in fact, it wasn't a tank at all. Just a big, oval, wading pool of sorts, about the size of, well, a public swimming pool's wading area, only a little deeper, a little bigger, and with, well, sharks swimming in it. And it was enclosed in glass or some kind of thick glass substitute, like Plexiglass, which, by the way, was first brought to market in 1933, by Rohm and Haas Company. Nowadays, since there are many, many brand names to choose from, it's referred to simply as acrylic glass.

Anyway, it was a good thing that it was enclosed by the stuff, as there were several families there with kids of all ages. Ankle biters everywhere, making for some quite unthinkable consequences should any of them try to take a dip: the kids, that is. "Sharks," thought Michelle, "seen one, seen them all. They're dangerous, stay away. End lesson."

Michelle and David, now holding hands, had seen enough of these fish; nothing to capture their imagination there other than scenes similar to everything already done in the *Jaws* franchises. They walked toward the other side, still accompanied by Beethoven, at least in David's mind.

As they entered the other side, the right as defined earlier, there were yet two more rooms to choose from. Those two rooms, as David and Michelle would soon learn, were connected. The left side contained separate educational kiosks of sorts, each interactive, describing different aspects of the sea or other oceanographic tidbits. It also contained the sea horse exhibit which consisted of several tanks with different types of fish in the sea horse family. The other side, the new right side, had several separate tanks, each containing different fish. And that's what they really came to see.

They walked in, still hand in hand, to the aptly named "Aquarium," the seventh movement of the musical suite "Le Carnaval des Animaux," French for "The Carnival of the Animals," composed by Camille Saint-Saëns.

Now, Saint-Saëns, concerned that the piece was too frivolous, suppressed performances of it and only allowed one movement, "*Le Cygne*," in English, "The Swan," to be published in his lifetime. Yet, going back to the music of "Aquarium," it was perfect for looking at Martians, David thought.

The melody is played by the flute—and yes, someone that plays the flute, in America anyway, prefers to be called a flutist—backed by the strings, on top of a piano's glissando-like, downward tricklings. And so they spent the next couple minutes looking at wolf and California moray eels, Califonia nettles, big, good looking, colorful, eye-catching, rhythmic, relaxing, pulsing jellyfish—moon jellyfish, bell jellyfish, lagoon jellyfish, and others—as "Aquarium" played in David's mind.

As they walked on, David thought back to Beethoven's string quartet that he had heard in his head when they entered the Aquarium. This time, he thought that the second movement, "*Allegro ma non tanto*," Italian for "Fast, but not so much," would be a good next piece to hear, especially about four minutes into it, a little before the lovely new section begins. It lasts but a minute; just enough time to take in some sea nettles, lion fish, and various sessile beings in the tanks ahead.

"Oh, look," Michelle said, as the music stopped in David's head. She let go of David's hand, pointing. "Uni." Their hands were getting a little sweaty and both needed a break.

"Uni?" replied David.

"Yes, uni. I love uni," Michelle said, pointing again to a sea urchin.

"I think that's a sea urchin," David pointed out.

"Oh, is that what you call it," Michelle said, smiling. "Every time I have sushi I order it. We call it uni."

"Funny," David said with a smile.

They moved to the next tank; it was larger than the previous on, and had several different types of starfish in it.

"*Bulgasali*," Michelle said in Korean.

"Bulgasi?" David replied.

"*Bulgasali*," Michelle said again, emphasizing the last syllable. "Starfish."

"Yes, starfish," David said. "Coolest animal on the planet. Look at that one there; it's called a brittle starfish."

"Brittle?" Michelle asked. "It's brittle?"

"It's named brittle," said David, "because you can move its arms to the left and right okay; but, if you try to move them up or down, they break off."

"Mmmm, frog legs," Michelle joked.

"Hahaha," David laughed, "sure, frog's legs."

"Tastes like chicken, eh?" Michelle said with a cute smile. David chuckled.

"You're probably sick of my lectures, Michelle, but would you like to hear something interesting about that other starfish?" David asked humbly.

"David, I love listening to you. You're gonna make a great professor someday," Michelle said sweetly.

David smiled. He really couldn't believe he was there with such a pretty girl, let alone that she liked him.

"Well, you can turn a starfish upside down, and, eventually, it will turn itself over back onto its correct side.

"Really?" Michelle asked innocently.

"Yup. They prefer to be on the side with those, uh, tube feet on their ventral side, which they use to, uh, walk with and to help them feed. That's also the side with their mouth. Biologists refer to that side as the oral side."

"Oh," Michelle said.

"Can you guess what the other side, the top is called," David asked.

"What was the first side called again?"

"The bottom with the mouth is called the oral side."

"Uh, anal?" Michelle answered, fairly sure she had it right.

"Anal?" David asked, acting surprised. "No! It's the aboral side!"

Michelle started laughing. She walked away a little with her hands on her face, still laughing.

David walked to her and grabbed her by the waist, laughing quietly into her ear. She turned around, still enveloped by David's arm, and kissed him on the lips.

"You're so funny," she said, as she returned the favor by hugging him. The two let go of each other and continued to walk to the next tank, which contained one sole beast, somewhat camouflaged in the same color as a rock it was affixed to near the back.

Yes, no Martian-watching trip would be complete without an octopus to view. We'll need some music to pair with this site. No, "Octopus's Garden" by Ringo Starr of Beatles fame will not do. No, there's only one piece that would correctly capture the mood, and it would have to be *"Le Jardin Mouillé pour la Harpe,"* French for "The Wet Garden for Harp," by Jacques de la Presle, an early- to mid-twentieth century composer. David knew nothing about the piece nor the man, other than it made for great octopus watching.

After just a minute or so of staring at this beguiling creature, a couple of kids came running in from around the corner, from the kelp tank ahead to the octopus tank where Michelle and David were standing, past them to their parents, who were just beginning to look at the starfish. The taller, and probably older boy, couldn't contain himself, and said loudly, "Mommy, mommy, there must be a star wars convention here, I saw a group of Jedi masters on the other room."

The other, smaller boy, his mouth smeared with chocolate from the Nestlé® Crunch® bar he had in his also chocolate-marked right hand added, "I saw them too!"

Michelle and David, and the mother and father, turned toward the end of the large kelp tank, which was at the end of the hallway connecting that room with the next, waited just a few seconds, when a group of monks came in the room to view the kelp tank. They were dressed in traditional monk clothes, technically called robes. Christian monks wear cassocks, ankle-length robes; but these were Buddhist monks, and they were wearing robes.

Michelle turned to David, the mother toward the father, and each began laughing. David and Michelle then turned to the mother and father, and laughed with them together, all four looking at each other, then to the little boys, then back to each other.

Michelle and David walked on, stopping to take in the humungous kelp tank installed at the end. Yes, it was hypnotic; but, they had some sea horses and dragons to check out. They turned the corner to the next room.

And now we; well, David and Michelle, are on their way to the leafy sea dragon's tank. The only music that could do them justice, David thought, as they passed some interactive, oceanographic-themed kiosks, is nearly the entire third movement of the String Quartet No. 16 in F Major, Opus 135, by, who else, Beethoven. The third movement, "*Lento assai, cantante e tranquillo,*" translates from Italian to English as "very slow and quietly singing."

Actually, thought David, there were many more pieces of music that would work just as nicely to fill the background during the leafy sea dragon viewing. His mind began to wander through the various scenarios.

He could easily imagine listening to the Adagio in G Minor, by Tomaso Albinoni.

Now, the Adagio in G Minor for violin, strings and organ continuo, David remembered, is a neo-Baroque—written in the Baroque style but post-Baroque time—composition popularly misattributed to the eighteenth-century Venetian master Tomaso Albinoni; but, in fact, composed entirely by the twentieth-century musicologist and Albinoni biographer Remo

Giazotto. Although the composition is usually referred to as "Albinoni's Adagio," or "Adagio in G Minor by Albinoni, arranged by Giazotto," he thought, the attribution was, and still is, reversed. Albinoni's contribution to the piece was only a fragment—Giazotto himself constructed the balance of the complete single-movement work around that fragmentary theme; he copyrighted and published it in 1958. It has thus been established as an entirely original work by Giazotto.

Out of the ordinary a story it was; but David's mind went back to Beethoven, as it always did. He thought, "Why not the slow second movement, the *Adagio*, from Piano Sonata No. 1 in F Minor, Op. 2, No. 1?"

Now, he reflected, this second movement was written in 1795, dedicated to Joseph Haydn, one of his later teachers, and opens with a highly-ornamented lyrical theme, a perfect musical metaphor for these graceful dragons. David knew that this *Adagio* was the earliest composition by Beethoven now in general circulation. It was adapted from the slow movement of a piano quartet from 1785.

David fixated on this subject for a moment, remembering how it was said that Beethoven didn't learn a thing from Haydn; he learned to write from small musical motifs, a lesson passed to him by studying the works of Haydn, not necessarily studying with him. And his playing ability? Well, Ludwig was a great virtuoso and improviser, developing his "chops" by playing in the salons of the nobility, often playing the preludes and fugues of J. S. Bach's *Well-Tempered Clavier*.

David's obsession, his possession, was based on the sheer number of works by Ludwig van Beethoven that David thought just as impressive as their quality: nine symphonies; nine or so concertos; thirty-two piano sonatas, only fifteen of which have extant manuscripts, the rest have been lost; sixteen string quartets; a significant amount of chamber music; more than twenty unpublished sets of variations; over thirty bagatelles, "*Für Elise*" included; only one opera, revised twice; choral works, numerous songs and folksongs, sacred vocal works, and even a couple pieces written for wind bands. All in all, he produced a mass of over eight-hundred individual works.

Or what about the third movement from Beethoven's String Quartet No. 16 in F Major, Opus 135—he couldn't get that one out of his mind—or even the slow second movement from his Piano Sonata No. 8 in C Minor, Opus 13, the "*Pathétique?*" Cripes, he thought, nearly any slow movement by Beethoven would do, whether to accompany the leafy sea dragon or just listen to on its own merit. For it was only Beethoven, David thought, that could so clearly realize through music such a vast range of emotions. Beethoven, above all other artists, conveyed the hopefulness that men and women have the ability to be better than they are.

Most exquisite of all, David thought, would be to hear the slow, second movement from Beethoven's Piano Concerto No. 5 in E-Flat Major, popularly known as the "Emperor Concerto." But, no, he had heard it many times before, and preferred unique accompaniment.

Perhaps "*Clair de Lune,*" French for "Moonlight," the third of a four movement suite composed by Claude Debussy in 1905, might make a good accompaniment. Yes, it would, he thought.

The "*Méditation*" from the Opera *Thaïs* by Jules Massenet might also fit well here. Said "*Méditation,*" thought David, is a symphonic *entr'acte*—meaning "between the acts"—performed between scenes of Act II in the opera *Thaïs*. In the first scene of Act II, Athanaël, a Cenobite monk, confronts Thaïs, a beautiful, hedonistic courtesan and devotee of Venus, and attempts to convince her to leave her life of luxury and pleasure and find salvation through God. It is during a time of reflection following the encounter that the "*Méditation*" is played by the orchestra. Following the "*Méditation,*" Thaïs tells Athanaël that she will follow him to the desert.

Fascinating as the opera is, David decided it wasn't a good fit for today's leafy sea dragon viewing, and his mind raced to the next potential selection, thinking at the same time how much Massenet accomplished. In addition to his thirty-four operas, of which only twenty-five survive, Massenet composed concert suites, ballet music, oratorios and cantatas and about two hundred songs. His claim to fame was being elected a member of the *Académie des Beaux-Arts* in 1878, to the exclusion of Camille Saint-Saëns.

Why not Mozart? Why not Wolfgang Amadeus Mozart indeed, he thought. Perhaps the second movement, the *Andante Cantabile*, from Mozart's Violin Concerto No. 4 in D Major, K. 218; or the *Adagio*, the slow second movement from his Violin Concerto No. 3 in G Major, K. 216; maybe the romantic and popular slow movement, the *Andante*, from his Piano Concerto No. 21 in C Major, K. 467; or even his slow second movement, the *Adagio*, from the Violin Concerto No. 5 in A Major, K. 219, the so-called "Turkish Concerto," very long for a second, slow movement, but why not stay and stare for eleven minutes. Eleven hours would work as well; but, sleep is necessary, he thought, raising his eyebrows and shaking his head as if agreeing with himself.

This action did not go unnoticed by Michelle, who wondered what he could possibly be thinking. She looked at him; all he could do was smile back, being caught in a fantasy. As they turned the corner just a few feet from the leafy sea dragon tank, presented with the entire sea horse exhibit before them, David realized that he had but a few more moments to set the scene with the perfect music. Perhaps they could stop and look at those sea horses for a while longer to buy some time. They did just that, without a word, looking, walking, stopping, looking some more.

Thinking about Mozart's Turkish Violin Concerto prompted David to recall why some composers' works were labeled that way. Indeed, why was Turkish music always lively and almost always a kind of march?

Turkish music is not really music of Turkey, David thought, but rather a musical style that was occasionally used by the European composers of the Classical music era. This music was modeled on the music of Turkish military bands, specifically the Janissary bands. Janissaries were infantry units that formed the Ottoman sultan's household troops and bodyguards; the Ottoman Empire lasted from 1299 to 1923.

This Turkish rhythm is the same rhythm as the stereotyped chant of marching soldiers: "Left...left...left right left." And this rhythm was contained in the third movement of the "Turkish Concerto," the movement that David wasn't considering.

But still, he thought, reminiscing his years studying music, it seems that at least part of the entertainment value of "Turkish music" was the perceived exoticness. The Turks were well known to the citizens of Vienna—where Mozart, Haydn, and Beethoven all worked—as military opponents, and indeed the centuries of warfare between Austria and Ottoman Empire had only started going generally in Austria's favor around the late seventeenth century. The differences in culture, as well as the Viennese peoples' general discordant feelings derived from the many earlier Turkish invasions, apparently gave rise to a fascination among the Viennese for all things Turkish. Thus the labeling of this and other works as being Turkish.

Yes, Mozart, David thought, born in 1756, and living only until 1791, was an incredible genius in his own right, and an almost teacher of Beethoven's. The story goes thusly: in March, 1787, when Beethoven was but seventeen and Mozart thirty-one, Beethoven traveled to Vienna for the first time, apparently in the hope of studying with Mozart, but the details of their relationship are uncertain, including whether or not they actually met. After just two weeks there Beethoven learned that his mother was severely ill, and he had to return home.

But David needed to hurry and think of some music to acoustically accessorize the leafy sea dragon viewing. Nevertheless, he thought, nearly anything by Mozart, with his six-hundred-plus works, including twenty-seven sublime piano concertos, forty-one orchestral symphonies, twenty-two ground-breaking musical dramas, nineteen masses, four horn concertos, eighteen piano sonatas, and various arias, songs, canons, fantasies, variations, rondos, and more, could nicely accompany the leafy sea dragons.

Just a couple more feet and they would be there. How about another movement from "*Le Carnaval des Animaux,*" by Camille Saint-Saëns? Maybe this time they could hear movement XIII, "*Le Cygne,*" French for "The Swan," the only movement from this work to be published in his lifetime? No, not that one either.

Wait just a minute, thought David. Bach! In all the commotion he forgot about Bach. Surely a short Bach piece would work well here. And yes, the "Air on the G String" would be perfect for these graceful beings.

The title comes from violinist August Wilhelmj's late nineteenth century arrangement of the Aria from Bach's Orchestral Suite No. 3 in D Major, which Wilhelmj arranged for violin and piano. By transposing the key of the piece from its original D major to C major and transposing the melody down an octave, he was able to play the piece on only one string of his violin, the G string. But, to David, it would best be heard as originally intended, for string orchestra.

And they were there. David and Michelle, and the leafy sea dragons: three, four, no five of them. In Michelle's mind; well, she probably heard some current Korean popular—K-pop—love song, maybe by SuperJunior, Girls' Generation, SNSD, Beast, MBLAQ, 2NE1, Wonder Girls, SS501, or something like that: upbeat, with lots of energy motivated by love, or the longing for it. Perhaps, even, she would be recalling an old flame to one of the songs from a very famous 2003 Korean movie entitled *The Classic*, a love story. It could have been "Confession" or "I am Yours, You are Mine," both performed by Delispice. In David's mind, however, the two stood there, in awe, looking at these graceful Martians—mythological though not fire-breathing dragons with variously sized living seaweed strategically sticking out from several body sites, attached at the mouth to a *dungchen*, a long horn used in Tibetan Buddhist ceremonies—these living, respirating, slowly swimming, filter-feeding, leafy sea dragon Martians, listening to *"Träumerei"* by Robert Schumann.

Träumerei is German for dreaming, and that's exactly what they were doing. The seconds passed. No one else, it seemed, was in the room. There were no other tanks, no other fish; and, yes, the leafy sea dragon is a fish.

Without saying a word, Michelle gently and slowly grabbed hold of David's right hand. And there they stood. Seconds passed. Seconds more. Half a minute. One full minute. Ninety seconds. Two minutes!

"Träumerei" lasts about two-and-a-half minutes, and that's how long David and Michelle stood there, hand in hand, staring at these wonderfully mesmerizing fish that periodically looked back at them with equal astonishment. Perhaps the fish marveled at how the two bipedal, bilaterally symmetrical, upright animals with only five appendages, fixed, forward-looking eyes and a face that could be infinitely contorted, could possibly stay alive so long out of the fluidity, let alone be covered in such differently textured, colored and sized plant material. From the perspective of the fish, perhaps the plant fiber that adorned Michelle and David served as some combination of camouflage, protection and mate attraction.

Still holding Michelle's hand, David took a couple steps back, as if to provide a one-on-one lecture from behind, and began to speak, "The leafy sea dragon, *Phycodurus eques*, is a salt-water fish in the family that also includes the seahorses and is found along the southern and western coasts of Australia. The long, leafy protrusions emanating from these fish are not used for propulsion; they serve only as camouflage. The leafy sea dragon propels itself by means of a pectoral fin on the ridge of its neck and a dorsal fin on its back closer to the tail end. These small fins are almost completely transparent and difficult to see as they undulate to move the creature slowly through the water, completing the illusion of floating seaweed. Their habitat includes rocky reefs, seaweed beds, sea grass meadows and sand patches near coral reefs covered with sea weeds. Since leafy sea dragons move so slowly they look like drifting sea weed, which makes this fish the only animal in the world which hides by moving. Even though they have the ability to camouflage, they are also equipped with long, sharp spines on their body to defend themselves."

"Leafy sea dragons have two eyes above their snout and these eyes have the ability to move independently. In short, this fish can look at many directions, at the same time. This amazing creature has no teeth, but a long snout, which helps them to suck in small fish, shrimp and plankton. They catch prey with the help of their ability to camouflage—their food thrives in the shade of the kelp forests where the sea dragons live—and it is sucked-up through the straw-like snout."

"During mating the female lays up to two-hundred-and-fifty eggs onto a brood patch on the underside of the male's tail, where they are fertilized. During each breeding season, male leafy sea dragons will hatch two batches of eggs. The male incubates the eggs for four to six weeks and gives birth to miniature versions of sea dragons. As soon as a baby sea dragon leaves the safety of its father's tail, it is independent and receives no further help from its parents. At birth the young are around twenty millimeters long, which makes them vulnerable to predators like fish, crustaceans and sea anemones; only about one in twenty survive to become adults. Young sea dragons grow fast, reaching twenty centimeters in one year and reach their mature length at two years. It is not known how long wild sea dragons live."

"Because leafy sea dragons are such fascinating creatures, some people illegally collect them for their aquariums.

Unfortunately, leafy sea dragons that are removed by divers usually die quickly because their captors do not provide them with the correct live food daily. Other major threats to leafy sea dragons include pollution and excessive fertilizer run-off, as well as loss of their sea grass habitat. They are 'Near Threatened' on the IUCN Red List of Threatened Species."

Michelle, who had been hanging on nearly every word of his, at the same time still watching the dragons, turned to him as he finished, smiled, and said, "David, you're so smart. How do you know all of this?"

He paused and smiled before saying, "I was just reading that from this sign posted over here," pointing to the large sign directly left of the tank, hidden from Michelle's view.

"I can't believe you," Michelle said laughing as she gently punched his arm. She continued to laugh, covering her face in the process and turning away from him. David began laughing too, as he gently hugged her from behind.

Still laughing, Michelle broke his hold on her, turned 180 degrees to look him in the face, reached with her right arm for David's left, and said, "Okay, funny guy, let's go eat."

With that, the two walked toward the exit, stopping in unison a couple feet from the tank, and then, without a word, both turned back to take one more look at the leafy sea dragons.

"They really are beautiful," Michelle said.

She didn't have to convince David, who added, "Yes, so peaceful too. I could watch them for hours."

"Me too," Michelle agreed calmly. Both smiled at each other as if finding a common bond.

They gazed at the dragons a few moments more, turned to walk out, stopped, turned back to look at the dragons again, then turned once more and walked toward the exit.

"Maybe next weekend we can go to SeaWorld, watch the dolphin and killer whale shows, and pet some other Martians."

"There's more?" asked Michelle.

"Oh, yes. They have stingrays in a big pond that you can feed and even pet."

"Do they bite?"

"Uh, no; but, they can hurt you with their barbed stinger that they have on the end of their tails."

Michelle looked confused. She opened her mouth but words did not immediately come out; it looked like she was about to sneeze. David took this action to mean that she wanted to say, "Why would they let people pet animals that could sting them." Yup, that's what she was thinking.

"Well, don't worry Michelle. All of the stingrays there have had their, uh, stingers cut off."

Michelle closed her mouth then smiled.

"And you can feed and pet them," he said. "Stingrays do have teeth but they are further back in their mouths. You hold a little fish — they sell you small fish to feed them for a couple bucks right by the exhibit — you hold it near their mouth and they just suck it right in. It's pretty cool."

Michelle giggled and said, "Oh, really? That sounds like fun. Yeah, rrret's go." David was a little shocked at first hearing her say the word 'let's' like that; but, seeing her smile, figured it was some sort of self-deprecating joke.

Better understanding and appreciating each other's humor, they were now outside, Michelle leading the way.

"Watch out for rattlesnakes, Michelle," David said.

She stopped, let him get to her side, took his hand, smiled and friendly said to his face, "If we see one, all I have to do is run faster than you and I'll be fine, right?"

"Yeah, that's right. Unless there's more than one."

They both laughed as they walked back to the shuttle stop. Michelle called her friend to let her know they were on their way. The shuttle arrived a few minutes later.

Karaoke

Michelle and David arrived at the restaurant "Seoul" at about six o'clock, after walking around for a little while. It looked like a typical restaurant on the outside: a two story, free-standing building, with the name "Seoul" spelled out in a neon sign, which was on. There were cheap window covers—tapestries—on the inside of the two windows adjacent to the entrance door, not so much to prevent people from looking inside; but, to set the mood for patrons who desired some privacy. The door had a copy of a two-page menu posted—in both Korean and English—for potential customers to review. David opened the door for Michelle, who smiled and felt a little giddy having had the door opened for her, and they walked in. The hostess looked like she knew Michelle.

"Ahn young ka seyo," the tall, thin, pretty Korean hostess said to Michelle.

"Ahn young ka seyo," Michelle said, smiling back. "This is my friend David," she said, motioning to him.

"Ahn young," David said, proud to have learned a new phrase. The hostess smiled. She looked back at Michelle and the two started speaking in Korean. David was a little uncomfortable.

Michelle turned toward David and said, "I'll be right back," warmly touching his bare arm.

"No problem," he said with a smile. Ah, the touch of a woman, he thought.

Michelle turned away and reconnected with the hostess in Korean. David took a couple steps back and fumbled through some of the magazines on the entrance-way counter; they were all in Korean. He picked one up that caught his fancy and began to page thought it. On the other side of the restaurant was a big, plasma television turned to a Korean cable channel, and on it was a thin, relatively tall, black-haired figure skater, in a one-piece short blue outfit, with a sequenced necklace attaching the front to — well, there wasn't much to the other side of the outfit — more sequences on the back that attached to the sides and bottom of her dress. There was a two-line English caption at the bottom of the screen that read "Yuna Kim, 2010 Vancouver Winter Olympic Long Program, George Gershwin Piano Concerto in F." David closed the magazine, but didn't put it back down on the table, captivated by the figure skater that had clearly won out over the magazine for his attention. He watched the skater while the girls talked to each other and, although the plasma screen was muted, he could hear the Gershwin piece in his head.

After a few minutes, Michelle turned back to David and said, "Shirley and Kimmy are already here; they're upstairs."

"David?" Michelle said, poking him.

"Oh, yes, I heard you," he said, still looking at the skater.

"You like her?"

"Well, what's not to like?

"That's the most famous person in Korea; we call her Queen Yuna," Michelle said with a proud smile.

The skating program ended, and Michelle and David continued to watch Queen Yuna skate to her coach, who hugged her. Queen Yuna walked with her coach to a booth, where they were met by an assistant carrying a jacket for Yuna. The coach high-fived the assistant, shook the girl's hand in midair; Queen Yuna hugged her, then they both sat down. The girl gave the jacket to Queen Yuna whereby the coach helped Yuna put it on, then patted her back. As Yuna was zipping up her jacket, the coach placed a bottle of water on a table directly in front of her; Yuna reached out for it, took it both hands, unscrewed it, then sipped from it by tilting her head back. She returned the cap back to the bottle, placed it on the bench she was sitting at on her right-hand side, waved to the audience with both hands, grabbed a tissue to dry her eyes of her joyous tears, and then waited for the score. As the scores were shown and announced — there was no sound — you could see Queen Yuna mouthing in English "Oh my God." She covered her wide-open mouth, first with both hands, then with only her right hand. She stood up, raised both arms with clenched fists, then let one arm down, and waved to the crowd with her right arm. Her coach remained seated, then eventually stood and gave her a hug. As they disembraced, the coach, who could be seen clapping for her, sat down; Queen Yuna remained standing, waving to the crowd.

As the clip ended, the screen cut to a Korean newscast.

"David," Michelle said, "Shirley and Kimmy are already here, they're upstairs."

"Upstairs?" he pointed.

"Yup. In one of the norebangs, uh, song rooms," Michelle quietly stated.

You see, karaoke originated in Japan about the same time as recording itself took off in the late sixties or early seventies. It is a blend of the words "empty" and "orchestra," although the machine wasn't patented by its first inventor, the Japanese Daisuke Inoue. It spread throughout Asia and the world, but was patented by a Filipino inventor, Roberto del Rosario, who developed then patented his "Minus-One" sing along system in the 1980s, which explains how much more popular karaoke machines are in the Philippines — one of the hallmarks of material good health of a family is having their own karaoke machine and its own room — than in the rest of the world.

Karaoke is very popular in South Korea, though folks from Korea prefer not to have it come standard with so much Japanese music, and instead store a great deal of Korean pop music, called K-pop. They also gave it the name "norebang," which translates to "song room," and Korean norebangs typically have a number of private rooms where patrons eat, sing, drink, and generally have a good time. Interestingly, the nation of *North* Korea issued an edict in 2007, banning karaoke bars from operating in the country to crush enemy scheming and to squarely confront those who threaten the maintenance of the socialist system. But that is neither here nor there, so let's get back to story.

David put the magazine back onto the table and Michelle led the way to stairs at the back. Before starting up the stairway, Michelle looked back at David, smiled, and reached back with her right hand toward David's left hand. She took his hand in hers and gently, gracefully led him up the stairs. Each smiled, though thought different things. Michelle thought her work was cut out for her and that he had a lot to learn. David, on the other hand, couldn't for the life of him know what she saw in him. Maybe practicing and studying all those years was indeed worth it.

"We're looking for *yodol*, uh, I mean, room number eight. Here it is." *Yodol* is Korean for the number eight.

Michelle smiled, opened the door, and her two friends Shirley and Kimmy sprang to life welcoming her like two happy dogs reuniting with their long estranged human.

The three said, "*Ahn young ka seyo*" at nearly the same time.

For Michelle, it was almost like going to a second home, or a special room in her house, like a family room. For David, it was like entering a small VIP room from a 70s style American discothèque, replete with its own spinning ball mirror.

"Shirley, Kimmy, this is that guy I was telling you about, David. David, this is Shirley," she said motioning to her with her arm, palm facing up.

"Hi Shirley, nice to meet you," said David.

Hi David," Shirley said with a smile.

"And this is Kimmy," Michelle said, motioning in Kimmy's direction with her hand, palm up.

"Hi Kimmy, great to meet you as well," David said.

"Hi David," Kimmy said, also with a smile, also kicking the air with her right leg, as if ending a subtle dance move.

Neither girl gave him the feeling that he was fat; just the opposite, in fact, they gave him the feeling that he was welcome and that they were interested in learning more about him. It was almost as if they were judging him to see if he was right for their good friend Michelle. Not his external appearance, mind you, but his heart.

"So, everyone, can you now tell me your real names," David requested.

Michelle took the lead. "Shirley's real name is Sang Hee Lee, Kimmy's is Eu-Ju Kim, and, hopefully you remember mine."

"Of course," David said without missing a beat, "Chun Hei Park, yes?"

There was a momentary pause and they all turned their heads to the video.

"Well, regardless of your names," David began, "you're three of the prettiest and smartest girls I've ever met."

"Straight up," Shirley blurted out. They all laughed.

David was beside himself, now the sole guy with three quite pretty girls. He tried not to stare at them, and, instead looked into their eyes and smiled, as if calling them cutie pies.

Of course there are other sides to the story. Michelle was charmed by David's piano playing; even here at the norebang she pictured him playing for her. Shirley had her own desires, but was happy for her best friend Michelle, and Kimmy was always good with everything.

The TVs in all the rooms were pumped continuously with old and current K-Pop music videos, and people in the rooms could only turn the TVs on or off, and control the volume. As David and Michelle entered, the last couple minutes to the video by 2NE1 called "I Don't Care" was playing, sung by a lead female singer, Dara, and three of her female friends. David was clearly in a new world; a good one at that, surrounded by women, thin and pretty all.

On the table where dinner would eventually be served, as had been ordered by Shirley and Kimmy earlier, were a bunch of Korean and Japanese candies including individually wrapped Hi-Chews — caramel green apple and caramel strawberry — different types of Kit Kat brand candy from Japan — not to be confused with a Nestlé® Kit Kat® bar — a melon chewing gum, and different types of individually wrapped ginseng candy. In addition, there were some *Zec* saltine crackers, *Kancho* chocolate center filled biscuits, *Choco* Chip cookies, some Korean brand chocolate-coated thin biscuit sticks, and other Korean labeled products all manufactured by the famous and popular Korean manufacturing company Lotte Confectionery Co., Ltd. As they got settled, the hostess came in with a tray full of a few cans of Coca-Cola®, glasses of ice, and some restaurant-made *yeot*, traditional Korean fermented confectionary, made from steamed rice, glutinous sorghum, corn, mixed grains, and sweet potatoes. This particular batch was covered with sesame seeds.

"Here you go, enjoy," said the hostess.

"Yummy, thanks," Kimmy said.

As the hostess placed tray's contents on the table, the next video to play was Park Bom's "You and I." David thought it sounded a lot like "techno-pop," and he was right.

"Bommie," Shirley bellowed out from her small frame.

"I love Bommie!" Kimmy exclaimed. "Hey David, have you ever tried *yeot*?"

David said, "No," and reached into the plate without disturbing the other candies and took a roll of *yeot*.

"Yo David," said Shirley with a smile, "eat *yeot*."

Both Kimmy and Michelle opened their eyes wide and covered their mouths as they laughed. The hostess was shocked but humbly smiled as well.

"Okay, what's up with that?" David asked.

Michelle, walked over to David, sat beside him, put her right hand on his left thigh, leaned toward his ear, and sort of whispered, "She just said 'Up yours.'"

He laughed, as did the others, and they looked at the hostess, who was also still kind of uncomfortably laughing, as she walked toward the door. As she got there, she said, "I'll be back in a few minutes with some dinner."

As the Bommie video ended, the next video to play was "So Hot" by the Wonder Girls, a fabulously popular group of five, well, wonderful girls.

"Is every girl pretty in Korea?" David inquired. The girls laughed.

"C'mon David," Michelle started, "No girl is ever pretty enough for her or her boyfriend. Did you know that plastic surgery is common in Korea?"

"Plastic surgery? Isn't that for car accident victims and old ladies looking to re-live their youth?" David said naïvely.

"You'd be surprised then," Michelle stated.

"Yup," Kimmy chimed in. "There's a fashionable street in *Apkujong* called "Plastic Surgery Street" where the almost beautiful people go."

"Almost beautiful people," Shirley said incredulously. "Funny!"

Kimmy exclaimed, "It's the media! A conspiracy theory!"

"Our ugly truth," added Michelle.

"So you guys have all had plastic surgery?" David said, turning his head as he looked at the girls' chests in order.

"Perv!" said Kimmy.

"Perv!" agreed Shirley.

Michelle just smiled. "Well, you never know," she said.

The three of them laughed. David felt comfortable that he could laugh too.

"C'mon Dave, none of us have had plastic surgery," Michelle said.

"I had my appendix taken out," Shirley excitedly said, standing up. "Look." She pulled up her shirt on the right side, holding it with her right upper arm, in the process showing the bottom of a purple bra she was wearing. Then unbuttoned and unzipped her pants and quickly brought the right side of her pants and purple bikini underwear lower than the left side. And there was the two-inch long scar proving that she indeed had her appendix taken out.

"Thanks so much for that, Shirley," David said, while thinking what a nice hard body she had, with a lovely shade of tan. The girls laughed while Shirley put herself back together.

"Tonsils," added Kimmy. Yes, she opened her mouth wide and showed everyone.

"Uh, I had braces, does that count?" Michelle asked sweetly. David just smiled.

Next up, "Kissing You," also performed by the Wonder Girls, though it really was a "cover," that is, it was originally performed by a eight-girl Japanese group named "*So Nyu Shi Dae*" and abbreviated SNSD in Japan, which translates to "Girls' Generation" in the states.

Michelle leaned toward David and kissed him gently on the lips. If there was a heaven, it was right here in this norebang.

Shirley stood up and sang along to the video and went close to Kimmy as if to kiss her. They both sang part of the song and kissed each other a couple of times. Michelle and David smiled and enjoyed the show. It's amazing what one beer does to skinny girls, thought David. Both Kimmy and Shirley approached David, though only Shirley kissed him lightly on the cheek; more like a peck. Michelle laughed.

The next video was of the song "Genie" by SNSD. David couldn't help himself as he stared at the performers' legs as they looked good in all the different shorts that they wore in the video. Very short, tight shorts.

Wouldn't you know it, the next video was of the song "Oh" performed by SNSD, Girls' Generation. David was truly having the time of his life. The only thing that could be better would be...

The door opened, and a mouth-watering waft of barbeque sauce instantly filled the room. The hostess was carrying a huge tray of a few large plates and several smaller plates and bowls all full of food fit for a king. In fact, one of the dishes was indeed originally for royalty.

As she walked into the room, everyone looked at the food. The biggest dish was called *Gujeolpan*, an elaborate Korean dish consisting of nine different foods assorted on a wooden plate with divided sections in an octagon. The individual foods were separated by color and ingredients, and were comprised of leafy vegetables, meats, mushrooms, and seafood. The center of that wooden plate had a stack of small pancakes made with wheat flour.

As the hostess put that first plate on the table, Shirley blurted out, "Tacos!" Michelle and Kimmy laughed.

The other big dish was *Galbi*, a full, hot—smoke was seen coming up—metal plate of pork ribs seasoned and lightly covered with Korean barbeque sauce stacked several ribs high.

The hostess put a dish towel in her hand before grabbing hold of this dish, then placed it next to the octagon-shaped plate. Still on the serving tray was a stone pot of soup, *kimchi jigae*, made up of *kimchi*, pork, and tofu, with an uncooked egg on top that boiled and hardened during the time it took to bring it to the table. There were a bunch of smaller plates and bowls of various appetizers called *Banchan* and *Anju*, the first of which included *kimchi* and the second technically side dishes for alcohol. She put them on the table one by one. The remaining metal bowls yet to be placed on the table were filled with rice.

Among the *Banchan* and *Anju* were cabbage, white blocks of fermented radish with no visible trace of their red covering, fermented cucumber, soybean sprouts, various noodles, and sugar-coated anchovies, called *myolchi*.

"More drinks?" the hostess asked pleasantly.

Michelle said, "More cokes."

"More beer!" said Shirley.

"Ok, I'll be right back."

As they began their feast, the next video to play was the same girl group performing "Run Devil Run," though this time they wore tight white then black outfits. David was captivated: the food, the girls on video, the girls in the room, take your pick. He wondered if they knew how excited he was. They did.

"Norebang!" Shirley yelled.

"No, let's eat," Michelle joked. "And we need alcohol before we sing, right David?! You have to sing too!"

"Uh, right," he said, knowing full-well that he would need some of that liquid confidence before doing any singing.

"Try the *myolchi* David," Kimmy suggested, pronouncing it "meerchee." Following Kimmy's finger, David grabbed a healthy portion of the anchovies with his chopsticks.

"You work those sticks nicely," Shirley said. David smiled, brought some of those critters to his mouth, and chewed.

"Mmmm," he uttered. The girls looked at him, looked at each other, and smiled silently as they started to bring some of the food to their plates. Michelle took control of the large octagon-shaped plate and started placing some of the different ingredients onto pancakes, passing them out as she did so.

And just then, the hostess entered the room with three cans of cokes and three bottles of Japanese Asahi® beer. She placed them on the table and asked, "Can I get you anything else?"

"More beer!" Shirley blurted out. "We'll polish these off in no time." The girls giggled. David did too.

"Ten-four," the hostess said. "I'll be right back."

Shirley abruptly stopped eating, turned off the video, and, with deliberation, grabbed a microphone, turned on the karaoke machine, chose her song, and got ready to sing. As the music began, it was easily identified by each of the three others as "Saving All My Love for You," the second hit single from Whitney Houston's debut album about a love affair with a married man. The singer is saving all her love for him.

"A few stormy moments is all that we shared,
You have your family, and they need you there,
Though I tried to resist,
Being last on your list,
But no other man's gonna do,
So I'm saving all my love for you."

Shirley walked over to David and stared right in his eyes. What a sexy little creature David thought, and Michelle didn't seem to mind the flirtatious behavior of either David or Shirley. Kimmy cracked up laughing, and Shirley walked back to the near center of the room in front of the table covered with still a great deal of uneaten food. Her beer was empty though no one noticed her drinking it. She continued singing:

"It's not very easy, living all alone,
My friends try and tell me, find a man of my own,
But each time I try, I just break down and cry,
Cause I'd rather be home feeling blue,
So I'm saving all my love for you."

Shirley walked over to Michelle this time and they high-fived each other. Shirley continued singing:

"You used to tell me we'd run away together,
Love gives you the right to be free,
You said be patient, just wait a little longer,
But that's just an old fantasy.

I've got to get ready, just a few minutes more,
Gonna get that old feeling when you walk through that door."

And believe it or not, the hostess came into the room just as Shirley finished singing those last few words, "through the door," with more cold beer. That was the most hilarious thing the four of them had seen that night, and certainly in a long time. They laughed and laughed. Michelle immediately spilled her beer, most of it in fact, because she hadn't been drinking too much of that second beer, and Shirley was on the floor kicking her feet and flailing her arms. The music kept playing. Kimmy was besides herself as well, though still seated. David, watching Michelle laughing, laughed himself at the coincidence, in addition to the big beer stain on Michelle's shirt, right across her chest, and all the way down to her pants.

As their laughter subsided, the hostess, who was still standing in the doorway, brought the four beers into the room and placed them on the table, Kimmy took the Microphone from Shirley, grabbed the wireless control from where the machine sat, and started looking for a song. The hostess, still chuckling to herself, left as Shirley asked for four more.

It was Kimmy's turn, as the three others focused their attention on the food and beer. Kimmy stood at the front of the table and looked for a song. She turned to the three others as the music to 2NE1's tune called "It Hurts," all in Korean, started. She sang it beautifully, for four solid minutes, and, when done, the three others clapped.

"That was beautiful Kimmy, Michelle said.

"Kind of boring and melodramatic, don't you think," added Shirley. "Hehehehe, just joshin' Kimmy. That was so sweet." As soon as she said that, she made a goofy face that's difficult to describe; suffice it to say, she made fun of Kimmy in Shirley's kind of way, with her tongue stuck out. It was done in good fun, and Kimmy took it well.

Kimmy handed the microphone and control to Michelle, who knew exactly which song she wanted to sing. Not to be outdone by Kimmy, she chose "Nobody But You," by the Wonder Girls, the English version.

"I want nobody nobody but you,
I want nobody nobody but you,
How can I be with another,
I don't want any other,
I want nobody nobody nobody nobody."

Gosh, pretty, smart, and a good singer, David thought. He couldn't help but smile and to feel something for Michelle. She was so cute, and, if she had one of those dresses, could be in that video looking and singing just as wonderful as, well, the real Wonder Girls.

"Why are you trying to, to make me leave ya.
I know what you're thinking,
Baby why aren't you listening,
How can I just, just leave someone else and,
Forget you completely,
When I know you still love me.

Telling me you're not good enough,
My life with you is just too tough,
You know it's not right so,
Just stop and come back boy,
How can this be,
When we were meant to be.

I want nobody nobody but you,
I want nobody nobody but you,
How can I be with another,
I don't want any other,
I want nobody nobody nobody nobody."

Kimmy and Shirley stood up beside Michelle and joined her in the repeat of the chorus, singing first to each other, then looking in David's direction, seductively.

"I want nobody nobody but you,
I want nobody nobody but you,
How can I be with another,
I don't want any other,
I want nobody nobody nobody nobody."

Michelle sang the next verse alone:

"Why can't we just, just be like this,
Cause it's you that I need and,
Nothing else until the end,
Who else can ever make me,
Feel the way I feel when I'm with you,
No one will ever do."

Kimmy and Shirley joined in again; all sang to David:

"Telling me you're not good enough,
My life with you is just too tough,
You know me enough so,
You know what I need boy,
Right next to you,
Is where I need to be.

I want nobody nobody but you,
I want nobody nobody but you,
How can I be with another,
I don't want any other,
I want nobody nobody nobody nobody.

I want nobody nobody but you,
I want nobody nobody but you,
How can I be with another,
I don't want any other,
I want nobody nobody nobody nobody..."

There was more to song. Kimmy, Shirley and Michelle were having a great time signing and imitating the actions of the real Wonder Girls, though, in David's mind, these were awfully wonderful girls in their own right.

David stood up to clap for the three musketeers as the song came to an end. Michelle jumped back to where David was sitting, and gave him a kiss, a longer, wetter kiss than before. David, not sure if the motivating force was romance or beer, didn't seem to mind.

"That was awesome," David told Michelle, looking directly in her eyes. "Hey Kimmy, Shirley, you guys rock!"

They all sat down and ate a little more. Michelle took a sip of beer, and everyone watched Shirley chug down her third or fourth beer. Shirley let out a short belch. Everyone laughed.

"We need more beer," Shirley said.

"She needs more beer?" David asked.

"Shirley is Shirley; we let her decide things like this," said Kimmy.

It's your turn David," Michelle stated with a devilish smile on her face. "Find something romantic," Michelle said as she handed David the Microphone. David stood up and dialed through the control to find a song. He looked for a while, and it wasn't long before Shirley returned with four more beers.

"Okay, I think I found one," David said as he turned around to face the jury and begin his song. "Are you ready?"

"Yeah," bellowed Shirley.

"Wooohooo," yelled Kimmy.

"Bring it home," said Michelle.

David prepared by trying to get serious, as Michelle and the other two musketeers prepared themselves for one of those hopelessly romantic songs. It wasn't long before a strong beat was heard on the speakers, the start of one of those hard-core rap songs. David began to sing:

"I like big butts and I cannot lie..."

As soon as he sang those words, the girls started cracking up. He looked at them; but, didn't miss a beat:

"You other brothers can't deny,
That when a girl walks in with an itty bitty waist,
And a round thing in your face,
You get sprung, wanna pull out your tough,
'Cause you notice that butt was stuffed,
Deep in the jeans she's wearing,
I'm hooked and I can't stop staring,
Oh baby, I wanna get with you,
And take your picture,
My homeboys tried to warn me,
But that butt you got makes me so horny,
Ooh, Rump-o'-smooth-skin,
You say you wanna get in my Benz?
Well, use me, use me,
'Cause you ain't that average groupie,
I've seen them dancin',
To hell with romancin',
She's sweat, wet,
Got it goin' like a turbo 'Vette,
I'm tired of magazines,
Sayin' flat butts are the thing,
Take the average black man and ask him that,
She gotta pack much back,
So, fellas! (Yeah!) Fellas! (Yeah!)
Has your girlfriend got the butt? (Hell yeah!)
Tell 'em to shake it! (Shake it!) Shake it! (Shake it!)
Shake that healthy butt!
Baby got back!
Baby got back!"

David stopped singing the song at that point and laughed with the girls.

Kimmy said, "You're crazy."

"Ya think you can find something a little more…" Michelle began, cut off by David who said, "Romantic?"

"Yeah," answered Michelle, "romantic."

"Okay, let me find something," David retorted. He started paging through the titles. In the meantime, the hostess entered again and before she could say something like, "Would you guys like anything else," Shirley yelled again, "More beer!"

"Go figure," the hostess said and left quickly.

"Here, I think I found something," David said.

"Bring it on," Michelle said. The girls were probably expecting another joke. But when the music began to play, they simmered down a bit to listen and watch.

The music to "Three Times a Lady," a 1978 single from the funk and soul band the Commodores, from their album *Natural High*, began to play, and David began to sing:

"Thanks for the times,
That you've given me,
The memories are all in my mind,
And now that we've come,
To the end of our rainbow,
There's something,
I must say out loud."

Here Michelle yelled "Wooohooo," Shirley yelled, "Take me!" and Kimmy shouted, "Owww." David continued with the chorus:

"You're once, twice,
Three times a lady,
And I love you,
Yes you're once, twice,
Three times a lady,
And I love you,
I love you."

"Wooohooo, that's my man!" yelled Michelle. She ran up to him in a bit of a stupor, and jumped on him, tightly hugging him, planting a big kiss on his cheek. David blushed a little and smiled. Michelle playfully jumped back onto the couch, landing onto both Kimmy and Shirley, spilling some beer and food in the process. They all laughed and he continued singing:

"When we are together,
The moments I cherish,
With every beat of my heart,
To touch you to hold you,
To feel you to need you,
There's nothing to keep us apart."

As the song got to the brief interlude, Michelle yelled, "Owwwww."

"He's mine!" Shirley shouted.

Kimmy added, "Woohoo."

"You're once, twice,
Three times a lady,
And I love you.
I love you.
Yes you're once, twice,
Three times a lady,
And I love you.
I love you."

The three girls clapped for him as he finished those lines. Michelle clapped the loudest. She said, "David, that was really nice, I didn't realize how romantic you could be. You have a really nice voice too."

Kimmy agreed, "Yeah, David, you're so sweet."

"I liked it better when you sang 'Baby Got Back!'" Shirley said. They all laughed.

"Let me try that one," Shirley said grabbing the microphone from David. She pretended that she was about to sing "Three Times a Lady," but instead surprised them:

"I like big butts and I cannot lie,
You other brothers can't deny,
That when a girl walks in with an itty bitty waist,
And a round thing in your face,
You get sprung..."

Shirley was shakin', and singin', and shakin' some more. Michelle, Kimmy and David were laughing the whole time, saying things like "Shake it," and "Go Shirley," and "Baby got back." A couple minutes of singing and laughing and drinking and shaking later, Shirley got to the end of the song.

"Baby got back!
Baby got back!"

"Woohoo!" yelled Kimmy.

"Wooooohoooooo!!" yelled Shirley, high-fiving Kimmy.

Shirley also gave Michelle a high five, then grabbed her beer and took a swig.

"You guys, I'm stuffed," Michelle said.

"Me too," interjected Kimmy.

"Bored," said Shirley. "I mean buzzed!"

"What do you guys wanna do?" asked Michelle.

It was then that the hostess returned with some take-out boxes, knowing that the chances were good that they were ready to go. She asked, "Are you guys finished?"

"Yup," said Shirley. "Those guys are finished but I'm gonna stay and drink for a couple more hours until I'm schmaded." Kimmy, Michelle and Shirley immediately began laughing hysterically. Shirley laughed so hard she snorted, which made the girls laugh even more.

David also laughed, the hostess too, and when the girls calmed down a bit, David asked, "What's schmaded?" That only made the girls laugh more, each repeating the word in their laughter.

As they calmed down again, Michelle said, "Shirley said that word the last time we went out. Toward the end of that night I said that I was fading, and then she said that she was schmading, and then at some point she said that she was schmaded. I forgot all about it till now."

"Schmaded," Shirley said again, laughing.

"Check please," Kimmy said once the giggling subsided.

"No problem," the hostess said as she put a few of those take-out boxes down on the table, giggling a little with Shirley, who was still giggling. "Just come downstairs when you're ready, the bill's there." She turned around and left.

"So, where do you guys wanna go?" Kimmy said.

The three girls looked at each other as if they knew. David didn't say anything; he was just sitting back, content.

Michelle mouthed a one syllable word obviously starting with the letter "L" to Shirley, who opened her eyes a little wider then looked at Kimmy. The three of them seemed to agree with their eyes, then together said out loud, "Lek's."

"Lek's?" David inquired.

"Rrrreks," Michelle loudly said to him, laughing.

"Rrrreks," Shirley and Kimmy said, also laughing.

"We're going to a Lek?" David asked incredulously.

"Rrrrek's" Michelle started, "It's a bar downtown. Drinking, more food, and, um..."

"Dancing!" Shirley shouted.

"Yeah, dancing," Kimmy added.

"Do you dance?" Michelle asked David.

"Uh," David said, looking around at the pretty girls. How could he say anything else but, "Yeah, for sure, I can dance." Well, he hadn't done that since a wedding a couple years ago, a real disaster he thought; but, heck, how could he say no.

The question would remain unanswered as Shirley shouted, "Rrrrek's. Rrret's go!"

The girls put the remaining food into the boxes, including the rice. Kimmy and Shirley grabbed some of the candy too. David didn't help, but he did take a couple pieces of the Hi-Chew candy; a couple of the caramel green apple and a few of the caramel strawberry ones. They left the uneaten *yeot* there.

The three girls grabbed their purses, put most of the leftovers in them, grabbed what didn't fit in their purses, and the four of them made their way out of the now messy room, and down the stairs. Shirley led the way, followed by Kimmy, followed by Michelle, who looked back at David, held out her right hand motioning David to take it. He did. It was warm, smooth and dry. She pulled him to her mouth and planted a nice, warm, wet kiss on his caramel green apple breath mouth, where they swapped a little saliva for a couple seconds. Michelle smiled, leading David to do the same, paused, looked around, then, realizing they were holding up the party, walked out of the room, far behind Shirley and Kimmy, who were already downstairs looking at the bill.

They showed and then shared the bill with Michelle; David didn't see it, nor was he asked for any money to help pay it. Nope, the three musketeers split the hundred-and-sixty-five dollar bill amongst themselves. They never planned for him to contribute; it was their gift. And what a gift he thought. It was the best night of his life, and it wasn't over yet.

The girls paid the bill and filed out of the restaurant in the same order. And the same ritual of Michelle leading David, hand in hand, followed, kiss included.

As soon as they were outside, a cab greeted them. The four of them got in, all in the back seat. When the driver asked them where they wanted to go, Shirley yelled out, "Rrrrek's."

The driver knew exactly where they were going, smiled, turned on the meter and sped off into the night.

Back to Lek's

"There it is," Shirley shouted out from the middle of the backseat. She pointed to the huge building slightly further up on the left hand side of the road and said, "Rrrek's."

The other girls were excited as well.

"And the line's not so long," Kimmy added.

"I'm not waiting in no rrrine," Shirley said. Michelle and Kimmy looked at Shirley and via their near-telepathy agreed. They were just going to walk up to the front of the line, wink at the bouncer, and walk right in.

"That bar over there doesn't have a line," David said.

"Mung's? Umm, no I don't think I wanna go there," Shirley said.

"It's called Mung's?" an incredulous David asked.

"Yup, there's the sign over there," Kimmy said, pointing to the sign of the millipede. "You can go there if you want, David, they have strippers."

"Oh, well, uh, no, you're right, I don't want to go there," he said, and kind of laughed. Of course he wouldn't mind seeing strippers; but, heck, he thought, would they be as nice as the three girls he was with?

The cab stopped slightly past the entrance so as not to block traffic; in front of the Lek's was that same yellow Hummer there when the girls went the previous week, followed by a yellow Lamborghini, a black Maserati, and a red Ferrari. On the same side of the street as the cab was Mung's, with just as nice cars parked in front of it: a black Mercedes Benz, black, convertible Bentley, and a Beemer.

The girls looked at him as they got out of the cab; Michelle paid the cab driver and led the way across the street to the front of the line.

"Oh, why yes," David began, "yes, that's how I'd imagine a sign of a place called Mung's to look," David said looking at the sign of Mung's, walking backwards to follow them. The girls looked back at David, then to each other, then to the door ahead of them, as they had no idea what he was talking about and, instead, were more concerned about getting in without having to wait in line, which they confidently did.

When David was stopped momentarily by the bouncer, Michelle, who was in front, walked back to the bouncer, smiled at him, gently touched his arm and said, "He's with us." The bouncer grinned, raised his eyebrows and replied, "Okay." ·

It was about nine-thirty in the evening and the bar was packed. As the previous song ended, the wall of individual conversations was drowned out again by the next song that blared out of the numerous speakers. It was "I know a Little," by Lynyrd Skynyrd, from their album *Street Survivors*.

Now, Steve Gaines wrote the song, becoming the band's guitarist in 1976; but, died in a plane crash in 1977. The crash was just three days after the album's release and it also claimed the lives of lead singer Ronnie Van Zant, Gaines's sister Cassie, who was a backup singer for the group, their assistant road manager, pilot and co-pilot.

The beginning of the song, with its southern rock swing beat given by the drummer's hi-hat cymbal pair and fast guitar solo excited nearly everyone in the bar. The four musketeers had big, authentic smiles on their faces as they scoured the bar for a table, taking in nearly the same sights and smells that the three musketeers had done the previous week.

And then they — everyone — could hear the singer:

"Yes sir!
Well the bigger the city, well the brighter the lights
The bigger the dog, the harder the bite
I don't know where you been last night
But I think mama, you ain't doin' right.

Say I know a little
I know a little about it
I know a little
I know a little 'bout it
I know a little 'bout love
And baby I can guess the rest."

Kimmy saw some people getting up in the back, got excited at the potential open table and pointed in that direction all the while trying to get the other three's attention. Making a connection first with Michelle, then Shirley, then David over the next few seconds, they made their way over.

"Well now I don't read that daily news
'Cause it ain't hard to figure
Where people get the blues
They can't dig what they can't use
If they stick to themselves
They'd be much less abused

Say I know a little
I know a little about it
I know a little
I know a little 'bout it
I know a little 'bout love
And baby I can guess the rest."

During the next minute or so listening to the guitar solo the four musketeers sat down, and simply looked around. It was a feast for their eyes.

There were people dancing on the main floor; cripes, people dancing everywhere. Waitresses bringing food to patrons were dancing; bus boys bringing dirty dishes back to the kitchen were dancing too.

The guitar solo led to a short, fast piano solo, which led back again to the singer:

"Well if you want me to be your only man
Said listen up mama, teach you all I can
Do right baby, by your man
Don't worry mama, teach you all I can.

Say I know a little
I know a little about it
I know a little
I know a little about it
I know a little 'bout love
And baby I can guess the rest.

Well I know a little 'bout love
Baby I want your best."

The song's end was greeted by a roaring, happy crowd. After standing to clap and yell, Michelle, David, Kimmy and Shirley became quite cozy and content in the booth together, like old friends at a school reunion.

"A pitcher of beer," Kimmy said when the waitress came to their table.

"Sure thing. Do you want any appetizers or other food with that? We're famous for our dish called 'the World,' a big plate of chips smothered in beef, chicken, mango salsa, guacamole, tomatoes, three types of cheese, sour cream, and onions. It'll take all of you to eat it."

They looked at each other, smiling, raising their eyebrows and opening their eyes large almost at the same time. They were still stuffed from the norebang; they all said, "No," at almost the same time, and laughed in their individual ways.

"Okay, I'll be right back," the waitress said, then turned around quickly and went to another table to get an order.

"Woohooo," Shirley yelled.

Just then another song came up loud on the speakers, without an introduction by the Deejay. It was again a Lynyrd Skynyrd tune, this time "Call Me the Breeze," a remake of an old blues song by J.J. Cale, about the benefits of having no responsibility, from their 1974 album *Second Helping*.

The crowd—seated and unseated, on the dance-floor or not—went crazy. The four musketeers smiled and grooved in their booth.

"Call me the breeze
I keep blowin' down the road
Well now they call me the breeze
I keep blowin' down the road
I ain't got me nobody
I don't carry me no load.

Ain't no change in the weather
Ain't no changes in me
Well there ain't no change in the weather
Ain't no changes in me
And I ain't hidin' from nobody
Nobody's hidin' from me
Oh, that's the way it's supposed to be."

The pitcher of beer arrived just as the first instrumental section began. Shirley grabbed the pitcher and drank a little; the others laughed. She then grabbed the stack of plastic cups and began to pour.

"Well I got that green light baby
I got to keep movin' on
Well I got that green light baby
I got to keep movin' on
Well I might go out to California..."

When the singer sang the word "California," many patrons on the dance-floor, seated at the tables, and standing at various places yelled "California" in response and...

*"…Might go down to Georgia
I don't know."*

…when the next instrumental section began with the piano, the place became even more alive with people shouting "yeah!" "owww!" and other words, phrases and utterances.

And then there *he* was. That really cute, buff, hot guy with the little butt and eight-pack abs that the girls saw the last time they were there. *He* was dancing, shaking, shimmying in the middle of the dance-floor, attracting attention from nearly all the girls. They would first eye *him*, then as nonchalantly as possible — given that they were dancing with their own partners — tried — struggled — to get near *him* and dance with *him*. It wasn't so nonchalant with some.

Kimmy, Shirley and Michelle were looking directly at *him*, and each knew the others were looking at the same guy. David thought they were just looking at all the folks on the dance floor, just like he was.

"*Chal sang gyuh dah!*" Kimmy said, which translates to "He's hot," in English.

"*Jinh chadah!*" Shirley replied, which is equivalent to "Seriously!" in English.

Michelle raised her thin eyebrows in obvious agreement.

"What's that?" David asked.

"*Wah! Chal sang gyuh dah!*" Kimmy answered, meaning "Whoa! He's hot." The girls laughed.

Michelle tried explaining it to David, "It's Korean for, uh…"

"It's Korean for Sean Connery," Shirley said, interrupting. The girls giggled.

"Sean Connery," Michelle said, widely opening her eyes. "*Mah juh! Chal sang gyuh dah!*" That means the same as above, except with a "Yes!" in front.

"*Jinh chadah!*" Shirley said. "I love Sean Connery."

David just smiled, sure they would never say that about him, though he didn't really mind.

Looking directly at David, Michelle said, "*Chal sang gyuh dah!*" Kimmy and Shirley looked at him and agreed by nodding their heads.

The four musketeers had some more beer, sat back, and listened to the rest of the tune.

The song ended with more enthusiastic, sweaty yells from the crowd. The Deejay, though they couldn't see him, came up on the speakers and said, "We'll be right back with more music; right now we're having a special on Bud Light®—order a pitcher for only five bucks. See you in a few minutes." The dance floor emptied of its smiling, satisfied patrons.

"So, David, do you dance?" asked Kimmy.

"Well," he said, "I dance kind of like I sing."

"Oh," replied Michelle, "you dance sweetly and nice?"

David smiled and laughed briefly, "Thanks Michelle, but, uh, I've danced at family weddings and in high school, but, uh, I don't think I'm very good. I'd probably look silly."

"We rrrike silly, David," Shirley said. They all laughed.

"You guys are falling behind! Drink up!" Shirley yelled, as she chugged what was left in her cup. The others pretty much followed suit; the pitcher was now empty as were all their cups.

"Should we get another pitcher of beer?" David asked, looking mostly at Shirley.

"No, I wanna dance," Shirley said, half serious.

A few moments later, as the four musketeers were looking around, taking in the sights, some "music" came up on the speakers, consisting of an electronic drum beat.

"Okay everyone, it's time to get back to the dance floor," said the Deejay. "Let's get the night going. I've got a mix to give you reason to come up and move. We're going to start with a new groove from Jewel Kid called 'Musica,'" which was playing now over the speakers, "followed by an oldie but goodie by Flo Rida, and some other surprises. So come on doooown."

The beat was inviting to the Shirley, Kimmy and Michelle. David just kind of went along with them, still happy being in their presence. If they liked the music, well, then, so did he. Numerous patrons walked onto the dance floor.

"Let's dance," said Shirley.

"Rrret's go," Michelle replied.

The four of them, led by Shirley, made their way to the dance arena, as the bar took on a different look and feel. The plasma screens were no longer showing sports programs; instead, they were synched with music videos and flashing digital designs.

Kimmy came out of her shell; she was moving gracefully — erotically even — to the techno-pop sounds. Michelle too was waving her arms with her mouth open as if singing along with sampled singing sounds from the "song." Shirley looked like a different person on the dance floor, her petite body now taking on a more expressive, rhythmic look.

David moved, but the most noticeable feature was his smile, being on the dance floor with three pretty, slender, young women. They were now dancing differently together, near the outer rim of the dance floor with more and more young women and men joining them.

The techno-pop ended after less than a couple minutes and blended nicely to an older Hip-Hop song — as promised by the Deejay — that patrons immediately recognized. It was the song "Low" by Flo Rida.

All the video screens showed the video from the song, though some had different versions; the deejay clearly had done some work mixing the song and synching it to at least three different videos, including one that showed the words of the chorus:

"Apple bottom jeans
Boots with the fur
The whole club was looking at her
She hit floor
Next thing you know
Shawty got low, low, low, low, low, low, low, low."

As with many common songs, everyone on the dance floor does similar things. On the words "low, low, low…" everyone crouched — in their own way — lower, lower and lower, some winding up on the ground.

These lyrics, the chorus, were repeated a few times in the song, and, each time, everyone on the dance floor got low. This was the first time David heard this song, and, upon hearing the chorus, and watching everyone get down, he joined in. By the last chorus, he pretty much had it down, having the time of his life with the three musketeers.

This song lasted about four minutes and was blended nicely into a link to an electro-dance remix by the Banger Brothers called "Supermassive," based on the electro-dance mix "Supermassive Black Hole" by Muse, which was featured in the movie *Twilight*, a modern-day love story between a teenage girl and a vampire. The "song" is pretty much just a heavy drum beat, a digital bass line, with one lead male singer and several backup singers singing the following lines in a high voice:

"Ooh baby don't you know I suffer?
But ooh baby can you hear me moan?
You caught me under false pretenses
How long before you let me go?

Oooohh, oooohhh, oooooh,
You set my soul alight!
Oooohh, oooohhh, oooooh,
You set my soul alight!

Glaciers melting in the dead of night;
And the superstars sucked into the supermasive
I thought I was a fool for no one
But ooh baby I'm a fool for you
You're the queen of the super'ficial
How long before you tell the truth?

Oooohh, oooohhh, oooooh,
You set my soul alight!
Oooohh, oooohhh, oooooh,
You set my soul alight!"

During this "song," nearly everyone on the dance floor slowed their movement down and became more expressive, including our four musketeers, though David surely didn't move as gracefully as the girls.

This remix lasted almost five minutes and was again blended into the drum beat — not much different from its own — of Jewel Kid's "Musica," which led to a relatively new song by La Roux, named "In for the Kill." This song started out with, you guessed it, a heavy drum beat that slowly varied into other beats with added musical ornamentation.

And then *he* came out onto the dance floor. Kimmy, then Michelle — because Kimmy tapped her arm — then Shirley — prompted by Michelle's knee to her thigh — noticed the guy from last week, that gorgeous, thin, chisel-faced hunk walking to the dance floor from the sides, alone, but not for long. For as soon as *he* started dancing, other girls waiting on the wings came onto the dance floor, and those girls — even those with partners — already on the dance floor, beyond just noticing *him*, moved in closer to *him*. *He* was moving toward the middle of the dance area, and it was like the entire group of individuals made way for *him*, to his respected place on the floor.

The whole ritual took place over the course of the seven-minute long song, when, by the time *he* was in the middle, most of the women on the floor were turned in toward *him*, with their partners turned out toward the rim of the dance floor.

Such was the case even with David's three musketeers. They were each staring at *him*, then looking at each other, as if saying telepathically, "Isn't *he* simply divine." Although David noticed them fantasizing, he made little fuss about it. After all, he was still having the time of his life, and it didn't really matter if he got lucky afterwards. He had his dissertation to write.

"Let's see if I can mix this smoothly to my favorite nasty piece of work from years past," the deejay said as he again utilized that same — though this time from a different section — groove from Jewel Kid. It linked to Nelly's "Hot in Herre" [*sic*], released in early 2002.

Immediately upon hearing the beginning of the song, the excitement was obvious on the faces of the folks on the dance floor. And the mood went from funk and groove, to the slow, expressive and erotic.

David was an astute observer. He entered college wanting to be a naturalist, having studied birds, small mammals, worms, spiders and insects in the wild, confined to backyard Chicago expeditions, where he grew up. There he would explore undeveloped neighborhood lots, focusing mostly on spiders, ants and such. In fact, he was especially hooked on biology from his youthful researches on spider webs, having learned that orb web weaving garden spiders built webs of silk — a natural complex of zippers, springs and Legos®, stronger than steel or even Kevlar® — with a fascinating type of reinforcement at many joints. These joints are actually made up of little dabs of liquid with extra webbing inside, allowing for the web to expand when dinner flies into it. The truly amazing thing about it was that these spiders built expandable joints into their first web, and every subsequent web, without instruction from a parent or teacher. No one sits them down on opposite ends of a small log explaining the facts of life. No, spiderlings spin silken webs with expandable joints right day one, motivated by nothing more than that universal of motivators, hunger.

Anyway, being so observant, he noticed that his girls were eyeing and moving closer to that other guy, as were nearly all the other girls on the dance floor. It seemed that nearly every girl did in fact make their way to dance directly with *him*, checking *him* out entirely from head to toe. When the following part of the song came up the second time, Michelle made her way to *him*…

"It's getting hot in here
So take off all your clothes
I am getting so hot, I wanna take my clothes off."

…and allowed *him* to subtly grind *his* upper thigh on hers. No doubt at that moment she thought *he* was the sexiest man alive.

Kimmy was next. Although she was the most shy among the three, you certainly wouldn't know that seeing her here. As she moved close to *him*, *he* grabbed hold of her right wrist first with his right hand, then took hold of her left, and pulled her close to *him*, bending her body backward, pressing *his* body to hers, then mimed kissing her from her neck to her belly as she bent backwards.

The two straightened up slowly, still embraced, and danced — thrust is probably the correct word — for the next few moments locked at the waist, their legs interlocked in the order of his left, her right, his right, her left.

Shirley's turn. She just looked into *his* eyes from *his* side, bumping into *him* from time to time until *he* grew bored and went back to Michelle for seconds. *He* grabbed her from behind, and danced with both *his* arms around her mid-section, tightly pressed to her backside with *his* front, gyrating first forward and backward, then side to side, then again to and fro.

As each of the three girls danced with *him*, they returned to David to, well, keep him occupied, in order.

As the song ended — it lasted only about three-and-a-half minutes — the deejay smoothly transitioned with electronic drumbeats — yes, it was Jewel Kid's drums sample again — to Rihanna's tune entitled "Only Girl (in the World)." Much less nasty than the previous songs, and formed more like a song too, it lightened the mood on the floor. Then again, with the mood changed to the romantic, all the girls wanted — yearned--for *his* time and attention just that much more, like the song conveyed:

"Want you to make me feel like I'm the only girl in the world
Like I'm the only one that you'll ever love
Like I'm the only one who knows your heart
Only girl in the world…
Like I'm the only one that's in command
Cuz I'm the only one who understands how to make you feel like a man, yeah
Want you to make me feel like I'm the only girl in the world
Like I'm the only one that you'll ever love
Like I'm the only one who knows your heart
Only one."

With all the girls vying for *his* time and attention, it was hard for David, who was taking it all in, to believe that all these girls could think that even if they had won *him* and *his* love that *he* would make them *his* only one.

Nevertheless, this was a bar, and apparently anything's possible on a dance floor. So, the girls in the bar continued to try to get *his* attention and time in the middle of the dance floor, no less or more than did Michelle, Kimmy and Shirley.

Still taking it all in, David thought about it at a higher level. Either the men on the dance floor were competing for possession of the best female, or the females were checking out all the males for the best one, or some combination of the two. A four minute song is hardly the perfect context to do field work thought David; but, looking at everyone on the dance floor reminded him of most birds and mammals in their ritual mating dances.

No, David thought, since here on the dance floor the best males were migrating toward the middle — *he* was now prominently there — with nearly each and every female checking *him* out, the dominant paradigm here was that of females agreeing upon and selecting males in preferential order. True, males were checking out all of the females; but, it was the females here that had the power of choice. They were the rulers of this land. By consensus it was the females that narrowed down the field, nudging *him* with their looks and movement to the coveted middle spot, the alpha domain.

Although nearly every male there would say yes to nearly any female, the reverse was most certainly not true. The males would have to pass muster — an old naval term meaning to pass an inspection, to be acceptable — in order to win the affection of nearly any of the girls there on the dance floor. *He* did with flying colors, which, to continue explaining metaphors, hails from the much older practice of a victorious fleet sailing into port with flags flying from all the mastheads in triumph.

Anyway, the song ended without a custom transition to the next song, and most of the patrons stood there on the dance floor. *He* walked slowly toward the bar to get a drink. As *he* did, so too did most of the women. That happens when the main attraction leaves.

The brief pause was broken by the sound of a ukulele playing a familiar chord progression and numerous "Oooh"s sung by the soloist, with a rainbow shown on the plasma screens. Michelle, David, Kimmy and Shirley walked toward their table as well. Kimmy and Shirley lagged behind hoping that *he* would return. *He* didn't.

The song was a recent version of "Over the Rainbow," by Israel "IZ" Kamakawiwo'ole. Lasting slightly under four minutes, it gave the four musketeers an opportunity to drink a little more.

"Oh, I love this song," Kimmy said.

"Hey David, do you know how to play quarters?" Shirley asked.

"Well, I won't say I didn't play when I was an undergraduate, but it's been a while," David replied.

"Okay, good," Shirley said, all perky. "I like playing with people that are a little rusty. The rules are simple. We pour a little beer into a small glass and put it in the middle of the table. Everyone gets a turn. If you're able to bounce the quarter on the table and have it land in the glass, you get to determine who should drink it. If you miss, you pass the quarter. We can make the person whose turn it is drink when they miss eventually if we want. Okay David? Are you in?"

"In," he replied.

Liking David's response, Michelle dittoed, "In." So too said Kimmy.

With that, Shirley got up, walked quickly to the bar and asked the male bartender for a small glass.

"Oh, would you like a tumbler or a rocks?"

"Uh, what's the difference?" Shirley replied.

"I'll get you one of each and you can choose," he said, walking to the stack of glassware a few feet over.

While at the bar, she looked over to *him*—*he* was still standing there alone at the end of the bar, drinking a glass of something—and they made eye contact. She smiled at him, and he returned the favor. The bartender, came back moments later and put the two glasses, a rocks and a tumbler, on the bar.

"This small one is a 'rocks' glass, for making drinks 'on the rocks'; this somewhat larger one is a 'tumbler,' for making mixed drinks," he said.

"Which one's better for playing quarters?" Shirley asked innocently.

"How drunk do you want to get and how quickly," retorted the bartender.

"I'll take the tumbler," Shirley said, grabbing the slightly larger glass. "Thanks." She took off back to the table, giving *him* a smile. *He* watched her walk back to her table, and she knew it.

Shirley returned to the booth, placed the tumbler down on the middle of the table with her right hand, and, before sitting, reached into her left-front jean's pocket, pulled out a small assortment of change that she just happened to have, grabbed a quarter with her right hand, put the rest of her change back into her pocket with her left, then took her end seat again.

Without missing a beat, she filled the tumbler with beer with her right hand that still held the quarter—she held the pitcher with her three fingers thumb to middle and the quarter with the end two—put the pitcher down, and quickly flicked the quarter on the table. No sooner had it landed in the glass that she passed the tumbler to David, who was seated opposite her. They all laughed.

"Gee, thanks," David said with a humorous smirk, as he grabbed the glass and gulped it down.

"My turn," Kimmy said. She missed by a long shot. The quarter rolled off the table and onto Michelle's lap. Michelle found the quarter between her legs, raised it with her right hand, and rolled it off her nose onto the table and into the glass.

"A gift for you Shirley," Michelle said, laughing. Shirley smiled and drank it like a pro, spitting the quarter out directly into her hand, immediately offering David the damp quarter.

"Your turn, hun," Michelle said to David, touching his upper left leg in the process. With great confidence he grabbed the quarter, concentrated, then, with three fingers on the edge of the quarter—those 119 grooves on the edge of a quarter are called reeds and they were originally created by the US mint to deter counterfeiting when precious metals were used in the manufacturing process, which they aren't anymore, though the reeding continues—slapped the quarter to the table and epically missed the glass. It simply bounced straight up and died straight down.

"Fail!" buzzed Shirley. They all laughed.

The music changed here to something a little more, shall we say, juvenile. It was "Girlfriend" by Avril Lavigne, kind of a fitting song, considering nearly all the girls in the bar wanted to be *his* girlfriend.

As the laughter subsided, and David reached for the quarter in the small pool of beer, there, at the end of the table, *he* stood.

"Quarters, how fun," the thin, chisel-faced man with the eight-pack abs said. "Bet these fine girls will have you drunk in no time," he said looking directly at David.

They all looked up to him in excited silence; the girls anyway. Shirley, being on the end, took a deep breath and almost fainted. Kimmy raised her eyebrows. Michelle was all aglow. The three of them looked at each other, all with raised eyebrows and widely opened eyes as if to telepathically say "Oh my God, it's *him*. Isn't *he* gorgeous?"

David, although he noticed the estrogen surge, simply said, "Yes, they're all pretty good at this game; maybe you can help me even the score."

"Do you mind if I join?" *he* said, looking around at the girls, ending with Shirley. She immediately made room for *him* on the end by squishing into Kimmy, who, in a significant understatement, didn't mind at all.

"How's everyone doing tonight?" *he* asked.

Shirley smiled and cried out, "Woohooo!"

Kimmy said, "I'm a little tired from dancing, but I'm, uh, much better now," raising her eyebrows and looking to Michelle.

"Great. Here, let me try," *he* said, requesting the quarter from David with *his* left hand, pouring more beer from the pitcher into the glass with *his* right. When *he* finished pouring, in one motion *he* took the quarter with *his* right hand, raised it, and tapped it into the table. The quarter went up then down, right into the middle of the glass.

"Bull's-eye," *he* said, as *he* picked up the glass. Looking around from right to left, from David, to Michelle, then to Kimmy and Shirley, *he* teased them all by offering it to each of them in turn. Then, *he* motioned the glass to Kimmy, but turned away at the last minute and gave it to Michelle.

"For you my princess," *he* said, coming up with the word from the song, handing her the glass, "Drink up." Michelle laughed and took the glass. She swigged it down quickly.

"More Beer!" Shirley said. *He* flagged down a waitress; she came immediately to the table.

"One more pitcher of beer for my friends, and another cup," *he* said. "This round's on me." The waitress, noticing how good-looking *he* was, gave him a big smile and said, "I'll be right back." She walked off to get them their beer without stopping at any of the other tables on the way.

"I'm John London," he said.

"I'm Michelle. These are my friends Kimmy, Shirley and David." Apparently she was the leader of the gang.

"Nice to meet you," John said, staring into Michelle's eyes. He stood to shake her hand, which he held for a couple seconds, long enough to make it known that he liked her.

"Hi Kimmy, Shirley and David," he added, finally letting go of Michelle's soft hand, looking at each of them in turn.

"Hi John," Shirley said, followed by the same hello from each of the other three.

"I'm staying in San Diego for the summer, taking time off from the real world. Are you guys students?"

"Yup," said Kimmy, "UCSD, all of us."

"I'm studying education," said Shirley.

"Undecided," Michelle chimed in. It was David's turn. John looked at David and expected a response.

"Here's your beer," the waitress said, interrupting, placing the new pitcher on the table. "And here's your cup," she said nicely to John, trying to earn some points.

"Oh, thanks, love," he said to her, looking in her eyes. She smiled and kind of blushed, which probably was more like a heat flash.

"Can I get you guys anything else," she said, staring at John.

"We're good here, thanks so much," John said, handing her a twenty.

"I'll be back with your change," the waitress said.

"That's okay, keep it," said John in quick reply. She walked off to help other patrons, though momentarily looking at him, then the girls as if silently saying, "He's dreamy, right girls?" Apparently they agreed.

John reached for and grabbed the pitcher, topping off everyone's cup with beer. He made eye contact with each of the girls as he poured their beer. With David, he just poured, looking at Michelle all the while.

"Cheers, everyone," John said, as they all touched cups and began chugging.

David returned to the conversation, "Oh, yeah, I'm a student. I'm doing my doctorate in evolutionary biology and teach a class in human evolution."

"Evolution?" John said with shock. "C'mon, that's just a theory; it's all swag."

There was a pause in which David thought about responding with a torrent of facts, and Michelle looked at him as if he was going to do just that, when John said, "I'm just kidding, David. I studied biology at Berkeley years ago. Did my graduate work there too. I'm originally from New York."

David was relieved; he may have found a new friend.

John continued. "But I eventually gave it all up when I entered the real world. I started a couple of dot-coms in the late nineties and early, uh, naughts, but I sold them all and now am looking for the next big thing."

He finished his drink — it was in a tumbler — and continued, "Like I said, I'm taking the summer off and living in the hills. It's a beautiful place, you should come by sometime."

"What are those?" Kimmy asked.

"Hills?" John asked incredulously.

"No," Michelle said, laughing, "what are the nuts?"

John laughed. "No," John said still laughing, "not the nuts; the *naughts*. It's a way of expressing a decade; it's easier to say than the 'two-thousands,' 'ohs,' or 'oughts.'"

"The naughts," Michelle repeated, "oh."

"You're so smart, John," Shirley said, obviously trying to earn more points than the other girls.

"You need more beer, Shirley?" Kimmy asked, trying to break Shirley's temporary grip on John.

Shirley laughed and said, "Of course; bring it on!" Kimmy grabbed the pitcher this time and poured the last of the beer into Shirley's outstretched plastic cup.

"A pitcher doesn't go very far these days," John said.

"We can always get more," Shirley said.

It was then that the deejay got on the microphone and said, "Here's a request from the Taylor party in the back here celebrating their twenty-year fraternity reunion." Applause and some shouts were heard from a large group of mostly guys on the second floor.

"It's the Violent Femmes," said the deejay, "from their 1995 tribute album *Saturday Morning: Cartoons' Greatest Hits*, but you'll probably recognize it from the Jetsons. For those trivia buffs out there, the song is from the 1962 episode 'A Date with Jet Screamer.' Rrrrastro!"

Again, there were more yells and shouts from the group. And then that memorable song came on. It didn't really fit the mood of the bar; but, hey, it was a request.

"Eep. Opp. Ork. Ah-ah.
Eep. Opp. Ork. Ah-ah."

The girls looked at each other; they thought the song was bizarre, but smiled and tried to understand what was going on. "Was this a new language?" they thought.

The bar livened up; a bunch of folks made their way to the dance floor, and nearly everyone in the bar started dancing. Those seated moved up, down and sideways to the music.

"Get in the capsule, baby
We are blasting off.

Eep opp ork ah ah
Eep opp ork ah ah
Eep opp ork ah ah
And that means I love you."

Michelle, Kimmy and Shirley were beside themselves watching the scene. It looked like everyone was having the time of their lives. Of course, the girls had no idea what was going on; but, it looked like so much fun.

"Well now, I took my baby for a ride in space
Eep opp ork ah ah
And met a little man with a funny, funny face
Eep opp ork ah ah
He taught us both to wail this way
Eep opp ork ah ah
Nobody digs a word we say
Eep opp ork ah ah.

Eep opp ork ah ah
Eep opp ork ah ah
Eep opp ork ah ah
And that means I love you.

Come fly with me
Up high with me
Come on fly with me
And now eep opp ork means I dig you."

Here's where the instrumental section started, lasting about forty seconds. People in the aisles were dancing, the fellows on the second floor were going a little crazy, chugging their beers and yelling various things.

"You guys wanna get out of here? Come to my place; it's really nice," John said sincerely.

Shirley blurted out, "Yeah, rrret's go to John's." The girls nodded their heads yes. David too thought it would be a good idea, as he was happy to have met a fellow supporter of evolution. There weren't too many people who understood the same concepts as he did, and he raised his eyebrows and shook his head in agreement.

The five of them stood up almost in unison and headed to the door through the raucous crowd dancing in excitement everywhere, led by John, with Shirley, Kimmy, Michelle and David following close behind.

"Yeah I read my baby loud and clear
Eep opp ork ah ah
She just said I love you dear.
Eep opp ork ah ah
Now when I reply the way I do
Eep opp ork ah ah
I just said I love you too
Eep opp ork ah ah

Eep opp ork ah ah
Eep opp ork ah ah
Eep opp ork ah ah
And that means I love you.

Come fly with me!
Up high with me!
Come on fly with me
And now eep opp ork means I dig you.
You heard the word
That crazy word
That word you heard
Eep opp ork means I love you."

Another instrumental section came next, lasting only a few seconds. The three girls looked at each other, halfway to the door, not really sure whether they wanted to stay or go. The music was new and fun; but, so was John. They walked on.

The song sped up a bit and modulated, meaning the key went up a half tone. "My how everyone was enjoying themselves," thought each of the girls.

After one more verse and the chorus repeated twice, the line *"Hop on baby, I'll put you in orbit,"* ended the song. They were safely outside the bar and looked back through the open door at the scene. The entire bar erupted in applause.

Michelle asked David, "Eep opp ork ah ah? I don't remember that from English class. Is that English?"

"No, no it's not," David answered, laughing. "Well, maybe kinda it is. It's from a cartoon. I can't really explain it other than to say there's a futuristic family named the Jetsons. George and Jane are the parents; their young boy Elroy writes these lyrics, or maybe it was the daughter Judy that wrote them. I don't remember. I think there was some kind of misunderstanding. Anyway, Judy wins a date with a rock star who sings that song."

John interrupted David, saying, "And don't forget Rrrastro, their dog." John was standing on the side of a big, yellow Hummer parked right in front of the bar, and was putting his cell phone back into his back pocket, having just made a quick call.

"Oh yeah, Rrrastro," David said.

"Rrrasto?" Shirley asked, emphasizing the "R." She looked at Michelle and Kimmy, who both seemed to silently agree with her that they were with two men who understood their humor.

The valet brought John his car keys; John handed him a five dollar bill as a tip, saying, "Thanks chief."

Facing Shirley, John added, "Astro is the family dog. He kind of looks like Scooby-Doo, and talks just like him."

"Scooby who?" asked Michelle. Both John and David smiled and laughed a little.

"Wow, is this your car, John?" Kimmy asked.

"Yup, terrible gas mileage, but a great ride. Come on in," said John, pressing the unlock button on his remote.

Shirley got in the front seat without looking at her three remaining friends. John walked over to the driver's door, opened it, and got in. David opened the rear passenger door for Michelle and Kimmy, who got in the Hummer in that order, then walked around to the other side, opened the door and hopped in next to Michelle.

With a roar of the engine, the car started, and they were off, no doubt talking more about the exploits of the family Jetson: George, Jane, Judy, Elroy and Astro, in the Skypad Apartments in Orbit City. Mr. Cosmo G. Spacely, Spencer Cogswell, Rosie the family robot too; oh, and, let's not forget the Great Gazoo.

It would have made for good conversation had they seen it; but, no one noticed. The personalized license plate of the custom, fully accessorized Hummer they had sped off in read "SPMKNG."

His House

"So now, how does Scooby-Doo fit into this?" Michelle asked.

John laughed. "No, Scooby-Doo was the dog in a different cartoon, called, uh, Scooby-Doo."

"*Scooby Dooby Doo, where are you,*" David sang. The girls all looked at him and laughed. Shirley, shoes off, sitting on her side with her legs bent underneath, was turned toward John in the front, but was looking over her shoulder at David, laughing. Michelle had her left hand on David's right thigh, scratching it gently, amused at his singing and previous description of the cartoons that they had been discussing during the ride.

"Yeah, that's right. *Scooby-Doo Where Are You* was the title of the cartoon," John said, focused on the next exit. "I haven't seen the cartoon in a long time, but Scooby-Doo was a talking great dane, and started every word with an "R," just like the dog Astro in the Jetsons: Rrrastro." The girls all laughed.

"Rrrastro," Shirley said laughing.

John continued, "He was owned by a dude named Shaggy, and together, they always had the munchies."

"The munchies?" Kimmy asked.

"Well, yeah, the munchies. Although it was a cartoon for kids, I think Shaggy was a dope-head, and when you smoke pot, apparently you get hungry; that's called the munchies. I wouldn't know anything about that," he said laughing.

"Oh, the munchies," Shirley said, giggling.

David added, "They always went for the Scooby snack."

"*Yeot*?" asked Shirley, laughing. The other girls giggled.

"Hey Shirley," David said, "eat *yeot*." Michelle squeezed his leg and laughed.

Shirley reached over to slap him, and, instead, David gave her a high-five. She was good with that.

"What were the names of the other characters? Do you remember David? There was Shaggy, Scooby..."

"Daphne was the smart one," David excitedly said.

"Velma! I always had the hots for Velma," John said, not realizing that he was referring to a cartoon character.

"You had the hots for Velma?" Kimmy asked.

"Well, hey, I was young and stupid." The girls laughed, liking that explanation.

They exited the highway, traversed the highway overpass, and then drove onto a steep road going up into the hills. They turned onto the first street, Royal Blue Court, and drove just a few blocks, passing some quite large and beautiful houses on the left; the houses on the right were much smaller-looking, as the bulk of each of those houses were undoubtedly hidden from view, embedded into the far side of the hill. Still, the three-car garages and windowed doorways of each façade laid claim to the probability that a multi-level mansion was behind.

The Hummer slowed and pulled into the driveway of one of a house on the right. David noticed the subtly blue-lighted address "1859" on a sign attached to the house between the left-most garage and the entranceway as they pulled in.

"Nice address," David said to John.

"Thanks," John said, thinking he was referring to the house itself, not just the address number.

"Jane, stop this crazy thing," David semi-shouted in a high-pitched voice. John apparently liked that and laughed.

"What the heck," Shirley said.

"Funny, David," John said, as the car came to a stop. "That's from the Jetsons," he said to the girls. After putting the car in park, he continued, "It's a recurring joke during the credits, you know, where they show the names of voices, animators, producers, directors, and such. Let's go inside." John got out of the car and waited for the group to join him on the left hand side of the car. Shirley put her shoes on and got out of the Hummer. David and Michelle got out on the left;

Kimmy got out on the right, waited for Shirley to put on her shoes, and walked with her to the other side, joining the group.

John continued the explanation as they walked toward the entrance, "George is walking Astro on leash on an automatic dog-walker conveyor belt outside the apartment. A cat appears on the conveyor belt and Astro chases it, causing the conveyor to speed up. George accidentally lets go of the dog leash as the conveyor speeds up even more, whereby both Astro and the cat jump off the conveyor leaving George alone on it. They both watch George forced to run for his life on the out of control conveyor screaming for Jane to 'Stop this crazy thing!' George eventually falls down on the conveyor and is carried by the treadmill's belt around its path, under the machine and back up again, over and over. It's pretty funny."

"I'll have to see it sometime, Michelle said, laughing.

"Me too," added Shirley.

"Ditto," Kimmy said.

John led the way past the unlighted, empty dolphin fountain and to the front door, house keys in his right hand.

"Oh, I love dolphins," Kimmy said.

"Yeah, me too," John said.

"Does it work?" asked Kimmy.

"Well, yeah, it does, but I leave both the water and the lights off to save energy. Everyone in California is energy conscious," John said proudly. He unlocked the top bolt, then, finding the other key, started to put it into the door knob.

"Ow," John shrieked, as he slapped the right side of his neck with his left hand and flung whatever creature had bitten him to the ground on his left.

"Sorry, cousin," he said with some pity in his voice. The four musketeers were silent, but glanced at each other. It seemed awkward for some reason, they thought.

"There's no place like home," John said with a smile as he opened the door.

Beyond the door was a fairly large landing with dark, solid wood floors; on the right, a table, chair, and some coat hooks. The five of them walked in and noticed, just behind John, a railing followed by a big open space, leading to a huge bay window yards away overlooking the lights of San Diego. To the left was a closet, and, to either side deeper forward, long and wide, semi-circular, off-white, Berber carpeted stairways leading down to the main floor.

In the middle of the landing, in front of the railing, was a big, black and tan stuffed dog, a German shepherd, seated, facing the door.

"Nice dog," David said.

"Yes, he was," John said.

"He was?" asked Michelle.

"Yup. That was my puppy dog Zack. Best, most loyal dog I ever had," John added.

"What happened to him?" Kimmy innocently asked.

"Well, it's kind of a long story," John began.

"Did he save your life?" asked Michelle.

"Not exactly," John said. "I had Zack for only a couple years; got him as a puppy when I entered grad school at Berkeley. He was a great dog. I taught him all the usual tricks: down, fetch, over, under, sit, paw, etcetera. Toward the end, as a graduate student in biology..." Michelle gently elbowed David, who smiled at her, "...I was studying the life cycle of various barnacles, with an interest in parasites, a simple, easy way to make a living as I learned." He paused, looking first at the dog, then at the expressions on the faces of his visitors. Both Kimmy and Shirley had their mouths open, Michelle looked a little confused by his comment about parasites, and David looked like he was just taking it all in: John's house, his car, the view, and his comment about barnacles.

John continued, "Anyway, although I had originally planned to write my thesis on barnacles, I grew much more interested in the genus of one-celled animals called *Leishmania*.

They are so interesting; you could say that I became a leishmaniac." Although he expected the gang there to laugh, or, at a minimum, be excited at hearing that, no one said a word. They were kind of amazed, however, their amazement was overshadowed by their apprehension. Not David though; he grew a little more interested.

"I can see you're not too excited," John said, "but, it really is interesting. The cool thing about *Leishmania* is that they use an insect, the sandfly, as a vector to infect vertebrates, where they reproduce and, hopefully, from their perspective, find another host or sandfly to continue the process. But the really interesting part is how they get through the host's — not the sandfly, but the human or other mammal it infects — immune system defense. Do you girls know how they do that?"

"Um, no," said Kimmy, kind of disgusted. Michelle shook her head no. There was a pause.

Surely Shirley could think of something funny to say here, David thought.

"Uh..." was all Shirley could say.

"Well, remember the macrophage?" asked John. There was a pause. The girls each looked at each other.

"Sure, the macrophage is part of the immune system that hunts down and eats invading microorganisms and other debris in the body," David said kind of proudly, but humbly. Michelle leaned up against him and grabbed his hand as if to positively reinforce him for his smartness.

"Yup, that's it," John said proudly. "Macrophages gobble up each and every *Leishmania* they can find, like the proud soldiers they are. Unfortunately, those little *Leishmanias* — there are a few different species — are much more insidious than the normal invading microorganism. They just let the macrophages gobble them up; but, instead of dying, they live in the macrophage and reproduce, eventually bursting out of them to be gobbled up by more and more macrophages, while the *Leishmania* themselves send out proteins to recruit more macrophages, until the whole host is infected. The results are dramatic; some *Leishmania* cause local skin infection, rashes or marks, while others cause serious fever and swelling, and mark the whole body with unsightly growths. Some even cause swelling of major organs like the spleen and liver. When this happens, death is almost certain." The girls were clearly grossed out, yet, at the same time wanted to hear more.

"But back to Zack. During my second year, as I was saying, I was studying *Leishmania*, and brought home — okay, I stole it from the lab — some infected sandflies to see how long it would take for them to die after being infected by *Leishmania*. I was timing them and wanted to know with some certainty how long they lived, or if they simply became carriers without being harmed themselves. I couldn't afford a video recorder at the time. My how things have changed," he said, looking around at the landing of his house.

"Anyway, I brought home a Petri dish with about ten of these sandflies; the Petri dish was in a brown paper bag, and when I got home I put it on the kitchen table. I took the Petri dish out of the bag and put it on the kitchen table. I stared at them for a while; nothing much happened. I grew tired and decided to take a nap."

"That was pretty stupid looking back. While I was sleeping, it seems that Zack grew hungry, curious too, for and in addition to eating his food, he must have somehow opened the Petri dish and let the sandflies loose."

"When I awoke from my nap, I noticed the Petri dish was on the floor, open, and told Zack what a bad dog he was. I was hopeful that they had all flown away to a dark corner of my house and died — they didn't — and took Zack to the vet, missing my classes the next day."

"The vet told me there was nothing I could do, that there was no cure, and that I should just assume that Zack had been infected and just put him to sleep. I couldn't do that, and, instead, just hoped for the best, that maybe he hadn't been bitten, nor I."

"Well, a few days later, he became ill; he didn't eat his food, and was vomiting. I put him in the backyard; my off campus house had one of those, and I just let him live out his days with *Leishmania*. I never did tell anyone at the lab, finished my studies, and graduated. That was more than ten years ago; gosh I was so young and stupid. Since that time, though, I started a few businesses, mostly those that send spam out to computer users. As you can see, I got pretty good at it."

"What about Zack?" asked Kimmy.

"Oh, yeah, Zack," John said, becoming a little depressed. "He looked terrible towards the end, though he lasted a couple months. Those damn *Leishmania* took over his body, eating him from the inside out. He died after a couple months; I brought his body to a taxidermist I found online. He did whatever it is that taxidermists do, cleaning him up a bit, and adding some fur from another dog so I could remember him as he was in his prime. I think I spent a few hundred bucks on it."

There was a pause, then, in Korean, Shirley said, "*Guh eh sookje gah jha shin eh geh dul muh guh sup ni dah,*" which created quite a stir among the girls.

"Hahahahahahaha," belly-laughed Kimmy, her hand over her mouth.

"Ahahahahaha. Puaahahahahaha," Shirley bellowed out from her small frame.

"Hahahahahaha," Michelle joined in.

"What? Why is that funny," asked an incredulous John.

"She said..." Michelle started explaining, but couldn't finish, "ah-hahahahaha."

"What?" John asked again.

The other girls stopped laughing, and each tried to explain to John what Shirley had said. But each time they tried, they laughed instead.

As the laughter diminished, Kimmy finally said, "Shirley said 'His homework ate his dog.'"

David then quietly laughed. John, of course, didn't; but, he did break a smile. It was funny, he thought; but, still, it was his dog, his best friend. How could he laugh?

Shirley, not to miss a beat, rubbed her tummy and said, "Mmmm, *Meongmeongtang*," which drew another round of laughter from the other two girls.

Kimmy covered her mouth and said in a louder than usual voice, "*Boshintang*," which seemed to spark a contest between the three.

"*Gaejangguk*," Michelle shouted.

Kimmy replied "*Sacheoltang*."

"*Gutang*," Shirley blurted out. David and John looked on helpless, not knowing what they were talking about.

Michelle looked at the other two and said "*Boyangtang*."

Not to be outdone, Shirley said "*Yeongyangtang*."

To which, thinking for a moment, Kimmy replied "*Dangogitang*."

The three thought for a second, obviously not coming up with any further way to respond. Ah, but it was Shirley that had the final say in the matter. "*Jiyangtang*," Shirley proudly proclaimed. With that last comment, the girls laughed together.

Of course, David and John, not knowing what they were laughing about, wanted to know. David was the one to ask.

"Okay, what was that all about Michelle," he asked.

"Hahaha," Michelle answered. "Wouldn't you like to know."

"C'mon Michelle, tell us," David said, leaning on her.

"Oh, okay," Michelle said. "Let's see, I think it was Shirley that started this. Some people in Korea still eat dog. Shirley said 'woof woof soup,' and we all gave synonyms."

John gave out a short laugh; David did too.

Michelle continued, "Kimmy then said '*boshintang*,' which translates to 'invigorating soup.' *Boshintang* is soup that uses dog meat as its primary ingredient; some people think it increases, um, vir…"

"Virility?" John asked, helping Michelle with the pronunciation.

"Yes, virility," Michelle said with a smile. "According to Chinese medicine, anyway."

"Everything increases virility in China," Shirley added. The girls laughed.

Michelle continued, "The meat is boiled with vegetables and Korean spices. The dish was common in Korea and has a long history, but is looked down on now by most people there."

"I hear it's delicious," Shirley said with a big smile. Kimmy and Michelle couldn't believe she said that, but laughed.

Michelle continued, "I think then we just came up with synonyms for that: dog soup, soup for all seasons, nutritious soup, sweet meat soup, and, um…"

"Land sheep!" Shirley yelled.

"Oh, yes, land sheep," Michelle said, holding back her laughter.

"Let's go downstairs," John said, happy there was a chance to get off the subject of his dog. He took another look at Zack, and then led the group down the right hand stairway. David followed John, then Michelle, then Kimmy. Shirley took the stairway on the left.

As they descended, David asked John "Why Zack? Why did you name him Zack?"

"Oh, yeah, Zack," John started. "Well, I first got into parasites by studying barnacles; specifically, Darwin's writing on barnacles."

"I read a lot about barnacles too," David said, increasingly finding much in common with him. "Are you referring to Darwin's work *Living Cirripedia*?" John turned around, having made it to the bottom of the stairway. Shirley came down and around to meet them; Michelle and Kimmy were right behind.

The stairways and floors they could see were adorned with Berber carpeting. Now, Berber carpet is commonly mistaken as a brand name of carpet fiber, but the term actually represents a specific weave of carpet originally made by the Berber tribe of Northern Africa. Berber carpeting contains big and small tufts with small flecks of dark color on lighter shades of background color, as was the case here in off-white wool.

"Yes, I read both volumes," John said. "While studying those barnacles I came across a really fascinating barnacle—a parasitic barnacle—that doesn't look much like a barnacle. It's called *Sacculina.*"

"I know there are parasitic barnacles, but never heard of *Sacculina*," said David.

"Well, *Sacculina*, the females anyway, parasitize hermit crabs. They essentially castrate the crab, and use it to make their own babies, and as a food source, effectively making the crab a zombie fulfilling its own needs. The male of the species doesn't parasitize anything—they're much smaller—and simply mate with the female who is attached to the crab. It's quite an elegant way to make a living, don't you think?"

The four musketeers just looked at each dumbfounded.

"Well," David said, "it is unique. But I never really thought about it in terms of elegance."

"Anyway, that's how I named Zack; it's short for *Sacculina*," John added. "And there are a whole lot more simple, elegant ways to make a living." David sensed foreshadowing in his tone.

The main room—the whole floor—was in the center of the house, connected to rooms at the front near the bay window, like the kitchen on the left, and hallways that led to other rooms directly under the landing. Those hallways probably connected to other floors as well.

The main floor was absolutely sumptuous. From this vantage point they could see the bay window and the magnificent view. The entire world was visible from it; well, the lighted-up world of San Diego, anyway.

Minimalist in décor, the living room furniture was comprised of three huge leather couches, replete with an array of pillows and what must have been scores of stuffed animals on the couches and on the floor, surrounding an enormous, rectangular fish tank. It must have been able to hold thousands of gallons of water. People on each couch could converse with folks on the adjacent couch, but the tank was at least five feet high, so it prevented anyone on one side of the tank to see or talk to anyone on the other side, assuming they were sitting down. There were wooden tables on the sides of the couches able to hold drinks, books, and other miscellany, though they were currently tasked with supporting, yes, stuffed animals. Some were recognizably animal, some not; more on that later.

There was also a huge, paper-thin, plasma television screen high up on the wall toward the kitchen, and a glass enclosed CD player on its own slender, tube-like stand, beneath the TV, with six CD receptacles, all full, one vertically on top of the other. There were two slender, tower-like speakers on stands, and a couple others at the room's corners. All the equipment was Bang & Olufsen: the speakers, CD player, and receiver.

"What can I get you all to drink? Beer? Wine? Something stronger?"

"What are you having?" Kimmy asked.

"How 'bout some wine. I have a few bottles of some good stuff that I've been saving for a while," John said. The girls shook their heads in agreement. "Well then, wine it is," John said, flicking a knob on the Bang & Olufsen receiver on his left before entering the kitchen. The four musketeers followed right behind him, as music began to fill the whole house.

"Mozart!" David exclaimed. It was the Overture to the opera *The Marriage of Figaro*. David knew it well.

"Good, you like Mozart," said John. "I put on a compilation CD, so there's other stuff on there. Do you fine women like Mozart?" They all shook their head in agreement, pretty much liking to be referred to as fine women.

"We like the Wonder Girls too," Shirley said.

"The Wonder Girls?" asked John. Shirley and the gang shook their heads "yes."

"I, uh, I don't have any of their CDs; but, we can change the music if you want. Feel free to look at my CD collection; it's on the rack in the living room next to the stereo under the TV.

"Thanks," Michelle said. After looking at each other to gain consensus, the girls remained there, though they appreciated knowing that they could make the change. Moreover, they had all heard and liked this particular piece.

"I love that opera," Michelle said, scoring huge points with both John and David.

The four musketeers looked around the kitchen: at the deep red hardwood floors, and the same stunning view as the main living room. It was tastefully done, thought the girls: expensive, black, polished marble countertops, glass cabinets revealing assorted dish and glassware, a huge, Sub-Zero® refrigerator with double glass doors on the top and two freezer drawers on the bottom built into the mahogany wall. Two islands, each with a wonderfully expensive, large, modern, illuminated — probably Swiss — faucet, double sink and built-in, countertop stove were in the middle, a short distance to the kitchen table with six elegant, wheeled, white leather chairs.

John opened one of the large, built-in, mahogany cabinets, revealing a full wine rack and asked, "Zinfandel, cabernet, or merlot?" There was no response; John figured they didn't know the difference. "Well," he said, "I have a couple bottles of Australian Shiraz that have been sitting in here for a couple months; low in tannins and high in acidity. You might like this; I was told it's easy to drink. Will that be okay?"

All the girls nodded "yes."

He pulled two bottles from one of the higher racks, placed them on the right-side island, then shuffled through a couple of drawers until he found a strange-looking piece of hardware.

"Here it is," John said, lifting up a pretty cool looking cork screw. It was in the shape of rabbit ears.

"David, grab a few wine glasses; they're over there," John said, pointing to the upper cabinet where the glasses were. Since the cabinets were glass, framed in a beautiful dark mahogany wood, David immediately saw them, opened the smooth, silent cabinet, and grabbed five by their stems.

"Let's go back in the living room and drink these bottles down," he said. Shirley led the way.

The view was overwhelming, and the four musketeers stood by the window and gazed for a couple moments as John opened the wine bottle.

"Yeah, I never can get over that view," John said, "Come on over and sit down, you can still see everything from there."

As they walked over to sit down, they saw a fairly large stuffed giraffe in front of the fish tank facing the bay window. The four of them walked kind of backwards over to the long couch in front of the kitchen. Although that couch sat four, Shirley walked to, and sat on the end of the other couch, which could comfortably seat three, next to John; Kimmy, Michelle and David sat, in that order, on the bigger couch.

With two bottles of fine red wine opened, John filled the five glasses in front of him and got up and hand delivered two at a time; one to David and one to Michelle; then back to collect two more, then one to Kimmy and one to Shirley.

As John was doing the pouring and delivering ritual, the four musketeers were busy taking in all the stuffed animals on the couches and tables. There were octopuses in various sizes and colors, dolphins too; some killer whales, crabs, snakes, tigers, lions, and, remember, that big giraffe at the head of the tank in front of the big, bay window. Oh, and a few teddy bears thrown in for good measure.

But there were also many other things in the mix strewn on the tables and couches; strange looking stuffed creatures. Some looked like spaceships with one, two, three, four, etc., legs, that looked like landing gear. In fact, a lot of the variously sized stuffed things, other than the recognizable animals, looked like spaceships; each had a head, long body, and a base with those legs attached. There were even some more comically shaped stuffed things there. Like a pink, round one on the table with eyes and fangs and six arms with attached five-fingered hands. And various fanged and unfanged worms. But there were many of the spaceship variety; David recognzed them as differently shaped viruses.

"I take it you're wondering what those are," John asked of the girls, judging by their inquizative faces.

"Is this a wine bottle?" Kimmy asked, lifting up what looked like a stuffed wine bottle with a few long tails.

"Uh, no, that's a, uh, virus," John said. Kimmy immediately threw it on the ground. The other girls laughed.

"No need to fear, I assure you," John said. "It's just a replica." The girls looked around at all the stuffed viruses. Yellow, black, red, purple, pink, white, orange, they were all over the place, in lots of different sizes.

John continued, with David and the girls listening intently. "Viruses have a really bad rap; but, they are also struggling to survive in the environment just like everything else. Actually, viruses aren't considered to be alive by any human definition because they are a molecular genetic parasite that depend on their host for replication or maintenance or both. The fitness of such genetic parasites resides in the survival of the network, not in individual elements. Thus, the fitness of any organism cannot be understood in the absence of the network of genetic parasites it faces."

David thought that this subject was simply fascinating. He said, "Yes, fitness is essentially the propensity to reproduce given the constraints of the environment. I can see how viruses can also be a part of the environment where it concerns other animals. But I never looked at it from the perspective of a virus before because they can't reproduce on their own without exploiting a host."

David paused briefly before adding, "Nothing brings out the fact that biologists lack of a good, distinct definition of life better than viruses due to that fact."

"Exactly," John said. "I studied viruses too for a while. I concluded that they're also trying to survive, doing their best to avoid decay into equilibrium before reproducing; there's no other explanation. They are just as unique, beautiful, and legitimate as any other organism, like us. And they're everywhere." His facial expression changed to dream-like as he added, "A flea hath smaller fleas that on him prey; and these have smaller fleas to bite 'em, and so proceed *ad infinitum.*"

David smiled and looked at the girls who were not too amused; but, they were still listening, sipping their wine, engrossed by the conversation.

The Overture to *The Marriage of Figaro* ended, and after a brief pause, a slow, beautiful piece began.

"I know this one; I love this," said Michelle. Kimmy and Shirley looked at the aficionado and smiled, happy for her. It did have a nice sound, they thought.

"Oh, yes," John said, "this is the famous second movement from Mozart's Piano Concerto Number Twenty-One."

"In C Major," added David.

"Yes, C Major," John said. "I always thought it was one of the most sublime pieces he ever wrote. It was very popular in his time too."

"Very romantic," added Michelle. She smiled at both John and David.

John looked at and tried to charm Michelle by adding, "The piece sculpts the air with romantic love." It worked on all the girls; they would have vocalized their sighs had David not been there. The girls looked at each other, each knowing that the others were thinking the same thing; that John was handsome, elegant, charming, buff, and his place was so beautiful and up in the hills.

As they listened to the music, eventually their thinking transitioned to their wine and the large tank in front of them. Everyone reached for their glasses and sipped at nearly the same time, taking in the dry, acidic texture of the red wine, then staring at the fish tank, enjoying their buzz.

John noticed most of them looking at the tank and said, "Oh yeah, my pets," John said, although he probably wasn't referring to the fish, as the girls and David were to find out shortly.

"Those are mostly snappers — spotted rose snappers — but there are other fish in there," John said.

"Snappers?" Kimmy asked.

"Yeah, snappers." John said. "Common fish; there are about a hundred different types mostly living in the ocean, though a few feed in freshwater. You probably eat them for dinner occasionally, though who knows if you're actually getting red snapper when you order red snapper. Most of the ones in the tank are spotted rose snappers; I use them for kicks and giggles."

"Kicks and giggles, kekekeke," Shirley said with a unique laugh added.

"What are those white things in there?" Kimmy asked.

"Oh, those," said John. "Well, snappers feed on plankton, small fish, and small crustaceans. Those white things are, uh, small and larger crustaceans."

"Crustaceans?" Kimmy asked.

"I'll field that one John," David said. Michelle, whose hands were at her side, reached over and tapped David on the side of his thigh, then looked at him with a smile. David turned to her, saw her smile, and smiled himself, brimming with confidence, in utter delight being in her presence.

"Crustaceans are essentially the insects of the water. Crabs, crayfish, lobsters, shrimp, krill, and barnacles: they're all crustaceans. Most notably, they all have exoskeletons, amongst other things like two-parted legs."

"Perfect, David," John said, "I couldn't have done better myself. Let me just add that, as you can see, their bodies are divided into three distinct regions, a head, thorax and abdomen. The first segment of the thorax is fused to the head. The remaining seven free segments of the thorax each have a leg on either side, which they use for locomotion and, uh, latching onto prey." John smiled when he said that last statement.

He continued, "The abdomen has five free segments, plus a fused sixth one. That last segment has kind of legs too, which they use for swimming and, uh, breathing. They have compound eyes, two pairs of antennae, and four sets of jaws." John paused, reached for his wine glass and took a sip, thinking of something to end the conversation.

He came up with, "It pretty much looks like a cross between a cockroach, an armadillo and a squished centipede, all white with much fewer legs and in the water, yes?"

Kimmy thought about it for a second, looked at the little white things in the tank, then looked back to John and said, "Yup, that's what they look like," shaking her head in the affirmative.

"You know, it is feeding time; hey David, Kimmy, would you like to feed my pets?" He said that with a little bit of a smile on his face, like he knew something they didn't. Shirley picked up on that; she looked over at the other three; but, her telepathy had malfunctioned. Kimmy, Michelle and David were too engrossed to notice. John stood up, walked over to the side of the tank where Kimmy was standing; Michelle and David rose. Shirley, not to miss out on the action, also got up and stood next to them.

"Here, let me get some food from the fridge," John said, as he walked into the kitchen. The four musketeers could hear him open then rummage through that really expensive, built-in Sub-Zero® refrigerator that they had seen earlier. They heard him take something out of the refrigerator, place it on the countertop, open a cabinet, take out a plate or bowl, open a plastic bag, and place some of its contents into whatever it was with a few taps, kind of like putting ice into a glass. They then heard him rustle the plastic bag closed, the sound of the fridge opening, the sound of him placing it back in the refrigerator, then the fridge closing. He walked back into the room with a bowl of cold fish, in various small sizes.

"Dinner time!" John exclaimed to the gang. Kimmy was a little excited; so too was Michelle.

"Would you do the honors, David" John said.

"Sure," David said, taking a couple fish from the bowl John handed him.

John lifted the lid of the huge fish tank, revealing bubble sounds and the bubbles from which they derived. Several fish swam to the top of the tank, which was right at eye level for Michelle and Shirley, and slightly below eye level for David, Kimmy, and John.

David dangled one of the fish into the tank. So far so good.

Then, one of the fish came up out of the water line from the back, opened its mouth, and...and one of those big, white segmented things came out of its oral cavity, raising its head and several legs, hissing, scaring the bejesus out of everyone.

David immediately dropped the fish he was holding.

"Ahhhh!" yelled Michelle, Kimmy and Shirley.

"Ewwww," shrieked Kimmy. The three girls gathered near the kitchen, freaked out. David too took a step back.

It looked like a lot of the other white crustaceans on the bottom of the tank, but was much bigger, about the size of a, well, about the size of a tongue. In fact, it was the tongue; well, a replacement of the tongue of that particular fish.

Michelle, Kimmy and Shirley were next to the wall, David a little closer toward the tank, and John; well, John was still at the tank, laughing.

"C'mon, you guys, isn't that cool!" John said, still laughing.

"Cool?" Kimmy asked. "You think that's cool? Ewwww."

Shirley started laughing and walking toward the tank.

"Kind of reminds me of my little brother," Shirley said. That broke the tension a little bit; the girls laughed.

"Well, that's interesting," said John. "Actually, all these fish have one of those in their mouths. But they're all female."

"They're all female?" asked Michelle.

"Yup, every last one of them," John said. The females are the tongues, they do all the dirty work, and the males hang out on the fish's gills. Pretty fascinating, eh?"

The girls looked at each other, then to David, who, admittedly, thought it *was* interesting.

John continued, "The crustacean *Cymothea exigua* enters through the fish's gills then causes the degeneration of most of the tongue of its host fish, oftentimes the snapper, and attaches to the remaining tongue stub and floor of the fish's mouth by hook like legs. It survives by drinking blood from an artery. Once the tongue has been gotten rid of, it attaches itself as a new tongue, and manipulates the fish's food and consumes the free food particles as the fish eats."

"Ewwww," reiterated Kimmy. The three other musketeers looked at Kimmy and smiled, somewhat engrossed by John's description.

John laughed as he continued, "There's no indication of reduced feeding or respiration in the infested hosts. Thus, these crustaceans serve as a mechanical replacement of the fish's tongue and are the first and only known case in animals of functional replacement of a host structure by a parasite."

The romantic Mozart piece ended, and another classical work began; but it wasn't immediately recognizable.

"C'mon, they don't bite; the fish or the crustaceans. Come on back and have some wine," John said, kind of laughing.

"Uh, can I change the music; I think I'll be safer over there," Kimmy said.

"Sure," John said, "let me show you how." He walked over to the stereo equipment; Kimmy walked to him, hesitantly.

"Here, you open the CD tower like this," John said. "The CDs are in that tower," he said pointing to the four-sided tower which contained hundred of CDs. "Just find something you like, stick it in the CD tower here, and just press play on this remote." He handed her the remote.

Kimmy started looking for a CD she liked among hundreds on the four sided CD stack; John returned to his seat.

"So David," John began — David, Michelle, and Shirley had taken their same seats while John was showing Kimmy the CDs — "David, don't you think those viruses and this example of a tongue-replacing crustacean, don't you think they make it difficult to define what a parasite really is."

David was struck by the question as he heard Kimmy take out a CD from the rack. David responded, "Well, I never really focused on parasites. I studied and teach biology; but, viruses don't really fit in a biology course because, as we discussed, they aren't treated as a form of life due to their inability to reproduce on their own. But, yes, I think you have a point."

Right as David finished talking, Kimmy, who had chosen a CD, went to put it in the CD tower and instead knocked it over into the speaker tower, which banged and crashed into the wall.

"Oh no!" Kimmy yelled. "Oh! I'm so sorry!" Kimmy said, blushing.

John laughed as he walked over to her and said, "No worries, Kimmy, that happens all the time. Those things are tough, bet it didn't affect them one bit."

The wall had a few short, light, and a couple long, heavy, black scuff marks; apparently, it *had* happened many times before.

"Here, let me help you," John said, as he approached her. David, Shirley and Michelle were also standing, but didn't walk over. John righted the speaker tower and then the CD tower. "No Doubt," he said referring to the name of the band of the CD that she had picked, "good choice. You put it in like this; gently, then simply press here." The song "Underneath it all" came up, a somewhat slow tune sung by Gwen Stefani of the group "No Doubt," with a reggae rhythm backing her up.

"Nice!" Michelle said.

"Oh, I love Gwen Stefani," Shirley said.

"Me too," John said.

David was silent, not knowing who Gwen Stefani or "No Doubt" was; but, he smiled, nodded his head, and went along with the team. They all grabbed their wine and took a sip.

"So what I'm saying, David, is that there are some fairly ambiguous definitions of the word parasite. The term "symbiosis" means living together, thus the crustacean and fish and viruses and humans, are symbionts. When both parties gain an advantage, then they are said to be mutualists, when one party gains and the other neither gains or losses, the party benefitting is said to be a commensal, and when one of the parties gains at the other's expense, well, that's a parasite. In the case of the tongue-replacing animal, although hard for most of us humans to understand, neither party is losing anything, except, of course, at the very the beginning of the relationship."

Shirley laughed in her individually way, "Kekekekeke," then added sarcastically, "at the beginning of the relationship," repeating what John had said, then exclaimed, "that armadillo ate the fish's frickin' tongue!" Everyone laughed.

"Yes, it did," John said. "But the fish isn't any worse for the wear, as evidenced by no reduced feeding, breathing or mating. How can we explain that?"

"I know!" Shirley blurted out, "they're here for us; we can just eat them both!" Everyone laughed.

David then said, "John, I think what you're trying to say is that the crustacean isn't a parasite because the fish isn't really harmed; it's a commensal."

"That's what I think, David," said John. "In fact, in nature, it's often hard to tell protagonists from antagonists. The parasitic lifestyle, from our perspective, looks deplorable, ghastly, inhumane. But it could very well be the ultimate way of life, innovative and strategic, even if disgusting. I can't think of a better, simpler, easier way to make a living than off the talents and energy — off the backs — of other beings. It could be that parasites are attracted to those members of a species that are maladapted in some way, or, better, those maladapted are attracted to the parasite. After all, not every member of a given species gets infected by the same freeloaders. Parasites might also serve as the major stimulus for other life forms to intensify a given function or to completely change it: to evolve. In short, parasites contribute to the increasing complexity of other life forms, while they themselves adapt."

"I like snapper," Michelle said, trying to change the subject. "Shrimp too." Kimmy, who was paying close attention to John, smiled when Michelle redirected the conversation.

David smiled at Michelle, placing his right hand between her two knees and cupping his hand behind her left kneecap; his forearm barely touched her upper-left thigh. Michelle smiled at him, allowing him to do so. In like Flynn, David assured himself. John happened to see David touching Michelle and gave a jealous look that neither of them saw; but, Shirley noticed. Kimmy returned to her seat.

And then the door bell rang.

David recognized it as the full hour chime — popularly known as the Westminster chime — heard from Big Ben, located at the north end of the Palace of Westminster in London.

As it was playing, John got up, said "Excuse me," walked over to the left stairway, and gracefully walked up the stairs, two at a time, reaching the landing before the chime had ended.

The girls commenced a private chit-chat in Korean as David focused on the musical chime, easily heard through the music playing on the CD. He thought about how the Westminster chime is typically believed to be a set of variations on the four notes that make up the fifth and sixth measures of "I Know that my Redeemer Liveth," from Handel's *Messiah*. David had heard that piece a few times and never could see the similarity, but knew that it was written late in the eighteenth century for a new clock in the University Church in Cambridge, but had no idea exactly who composed it. He had, however, committed to memory the words written on a plaque on the wall of the clock room in the Big Ben: "All through this hour, Lord, be my guide, And by Thy power, No foot shall slide."

David, Michelle, Kimmy and Shirley heard the door open.

"Hello gorgeous," John said enthusiastically.

"Hi there John," said a female with a happy tone, eerily familiar to David and Michelle.

"How did you get here; I don't see any cars in the driveway besides mine," John said.

"I flew," said the female.

"Funny," said John from the second floor landing.

"What a beautiful house you have John, I had no idea," the mystery guest said.

"The better to keep all my pets and entertain, my love. C'mon in." And, with that, John led her down the left side stairway. That is, the left side stairway from the four musketeer's perspective; it was the right side for John as he led his newly arrived guest by the hand. Shirley, Kimmy, and, especially, David and Michelle, watched first with no emotion, and then in horror, as first John came down the stairs, and then, after a thin leg in jeans was seen, in slow motion the other leg, then body, pink purse with thin, pink strap, ends of hair, neck, and face of a young woman was seen. And then they saw that long nose. In slow motion, *she* became recognizable.

It was *her*, that preacher David and Michelle met on the Biomedical Quadrangle, adjacent to the Paris Green.

"Ahhh!" Michelle yelled in shock. Kimmy jumped up off the couch; Michelle's scream took her completely by surprise, spilling her wine on the couch and floor. Shirley looked at Michelle and wondered what was going on. David sat there with his eyes and mouth wide open.

The preacher laughed. "Oh, hi there," she said.

As he followed her down the stairs, John simply said, "I see you know each other."

"Yeah, I saw her earlier today," the preacher said, motioning to Michelle. "And him too," she said tilting her head toward David. "Hi there, remember me?"

"Yes, I remember you," David said. "What are the odds?" He looked at Michelle, shaking his head. Michelle shrugged.

Making the best of a strange situation, David stood up and formally introduced himself, "Hi, I'm Dave Bennett. These are my friends, Michelle, Kimmy and Shirley. We all go to UCSD."

"Nice to meet you David, Michelle, Kimmy, Shirley," she said, shaking each of their hands in turn. "I'm Ann Opheles."

John reached for some paper towels that were at the foot of the snapper tank, grabbed the roll, unrolled a few, handed some to Kimmy, who started wiping up the mess, and then took some for himself to help clean.

"It's such a beautiful house, isn't it," Ann said, oblivious to how David and the girls were receiving her.

"Yes, it is," Michelle said politely.

The song ended here, and, after a brief pause, the next song came up. It was "Cool," also by Gwen Stefani, and apparently also on the compilation CD.

Shirley and Kimmy walked over to Michelle and started conversing in Korean; Michelle was probably explaining how she and David met Ann near the Paris Green where they debated evolution. No doubt she told them that David won.

"Are those your pets, John?" Ann asked, referring to the fish.

"Why yes, those are my, uh, pets," John stated.

It was obvious to David and the girls that Ann did not know about John's *real* pets.

"Would you like some wine Ann?" John asked, trying to make her comfortable.

"Sure," Ann replied.

"Let me get you a glass," John said, walking into the kitchen, leaving the four of them alone.

A moment of uncomfortable silence later, looking at the girls, Ann said, "John's so handsome, isn't he."

The girls looked at Ann inquisitively for a moment; all four of the musketeers then looked around at each other as if waiting for one of them to provide guidance in this situation. It was Shirley that said, "He sure is," giddily. Michelle couldn't help but to smile and nod her head in agreement, as did Kimmy.

"I love this song," Kimmy said, as the real melody began, trying to break the continuing strange feeling in the room. She looked around at David, Michelle, Shirley, and Ann, who all seemed to show their agreement in different ways, mostly by head nodding and smiles.

John walked back into the main room with a glass for Ann, poured some wine into her glass, picked up his own glass, and proposed a toast.

"Here's to new friends," John said.

Looking around at the girls and David, Ann added, "And potentially, new hosts."

David thought that comment was strange, though the girls didn't seem to notice. Ann didn't say "new hosts" and look at John; she said "new hosts" and looked at everyone else. Maybe he was being too analytical for a social situation. Still, he wasn't sure what that comment meant. Nevertheless, they all raised their glasses and sipped some wine. Shirley chugged hers down and motioned John for a refill.

"Here you go," John said, lifting up the bottle and pouring out what remained.

"Thanks," Shirley said, taking another sip and placing the glass down on the table.

"So, how do you folks know each other?"

"We had a lovely conversation on campus," Ann said.

"Yeah, lovely," David added. "John, I think you would have appreciated it."

"Really," John stated.

David replied, "Your friend here holds some antiquated notions, such as how the Earth is only a few thousand years old and that God created everything in one fell swoop." David reached for his wine glass.

"Oh, yeah, well, of course I don't believe any of that," John said. You could see the relief on David's face.

"We all need something to do on Sunday mornings," John added. "Ann is visiting as part of a church group that I sponsor; we invite different youth groups to stay in California from time to time. Ann, where are you from?"

"Utah," she quickly replied, enamored with him.

"Utah, that's right," John said, winking at Ann.

Returning his attention to David, he said, "I try to show them aspects about life that they may be missing living in other parts of the country. You know, broaden their horizons. In exchange, some do work in the local community like feed the homeless, or, uh, give seminars."

"Seminars," David said sarcastically. "She was on campus proselytizing."

John laughed. "Ann, were you proselytizing?"

"Who me?" Ann innocently asked. Ann tried to convert the skeptical looks she received by adding, "Well, my father was a priest in the Christian church, and his father before him. My last name comes from two Greek words, one meaning 'not' and the other meaning 'profit,' thus my father led me into nonprofit work. That's what I was doing at the University: my non-profit work." The four musketeers remained unconvinced.

"It's a necessary evil, David," John began. "She doesn't mean any harm, she's just trying to make a living. She gives back to her church, and they put her in touch with other folks to expand her network, thus expanding the reach of the church. She gets to learn, and we get people who make a difference in local communities throughout the country. It's a win-win."

Michelle, Kimmy, and Shirley were listening intently; other than Michelle, they had never seen that before. It was believable; well, maybe it wasn't, but, coming from John's mouth, it sure seemed so.

"You don't really believe all that God stuff, do you Ann?" John asked.

"C'mon, John, you don't really believe that we came from apes, do you?" Ann retorted.

"Lungfish maybe, but certainly not apes," John said.

David laughed. "Yeah, lungfish; there's a really old one at the John G. Shedd aquarium in Chicago. I think it's still alive."

Michelle rubbed David's kneecap with her left hand.

"Rrrungfish?" Shirley joked. "Are they de-rrricious?" Everyone laughed.

"Really, John, c'mon, we're primates," David said.

"Yeah, I'm just kidding, we're primates," John said. "But with all the studying I did, with all the research you've done, David, it's hard to get along with the larger masses of society talking about those sorts of things. Ya gotta go along with the flow sometimes, especially Sunday mornings. What would we spend our time on if it weren't for the church?"

"Sleeping!" Shirley said. They all laughed.

"What are all those?" Ann asked, referring to all the stuffed animals strewn about.

"Oh, those," John said. "We were just talking about those before you came in, Ann."

The song "Cool" ended just there, and another Gwen Stefani tune came up, "Just a Girl."

"Woohoo," Kimmy exclaimed, "great song." Shirley and Michelle agreed with head nods while dancing in their seats.

John continued, "Uh, Ann, those are just some of God's various creations. You know, viruses, worms, teddy bears."

David liked the fact that he was making fun of Ann.

"Teddy bears?" Ann asked. I think we can all agree that God had nothing to do with teddy bears."

"Sure, Ann. We finally reached agreement. No teddy bears," David said sarcastically.

"*Cause, I'm just a girl,*" Shirley sang along with the song, shaking her head as if not paying attention to the discussion. Michelle and Kimmy laughed; John, David and Ann smiled.

"I know you don't believe in God, David, but why do you insist on destroying the faith of those of us that do? This is the United States of America after all, we are free to believe in whatever we want," Ann said passionately.

"Part of the reason is that I'm studying to be a professor — I'm an educator — and when *you* go to a college campus and spew your non-knowledge about, when you add your granules of non-reality to the Everest of non-contributions, there's no choice but to respond with the truth. People should be more critical, they should be able to think for themselves given the facts," David said with equal passion.

The girls were listening to every word; if they had pen and paper, they would have been taking notes.

Ann said, "Well, everything can't be broken down into bits and pieces; faith handles some things better."

"You mean people should believe what they are told," David replied.

Ann thought about that for a moment and then said, "Yes, I suppose that's what I meant."

Michelle looked at Kimmy and Shirley; they then looked at each other, and then back to Michelle and smiled as if saying, "Yes, David is smart and eloquent; way to go Michelle."

"Well, I think David won this round, followed closely by Shirley," John said. "Ann, I think you're in last place, maybe you need to drink a little more."

"I think I've had enough, John. When can we be more, uh, alone," Ann said noticeably perturbed.

Seizing the moment, Michelle said "We have to get going anyway; David's going to play for us."

John looked friendly, but was livid inside. He wanted them to stay, especially Michelle. Even he didn't want to spend much time with Ann, as he found her to be obtuse.

"David's going to play for you? What do you mean?" John asked sardonically.

"He's a pianist," Michelle said proudly.

"A pianist?" John said, somewhat surprised.

"Well, hold on there a minute," David replied, "I'm not really that good; I practiced a lot when I was younger, now I just play the repertoire that I learned back then."

"He's awesome," Michelle said, eyes wide open, smiling seductively. Her facial expression and statement inflamed John all the more, and now it showed.

"Awesome, huh?" John said, clearly not believing it.

"Oh, c'mon, Michelle, I'm really not that good."

"I think you are," Michelle said with a slow blink of the eyes and a humble smile.

As if it were a competition, John admitted a little defeat by saying, "I never learned to play an instrument," which only made Michelle look more fondly upon David.

"He plays 'Moonlight Sonata' beautifully," she said, "the whole sonata, not just the slow part." Ann now understood why David knew so much about Beethoven and had schooled her in their debate earlier in the day.

"Do you have a piano in your dorm room David?" John said in the same sardonic tone as previously.

"Funny, John," David replied. "No, not in my, uh, dorm room. I have a key to the old Music Building; there are still a bunch of practice rooms there, up on the second floor. That's how I met Michelle."

"Where's that?" John asked.

"They built the medical school on the old music campus, before they moved it," David said. "The Music Building is still there, though the first floor has been converted to offices for medical instructors and staff. It's right by the Paris Green."

"The Paris Green," John stated. "I bet it's a great place to hang out; I never go there myself."

"Can you take us there, John. We're gonna go listen to David play. Maybe we can come back another time," Michelle said. Kimmy and Shirley, nodding their heads in agreement, stood up to get the show on the road.

"Sure, I—we—can take you there," John said, looking at Ann with fully opened eyes. Ann certainly wanted them to leave, and was happy to help them out.

John got up and turned off the stereo—nicely timed with the song's end—and led the four musketeers plus one to the stairways. Michelle, Kimmy and Shirley stopped and turned to take in the view, causing John, who was now on the third step of the right stairway to stop, as did Ann, just behind him, and David behind her. The stunning, densely lighted, nighttime San Diego Bay view together with the evening's alcohol easily put anything negative seen or discussed behind the girls as they turned, telepathy on, smiling at each other. "This is heaven on Earth," they thought as Michelle led them to the other stairway. And so that's the order they left; John and Ann walking up the right stairway, and the four musketeers, Michelle, Kimmy, Shirley and David, walking up the left.

Let's Call it a Night

Not two seconds after both doors closed and the Hummer sped off, Michelle asked cute little Shirley, *"Meongmeongtang?"*

Shirley smiled, covered her mouth and giggled. "Yes, woof woof soup. My favorite!"

"He's so handsome," Shirley added.

"Mah juh, chal sang gyuh dah," Kimmy added, which meant "yes, he is hot."

"Chal sang gyuh dah, yes, but...creepy when you think about it. I'm glad we left. Hey David, are you ready to play for us?" Michelle asked innocently.

"Sure," David offered, thinking to himself how cute she was. Cripes, he thought, how cute they all were. He scratched his head wondering why they were with him.

"Rrrets go," Michelle joked. The three musketeers with their newly dubbed knight David began their walk on the Paris Green to the Music Building, guided only by distant streetlights and a bright crescent moon in the sky. Surrounded now by the medical school campus, walking on familiar Paris Green, they were safe. It was Shirley that, fumbling first to unwrap a caramel green apple Hi-Chew, started singing as if at the norebang, though the song wasn't on their original play list.

"Feerrings, nothing more than feerrings," Shirley sang and laughed. Michelle, Kimmy, and David laughed with her. Shirley put the Hi-Chew in her mouth and sang some more, though it sounded more like dry gargling, *"I rrrike big butts, ba, ba, ba, ba, ba, ba, ba, ba."* They all laughed.

"And I cannot lie," David sang in response, *"shake it."*

"Shake it," Shirley answered.

"Shake it," David repeated.

"Shake it," both Shirley and Kimmy answered.

"Shake that healthy butt," David replied, cracking up.

"*Baby got back!*" Shirley yelled hysterically.

They all stopped, put their hands on their heads, and shook their booties like the girls in the video did. They laughed and continued walking.

Michelle then started singing a familiar Korean love song, not sung during karaoke, in Korean.

"Ewww," Kimmy said. There was no one in sight.

"Ewwwww!" Shirley added. David looked over in surprise, adding nothing but a smile.

They reached the Biomedical Quad with no one in sight, felt a cool ocean breeze, and looked around at the safe and calm setting. They walked toward the hallway with the sliding glass doors on each side separating them from the Music Building.

"Look," David said, "just beyond those doors: it's the…"

"Hahaha," Michelle laughed, "it's the mucous building. Isn't that what it is David?"

"Seems that way sometimes," David said, kind of giggling. Kimmy and Shirley didn't get the joke, but laughed anyways.

"I'm so drunk," David said. He didn't know how he was going play the piano.

Michelle sang as they crossed the Biomedical Quadrangle, "*Nobody, nobody but you,*" clapping her hands twice with a pause before she clapped once again, just like in the video.

"*Nobody, nobody but you,*" Kimmy replied.

"*Nobody, nobody but you,*" the three musketeers sang in unison, looking at David. He blushed. Gosh they're so cute, he thought. And my how drunk he was, again thinking that he will not be able to play that piano, as he took his wallet out of his back pocket as if on automatic pilot.

They reached the sliding glass door of the Biology Annex. David pressed his wallet to the black, square scanner on the right, and the large, sliding glass door slid open rather quickly. The four musketeers walked in and directly toward the second sliding glass door, which would lead them back outside and a short walk to the Music Building. Although lit from the outside, the inside of the hallway was much darker — it was late at night, after all, and the smart, connected facilities program covering the entire campus was sure to keep light usage down to a minimum at this time — and my how it echoed.

Shirley let out a long, loud belch that filled up the hallway with sound. David, Kimmy and Michelle laughed.

"What a talented girl you are," David said to Shirley.

"Why thank you, Scooby-Doo!" Shirley said, getting the full echo effect in the hallway. She was dying to finally use that new name in a sentence. The girls giggled.

Shirley hit the green "open" button on the wall next to the other sliding glass door; the door slid open as fast as the previous one, and a light went on outside, illuminating their way toward the Music Building. David took the lead.

"Jane, get me off this crazy thing," Shirley yelled.

It was just, say, forty or fifty feet on the paved walkway from the Biology Annex to the Music Building. As they walked, they could see the outline of a tall, thin statue about twenty feet away to the right and the Pharmacological Sciences tower further off in that distant direction; a parking lot with few cars could be seen on the left. In front, there it was, the two story, old, non-descript, red brick Music Building.

Shirley felt a sudden, sharp pain on her back and shouted, "Oww!" She awkwardly used both hands to knock away whatever small insect was biting. They all looked at her.

"I guess the mosquitoes are out tonight," Shirley said to David, trying to regain her composure.

"Don't look at me," said David. "Of the few thousand mosquito species, only the females suck blood. Don't worry, though, none of the ones in California carry serious diseases.

"Owww!" Kimmy yelled, "she got me too!" Shirley laughed.

"Not funny!" Kimmy said with a stern voice. They continued walking.

"You guys, I don't feel so good," Shirley said moments later, as she walked over to the grass.

Kimmy, her hand pressed to her back, walked up to Shirley. David and Michelle walked up to the both of them; they all formed a circle around her in the grass.

"I'm dizzy," Shirley said.

"One too many beers," Kimmy said, laughing.

Then Shirley started dry heaving. To see this small-framed girl now hunched over with her hands on the ground significantly changed the mood.

Then Kimmy said, "I'm feeling a little dizzy too."

Michelle and David looked at each other.

"What were you saying about mosquitoes, David?" Michelle asked in a serious tone.

Shirley fell completely on the ground.

"Oh my God! Shirley! Are you okay?" Kimmy shouted.

Shirley didn't answer. Kimmy then hunched onto the ground, her hands bracing her descent, and she too began to dry heave.

"David, what's going on?" shouted Michelle.

Before he could answer, Kimmy fell completely to the ground and passed out.

"David, call an ambulance," Michelle said frantically, bending over both girls now unconscious on the grass.

"Michelle, I, uh, I don't have a cell phone," David said, trying to remain calm.

Michelle, confused, desperate to help her friends, stood up and not so calmly said, "I'll try mine." As she fumbled through her purse for her cell phone, she heard David yell out...

"Ahh!" Instead of swatting whatever it was on his calf, however, he slowly pulled out small a plastic dart. He held it in front of himself with his right hand, catching Michelle's gaze.

Said David, "I don't think this is a mosquito. I think someone's shooting at us." With that, the dizziness kicked in; he moved slowly backwards toward the Music building.

Michelle watched in helpless agony as he stumbled further back, tripped and hit the ground with a thump onto a small heap of dirt. She thought he would hit his head on the side of the brick building; but, thankfully, he fell short. Still looking at him, she was obviously torn between staying with her friends, walking over to him or calling for help.

Imagine for the moment David lying face up, his head and upper body supported by some sort of mound. He turned his head to the right and just barely made out a big, yellow Hummer in the distance as his vision began to blur. He heard footsteps rushing toward his general direction, yet no one else was visible. Some sort of scuffle occurred close by; and then, not a sound. He heard footsteps once again diminishing to silence. David was now completely unconscious.

Although it was dark outside, there was just enough moonlight to make out David's lifeless body on the ground. Picture zooming-in to his right shoulder in the silence. Stop there. Wait. A couple seconds tick forward, and then a single ant — a scout — can be seen climbing up from the David's back to the top of his shoulder, waving her two long, slender L-shaped antennae in the air and then touching them to David's shirt. She was investigating the scene and the intruder.

No, it was not an Argentine ant; this ant was far too large. It was, in fact, a leafcutter ant — a soldier leafcutter ant — with large, menacing mandibles. Her friends, one, two, then three, slowly joined her, performing the same ritual. They were soon no longer investigating; they were biting.

- - - - - - - - - - - - - - - - - -

"Thirty-one is too young to leave this world," thought the elder Alvarez as he pulled his old, four-seater into the Pharmacological Sciences Building parking lot. The two — Luis and Walter — were listening to a version of Schubert's "Ave Maria," sung by a wonderful female soprano, with solo piano accompaniment, emanating from Walter's vintage AM/FM stereo cassette deck; the car's stock AM radio simply wouldn't do the trick. We met these two distinguished gentlemen earlier in our story near Geisel Library.

Still, even at thirty-one, Franz Peter Schubert composed over a thousand individual works: six-hundred or so Lieder, nine symphonies, sacred music, operas, incidental music, various chamber and solo piano works.

Schubert had a respite from his poverty in 1825, during his prosperous holiday in Austria. It was during this time and setting that he composed his "Songs from Sir Walter Scott."

Walter Scott's poem, *The Lady of the Lake*, was set to music by Franz Schubert in his work entitled *Liederzyklus vom Fräulein vom See*. This work of seven songs included the three "Ellen Songs," written in German: "*Ellens Gesang I*," "*Ellens Gesang II*" and "*Ellens Gesang III*." Known by the song's first two words, "Ave Maria," "*Ellens Gesang III*" is now commonly referred to as "Schubert's Ave Maria," however, the music became famous in a later adaptation that replaced Scott's text with the Latin text of the Catholic "Ave Maria" — the "Hail Mary" — prayer.

It's a few hours later; Luis and Walter Alvarez, contractors at the University, are taking their ritual sunrise walk along the beach and through campus.

It was a beautiful morning, like most mornings in San Diego. The Sun was just coming up; it was about six-twenty. Both were dressed in faded jeans and T-shirts, and both wore their University badges. Luis, the taller of the two whose gray hair distinguished him more so than Walter, wore badge number nineteen-eighty around his neck, hung by what looked like a plain, black, wide but thin shoelace, about the same length. Well, everything is called something; that sheath on the end of a shoelace there to hold the ends together tightly in order for it to be easily thread into a shoe's holes is called an "aglet." Similarly, that wide, thin, shoelace-like thing worn around Luis's neck purposed to carry his badge is called a "lanyard."

Walter didn't have his badge held by one of those; he wore it on his belt, via a "retractable badge reel" as they're known. The badge was partially hidden by the somewhat archaic, portable radio he was now carrying.

Although they typically parked at the Pharmacological Sciences Building or the hang gliding center on the cliff overlooking the Pacific Ocean, and sometimes walked past the medical campus, they didn't typically walk on any quadrangle, though they often walked past the Paris Green. This morning, however, fortuitously for some as we shall see, Walter seemed to be called to a statue that had been installed sometime ago. He had seen its outline a few times; but, had not really seen it in detail. Today, however, to the sacred delight of Schubert's "Ave Maria," they were going to give it a more formal viewing.

The statue was right across the street from the Pharmacological Sciences Building, where they had just parked, between the Biology Annex—the one with the sliding glass doors—and the Music Building. It was a unique statue, a fountain, created and christened "Standing" by Kiki Smith in 1998. The music played on.

Smith's fountain features a female figure, standing arms open, in a Madonna-like pose, on top of a twelve-foot high tree-trunk-like column. Ribbons of water—the source of life—flow gently from her arms, splashing onto a base of pale stones.

A grouping of starfish-headed pins, placed in the shape of the constellation Virgo, pierces the figure's flesh, calling up numerous metaphors: acupuncture, self-adornment, assault, martyrdom. The delicate pins, with their tiny, starfish caps, suggest yet other metaphors derived from both the ocean and heavens, images that speak to mind and body, flesh and healing. Smith used the creation to question what is concealed and revealed, celebrated and censored in daily human life.

A few moments of inspiration later, "Ave Maria" ended. Walter switched his vintage radio to FM, which was already tuned to his favorite station. A version of "Ella" performed by Alejandro Fernandez, backed by a full Mariachi band began.

Walter smiled at Luis who approvingly smiled back at him. You see, he knew that the original version was performed by José Alfredo Jiménez in the introduction to the 1966 movie *Me Cansé de Rogarle*. Walter turned up the volume and gazed at the fountain. He watched the water hit the ground, following the water back up in the opposite direction to the arms.

"Me cansé de rogarle, (I grew tired of begging her)
me cansé de decirle (I grew tired of telling her)
que yo sin ella (that without her, I)
de pena muero... (would die of a broken heart)"

And then, while taking in the view, something caught Walter's eye to the right by the Music Building. It was a shirt; a pair of crumpled up jeans. No, it was a couple different shirts…

"Ya no queria escucharme... (She didn't want to listen)
si sus labios se abrieron (her lips opened)
fué pa' decirme... (only to say)
ya no te quiero. (I no longer love you)"

Wait. Wait, there were people in those clothes. Small, thin people, with black, shiny hair, curled up in little balls. He walked over to investigate; maybe they were sleeping off a night of heavy drinking, unable to make it home…

"Yo sentí que mi vida (I felt my life)
se perdía en un abismo (slipping away into an abyss)
profundo y negro (deep and black)
como mi suerte... (just like my luck)"

Walter gave a desperate look to Luis who at first didn't seem to notice anything unusual. Then, in a single instance, as Walter pointed to the carnage, Luis came running over…

"quise hallar el olvido (I wanted to find oblivion)
al "estilo Jalisco" (Jalisco style)
pero aquellos mariachis (but that mariachi band)
y aquel tequila (and that tequila)
me hicieron llorar. (made me weep.)"

As the instrumental section began, Luis and Walter looked at each other in panic. There was a third body lying on the ground, covered in what looked like a thin, moving layer of black oil with red highlights. The two walked closer to that body partially behind large bushes abutting the red brick, two-story building, in the dirt, on a mound. The oil covering the body seemed to ooze in all direction. And then, as they approached, the oozing oil morphed slowly to movements of non-descript red and blackness, then, finally, to individual swarming, biting, stinging, frenzied ants.

"Catastrophe!" Luis said slowly and quietly. Neither could believe the input carried on waves of billions of photons, at the speed of light from the sun, reflected on the gruel-covered body, through their saccading eyes to their brains.

Walter thought about how the light carrying the image effortlessly pierced the conjunctiva and cornea via his pupils through his lenses, refracted through the viscous, vitreous humour, landing upside-down on his retinas' foveas, through the one-hundred-and-twenty-six or so million photoreceptors, consisting of twenty times more rods than cones, to the million or so fibers making up his optic nerves, the left-most fields of view from both eyes drawn together separately from the right-most field of view of both eyes at the optic chiasma, landing inverted on the both sides of his primary visual cortex.

No, neither Luis nor Walter could believe the result in their primary visual cortexes, that single, shared, inverted view that their brains somehow now instantly righted into the terribly wrong perception of an ant carpeted and two other lifeless bodies of formerly vivacious, young students.

Luis reached into his pocket and pulled out a small cell phone. He called 911, no doubt, and could be seen talking excitedly, using his free arm to help describe the tragic scene.

Imagine moving straight up, as if viewing the scene from a long, extending camera boom. Up, up, up further, until we see the two men, the statue, and the one, two, three bodies surrounding the old, red brick Music Building.

"Me cansé de rogarle... (I grew tired of begging her...)
con el llanto en los ojos (with tears in my eyes)
alcé mi copa (I raised my glass)
y brindé...por ella... (and drank...to her...)
no podía despreciarme, (she couldn't scorn me)
era el ùltimo brindis (it was the last toast)
de un bohemio... (from a misfit)
por una reina. (to a queen.)

Los mariachis callaron... (The mariachis became silent)
de mi mano, sin fuerza, (from my limp hand)
cayó mi copa (fell my glass)
sin darme cuenta... (I didn't know)
ella quizo quedarse (she wanted to stay)
cuando vió mi tristeza. (when she saw my sadness)
pero ya estaba escrito (but it was already written)
que aquella noche (that on that night)
perdiera su amor. (I would lose her love.)"

As the music ends, and we're viewing the scene from higher and higher up, one, two, three, then many more police are seen running to the lifeless bodies. Some congregate around the one covered in ants. Those there work to rid the body of the gruel with their shirtsleeves, arms and hands. More and more people show up, some in official uniform, some not.

Paroxysms and More

One week later: Saturday afternoon

Envision fading-in to a large, fluorescently lighted hallway; at the end is a single room, its door closed, which is itself in the middle of a perpendicular hallway. A single male voice is heard singing in Gregorian chant style:

*"Kýrie eléison
Chríste eléison
Kýrie eléison
Kýrie eléison"*

He is singing the *Missa Orbis Factor,* the eleventh setting of the Ordinary of the Mass, a setting for Ordinary Time. Kýrie eléison is translated to "Lord have mercy." Chríste eléison means "Christ have mercy." The phrase is the origin of the Jesus Prayer, beloved by some Christians. The biblical roots of this prayer first appear in 1 Chronicles 16:34: "*...give thanks unto the Lord; for he is good; for his mercy endureth for ever...*"

The prayer is simultaneously a petition and a prayer of thanksgiving; an acknowledgment of what God has done, what God is doing, and what God will continue to do. It is refined in the Parable of The Publican, Luke 18:9-14, "God, have mercy on me, a sinner," which shows more clearly its connection with the Jesus Prayer.

Several different wheeled pieces of equipment with tubes, wires, and lots of dials standing unused in the bleached-clean smelling hallway are seen, and is all the evidence needed to know that we are in a hospital.

The *Orbis Factor* lasts a little under two minutes, enough time to see the equipment in the first hallway leading to the room, and various pieces of equipment in the abutting hallway, and, if you can imagine for the moment viewing this as a movie, as soon as the chant ends, another sacred piece begins, and the camera begins to move. It goes over the door and peers into the room from the top. We are listening to Rachmaninoff's "Vespers," No. 1, "O Come and Worship," sung in Russian.

The camera stops just above Shirley, or what looks like Shirley, connected to all sorts of machines by tubes. There's a nurse on either side of her bed. She's sweating profusely; her former beautifully shining straight hair is twisted, wet, and going in all directions. Some is stuck to her forehead, her cheek, her neck, and some is bent away from her head. All her covers and top sheet are at the foot of the bed, noticeably pushed by her feet to form a little cotton-polyester hillside. You can't help but hear the fast beeping of her heart monitor.

"I'm so hot," she is heard to say, and one of the nurses hands her a glass of water. She does her best to reach for it through her weakness and dizziness and grabbed it while the nurse kept a hand on the glass. Both worked together to help her drink; Shirley was content taking only a few sips, spilling about the same amount on the bed sheet.

The camera moves to the next room from above, and, yes, it is Kimmy. Everything about the room is the same as Shirley's: the machines, the tubes, two nurses, and the hair, although hers is longer. Everything is the same; everything, that is, save one exception.

"I'm so cold," she yells. Kimmy is already under a stack of covers; one of the nurses places yet another cover over her.

The camera moves to the next room from above Kimmy's head. We see the foot of the bed and then the patient's two feet, wrapped separately in gauze. In fact, as we move further toward the head, we see that the whole body is wrapped in bandages. The patient was unrecognizable; but, the equipment looked the same as that in the previous room. So too the balloons and flowers sent by well-wishers.

There were no nurses present; other than a white milky tube emanating from the mouth, this person's head was completely covered in wound dressings, as were the arms, which were resting at the sides of this person's bandaged torso. The patient looked calm, and was either medicated or in a coma, but definitely not asleep, for who has ever seen a person at sleep on his back like that, with the sheet so neatly pressed under the body, and head so centered on the pillow? According to the chart, the mummy under those bandages was David.

The music ends just as the camera focuses on a digital clock on the night stand. It reads "4:00 p.m.," and is the last thing we see here as the scene fades to black.

Moments later, we fade back in to the same room, only the clock reads "7:00 a.m." We have moved fifteen hours forward in time. Nothing else has changed, save the bright light coming in from the morning sun. Imagine "The Flower Duet," a famous duet between characters Lakmé and Mallika, from the opera *Lakmé*, by Léo Delibes, beginning to play.

Two short, somewhat obese nurse's aides walked in, one carrying a couple of white bed sheets, the other just finishing up eating something. They move to opposite sides of David's bed and synchronously lower the side rails in order to change David's bottom sheet.

The nurse on the left hand side pushed to tilt David's body toward the nurse on the other side, who pulled and held him as the other nurse then began to untuck the bottom sheet from the top to the foot of her side. While bottom sheets normally are "fitted," this hospital saved costs by utilizing one type of sheet for both bottom and top. Light red and yellow stains could be seen now on David's wound dressings, which explained why they were there changing the bottom sheet: to see how the bandages were holding up. Actually, that's not the only reason. You see, bedridden patients need to be moved periodically to minimize muscle atrophy and prevent decubitus ulcers, commonly known as bedsores. They would be back to change his dressings later.

Now untucked, the nurse pushed the sheet from top to bottom toward the center longitudinal line of the bed and bunched it under David's side, while the other nurse kept holding on to make sure he didn't fall back or forward toward her. The nurse who had just bunched the sheet under David then grabbed hold of the fresh sheet that had been placed on David's side by the other nurse, unfolded it, and placed it first at the head of the bed, then the foot of her side, and spread it out evenly on her half of the bed, allowing about a foot of overhang at the head, side and foot. She bunched the other half of the sheet under the old sheet, which, of course, was bunched beneath David's side.

She tucked about half of the draping sheet under the head of the mattress then pulled a point of the sheet hanging over the side — the sweet spot — and draped it over the bed. There, she flattened it out on top of the bed, tucked in what was left hanging under the mattress, then grabbed the sheet from the same sweet spot and let it hang again on the side. She then tucked this part of the sheet under the mattress as well, completing the first of three clean, neat and calculated forty-five degree hospital corners.

She tucked in the rest of the sheet hanging over the side as she moved to the foot of the bed and performed the same series of actions there resulting in a near mirror image of the hospital corner at the head. She smoothed out the sheet with her right arm going up toward the head in anticipation of the dance's climax.

In a choreographed maneuver that the two must have rehearsed countless times a day, they turned David back onto the new sheet, and changed roles; the nurse on the other side of the bed now pushed to tilt David on his other side as the nurse that had just completed her two hospital corners pulled and held him on his now right side. The nurse that did the pushing completely removed the old sheet, let it fall to the floor, then grabbed the new sheet underneath from where David was just lying, and went through the exact same steps as the previous nurse, ending up with a hospital corner at the head and foot of her side of the bed. With her right hand and lower arm, she smoothed out the sheet, and then together with the other nurse, carefully lowered David back onto the center of the bed, being sure not to disrupt the bandaging, the probable wounds beneath, or the plethora of tubes going in and out of his body. They adjusted his body on the bed and pillow, made sure all the tubes were where they needed to be and in good working order, raised the side rails, re-checked some of the tubes, then made their way toward the door; the nurse on the far side grabbed the old sheet from the floor, looked one more time at the finished product and smiled. Viola.

Their dance lasted two minutes of the duet that lasts almost four, a performance surprisingly well-synched to the music. A couple seconds after the nurse's aides had left, the camera begins moving in reverse along the same path it traversed fifteen hours earlier.

"I'm so hot," said Kimmy, continuing to push the covers and sheet with her feet but not noticeably changing the height of the cotton-polyester, though changing the configuration a little and driving them off the bed a little more with each kick. The one nurse with her left the visible area—to the bathroom, no doubt—and returned a few seconds later with some water. Kimmy grabbed the water desperately with both hands and tried to chug it, though her fever kept her from sitting up for more than a second, and she spilled more than she was able to drink.

"Ice! Can I have some ice?" It was uncomfortable for anyone to watch her, and the nurse was relieved to have the opportunity to leave the room to get some ice.

As the nurse left the room, the camera, which was temporarily stationary, moved back again over Shirley's room.

There was little intelligible sound coming from Shirley, though she was shaking with chills under her covers, and you could see and hear her clattering teeth. A nurse stood by with additional covers to put on top of the extra covers that already adorned the small frame of this pitiful creature. This too was difficult and painful to view.

The camera pulls out of the room at a ninety-degree angle, the same way it had entered from above, and returned to eye level pointed to the closed door. It then moved backwards, away from the door.

The music ended; just under four minutes had passed. The camera stopped about fifteen feet from the door and all that you could hear was the incessant beeping from Shirley's heart monitor.

Then, five seconds later, that repeating beeping sound stopped and was replaced by one long "beeeeeee..." Shirley's heart had stopped.

The door opened seconds later, and the nurse quickly exited. With the camera still stationed with the same view of the open room, that same nurse, with three other nurses, rushed back into the room with a large piece of wheeled equipment, probably a defibrillator, and you could just see the nurses performing CPR on the tiny girl known by her family and friends as Sang Hee Lee.

Another man, a doctor, and another nurse could be seen running into the room, starting this time from behind the camera.

Our Hero Awakens

Four days later: Thursday

"Someone get the doctor, I think he's finally waking up," a female voice was heard to say.

Imagine for a moment you are in David's place. You hear a couple of nurses talking about you, how you're moving and trying to wake up; in fact, you just heard one of the nurses instruct the other to get the doctor. You try to open your eyes, and, as you do, two things stand out in your blur: a slight pressure from your arms, legs, stomach, back—in fact, all over—with the most distinct pressure emanating from both inside and outside your private parts, and a waxy, crusty substance on your eyes that is making the waking up ritual all the more difficult.

You continue the struggle, fighting to open your eyes, when an older, distinguished looking doctor rushes into your room, his white lab coat flailing in his own generated wind. He comes to your side somewhat frantically, grabs your shoulders, and as if he was going to deliver some terribly urgent news, he widely opened his mouth as if directed to do so by something inside, and one of those gnarly, white crustaceans David saw back in John London's house lunges out and starts biting his face and making terrible hissing and screaming noises. Horrible, awful, painful, loud, messy, wet, it was clawing, and biting, and hissing, and clawing...

All of it rubbish, of course. You can stop imagining being in his shoes now. Yes, David was still trying to wake up from a long sleep and had that nightmarish vision in the split second that he heard the nurse request the doctor. And now he opened his eyes abruptly, feeling pain in his eyelids from nearly tearing them from the waxy substance that attached quite firmly to the skin just under the eyes. There was a nurse right there, the one that had the other nurse get a doctor, dabbing his eyes with a warm washcloth at that very moment.

"Oh, it's okay David," she said with great empathy. She was the kind of nurse that everyone would want should they need someone to care for them. She continued to dab his eyes of the crust that had built up over the last couple weeks. That sleepy-dust by the way is "rheum," a dried combination of thin mucous naturally discharged from the eyes, blood cells, skin cells, and dust. As the nurse gently wiped away the rheum, and David's vision adjusted to the light, he found the sleepy-sand to be far from his worst problem.

The top of his body was raised significantly, thanks to the wonders of adjustable beds, allowing the nurse to be able to sit on his bed and clear his eyes of rheum without straining herself. As he calmed down, he could see why he felt that slight pressure all over his body: it was the bandages. On his arms, head, face, legs, back, stomach; bandages everywhere. And what of that pressure emanating from his private parts? Well, that was in fact caused by a catheter inserted into his penis, which in turn was connected to a long, winding clear tube, which in turn was connected to a urine collection device.

The nurse, having finished clearing the debris from his eyes, stood up and began to leave. "I'll check to see if the doctor can see you now. You two have a lot to discuss," she said, smiled, and left.

This brief solitude allowed David some time to orient himself to his location and predicament, though he couldn't stop thinking—or looking—at the middle part of his body, and that thing inside it, surrounded by what felt like tape. His entire body was covered in a sheet and blanket, so he just saw the outline of his midsection; but, his imagination did a good job of approximating the chaos that was his catheter.

It's easy for the mind to wander when confronted with something like this for the first time. Like the fact that urine is sterile until it reaches the urethra, where the epithelial cells lining the urethra are colonized by bacteria. Or that although urine is not toxic, it is a waste product and contains compounds undesirable to the body and irritating to skin and eyes. After suitable processing, however, it's possible to extract potable water from urine for drinking. Urine is, after all, ninety-five percent water.

David looked to the door to see if the doctor was there. Nope, no doctor yet.

He thought about it a little more. Numerous survival instructors and guides advise against drinking urine for survival. These guides explain that drinking urine tends to worsen, rather than relieve, dehydration due to the salts in it, and that urine should not be consumed in a survival situation, even when there is no other fluid available. In hot weather survival situations, where water is also hard to find, soaking clothes in urine—a shirt for example—and putting it on your head can help cool the body. Oh, and there was the fact that urban myth states that urine works well against jellyfish stings. So false, he thought, as at best, it is ineffective, and in some cases this treatment may make the injury worse.

The doctor was still not there. Well, that's okay, there was one more thing to add, David thought.

The effect of eating asparagus on one's urine has long been known. Certain constituents of asparagus are metabolized giving urine a distinctive smell due to various sulfur-containing degradation products, such as ammonia. All individuals produce the odorous compounds after eating asparagus, but only about forty percent of the population have the genes required to smell them.

And then they walked into the room. If David could have straightened up and be respectful, he would have. The inorganic tubes connecting him to various life-sustaining fluids and machines that went "beep," not to mention the pain he felt in his red polka-dotted arms when they moved, however, voluntarily or not, prevented him from doing so.

"Hi David," said Professor Ross, placing a few heavy books on the wheeled over-bed table, situated near the foot of David's adjustable bed, titles hidden from his view. "We've missed you terribly. How are you?" Professor Ross was the epitome of a sincere and humble man in David's eyes.

"Hi Professor Ross!" David said, struggling to hide his pain. Professor Ross gave his trademark, comforting smile.

"I'm okay, but in need of some answers," David added.

"Well, we have some of those David," Professor Ross said.

"Hi David. I'm Dr. Martino," said the bespectacled, perfectly coiffed gray and black-bearded doctor. The doctor's white lab coat with "Dr. Salvatore Martino" stitched into the upper-left pocket in blue mostly hid his slacks, white shirt, and matched solid, blue silk tie. He was much shorter than Professor Ross; not thin, but not fat either.

"There's a lot to discuss, David. Are you up for it today?" the doctor asked.

"I don't have any plans, sure," David said, calling to his existing reserve of humor.

"Okay, David. I must say, you do look a lot better than when you first came in," the doctor said, reviewing David's head-to-toe red polka dots that resembled the fissures and pin hole perforations seen in acoustical ceiling tiles.

"You've been in a coma for about ten days, David, do you remember anything," Dr. Martino asked.

"Ten days? Well, bits and pieces," said David, struggling to remember.

"That's okay, David. Most of your memories will come back, and you should become re-oriented soon," said the doctor. "The important thing is that you regain your strength and not become infected. We're going to keep you here for a few days to accommodate that."

"Okay," David replied.

"As I was saying, you were in a coma for a couple weeks, brought on by a combination of alcohol…"

"Oh yeah, alcohol. I remember," David interrupted. "We were at a bar; Michelle, Kimmy, Shirley and I…"

"Yes, David, that's good," Professor Ross said.

"David, it was the combination of alcohol and, uh — we found a drug in you: phenobarbital — it was that combination that kept you in a coma until today. Do you remember taking any drugs that night?" Dr. Martino asked.

"Phenobarbital? No…No! I don't take drugs. I didn't take any phenobarbital. I don't have a prescription for that," David said, agitated.

"Okay, okay, I believe you," Dr. Martino said quietly, believing him.

"Anyway, when they found you, you were passed out, lying on the ground on campus, by the Music Building. Do you remember that?" the doctor asked.

"Uh, kinda. Oh, yeah, now I remember, I played the piano for my friends — oh, wait; no, no I didn't — I was *going* to play the piano, for Michelle. For Michelle and Kimmy…and Shirley. Are they okay?"

"We'll get to that David. There's still more," said the doctor calmly, smiling now that David's higher-level reasoning and cognitive abilities were noticeably undamaged. David could be seen trying to recall other events; his eyes were moving to the upper left and right under raised eyebrows.

"Do you remember lying on the ground?" Dr. Martino asked.

"No," David said, shaking his head left to right.

"Well, David, I'm sure you're wondering how you came to have chicken pox, aren't you?" asked the doctor.

"Chicken pox? I have chicken pox? This doesn't look — or feel — like chicken pox. And I did have that when I was a kid," said an incredulous chicken-poxed, very *thin* man. He was, after all, noticeably thin, even in bandages. More on that later, thought the doctor.

"Well, David, there's really no easy way to say this. You, uh…"

"Just tell me doctor; I think I can take it," said the chicken-poxed man, the very brave chicken-poxed man.

"Okay, David. Here goes." The doctor took a deep breath, exhaled, and then took another long, deliberate one. "When we found you, you were covered in ants."

"Leafcutter ants, David. Leafcutter ants," the professor said with a slight exuberance in his voice.

"Leafcutter ants?!" David asked, exclaimed.

"Yes, they were leafcutter ants," Dr. Martino confirmed. We had an entomologist validate that.

"You mean Professor Ross?" David proudly asked.

Professor Ross humbly laughed, adding, "No, it wasn't me, David. But, I did take a look at the specimens they collected."

Said David, "I heard that leafcutters had invaded the area; but, I didn't think that they were on campus."

Dr. Martino responded, "Well, they were, they are, here, or, well, they did bite you and they were found all over you. You're quite lucky to be alive, considering that they bit and stung you on nearly your whole body. They do have stingers, right professor?"

"Yes, stingers are nearly universal in ants," Professor Ross answered. "Biting is a technical term; the leafcutters have large mandibles that pierce, but those mandibles have sharp teeth on the ends, so, yes, you could say that the ants bit and stung him."

"Fascinating," Dr. Martino said. "Anyway, the people that found you pretty much saved your life; they happened to be taking a walk early in the morning. We estimated that you were there sometime after midnight; you had ants biting you for several hours. No one really understands how you got there or why the ants bit and stung you, but they did."

"Well, that might be a good thing," David said, capturing the attention of both Dr. Martino and the professor.

"How's that?" Dr. Martino inquired in a higher pitch.

"Well, we know that I didn't contract a new strain of chicken pox," David joked. They all had a quick laugh.

"Good one, David," Professor Ross said, smiling.

"Hey professor," David said looking to his teacher for help, "what about these ants? Why in the world did they do this to me? How'd they get there? I thought they were mostly a tropical bunch."

"We know a lot about these ants, David," Professor Ross began. Why they're here, however, that's; well, we don't know how or why. Maybe someone brought them over delivering coffee. Maybe someone let their leafcutter pets go free. Who knows. All we know is that they're here."

Imagine now Dr. Ross narrating a short leafcutter ant documentary, as David and the doctor did. His good friend, E. O. Wilson of *Biophilia* fame—a book suggesting an instinctive bond between human beings and other living systems—had written a Pulitzer Prize winning compendium on the subject titled *The Ants*. And that was the large book that Professor Ross had carried in with him; it was the book on the bottom of the stack on the wheeled over-bed table. The huge book had a few pages with different colored tape-like tabs on them; he opened it up to one of the red-tabbed pages and began to read.

"Ants are everywhere, but only occasionally noticed. They run much of the terrestrial world as the premier soil turners, channelers of energy, dominatrices of the insect fauna—yet receive only passing mention in textbooks on ecology. They employ the most complex forms of chemical communication of any animals and their social organization provides an illuminating contrast to that of human beings, but not one biologist on a hundred can describe the life cycle of any species. The neglect of ants in science and natural history is a shortcoming that should be remedied, for they represent the culmination of insect evolution, in the same sense that human beings represent the summit of vertebrate evolution."

Dr. Martino was instantly captivated, as was David.

Professor Ross turned to the page with the blue colored tape-tab on it and read on. "Of the roughly twenty-five thousand species of ants, about forty different types of enormously successful leafcutter ants have been identified, and these are a specialized bunch which can be thought of as insect agriculturalists. Although they cut and bring plant matter back to their homes, they don't eat it. They actually use the plant material to feed a particular fungus, which they care for, nurture, and in turn, feed to their young."

"In short, the main properties of the leafcutter-fungus symbiosis can be stated as follows. Adult ants are fundamentally nectar feeders, predators, and scavengers. Their entire digestive system is geared to this dietary commitment. They are ill-suited to be herbivores. The fungus, in exchange for protection and cultivation, digests the cellulose and other plant products normally inaccessible to leafcutters and shares part of the assimilable metabolic products with them."

"How do they do that? The ants do not permit the fungi to form the mushrooms or other spore-bearing bodies under natural conditions. Instead, the ants feed exclusively on the special tips of the fungus, a preference that appears to have resulted in loss of the ability of the fungus to produce fruiting bodies. Reciprocally, the fungi utilize the ants for transport and do not have to depend on windborne spores to transfer themselves from nest to nest."

"The fungus-growing ants of the tribe Attini, to which *Atta* belongs, are of unusual interest because they alone among the ants have achieved the transition from a hunter-gatherer to an agricultural existence."

"Fresh leaves and petals require a whole series of special operations before they can be converted into substrate for growing their fungi. They must first be cut down, then chopped into fine pieces, next chewed and treated with enzymes, and finally incorporated into the garden comb. Beyond the harvesting process, the fungus must also be provided with constant care after it sprouts on the substratum."

"The Atta workers—all female—organize the gardening operation in the form of an assembly line. Tough vegetation can be cut only by workers with head-widths of 1.6 millimeters or greater. At the opposite end of the line, the care of the delicate fungal hyphae requires very small workers, and this task is filled within the nests by workers with head widths predominantly 0.8 millimeter. The intervening steps in gardening are conducted by workers of graded intermediate size. After the foraging ants drop the pieces of vegetation onto the floor of the nest chamber, they are picked up by workers of a slightly smaller size, who clip them into fragments about one to two millimeters across. Within minutes, still smaller ants take over, crush and mold the fragments into moist pellets, and carefully insert them into a mass of similar material."

You could hear Professor Ross turn to another page in the huge book. He continued, "The remainder of the gardening cycle proceeds. Worker ants even smaller than those described pluck loose strands of the fungus from places of dense growth and plant them on the newly constructed surfaces. Finally, the very smallest—and most abundant—workers patrol the beds of fungal strands, delicately probing them with their antennae, licking their surfaces clean, and plucking out the spores and hyphae of alien species of mold. These colony dwarfs can travel through the narrowest channels deep within the garden masses. From time to time they pull loose tufts of fungal strands resembling miniature stalked cabbage heads and carry them out to feed their larger nestmates."

"Although the assembly line of fungal cultivation is the core of caste and division of labor in the leafcutter colony, it is far from the entire story. The defense of the colony is also organized to some extent according to size. All the size groups attack intruders, but in addition there is a true soldier caste."

"The ultimate size reached by the Atta nests is enormous. Some can reach more than a thousand entrance holes, with a-thousand-plus chambers, of which hundreds can be occupied by fungus gardens and ants, forty-thousand males and five-thousand virgin queens, and millions of workers, all female. Of course, the males do nothing, and are only active when the queens go on their nuptial flight, try to mate with them before they found their own colony, and die soon after. Each male is born into full maturity with all the sperm he will ever possess, which they normally try to give to one, or at most a few queens, which results in severe competition."

"Colonies typically last as long as the queen remains alive, which for some species can be up to thirty years; the average leafcutter queen lives about fifteen years."

"It can be said that a principal difference between human beings and ants is that whereas we send our young men to war, they send their old ladies."

Dr. Martino let out a muted laugh; David smiled. Professor Ross turned the page and continued with that calm, steady voice.

"Why are there sterile workers? Isn't this the opposite of natural selection occurring at the level of the individual? Isn't this evidence that Darwin was wrong?"

"No," Professor Ross said as he continued to read. "According to Darwin, if some of the individuals of the family are sterile and yet important to the welfare of fertile relatives, as in the case of insect colonies, selection at the family level is inevitable. With the entire family serving as the unit of selection, it is the capacity to generate sterile but altruistic relatives that becomes subject to genetic evolution. To quote Darwin, 'Thus, a well-flavored vegetable is cooked, and the individual is destroyed; but the horticulturist sows seeds of the same stock, and confidently expects to get nearly the same variety; breeders of cattle wish the flesh and fat to be well marbled together; the animal has been slaughtered, but the breeder goes with confidence to the same family.'"

David nodded his head in agreement. Dr. Martino seemed to look to David and Professor Ross for confirmation of that fact; he wasn't a student of evolution, after all.

Professor Ross turned the page and continued speaking, "Upon reflection it is impressive how nearly pure the ants keep the fungal growth in their nest chambers. They build this monoculture by a variety of techniques: the plucking out of alien fungi, the frequent inoculation of the correct fungi onto fresh substrate, the manuring of the substrate with enzymes and nutrients to which the correct fungi — *Leucocoprinus* — are especially adapted, the production of growth hormones, and the production of antibiotics to depress competing fungi and microorganisms."

Professor Ross closed the book with a smile and noticed that both Dr. Martino and David were both staring at him — Dr. Martino's mouth was open too — hanging on his every word.

Professor Ross now spoke in his own words, "We've found data that suggest that the fungi itself produces toxins — antibacterial agents — that depress other fungi, but the ants themselves sample bacteria from the soil, selecting and maintaining those species that make useful antibiotics. And here's the point of this discussion. The lab came back with a positive match to one of those bacterial strains, *Streptomyces achromogenes*, in your blood, David. I'll let the doctor take it from here."

"Yes, that's right," Dr. Martino began, with barely half the confidence or charm of the prior speaker. "And we found that bacteria, among many others common to the leafcutter ant in your blood. Luckily, we were successful in removing them from your system with antibiotics manufactured from, uh, other bacteria and fungi via several blood transfusions."

David looked pitiful. Not knowing what to say, he simply stated, "So, you found some bacteria in my system." He said that with little drama, trying to come to terms with what it meant. Looking at the faces of both the doctor and his professor gave him the impression that they knew what was wrong with him, besides being covered head to toe in pock marks testifying to him having been bitten by thousands of ants. Female soldier leafcutter ants.

He looked at his red polka-dotted arms, and asked, "What else is wrong with me?"

Dr. Martino paused, looked down at the ground, then back into David's eyes, and began his briefing.

"Well, we isolated one of those toxins the ants inoculated into your body, and found it to be streptozotocin, a, uh," he let out an uncomfortable, nervous laugh and said, "well, scientists use the synthetic form to, uh, use on rats to model...diabetes."

Silence. Neither of the three had anything to say for a few uncomfortable moments. Professor Ross was looking at the floor. Dr. Martino too.

David kept his composure, though it was hard for the two other gentlemen to perceive composure as they simply saw a pitiful-looking, red polka-dotted, thin, young man with a serious case of chicken pox or the measles or ceiling tile syndrome.

"You're saying that the ants gave me diabetes?" David eventually, quietly asked.

The doctor paused for a moment, and then quietly replied, "Yes...you have diabetes."

Another uncomfortable pause later, the doctor continued, "A few days before you awoke from your deep sleep, we found your urine collection device filling up too rapidly. In adult humans the average production is about one to two liters per day. We found you to be producing more than two-and-a-half liters per day with the same hospital nutrition given to you as the previous days. That extra urine production is termed 'polyuria.' When we analyzed that urine, standard operating procedure here, we found that it contained significant amount of ketone bodies, and lots of glucose, which is the result of burning predominantly fat for metabolism, instead of carbohydrates."

Another uncomfortable pause later, Dr. Martino added, "There was something else." David just looked at him, glassy-eyed, expecting more bad news. "As we were treating you for the bites and stings and noticed the extra volume of urine, we saw that you were getting thinner. I think all in all, you've lost about thirty pounds...in a week."

David tried looking at himself; but, all he could see were the tubes going in and out of his arms and bandages.

"You'll have to believe me on that one, David," Dr. Martino said, noticing that David was trying to see if he had lost any weight. "We'll weigh you when you're up to it." They both smiled.

Dr. Martino continued, "Your blood sugar was so high, when we finally tested it, that your body drew energy reserves from your fat cells. You still have those same fat cells, but most of the fat from them are gone. And, by the way, it's not the raised blood sugar that does the harm, it's the ketoacidosis, a very serious condition caused by ketone bodies, the residual molecule after fat is burned, that does all the damage."

Professor Ross interjected, "Some animals do quite well with high blood sugar, some even with very high blood sugar. Take the hummingbird, for example. Unlike humans who have, uh, uncoupled food intake from functional needs, animals that must flap their wings fifty times a second in order to feed have a hard time staying fat, nor do they develop diabetes, at least as we know it."

"Fascinating," said the doctor.

"But, of course, we're talking about glucose, at least in the body," Professor Ross said. "Who knows what would happen if hummingbirds were forced to eat table sugar, or any other processed sugar that our species likes to indulge in. W culd they become adapted to it over time, or would they succumb to the same diseases that we experience: obesity, diabetes, heart disease, cancer, others. It doesn't take a genius to realize that we — most of us anyway — are maladapted to eating any of the processed foods that persist in supermarkets and restaurants. Yet we eat it nonetheless."

"Some of it tastes pretty good," Dr. Martino said as if to give a reason people indulge in sweets, not necessarily in defense of it.

The three thought about his statement for a moment, and then David replied, "But most of us *are* maladapted to it in all forms: ice cream, candy, cake, pudding, pasta, bread, rice, and the list goes on and on. We may eat it because it tastes good, or maybe because everyone else is eating it, or because it's inexpensive, but sugar really doesn't do us any good. Maybe in a few thousand generations we'll be able to adapt to it as a good energy source, but we're just not there yet. I think it was Lenski that showed that experimentally."

"Good David," Professor Ross said.

"Who's Lenski?" Dr. Martino asked.

"Lenski experimented with bacteria, essentially showing how they adapt over generational time when given a different food source," David answered.

"I see," Dr. Martino said with interest.

"Professor, tell him about Lenski; you tell the story best," David said.

Professor Ross gave a slow, hearty laugh, appreciative of being called upon to shed light on a subject.

"Yes, Dr. Martino, David's right," Professor Ross said, "Lenski showed how adaptation is evolution in action. I tell this story in my graduate microbiology course, but I can share it with you. David, let me know if I miss anything."

"Sure thing, professor," David said. The two doctors were happy to hear that David still had some spirit.

Professor Ross began, "Michigan State University biologist Richard Lenski and his colleagues and students provided a beautiful demonstration of adaptation. Lenski started off with a single bacteria of *E. Coli*; after it divided a few times into identical clones, he started twelve colonies, each in its own flask. Each day he and his colleagues provided the bacteria with a little glucose, which the bacteria ate by the afternoon. The next morning, the scientists took a small sample from each flask and put it in a new one with fresh glucose. They did this for more than twenty years. It's probably still running." Professor Ross looked at both Dr. Martino and David. They were both actively listening and expecting more.

He continued, "Lenski expected that the bacteria would experience natural selection in their new environment. In each generation, some of the microbes would mutate. Most of the mutations would be harmful, killing the bacteria or making them grow more slowly. Others would be beneficial allowing them to breed faster in their new environment. They would gradually dominate the population, only to be replaced when a new mutation arose to produce an even fitter sort of microbe."

"Over the generations, the bacteria did indeed evolve into faster breeders. The bacteria in the flasks today breed seventy-five percent faster on average than their original ancestor. Lenski and his colleagues have pinpointed some of the genes that have evolved along the way; in some cases, for example, the same gene has changed in almost every line, but it has mutated in a different spot in each case. Lenski and his colleagues have also shown how natural selection has demanded trade-offs from the bacteria; while they grow faster on a meager diet of glucose, they've gotten worse at feeding on some other kinds of sugars."

"So," Dr. Martino said, "these bacteria adapted to their new environment — a flask — by becoming faster breeders."

"Yes, they did," Professor Ross answered. "But that's not all. In addition to becoming faster breeders, they also became larger. And then, out of the blue, the bacteria had abandoned their glucose-only diet and had evolved a new way to eat."

"After 33,127 generations, Lenski and his students noticed something strange in one of the colonies. The flask started to turn cloudy. This happens sometimes when contaminating bacteria slip into a flask and start feeding on a compound in the broth known as citrate. Citrate is made up of carbon, hydrogen, and oxygen; it's essentially the same as the citric acid that makes lemons sour. Our own cells produce citrate in the long chain of chemical reactions that lets us draw energy from food. Many species of bacteria can eat citrate, but in an oxygen-rich environment like Lenski's lab, *E. coli* can't. The problem is that the bacteria can't pull the molecule in through their membranes. In fact, their failure has long been one of the defining hallmarks of *E. coli* as a species."

"If citrate-eating bacteria invade the flasks, however, they can feast on the abundant citrate, and their exploding population turns the flask cloudy. This has only happened rarely in Lenski's experiment, and when it does, he and his colleagues throw out the flask and start the line again from its most recently frozen ancestors."

"So in one remarkable case, they discovered that a flask had turned cloudy without any contamination. It was *E. coli* thriving on the citrate. The researchers found that when they put the bacteria in pure citrate, the microbes could use it as their sole source of nutrition and energy."

"What was going on? What was it that suddenly happened to that one tribe? If a mutant could discover how to deal with citrate, a bonanza would open up for it. This is exactly what happened with that one tribe. This tribe, and this tribe alone, suddenly acquired the ability to eat citrate as well as glucose, rather than just glucose. The amount of available food in each successive flask in the lineage therefore shot up. The only explanation was that this one line of *E. coli* had evolved the ability to eat citrate on its own."

Even though David had heard this story before in Professor Ross's class, he was still rapt by it. David looked at Dr. Martino; apparently he was just as impressed. It took a couple moments before one of them responded.

"I see, Professor Ross," Dr. Martino said. "You're saying that adaptation is possible; but, that it takes a long time. Some of us can eat sugar in all its forms and look good at the beach because we are relatively adapted to eating them. And some of us, probably more like most of us, cannot; we haven't adapted to the use of sugar as a nutrient or energy source.

"Yes, that's exactly what I am saying; that's what the evidence suggests," Professor Ross replied.

"And I was perfectly adapted to eating whatever I wanted before those ants got to me," David said. Both the professor and Dr. Martino smiled.

"But now I'm maladapted to anything that has sugar in it," David said. He took a breath and asked, "Is there a word for that maladaption?"

"Well, in your case, David, I don't see it as maladaption; specifically, you are unable to process carbohydrates as a result of insulin deficiency," Dr. Martino said, "and that insulin deficiency was brought on by toxins that destroyed the beta cells in your pancreas. Instead of maladaptation, you have a condition: type I diabetes. Of the four known mechanisms — genetics, infection, toxin, and deficiency — you became insulin deficient by toxin."

"But it is still inadvisable for me to eat carbohydrates, because I don't produce insulin, yes?"

Dr. Martino responded, "That is correct, David. Now, you certainly can eat carbohydrates and inject a corresponding dose of insulin to remove that sugar from the blood, which is what the diabetes treatment industry says, or you can just avoid carbohydrates. Your choice."

"So," David began, "the real question to ask is: are carbohydrates essential?"

"If you ask me," Dr. Martino said, "unless you want to run a marathon or be some sort of athlete, no, carbohydrates are not necessary."

"David," Professor Ross began, "what do we tell our students about the diet of early humans; maybe that will help."

"We tell them there is evidence based on jaws and teeth that archaic species probably ate fruits, herbs, leaves, grass, succulents, seeds, and perhaps tubers, roots, lichen, and bark. They ate more quantity, or roughage, to make up for poor nutritional quality. When available, they also ate insects — mainly grasshoppers, termites, and grubs — honey and perhaps small vertebrates. The only real evidence we have for an archaic *Homo* species eating predominantly flesh is from the *Homo neanderthal* line. They have tooth wear similar to Inuits and other groups that mainly eat meat; we know that because plant foods are available for only a short portion of the year in cold habitats."

"Brilliant, David," Professor Ross said.

"Why, yes, that is interesting, David," added Dr. Martino.

"I can't imagine a group of cavemen sitting by the fire a few hundred thousand years ago eating pasta," David said. Dr. Martino and Professor Ross laughed.

"No," Professor Ross added, "no, I don't suppose they would have. To answer your earlier question, us *Homo sapiens* never need to eat carbohydrates; we can convert protein readily to all the glucose we need within reason, and can do quite well getting our energy from fat. Of course, as Dr. Martino said, if you want to run a marathon, or be an athlete, then you're going to need to eat carbohydrates. If not, then you just don't need them. And those folks that have a metabolic problem, those with insulin anyway, get fat from eating carbohydrates, not from eating fat."

"So, carbohydrates didn't cause my disease, it was caused by the toxin of a bacteria that an ant uses to protect its food;

and, there's no discernable problem until and unless I eat carbohydrates, which I don't need," David stated.

"Yes, David, that's the way it is," Dr. Martino said.

"That sounds so psychotic," David said. He paused and thought about that for a moment.

"I'm fine if I do nothing; but, eating sugar will make me...*glycotic*," he said. Both Professor Ross and Dr. Martino were astonished; he had just coined a new word yet they understood exactly what he meant.

"Diabetes," David said in resignation, letting out a deep breath through his nose.

"It's really not that bad, considering," retorted the doctor quickly. "We have hundreds of patients that do quite well with it, and there are millions of folks with it now in the world."

"Well, I never thought I would get it; not from ants, anyway," David answered.

"No, I can't imagine that you would," the doctor replied.

"So, what do I do now?" David asked.

Dr. Martino was pleased that David had accepted his new constraint and simply said, "I've scheduled a diabetes educator and a nurse to stop by and give you more information and perhaps a demonstration. It will be instructive to hear their viewpoint, however, remember, you alone are the one to decide how best to treat yourself. They'll be here momentarily."

"Great. When can I get out of here?"

"We want to keep you here for a few more days to run further tests to see if you've developed any other negative side effects or complications from the invading bacteria, its toxins, or the treatment we provided while you were unconscious these past couple weeks. We want to make sure you're stable."

"Will these polka dots heal, or will I be scarred for life?" he inquired quite naturally, playful even.

The doctor gave a comforting smile that seemed to transcend his trained bedside manner. Professor Ross, who had been quiet and motionless during David and the doctor's exchange smiled too.

"Yes, David, the scars will heal for the most part. I'm a little concerned with you getting an infection if you, uh, pick at some of those still not completely healed bites; but, yes, all in all, you should be fine. And, as I said, it looks like the diabetes will be with you for life, as the, uh, rats that are used to model the disease inoculated with steptozotocin never recover. The beta cells in their pancreas's are burned out for life. But, as I said, we've got some very good support staff here that will enable you with the tools to successfully manage the disease, so I think you'll be fine."

The doctor did his best and waited for David's response to see if he bought it. David, looking like a combination of relief and defeat, offered, "Thanks for your honesty, doctor."

The doctor smiled, walked closer to him, gently touched his shoulder and said, "Anytime, David. I'll leave you in the hands of the nursing staff from here; but, I'll be back before your discharge to make sure you're off on the right foot."

"Okay, thanks again doctor," David said.

With that, the doctor left. He had scores of other people to give his good, bad, or worse speeches to, David thought.

"Have I missed much, professor," David asked.

Professor Ross laughed and said with that gracious, humble smile, "No, not much David. Don't worry, I covered for you personally these past couple of weeks, and I'll be happy to cover for you this week and next. But I really want you back teaching." David loved that reassurance from him. Professor Ross was the embodiment of a kind, caring, trusted father-figure, and he was glad to have him there.

"Thanks professor. Thanks so much for coming. Oh, wait, what about Michelle? And Kimmy. And Shirley?" Suddenly David was fully cognizant of the time he was unconscious.

Professor Ross didn't want to give him more bad news after he had heard so much already and simply said, "David,

I'm not going to lie to you. But do you think you can you handle more right now?"

"Yes, please, please tell me. How's Michelle?"

"Michelle?" Professor Ross asked.

"Yes, Michelle. I remember going out with her; where is she? Is she okay?"

"I haven't heard from Michelle. But Kimmy is fine."

David knew he had more information and asked, "Professor, what happened?"

"Well, the police are trying to put it all together. Are you sure you're okay? Can I get you anything?"

"Please, professor, please tell me."

"Okay, son," Professor Ross said, defeated. "I'll tell you." David looked at him ready to hang on his every word.

"We don't know where Michelle is, David. The police are still trying to put it all together. When they found you, they also found Kimmy—who's fine by the way—and Shirley, but not Michelle. As I said, the police are still trying to piece it together; I'm sure they'll have questions for you. I've been coming here every day to see how you're doing, and I've seen a couple of investigators here waiting for the same."

"Shirley! Where's my little pistol Shirley?"

"David, I don't think you understand," Professor Ross said, a little frustrated. "And there's so much to understand."

"Please, Professor Ross, please tell me. You know, I'm a pretty smart guy."

"Yes, David, you are, that's a fact. None of my graduate students can match your insight."

David smiled though his polka dots. "Thanks Professor, you know that means a lot to me. Shirley?" He knew something was wrong and had to know what.

"David, it's all so complicated and no one has much of anything resembling an answer; but, Shirley and Kimmy both contracted malaria, as did you."

"I have malaria!?"

Professor Ross hesitated for a moment, then answered calmly, "No, David, you *had* malaria. It's amazing how fast modern medicine can dispatch those nasty little parasites, although probably nothing is as good as nature, right?"

Quickly letting go of his shock, David smiled. Like always, he could come up with the answer. "Right, professor. Plants are the true lords of life and have had much more time developing their defenses than us. That's why most medicines come from them or some other modern species of long-lived lines like bacteria and fungi. They perfected the antidote to malarial ancestors before primates existed. Plants want to survive no less than any other organism, and even some of them enjoy the parasitic way of life, making their living off the backs of other plants. They even make use of animals to do their scurrying for them, and flowers, with their beauteous colors, shapes and scents, are the instruments of their manipulation. Not to mention their fruit, which they use to bribe animals into spreading their seeds."

Professor Ross presented his trademark laughter and said, "That's right, David, and now we have quinine."

"Quinine," snapped David. "A plant makes quinine, a compound that kills those little malarial demons."

"Manufactured by the cinchona tree."

"Oh yeah, the quina tree, of course," retorted David with the alternative name of the same tree.

"I see those ants haven't stolen your sharpness," Professor Ross said with that warm smile. "You should lend some of that ingenuity to help the world find a better solution to the malarial problem. They cause about a million deaths per year, mostly in Sub-Saharan Africa, and infect hundreds of millions of people. I don't know why disease control authorities always go after the mosquitoes instead of the root cause."

"You mean food and reproduction," David said.

The professor laughed. "Yes, David, reproduction and food. A single-celled animal infects a female mosquito. The mosquito then seeks out vertebrates like us from which to take a blood meal, not realizing that it's being used as a transport vehicle for that single-celled animal, which in turn uses us as a breeding ground. Female mosquitoes that don't have one of those different species of *Plasmodium* infecting it, are — if they happen to be looking for a blood meal in a population of people infected by it — in turn infected, thus completing the cycle."

"So you're saying to heck with the mosquito. It's like trying to rid the world of bank robbers by going after getaway-drivers. We should really be going after the thieves, or at least making the banks — our bodies — more resistant to them."

Again, the professor laughed. "Yes, that's exactly right. Now, some isolated populations did develop a natural form of opposition and still do — a sickled red blood cell that prevents those animals from reproducing — my own family has a history of that paradoxical disease — but, it was and is an imperfect defense. Some of those people — those that inherit the sickle cell gene from both of their parents — succumb from complications of having that very ability. So, it's something your generation will have to solve. Mine only worked on the self-interested accomplices, the ones that just go for a meal, inadvertently picking up or delivering the real problem. We simply made agents that kill mosquitoes or made better, less expensive netting to keep them from unwittingly delivering their payload." They both smiled in agreement.

"So, professor, Kimmy and Shirley are okay?"

"Kimmy pulled through fine," the professor said. He paused, and then, looking at his prize pupil's face, now a combination of chicken pox and pleading puppy dog, he quietly provided the information that David didn't want to hear. "Shirley didn't make it."

David's eye's swelled with tears and his face became red. "She didn't make it? No. No! Nooooo!" He tried to turn over but the tubes going into his arms wouldn't allow the maneuver. He buried as much of his face into his pillow and cried.

Professor Ross walked over to David's side in much the same way that Dr. Martino did earlier, placed his hand on David's shoulder, and said, "David, Shirley was just too small to survive the attack."

"That's such bad news, professor," he said through his tears.

"Yes, I know. And now it's in the hands of the police." The professor removed his hand from David's shoulder and took a step back.

"I'm tired; I want to go to sleep."

"I understand David. I'll come back tomorrow to check in on you. I'll leave all these books here for you to read too if you have the energy. Try not to think about your class load, it'll be there when you're feeling up to it."

"Thanks Professor. Thanks for coming. I really appreciate it," said David without looking at the professor.

"No problem, David. See you tomorrow."

And with that, Professor Ross smiled compassionately, tapped the books a couple of times with his left hand, then quietly left the room.

David fell asleep moments thereafter, somewhat hopeful that he had heard enough bad news; but, not entirely ruling out hearing more.

- - - - - - - - - - - - - - - - - -

A couple hours later David awoke to the smell of food. Hospital food, yes; but, food nonetheless. Good thing, too, as he was hungry. There would be no monster waiting for him as if still in a dream.

"Hi David. Are you awake? It's lunch time. And we have a couple guests for you to meet," said a nurse that he had met earlier in the day.

"Yes, I'm awake," he mumbled. "That smells pretty good. What's for lunch?"

"Well," began the same nurse, "we have a balanced meal according to the USDA's New Food Guide Pyramid consisting of a hamburger, mashed potatoes, some green beans, salad, an apple and skim milk. But I have some other people here that want to meet you. Can I send them in?"

"Sure, why not."

In walked three nurses, two in regular white nurse uniforms, and another in maroon. The one in the maroon outfit was a little taller than the other two and had a fair complexion; of the other two, one was white, and the other a light shade of brown. All three of them were different shades of fat.

"David, this is Sue Robeson, our staff diabetes educator; Brenda Michaels, our nutritionist; and Rolanda Evergreen, a nurse's aide.

"Hi everyone. Welcome to the party."

"Hi David," each of the women said in succession.

The diabetes educator, Sue Robeson, took the lead. "David, we're here today to teach you a little about diabetes, and show you how easy it is to treat the disease, and also to show you that you can eat and enjoy the same foods you used to eat," she said passionately and sincerely with a smile plastered on her face.

"Okay, bring it on," David responded.

The nurse moved the wheeled over-bed table with the metal-covered food tray from the right side of his bed to directly on top of his chest, with a few inches to spare, as if rehearsed on queue by her and the other two before. She then bent over to reach for and grab the hand control of the adjustable bed which was dangling from the head of the bed railing—wherein David noticed an unopened Hershey's® Reese's® Peanut Butter Cups® wrapper in her right hand nurse's jacket pocket—then hit the button that raised the upper body, so that David could more easily view the food and the three hospital staff members.

"Are you comfortable, David?" asked Rolanda.

"Yes, I'm fine. It only hurts when I move."

"Oh dear, did I hurt you?"

"No, no, I'm just kidding. The smell of the food dulls the pain, don't worry."

They all laughed a little, and appreciated that David still had some humor in him.

"Hey, that reminds me of an old joke I heard in nursing school," said the diabetes educator, Sue.

"A very tired nurse walks into a bank, exhausted after an all-night shift. Preparing to write a check, she pulls a rectal thermometer out of her purse and tries to write with it. When she realizes her mistake, she looks at the teller, and, without missing a beat, says, "Well, that's great, that's just great. Some ass has got my pen!""

All the nurses seemed to like that one; David, however, was starting to think they had rehearsed the whole scene, though he gave a polite laugh.

As the laughter subsided, Sue began her routine, "Okay, let's begin, shall we? You look hungry and we certainly don't want to keep you." The nurse's aide, Rolanda, removed the metal cover from the plate, and placed it on the table behind her. A wonderful hamburger-cheese-potatoes-gravy smell filled the room.

"These are the tools of the trade, David," Sue said, as Brenda started placing things on the tray on the wheeled over-bed table, next to the plate of food growing cold.

Pointing in order to the accessories that Brenda had placed on the table, Sue instructed, "This is fast-acting insulin that you will be taking before meals, here is a vial of long-acting insulin that you'll take at night to mitigate your eventual morning's high blood sugar, a syringe, alcohol wipes, lancet, and blood sugar meter. This particular device is an ACCU-CHEK® Compact Plus meter system with a load-and-go drum of seventeen preloaded test strips and detachable lancing device."

Sue continued, "The first thing we need to do, David, is to test your blood sugar. I'll do it for you this time, but remember that you'll need to do this many times during the day to figure out how much you can eat and how much insulin you'll need to take to balance the load." David was paying close attention but was also growing skeptical.

Sue carefully grabbed hold of David's left wrist, still connected to an IV drip at the upper end, with her right hand and said, "Make a fist but leave your index finger extended." David obliged.

Brenda opened the alcohol wipe packet and handed the wipe to Sue, who professionally cleaned his index finger with it with her left hand, still holding on to his wrist with her right hand. She then slid her right hand to the base of David's index finger, as Brenda handed her the lancet device.

"This shouldn't hurt much, as it's on level three," Sue said, then pressed the tip of the device to the tip of his finger and pressed the trigger-top, which made a short clicking sound. Sue handed the lancet device back to Brenda, who gave her the blood sugar meter in exchange, which had just beeped. Sue gracefully slid her hand to the tip of David's index finger and squeezed, releasing a perfectly half-spherical dab of blood from which to draw into the test strip of the blood sugar meter, which she accomplished with her left hand.

Sue and Brenda exchanged the blood sugar meter for another alcohol wipe, which Brenda had prepared while Sue was drawing the blood. Sue wiped the blood from David's finger with the alcohol wipe and said, "hold on to this until the blood clots and then throw it away, or place it on the tray."

The blood sugar meter beeped again, and Brenda showed it to Sue and David. "One-twenty, not bad," Sue announced. "The American Diabetes Association says to keep your blood sugar in the seventy to a hundred and ten range between meals, and no more than a hundred and forty immediately after meals, which is called 'post prandial.'"

"Post prandial," David replied, "that's a good one."

Sue smiled, as did Brenda and Rolanda.

"So, now comes lunch," Sue began. "I'll defer to Brenda for that part." She and Brenda changed places; Brenda was now on the left, Sue in the Middle, and Rolanda on the right.

"Okay, David, lunch time," she said. "First, diabetes is a chronic, lifelong disease marked by high levels of sugar in the blood. Diabetes can be caused by too little insulin, resistance of the body to its own insulin, or both."

"Or ants," David replied in disbelief of his predicament.

"Ants?" asked Rolanda. "No, not ants!" She laughed, oblivious to David's predicament, looking to both Sue and Brenda for guidance.

"Well, I don't know about that, David," Sue said, "but moving along, what kind of nutrition do you suppose a diabetic needs?"

David though for a moment, and replied, "Hamburgers?" The three nurses laughed.

"Well, yes, and no," said Brenda. "Diabetics need the same nutrition as non-diabetics. A balanced diet is best to make sure you get the amino acids, fiber, vitamins and minerals you need to function. So, we've prepared this lunch for you, which contains protein in the hamburger, complex carbohydrates in the bun and fiber in the green beans and salad. And since fat has been shown to increase cholesterol, we've given you skim milk. Oh, and we even have an apple for you for dessert." Brenda paused. David looked skeptical; but, said nothing.

She continued, "So, here's the insulin and a syringe; we're going to estimate the number of grams of carbohydrates and match that with a bolus — a dose — of insulin."

David continued to politely listen and watch.

"So, David, we have a lean quarter pound hamburger, which should give you, say, fifty grams of protein and a little fat — it's lean, so it won't give you too much saturated fat, which you'll need to keep real low to avoid getting atherosclerosis at a young age—twenty grams of complex carbohydrates from the wheat bun, about forty grams of carbohydrates from the mashed potatoes, thirty grams of fiber from the green beans, and some more protein and calcium from the milk with an additional ten grams of carbohydrates. And, for dessert, an apple, for vitamin C, more fiber and carbohydrates for energy."

"Given that load of carbohydrates, I estimate you'll need about five units of insulin, and we do it like this," Brenda said, as Sue picked up the fast-acting insulin and syringe.

Said Sue as she demonstrated, "Pull the syringe back until it has about ten units of air, like this, inject it into the vial of insulin, and then draw five units of insulin into the syringe. Take out the syringe, hold it upside down, and, flicking the top with your other hand, squeeze it until all the air is out and only the five units of insulin are in, and viola, you can now "pinch an inch" of fat in your abdomen or thigh, and inject the insulin directly under the skin and into your fat." The three nurses looked so proud of their presentation.

David, on the other hand, was incredulous. Having studied organic chemistry, and biochemistry, not to mention his years of anatomy and taxonomy, he knew that everything she just said was a load of crap. He kept it simple, asking, "So, you're saying to inject myself with insulin, and then eat a balanced meal? Well, you don't really believe all that, do you?"

"That's what they teach us in nutrition school, David," Sue said, confirmed by a nod of the head by Brenda and Rolanda.

David thought about her answer for a moment, then, still looking like he had recently survived a serious case of chicken pox, asked, "What would happen if I didn't eat any of those carbohydrates? Would I still need to take the insulin?"

Brenda retorted, "You need carbohydrates, David, they give you energy, and you need the insulin to act as the key to let the carbohydrates into your cells."

"I don't buy that," David said emotionlessly, shaking his polka-dotted head. "I mean, yes, I agree that you mostly need insulin to get glucose into the cells; but, we humans evolved pretty well without eating much in the way of carbohydrates. Plants eat photons from the sun, herbivores eat plants, and carnivores eat herbivores and other carnivores. We can get almost everything we need from eating herbivores or carnivores. For vitamin D we can just walk out in the sun. And you've contradicted yourself from the very beginning by telling me that diabetes is a disease, in your words, marked by a high level of sugar in the blood. So, why on Earth would I then eat sugar to compound the problem?" He was happy with his logical, coherent reply, though that apple looked mighty good.

"Well, like I said, David," Sue began somewhat agitatedly, since she wasn't used to a patient challenging her, "you *need* carbohydrates for energy, just like a person without diabetes."

David didn't agree, saying, "No offense, Sue; but, carbohydrates from the external world are not essential for life. We, like all carnivorous animals can get all the sugar—the carbohydrates—we need from eating protein, which is then converted by the liver into glucose, a simple sugar. Although carbohydrates certainly do look, smell, and taste pretty good, we just don't need them."

"David," Sue began, "I—we—don't agree, and advise that you should follow our instructions."

"Again, Sue, no offense intended; but, I'm not convinced."

"Well, David, you're ultimately responsible for the consequences of your behavior," Sue said. "All we can do is give you the treatment guidelines that have helped hundreds of our patients here and at our clinics; but, again, the implementation is your responsibility. We've done our job."

"Well, I do appreciate it," David said. "It just doesn't make any sense to me."

Brenda chimed in this time, "We can leave you with some literature and some helpful links to web sites like the American Diabetes Association. For now, we have other patients to train, so, best wishes and thanks for your time."

"Nice meeting you David, good luck," Sue added.

Rolanda said, "Bye David, take care."

"Bye ladies," was all David said, looking at them and the heap of food, medicine, devices, and garbage that had piled up on the tray sitting atop the wheeled over-bed table.

The three blind mice filed out of the room without cleaning up. As they got to the hall, David overheard one of them—Sue, he figured—say, "Don't fret Rolanda, not all patients are annoying. Some are unconscious." He heard them giggling too in the distance; but, gave it no quarter, aside from a short downward smirk on the left side of his mouth.

David reached for the hamburger patty with his right hand, and, grabbing it, took a bite. With his other hand, the index finger still stinging a little, he reached for the television remote control and turned it on. After the end of a commercial promoting Keebler® Cheesecake Middles Original Graham Cookies®, a rerun of "Who Wants to be a Millionaire" came on. David watched it while finishing the hamburger patty, eyeing the mashed potatoes and apple still on the tray in front of him. He pushed the wheeled over-bed tray away from him to the right, and then tried to get in a comfortable position which allowed him to lie on his left side to watch TV without pulling too hard on any of the tubing going to his body.

After a couple tries, he found the position which maximized his viewing ability while minimizing pain. Were it not for the rail, he could have found something even better.

Television still on, burger patty down the hatch, it wasn't long before he fell asleep.

The Investigation

"David, are you sleeping," asked a female voice.

David awoke, his left arm asleep from having it sandwiched between the left-hand side bed rail and his red polka-dotted body. He groaned.

"David, I'm Detective Sharon Bennett, we'd like to ask you a few questions if you have the energy.

"Yes, I'm awake," he said, not entirely awake, wriggling his left arm to get it working again. He opened his eyes facing the front of his bed, where an African-American woman and Caucasian man in noticeably plain-clothes police outfits were standing.

"Hi David," Sharon said again. And this is Lance Smith, Detective Lance Smith."

"Hi David," said a nice, humble gentleman with short, black hair. "I'm Lance."

"Hi Lance, Hi Sharon, happy to help if I can."

"Are you in any pain; would you like us to come back later?" asked Lance.

"No, I'm okay, but I could sure go for some ice cream."

"We can call a nurse if you want," Sharon said.

"No, I'm just kidding; apparently I have diabetes, and probably shouldn't be eating that stuff."

"Oh, my mom has diabetes," Sharon said. "She's type two, so she can have a little fruit now and then; but, she takes great care of herself by not going too heavy on carbohydrates. Are you type two or type one?"

"I think I'm type one, at least that's what the doctor told me this morning; but, I'm not sure. Which is the type you get from ants?"

"Yes, we heard about that," Lance said. "That's part of the reason why we're here."

"Well, the doctor said all the beta cells in my pancreas are toast. He took a test—I think he called it a C-peptide or something like that—basically, he said I no longer produce any insulin."

"Yes, that's type one," added Sharon. "You can treat it pretty well by just not eating carbohydrates, like my mom; but, you have to be vigilant."

"Yeah, that's what I thought; but, don't tell the nurses around here that. They want me to take insulin and eat all the carbohydrates I want. After all, according to them, I need the same nutrition as a person without diabetes."

Sharon laughed. "My mom heard that when she was first diagnosed; but, after a while, she just stopped eating them, except, of course, on her birthday when she eats cake and ice cream."

"Yeah, ice cream. Do you have any? Chocolate chip?" The three of them laughed.

"So, how can I help you?" David inquired.

Lance chimed in, "David, just tell us what you remember, what was the last thing you remembered doing?"

"Well, the four of us, Kimmy, Shirley, Michelle, and I were having dinner, singing karaoke, er, uh, norebang…"

"Norebang, David?" Sharon asked.

"Oh, yeah, norebang; it's the Korean version of karaoke. Anyway, we were eating and singing, and then went to this bar, and then a guy's house, and then I was going to play piano for the girls in the Music Building, when, I, uh, don't remember anything after that. Except for being here, learning that Shirley passed away, Michelle is missing, more about ants, and, well, having diabetes." Tears began to swell in his eyes.

"You're very brave, David, thanks for that; yes, we heard about the ants. And we're very sorry about Shirley," Sharon said with compassion.

"Again, that's why we're here, David," Lance said. "We want to find out how Shirley and Kimmy got malaria, and find out where Michelle is. Anything you can remember would be valuable. So, where were you before you got to the Campus, before you were by the Music Building?"

"Well," David thought hard to remember, "we were at this bar called Lek's downtown, then met this guy there that had met Michelle before. We went to his house, then left, then, uh, went to the Music Building, then, well, I'm here."

Sharon asked, "Tell us about this guy you met, like what was his name?"

"Uh, let me see," David said, closing his eyes in thought. "It was Jack...Jack London...*John* London. Yes, John London."

"Good, David, that's what Kimmy stated," Lance said. "That's a famous name up north; he was a writer, ever hear of him before that night at Lek's?"

"No, I've never heard of a Jack or John London before nor have I ever met him."

"Okay, thanks David," said Lance. "Kimmy doesn't remember the exact address where he lived, do you?"

"Uh, no; wait, yes, it was, Royal Albert Hall, King's Court..."

Lance cut him off, "Royal Blue Court?"

"Yes, that's it, Royal Blue Court," David said, smiling, then wincing in pain from having smiled.

"I know where that is, David, good, Kimmy also told us it was Royal Blue Court," Lance said. "Now, tell us David, where on Royal Blue Court?"

"Oh, I really don't remember," David said.

"Try harder David," Sharon said, dropping her compassionate tactic and went for the jugular. Lance looked at her with a hint of disdain, perhaps rehearsed.

David said, "Really, look, I don't remember," as he shrugged, turning his palms up, then dropping both intubated arms beside him on the bed.

Lance took control again, saying, "Okay, that's okay David, tell us more about what happened at the house."

"We weren't there too long, I remember that," he began. "We were looking at his fish," he suddenly saw one of those copepods beginning to come out of Sharon's mouth. He blinked his eyes a couple of times and the vision was gone.

"Where was I…oh, yes, we were looking at his fish…"

"John London's fish, David?" Sharon asked.

"Yes, John London's fish, at his house," said David, "and these fish had other, uh, fish inside them, inside their mouths."

"There were smaller fish inside the fishes' mouths? You mean food, David?" Sharon asked.

"No, not food," David said with certainty. "They were fish, or, rather, copepods, a type of crustacean that lives in the mouth of a fish. I'm not familiar with the species, but John London explained that they are the only parasites that eat then replace the tongue of other fish. Can you guys open your mouths so I can see if you have them?"

"David, I don't have any bugs in my mouth; see, this is my tongue," Sharon said, sticking out her tongue.

"Me either, David." Lance performed the same exercise, sticking his tongue out for David to see.

"Oh, yeah, sorry. This guy John, he really did have these things in the fish tank, and they were in some of the fish. I swear," he said sincerely.

"We believe you David," Lance said. "So what happened after you looked at his fish?"

"Uh, we were looking at the fish, and this guy John said they were his pets, that parasites have the best strategy in life, living off the hard work of other life-forms, not having to create anything, just taking advantage of the skills of other beings."

"So, the parasites were his real pets?" Asked Sharon.

"Well, at the time, he didn't say, but looking back on it, yes, I think those were his real pets. At some point John gave us some fish to feed his bigger fish — snapper — in the large tank. I thought I was feeding those larger fish; but, it turned out, as he explained later, that I was feeding the host of his real pets. Yes, that's how it worked. It really freaked-out the girls, especially Kimmy. Right after she saw the fish with tongues made of still smaller fish — crustaceans — she became jittery. When she went to put a CD in the really nice CD tower, she knocked it over into a large speaker, which banged into the wall causing a large, black scuff mark. John thought that was funny and told Kimmy to forget about it, as he had done it many times before." David tried to smile, happy with his explanation and truthfulness.

David took a breath and continued, "Anyway, we were talking about how parasites were the true protagonists of the world, the top of the food chain, that they were the oldest, and most successful creatures, having eaten plants, animals, dinosaurs, fish, and even people. Then he talked about his — well; no, before that we saw his dog, his dead dog…"

Sharon interrupted, "You saw his dead dog there?"

"Well, yes, and, uh, no. His dog was preserved: stuffed. It was near the entrance. A big, beautiful German shepherd. "Zack" was his name; it was short for "*Sacculina*," which was another parasite he happily explained to us."

"He liked parasites, David?" asked Lance.

"Yeah, I assume so. After the fish incident — which was after he talked about his dog — and the tongues in the fish tank, he told us about his old company, how he was a spammer in the late nineties and early naughts. Then the doorbell rang, and *she* came in."

"She?" asked Sharon.

"Yes, *she*," David said with a scowl on his face.

"Okay David, good. Can you tell us who she was," Lance asked sincerely.

"She — her name was Ann, Ann Opheles, a Bible thumper I — we — Michelle and I, had met the week before."

"You knew this girl Ann?" asked Sharon.

"Yes, Ann was a preacher we met on the Quad earlier in the day."

"Good, David," Lance replied sincerely. "You met her on the Quad earlier that day. Say, uh, David, has anyone told you how long you've been here?"

"Yeah, the doctor told me earlier that I've been in a coma for about ten days."

"That's right, David," Lance confirmed. "You've been unconscious that long. So, you're saying that you met this Ann Opheles girl about ten days ago, earlier in the day you met with Michelle, earlier from when you had dinner with Michelle, Kimmy, and Shirley, who you went to Lek's with. You then met this guy John, then went to his house, then met this girl Ann again at his house. Is that right, David?"

David was following every word of Lance's. "Yes, that's right. Exactly."

Lance continued, "And Ann was a preacher on campus. John was older and the four of you met him at the bar, and you all went to his house? Is that right David?"

"Yes, that's right Lance. John invited us to his house for a nightcap, and to escape the loud, crowded bar."

"You went to John's house, a stranger that you met at a bar, to look at parasites?" asked an incredulous Sharon.

"Yes, well, no, we didn't go there to hear about his parasites, only to have a nightcap. He also bragged about his view. Michelle had seen him there at the bar last week, uh, a week before we all went out. But she didn't know him."

"Okay, David, good," Lance said with his now consistently polite demeanor. "How did you get from the bar to his house?"

"John took us there, in his Hummer. It was a big one, with huge tires, that famous, dark yellow color. The girls were impressed with it; and, yes, I suppose I thought it was cool too."

"Did you get the license plate number on that Hummer?" Sharon asked.

"No, it didn't seem relevant at the time, sorry."

"That's okay, David," Lance reassured him. "Just tell us what happened when you left. Where did you go from John's house."

David was still happy to help, but was getting a little tired from the back and forth. "John and Ann took us back to campus. I remember coming down from the hills, the highway, then to the Paris Green, where they dropped us off."

"So you're saying that John and Ann took you from the house, back to campus, to the Paris Green," Lance said.

"Yes," replied David.

"Where's the Paris Green, David?" Sharon asked.

"Oh, the Paris Green is the area by the Biomedical Quad, which is by the Music Building. We were going to the Music Building; I was going to play for the girls." David proudly said.

"You play piano?" Sharon asked, relaxing her posture.

"Yes, I used to play and study piano as a kid. I still do, but most of my time now is spent studying and teaching."

"What program are you in?" asked Sharon.

"I'm in the evolutionary biology doctoral program at the Darwin Institute of UCSD. But I still practice when I can. I'm hoping to not forget any of music I can play now; but, I don't really have much time to learn new music."

"What do you play?" asked Sharon.

"Beethoven's my favorite. I can play a few of his sonatas, and some Mozart and Bach; oh, and Chopin too." His spirits were improving to that point until he was reminded of those tubes going in and out his polka dotted arms.

"Are you in much pain, David? We can come back," Lance said compassionately.

"No, I'm okay," David said, sighing. "Let's finish this, and then I'm just going to sleep."

"Okay, David, not too many more questions," Lance said. You saw John and Ann at John's house with Michelle, Kimmy and Shirley. We have that. All six of you then drove back to campus, the Paris Green. Then what? Did John and Ann go with the four of you?"

"No, I don't remember them coming with. John and Ann dropped us off at the Paris Green, then drove away. We walked from the Paris Green, to the Biomedical Quad, through the Biology Annex hallway—it's just a hallway with sliding glass doors on each side—then to the Music Building. That's all I remember. I don't think we made it into the building, at least I don't remember playing that night."

"Good, David, that's helpful," Lance said. "Now, all we need to find out is John's address. We have Royal Blue Court. Do you remember the address? We'd like to find this John London and Ann Opheles. Do you think they had any reason to hurt you or your friends?"

"Well, we did have a disagreement with Ann earlier in the day, but not with John," David said unemotionally.

"Ann was the preacher you met, right David?" Sharon said. "What did you argue about?"

"She was preaching by the Paris Green, on the Biomedical Quad, and I didn't agree with her, with what she was saying." He paused. "She said something about Beethoven that was crap, and I told her the truth. Professor Ross was there too, and he didn't agree with her either. She called us fornicators. I think I may have dug into her a little bit, but I didn't swear at her or anything like that, although I wish I did. She was pretty stupid out there. But there were lots of other people there too saying much worse things than me."

"Okay, David, good, I think we have enough for now," said Lance. "We'll follow up with you again soon."

"I'll be here," David said with a slight scowl.

"Bye, David," Sharon said as the two of them started walking to the door.

Before they reached the door, David perked up a little then said, "1859! The house was number 1859!"

Sharon and Lance stopped, turned around, and Lance said, "1859. The address was 1859 Royal Blue Court? Are you sure?"

"1859 Royal Blue Court. I'm sure. I remember it now. 1859 is a very famous year in biology. I remember it because I saw it when we pulled into his driveway, and it stood out for me because there was everything that was believed by people before 1859, then the one simple explanation thereafter."

"You remember his address from biology?" Lance asked.

"Yes," David said, smiling. "1859 is a famous number. I remember. 1859 is famous in biology. It's the year that *On the Origin of Species by Means of Natural Selection* by Charles Darwin was published. Yes, it was 1859 Royal Blue Court."

"Good David," Lance replied, "1859 Royal Blue Court. We're on our way." Lance and Sharon looked at each other and smiled.

"Thanks David," Sharon said.

"Yes, thanks again, David. You did great," Lance said as they walked out of the room, passing a nurse who was making her way in, who popped a Wrigley® Altoid® into her mouth with her left hand, closed the case with both hands, then put it back into her hospital uniform jacket with her right.

"Hi David, how are you feeling this morning?" she asked.

- - - - - - - - - - - - - - - - - -

"These houses don't look like much from here, do they," Sharon said. Lance and Sharon were driving up in the San Diego Hills looking for John London's house.

"No, they don't," Lance replied from the passenger seat of the unmarked, silver Crown Victoria police car Sharon was driving.

"1840, 1842, 1844...it must be up there on the left," Lance said, pointing with his left hand, though Sharon didn't see his point. "1855...1857...1859, this is it."

"There's everything before it, and only one simple explanation thereafter," Sharon said trying to imitate David.

"Let's hope that's the case," Lance said. They smiled at each other.

The house they stopped at had a big mailbox, and a deep, wide driveway, leading to a three car garage on the right hand side, a fountain with dolphins in the middle, and a small storage area for rubber garbage bins hidden by a wooden gate on the left. The front door was behind three wide steps, behind the fountain, which, although it contained water, was not turned on. The number "1859" was clearly visible from the street in big, black block numbers arranged vertically on the right-hand side of the entranceway. They pulled in, and parked next to an old, though fully restored Pontiac Woodie, gray in the front, with what looked like real wood trimmed doors, with a bunch of stuff in the back.

Sharon and Lance got out of the car and walked to the fountain, where they stopped for a moment, looking at each other as if to say, "This is where the other half lives," then continued to the door, a tall, sturdy door with no side windows, though it did have a large fan-shaped, stained glass window on top. Lance reached out with his right hand and rang the bell. Funny, it sounded just like they thought it would, like the long chime from Big Ben.

They didn't have to wait long before the door opened. And there, confidently peering out from behind the door was a thin, older-looking man with a healthy head of natural blond hair who greeted them with, "How can I help the police this morning."

"Good morning," Sharon replied, somewhat shocked from the greeting. "I'm detective Sharon Bennett with the San Diego Police Department, and this is my partner, Lance Smith. We'd like to ask you a few questions if you have the time."

They looked him over; he didn't look anything like the description given to them by David. This was a much older gentleman, probably in his sixties. He was wearing blue "tennies" — VANS® brand canvas, thick-soled, lace-up shoes — without any socks, faded Levi's® blue jeans and a t-shirt. He looked like something left over from the sixties, though his hair was probably too short, and, instead, reminded them both of a surfer who never found anything better to do. Judging from the size, location and beauty of the house, both detectives thought he was just the caretaker.

"Is the owner of the house here?" Lance asked.

Donny smiled and replied after chuckling to himself, "I'm the owner; this is my place."

Surely he won the lottery, Lance and Sharon thought.

"I'm Donny White. Come on in. Can I get you anything? Uh, I don't really have anything here, so how about some water?" he said.

The place was empty and immaculately clean, at least on the landing that they were on. The entranceway was on the second floor, as most luxury houses on the hill overlooking the valley and Pacific Ocean had a second floor landing, with the rest of the house hidden from street view, built into the hillside. The wood-floored landing, from right to left, had a mirror built into the wall over a table, with a bench for sitting, and a coat rack. As they entered, they could see a closet on the left, then further forward, was a double stairway leading to the main level from either direction, right or left.

"Sure, some water would be great," Lance said.

"Right this way," Donny said. He led them down the right-side semi-circular stairway to the main floor.

As with the landing, the rest of the house visible as they descended the stairway was immaculate. No furniture, no wallpaper, no picture or works of art, just carpeting covering every inch of ground. And, hard to miss, a big bay window allowing them to take in nearly the entire Pacific Ocean at the back. It was gorgeous.

Sharon and Lance stopped in the middle of the room, in front of a big, rectangular outline of something that had significantly depressed the carpeting leaving a completely flat impression.

"I'll get you some water, hold on," Donny said as he continued in the kitchen, which was visible from the main room on the left.

As he went into the kitchen, Sharon turned toward Lance, then both of them looked down at the carpeting. Lance said, "What do you suppose could have done that?"

The sound of a refrigerator ice dispenser quietly thumping ice into something that suppressed the sound was heard from the short distance away.

Sharon widely opened her eyes, shook her head slightly up and down, then said, "A fish tank. A really big fish tank."

Lance too shook his head and smiled, happy that his witness had told them the truth. He looked over to the wall behind him and, to the right, he saw several marks.

"That must be where Kimmy knocked over the CD player into the large speaker," Lance said, walking over to the wall with Sharon. The wall had a few short, light, and a couple long, heavy, black scuff marks.

Sharon added, "Which must have banged into the wall." They walked back to the depressed carpet area and looked at it some more waiting for Donny.

Donny re-entered the room moments later with two short Styrofoam cups full of ice water and a beer for himself.

"Yeah, I don't know what to make of that; hopefully it'll come out when I have it steam-cleaned," Donny said as he handed them their water.

"Thanks," Sharon said as she took hers.

"Oh, thanks," Lance said taking the water from Donny.

"I'm sorry this is all I have for you. My summer tenant just recently left, and this is all I have. So, how can I help San Diego's finest today?"

"Actually," said Sharon, "That's why we're here today. What can you tell us about him? What was his name?"

"John London was the name he gave me. Did he do something wrong?"

"That's what we're trying to find out. We'd like to ask *him* some questions, but first we need to find him. Do you know where he is?"

"Uh, no I don't," Donny said.

"You don't know where he is?" asked Lance skeptically. "Don't you have a forwarding address?"

"Actually, no, I don't."

"Certainly there's something on his rental application; can we see it?" asked Sharon.

"Oh, yeah, the rental application. Well, I, uh, don't have one of those for him."

"You don't have a rental application?" asked Sharon.

"Well, I know, normally, us landlords are supposed to get those sorts of things, do a credit check and the like, but this guy was different, and I was just renting the place out for the summer," Donny said, hoping that now he wasn't a suspect in anything criminal.

"How was he able to rent a place like this; don't you check out references, or do some due diligence before you give someone the keys to the kingdom?" Lance asked.

"Well, normally," Donny said with a nervous laugh, "normally, yes, I do. But this guy was different."

"How so?" Sharon quickly asked.

"Well, I met him on a Friday before the summer season started. He looked at the place, and said he would have a cashier's check for me later in the day to prepay for three months. It's hard to say no to a three month check. I believed him; he was a good looking young man, in a Hummer, so I had no reason to doubt him. And when he showed up that same afternoon with a check for eighteen-thousand dollars; well, I just took it and gave him the keys. I told him to be out by September, and; well, here we are in September, and he's out."

"A Hummer?" Sharon asked.

"Yep, one of those big, gnarly yellow Hummers, with really big knobby tires. I thought it would add to the character of the house and neighborhood nicely," he said with that same nervous laughter.

"I suppose I can see that," Lance said compassionately. Clearly it was becoming noticeable that he was the good cop to Sharon's bad.

"How about that Hummer?" Sharon asked. "I don't suppose you have the license plate?"

"No, uh, no I don't. Just his name, John London. He said he was doing some research for a book, that he was visiting the campus of UCSD, and that he used to work in New York."

"And he gave you a cashier's check for eighteen-thousand dollars, without showing you any identification, and you gave him the place?" Lance asked.

"Yeah, that's right. Money talks," Donny said. "With the recession in full swing, I kind of needed the money; folks haven't been buying a lot of surf boards or accessories these days, and eighteen-thousand dollars goes a long way in terms of flights and hotels in Hawaii."

"You're a surfer, Donny?" Lance asked.

"Sure am. Ever since I can remember. I surfed, and then taught it for a while, eventually opening a surf shop right down there," he said, pointing out the window toward the ocean. "Now I own ten of 'em: San Diego, Huntington Beach, L.A., Monterey, Half Moon Bay, Malibu, Santa Monica, Venice, and two in Hawaii. I used to make fun of the rich people in the hills and their opulent houses; now, I'm one of them," he said with a smile, looking around at the bare walls and then at the view.

"So, you rent out this place only during the summer; do you live in it the rest of the year?" Lance asked.

"I travel quite a bit, mostly to my shops, and I'm never really home much anymore. Since the downturn, I learned that us folks up here in the hills can rent out our places weekly or monthly during high season and command some pretty good rents. So I rented it out last year, and, well, this year too. Apparently I'm not as efficient as I need to be; next year I'll, uh, have my tenant fill out an application."

"Okay, Donny, that's all the questions we have," Lance said.

"I'm not in any trouble with the law, right?" Donny asked timidly. "It's been a while since I had that kind of excitement."

"No, Donny, the San Diego Police Department has no problem with you," Lance said, smiling. "Just let us know if you hear from John London again. Let us know immediately if you hear from him, or if you find out where we can find him. We'd be, uh, stoked if you'd let us know."

Donny laughed at Lance's use 'stoked,' and was happy he wasn't in any kind of trouble. "Will do, detective."

"Thanks for your help Donny," Sharon added, as she reached to shake his hand. Lance too shook his hand and then the two of them walked up the right-side stairway, opened the door and exited.

As the door closed, Sharon turned to Lance and said, "I sure would be stoked if we can find that John London."

Lance smiled and said, "Well, I surfed a little too when I was younger."

"Didn't we all," Sharon said.

They got in to the car, Sharon again at the helm, and left to fill out whatever paperwork was required for the day.

It wasn't long into their shift the next morning—the Sun had just come up in the east behind them—when Sharon and Lance drove up to an area where eight marked police cars were parked at the far end of Mission Bay, not far from SeaWorld. As they parked their car, they saw a small area in the distance on the water's edge cordoned off by orange cones with metal poles inside attached awkwardly to yellow police tape.

They exited their car and walked toward the gathering of police officers huddled over a yellow tarp within the yellow tape perimeter. As they neared, one of the police officers made a kicking motion at a small white bird, which flew away.

Sharon said, "Protect the crime scene, if it is one, but be nice to the birds, we don't want to piss off any conservationist who has a fancy for Least Terns," referring to the California least tern, a small seabird related to gulls and skimmers, endangered since the seventies, and now up to a more healthy population of some thousands.

"I don't know the difference between a least tern and any other tern, but let's just not hurt any of them to be on the safe side," Sharon added, as they reached the group. Sharon and Lance stepped over the yellow tape, went up to the body, and intended to take a look.

"What do we have here gentlemen," Sharon asked. All the other police officers were male, and all were in uniform.

"It doesn't look like a floater, ma'am, it looks like it was dumped here," said one of the senior uniformed officers.

"Let me see," Sharon said, as she pulled the tarp up and then down, uncovering the head, neck and torso.

They were gathered on a jetty, a word deriving from the French word *jetée*, meaning "thrown," and signifies something thrown out, which is how the body looked to both Lance and Sharon. A jetty's function is to slow down beach erosion.

"So young, again," Sharon said, referring to the last body discovered, though it was a male who committed suicide.

"Are there any signs of homicide?" Sharon asked.

"We haven't moved the body, ma'am, but we didn't see any obvious marks, cuts or bullet holes on this side of her body, the visible front or back," said one of the more senior officers. "That narrow pink strap around the right side of her neck probably leads to her purse, which she's probably lying on."

"A purse? Well that would rule out robbery if we find it there," Sharon stated.

The body itself was that of a girl, twenty to twenty-five, dirty-blond hair, average height, thin, in a t-shirt and jeans, wearing boat shoes, no socks. She was lying on her side, her left side, on top of her left arm, and her right arm just sort of dangled over her body. She was white as a ghost, with just a little seaweed on her hair and face.

"Okay, roll her over toward me; I'll check for bullet holes, someone else check her pockets for identification," Sharon instructed. And you, if there's a purse under her, please grab it and check for an ID.

As the team rolled the body over, her shirt became legible. It read in pink letters, over a large pink ribbon—which Sharon, and probably all the police officers first thought was a message about breast cancer—in quotes: "I can do all things through Christ who STRENGTHENS me." Underneath the quoted words was the source; it read "Philippians 4:13."

A police officer took several pictures from a Polaroid camera before they turned the victim, and more after they turned the victim. He had another camera, which was not Polaroid, and took several pictures with that camera as well.

"There's the purse," an officer said. It was a small, pink, alligator—or snake or lizard or crocodile—skin purse.

"No, obvious trauma, or tears or holes in her clothes," Sharon said. To which another officer in the group remarked, "Maybe she died of breast cancer," which was greeted by some chuckles, but only a disdainful smirk from Sharon.

"I have an ID card from a wallet in her purse," another officer said. "It's a Utah Driver's License. Ann Opheles. Uh," he said doing the math in his head, "twenty-five."

Sharon looked back at Lance, who returned the look at the same time.

"Ann Opheles?" Lance said to Sharon. "Now there's a coincidence."

"We're investigating a suspicious death and whereabouts unknown case at UCSD and this is somehow related," Sharon said to the group. "Bag and tag everything around here, and someone call the coroner."

Can I get one of those pictures," Sharon said to the photographer, a fellow policeman. "We need it to confirm her identity with a possible witness.

"Sure," the photographer said. "How's this one?"

"That'll be fine," Sharon replied. She turned toward all the officers and said, "We're going to go talk to a witness, please make sure you get everything. Keep the scene secure, and hand over the body to the coroner when he gets here."

"I'll take it from here, detective," a senior officer said.

"Great" replied Sharon.

Sharon turned to Lance and said, "We should wait to hear from the coroner before passing judgment; but, it doesn't look like robbery, an opportunistic killing, or that she was murdered and dumped here."

"Agreed," Lance replied. "She looks so young; but, maybe she was just walking along the jetty, slid and hit her head on the rock. Maybe it's as simple as that."

"Or maybe she collapsed from something else."

"Malaria?" Lance offered.

"Maybe. Maybe just good, old fashioned natural causes."

"Anything's possible," added Lance. "Twenty-five. Pity."

"True that," agreed Sharon.

The two walked back to their car without a word, knowing exactly the task before them, leaving the busy scene to the uniformed officers for the hospital.

- - - - - - - - - - - - - - - - - -

As Lance and Sharon walked past the nurse's station, they noticed two of the nurses sharing a bag of Frito-Lay® SmartFood®. Lance stopped behind Sharon for a moment to get a better look; they were Honey Multigrain Popcorn Clusters, and, while he was focusing on the package, one of the heavy-set nurses there noticed him looking and offered him some.

"Would you like one?" she asked.

"Sure," said Lance. The nurse picked up the bag without spilling any of the clusters, offered it open side to Lance, who reached in and grabbed a few, dropping a few crumbs on the table.

"Thanks," he said, popping a few small pieced into his mouth. He closed his right fist as he chewed to save some for a few moments later.

"Complex carbohydrates for energy, lactose free, and a great source of energy," the nurse said.

"Great, thanks again," he said.

He caught up to Sharon and together they walked into David's room.

"Hi David," Sharon said first. "How are you feeling today?"

"I'm okay," he replied, still just as polka-dotted as the previous day. "They changed by dressings this morning; it was a little painful, but they gave me some more meds, so I'm not in any pain. Feel pretty good as a matter of fact."

"We'd like to show you a couple pictures this morning," Lance said, as he put the rest of the lactose-free complex carbohydrates into his mouth and crunched.

"Bring it on," said David.

Lance wiped his hand on a napkin sitting on the wheeled over-bed tray that was now on the left hand side of the bed. He reached into his right jacket pocket — he was wearing a blue suit — and pulled out one of the Polaroids that was taken earlier that morning.

"Do you recognize this woman, David," Lance asked.

"Yes, that's the girl!" he exclaimed. "That's Ann Opheles. Is she okay?"

"No, David, she's not," Lance said.

"We found her on a jetty in Mission Bay this morning," Sharon informed him quietly. "Dead, in Mission Bay."

"She's dead?" asked David, kind of caring, kind of not.

"Yes, David," Lance said. "Her body looked like it was dumped there sometime last night or early this morning; based on the currents, we don't believe she floated there. She was probably placed there."

There was an uncomfortable pause.

"Well, you don't think I did it do you?" David said with raised eyes and eyebrows. "I've been here all night!"

"No, David, no!" said Sharon. "We know you didn't do it, relax. We don't know how she died, only that she was dumped there. Her body is with the coroner now, and we have to wait to find out what she died of; we just wanted to confirm that this was the girl you were with the night you were, uh, attacked."

"That's her," David said. "I'm really sorry. For her and her family."

"We found her with a Driver's License from Utah," Lance said.

"Utah?" David inquired. "I thought she might be a local preacher; we get a lot of those types coming to campus from time to time, telling us students to repent. I usually don't pay them any attention, but they do create a stir."

"I'm sure they do," Lance replied.

"That's not all we found since we visited you yesterday, David," Sharon said. "We also went to the house at 1859 Royal Blue Court."

"So you arrested John London," David said looking relieved.

"Not exactly," Sharon answered, slightly hesitating.

"He wasn't there, David," Lance added.

David looked puzzled.

"No," continued Lance, "he moved out a week or so ago. We met his landlord. Did you know him?"

"No, I never met John's landlord. We thought he owned the house."

"Well, that's okay, David," Lance began. "We confirmed that a John London matching the description you gave us lived there, and that there may have been a large fish tank in the main room of the house; but, other than that, the whole house was immaculate. There were no dogs, parasites, or anything else there that we can go on."

"You don't believe me," David said with resignation.

"We believe you David," Sharon said. "But we have no evidence of how you contracted malaria or if John London is related to it. All we have now is a missing girl, Michelle, a dead body of Ann Opheles, and, well, your friend Shirley too. But we have no evidence linking those things to John London, though we would like to find him to ask him some questions."

"Michelle," David said closing his eyes. "I really miss Michelle."

"We can see that, David," Lance said empathetically.

"Help us find her, David," Sharon added. "What else do you know about John London? Help us find him."

"I've told you everything I know," David said, becoming agitated.

"Try to remember anything, David," Sharon said. "Maybe something from your conversation with him at the bar or at his house can lead us to him. Did he tell you where he was from, for instance?"

"I really don't remember," David said, turning over to his side as if to hide from them. "He told us he owned a company and that his company made money by sending out spam; but, I don't remember the name."

Said Sharon, "Good, David. Where was the company located?"

"He didn't say."

"Anything at all David, even the most innocently mentioned comment can be used to find him," she said.

"Really, I don't know anything," David said, closing his eyes.

"So, we're looking for John London; but, we don't know where he's from, so anything you can add would help us a great deal, David," Lance said.

David's eyes were closed, and he was going over the night he went out with Michelle, Kimmy and Shirley. He remembered going to dinner, the norebang; he remembered Lek's and going to John's house. Then, he remembered walking up to the house door, where something didn't quite fit. He opened his eyes then squinted, which didn't go unnoticed by Sharon or Lance, trained observers of the human condition.

"What is it David?" Lance asked.

"Well, it's probably nothing."

"Like I said, David," Sharon held, "even the most innocent comment could lead us to him."

"Well, I, uh, remember walking up the stairs to his house…"

"Yes, we were there, David. In front of the fountain, with that pretty stained glass window over the door," Sharon said.

"We walked up to the door, and, uh…"

"Yes, David," Lance said, keeeping the momentum going.

"Well, he swatted a mosquito that was apparently biting his neck, and said something strange."

"What was that, David?" asked Lance.

"He said," David paused, "he said, 'Sorry cousin,' as he swatted it, and threw it to the ground. That seemed strange."

"He said 'Sorry cousin' to a mosquito that he swatted to the ground, David?" asked a surprised Sharon.

"Yes, 'Sorry cousin,'" David confirmed.

Lance and Sharon looked at each other simultaneously. "DNA" each thought.

"Well, that's great, David," Lance said. "Maybe we can find that mosquito, bring it to the lab, and find a DNA match. Anything's possible."

David smiled through his polka dots. "DNA. Yeah, I suppose if you find the mosquito you can extract the dried blood and analyze its DNA. It's possible, assuming that the DNA hasn't degraded too much. At least that's what they teach us in biochemistry class."

"Good, David, we'll try that. We'll go right now," Sharon said.

"Oh, one more thing," said a calm and lucid David.

Lance and Sharon gave their complete attention to him.

"I also remember seeing John's Hummer at the scene, just after I fell on that ant mound," said David.

"You saw his Hummer," stated Lance, confirming what David had just said.

"Yes, I did," David confirmed. "I'm sure there are plenty of yellow Hummers in town; but, on campus they, uh, pretty much stand out."

"Yes, I'm sure they do David," Sharon agreed.

"The bites we felt that night," David said, "those probably weren't bites."

"We don't think you were bitten either, David," Lance said.

"And I don't take drugs, detective," David said.

"We know," Lance said, being very empathetic and compassionate to David.

David was putting it all together.

He thought for a moment or two, and then declared, "So, we must have been shot some way with a tranquilizer gun or something like that. A phenobarbital delivery device."

"That's what we think, David," Sharon said with Lance agreeing next to her.

"But you don't remember actually seeing anybody do the shooting; you didn't see anybody take Michelle?" Sharon asked.

"No," David said, "I didn't see anyone. I saw Shirley get bit by something; we all thought it was a mosquito. Then we saw Kimmy get bit. Both of them eventually fell to the ground.

Then I got bit. I remember falling backward. I remember the yellow Hummer. I remember some footsteps, then a scuffle of sorts, then more footsteps. Then, well, this," he said, motioning to the tubes going in and out of his arms, the hospital room and again to his body. "That's it."

"Good David," Sharon said, "that's helpful information."

Lance was already on the phone contacting a crime scene unit to meet him at the house.

"We'll have to get back to you, David," Sharon said. Lance, still on the phone, waved goodbye to David. David just raised his head to acknowledge him as Lance and Sharon left.

David was pleased that they believed him; but, pessimistic that they would find anything, least of all Michelle.

- - - - - - - - - - - - - - - - - -

Arriving at 1859 Royal Blue Court again, Lance and Sharon knew exactly where to go. The clearly marked "Crime Scene Investigation" van was already there, though the two officers were still inside waiting for instructions. As Lance and Sharon pulled into the driveway in the third spot next to the van, which was next to the Pontiac Woodie, the two crime scene investigators in uniform got out of their van to greet Lance and Sharon. After introductions, the two crime scene investigators grabbed their gear and the four of them walked to the door. While Lance rang the doorbell, one investigator started combing the entranceway with a magnifying glass while the other took pictures with a digital camera.

Donny White opened the door to the excitement, and said, "Cool, a party."

"Hi Donny," Lance replied.

"Hi detective. What's going on?"

"We're acting on a tip. You wouldn't mind if we have a look around the front of your house, would you?" Lance asked.

"Not at all. What are you looking for? Can I help?"

"No," Sharon said. I think we have everything under control."

"What are you looking for?" Donny asked again.

"We're looking for that needle in a haystack this morning," Lance said.

Then, one of the investigators on the left hand side, by the garbage bins, said, "Got it."

"Make sure that you pick up every dead bug there," Sharon directed. There were other insects in that area; but, apparently only one squished mosquito.

"You're looking for bugs?" asked Donny.

"Just one special bug," Lance said. "Have you cleaned this area up in the last couple weeks, Donny?" Sharon asked.

"Well, no," Donny replied. "Garbage is collected twice a week by the city, but I just got back a few days ago and haven't had a chance to clean up that area."

The technicians put everything they found on the ground into different paper bags—paper, because plastic bags retain moisture, which can damage DNA—of different sizes: leaves, grass, dirt, a dead-on-its-back cockroach here, and a few ants. Not leafcutters. The mosquito was placed carefully into one of the smaller paper bags.

"That's all we need," Lance told Donny.

"Well, that was a fast party," Donny said. "You know I bought some beer and groceries yesterday, maybe you could stay a while; it'd be better than just water like last time."

"No thanks," Lance said under a slight laugh. "We'll take a rain check on that."

"Okay," Donny said. "But come back anytime. I brought some of my old surfing movies I made when I was younger. I've got some gnarly footage from the early Mavericks and some Van's Triple Crown highlights from even earlier than that. Pipe Masters and Billabong too. I wish I could have been at the early Makaha International Surfing Championships; but, that was before my time."

"Will do, Donny, thanks," Lance replied.

The CSI technicians headed to their van.

"Thanks for helping us out today," Sharon said.

"Yes, thank you Donny," Lance added.

Donny smiled, offered them an obligatory, "Thank you," and resigned himself to spending the rest of the morning alone, cleaning, watching television, drinking beer, and napping. The house was perfectly clean, he thought, so maybe he could skip that one. Yes, TV, beer, movies, and sleep, what a perfectly good combination.

Donny watched them leave and slowly closed the door; his mint condition, rebuilt Pontiac Woodie being the last proud vision he saw from the outside. The smile dissolved from his face as he reflected for a moment in the doorway. Old surfers do just fade away, he thought.

- - - - - - - - - - - - - - - - - -

Both veteran detectives, Sharon and Lance had a great deal of experience with crime labs. They knew that a personal touch with the technicians went a long way to getting them to work on their case load. From a forensic technician's perspective, knowing the case, and hearing the background from the detectives, helped them understand the context and feel like part of the team. In short, it gave meaning to their work, of which there was plenty.

For example, in 1995, there were ninety-one murders in San Diego, about one of every three unsolved murders in San Diego's last half century happened during crime boom of the 1990s. Compare that to 2009, when San Diego police solved more murders than happened. Forty-one people were murdered — crime levels have dropped significantly from the nineties — but police cleared forty-eight cases. Modern forensic tools have made the difference.

Two decades ago, San Diegans saw the largest crime wave in recent history. Law enforcement authorities say a rising population of young adults and rampant cocaine abuse contributed to staggering violent crime across the country. San Diego, with a historically low number of murders for its size, soon became part of this trend.

Between 1990 and 1995, the city had an average of one-hundred-thirty murders each year. Compare that to the years between 2004 and 2010, when the city had an average of fifty-six murders each year. In the early nineties alone, seven-hundred-eighty-one people had been killed. About three-hundred of those cases still remain unsolved.

These days, the San Diego Police Department has twenty-two detectives dedicated to homicide, with two of them specialized in cold cases. Despite the continued fall in the number of murders, the homicide unit had been spared from the city's budget cuts, and police have used advanced DNA technology, and a huge staff of forensic technicians, to find new leads in unsolved murder cases and close new and old cases.

And so, here we are with Lance and Sharon meeting with Lisa Rosen, a senior forensic lab technician in the San Diego Crime Lab's Forensic Biology Section, hand delivering her the current case file, and letting her know that the field technicians had just entered the paper bags of evidence gathered from Donny White's house into the Central Evidence Reception Facility.

"Hi Lisa. I'm Lance Smith, and this is Detective Sharon Bennett. We're here to talk you through an interesting case.

"Hi Lance, hi Sharon," Lisa, a demure, young woman of thirty said from behind her wire-framed glasses. "What do you have for me on this beautiful Friday?"

Sharon took her through what they knew to date. "Missing person, one, possibly two homicides, and aggravated assault to start with. Do I have your attention?"

"Oh, yes, such intrigue!" Lisa said with a combination of dark humor and professional style. "Please, go on."

Sharon continued, "We have three victims at UCSD that were possibly drugged with phenobarbital who contracted malaria from an unknown person or persons, two of which are still alive, one deceased. They had met two potential perpetrators, one of which we found deceased at Mission Bay this morning, which is now with the coroner, and another possible perp still at large. We have an alias on that one—John London—and we might have a blood sample of his for you to test. That's all we have, and that's why we're here."

"You have a blood sample?" Lisa inquired.

"We hope so," Lance said. "That's a story unto itself. One of our vics remembered him being bit by then swatting a mosquito in a doorway. We think we found that mosquito and have it in one of those bags of tricks the technicians should have entered into the system by now."

"A sample of blood from a mosquito. Nice!" Lisa said. "How old do you think it is?"

"It shouldn't be older than about a week," said Sharon.

"Well, that's not too bad. Blood takes a while to degrade completely, so maybe we have a chance. Do you know where the perp is?" Lisa asked.

"Well, that's the second part of the story," Lance said. "We think that the perp's name, John London, given to us by one of the vics is an alias. We were hoping that someone like him has a prior, and that you can match his blood to something already in the system. It's a long shot, we know."

"Well, this is an intriguing case. Just a couple things to point out," Lisa said smiling, knowing that if anyone can help them it was her. "Blood cells don't have a nucleus, so RFLP and STR testing are out because they require DNA found in the nucleus of a cell. I'll use mitochondrial DNA analysis, which uses DNA from a cell's mitochondria." She paused, taking off her glasses, holding them by the frame in her right hand.

"If I can process that sample, I can then compare it to DNA profiles stored in the State DNA index system named SDIS. It contains forensic profiles from local laboratories in California, plus forensic profiles analyzed by the state laboratory. The state database also contains DNA profiles of convicted offenders. Finally, DNA profiles from the states feed into the National DNA Index System, the NDIS."

"Now, the FBI developed a technology platform known as the Combined DNA Index System, or CODIS. The CODIS permits laboratories throughout the country to share and compare DNA data. It also automatically searches for matches. The system conducts a weekly search of the NDIS database, and, if it finds a match, notifies the laboratory that originally submitted the DNA profile. These random matches of DNA from a crime scene and the national database are known as 'cold hits,' and they are quite important. Some states have logged thousands of cold hits in the last twenty years, making it possible to link otherwise unknown suspects to crimes."

Lance and Sharon were hanging on Lisa's every word. Lisa thought for a moment and then delivered a short conclusion, "The analysis of the blood will only take me a couple days; but, finding a match in CODIS may take a week or more. I'll call you if and when something comes up." Sharon and Lance were both relieved that Lisa would do that.

"Great," Lance said.

"Thanks Lisa, it's a relief to hear some good news for a change," Sharon added.

"I'll follow up with you in a week regardless," Lisa said, trying to remove any apprehension still present in her two internal customers.

"Thanks so much Lisa," said Lance.

They each shook Lisa's hand and professionally walked to the exit. Lisa put her glasses back on, walked over to her desk, grabbed a file and went back to work.

The Investigation II

"You know, I've been eating these my whole life and I still can't get enough of 'em," Lance said, putting another hot sauce covered oyster into his mouth and slurping it down.

"Yeah, these are pretty good," said Sharon.

Sharon and Lance were sitting at the bar of a restaurant on Ocean Boulevard eating lunch and talking about the week's case load overlooking the beach and Pacific Ocean. They thought about how they were just northeast of Sail Bay, which is slightly just northeast of Mission Bay, where they had found the body of Ann Opheles just last week. That was, of course, a day after meeting David, who four days earlier woke up covered in painful, red, ceiling-tile-like fissures and pin hole perforations, resulting from invading an ant colony eight days before that, having met the girl of his dreams, Michelle, eight days before that, who was still missing.

The busy summer season was over; restaurants and bars in the area were now only doing an average business. The restaurant they were at had plenty of seats open though it was early in the afternoon, quiet, still, with a periodic cool ocean breeze whirling throughout.

And then Lance's cell phone rang.

"Lance! Lance!" Even Sharon, sitting next to Lance, could hear the scream emanating from Lance's cell phone.

"Hey," Lance said, staring and talking into the cell phone he held in front of himself.

"Lance! We got a hit! A cold hit!"

"Lisa?"

"Yes, of course it's Lisa. Do you get cold hits from anyone else?" asked the person on the other end of the phone.

"We got a cold hit?"

A calmer Lisa explained, "Lance, remember when you were here last week, I said it would take a couple days to analyze the sample, then about a week to search the Combined DNA Index System?"

"Yes, I remember, Lisa."

"Dude! We got a cold hit! That means there's an exact match of the specimen to a file in the database. Here, I have it right here, hold on, it's, it's, uh, Fal-cip-a-rum," Lisa said, sounding out the name. "Peter Falciparum. He has a San Diego, California address. No aliases listed. Is this your guy?"

"We were looking for a John London, but that's ok, Lisa. It could be that Peter, uh, what was his last name?"

Lisa sounded it out again over the phone for Lance, "Fal-cip-a-rum."

"Got it, thanks," Lance said, looking at Sharon. Both were writing down information with pens on their memo pads.

"Could be that Peter Falciparum is this guy's real name and John London is the alias. Anyway, thanks so much, Lisa, great work," said Lance, who was standing up and looking at Sharon at this point.

"Give me the address and I'll take care of the arrest warrant for Peter Falciparum in San Diego. Sharon and I can take care of that from here.

"No Problem Lance. Do you have a pen and paper?"

Lance smiled at Sharon and said, "She wants to know if we have paper and pens." Sharon smiled.

"Shoot!" Lance said.

Lance wrote down the San Diego address and showed it to Sharon, who nodded and used her hands as if pointing to where the address was located.

"Okay, got it, thanks so much Lisa!" Lance said.

Sharon could no longer hear Lisa's voice emanating from the phone.

Lance replied to what Lisa had just said, "Sharon and I will take it from here. We're going to get the warrants together now and will let you know what happens."

"Thanks again Lisa, take care," Lance said, hitting the "end call" button, and then placing the cell phone back in his pocket.

"Okay Lance, let's get our story straight. We can call Judge Robertson for the warrants," Sharon said.

"Agreed."

"And, exactly what do we have?" Sharon asked, ready to play devil's advocate.

Lance smiled as he gathered his thoughts while flipping through his memo pad.

"Okay, we have a witness that has ID'd a vehicle—a yellow Hummer—near a crime scene, at the time of the crime, in an area—a college campus—where that sort of vehicle is rare. That crime scene is where one missing person, presumed alive, was last seen after some sort of scuffle, as described by the witness. In addition, three unconscious but living victims were found Saturday morning, two females of Korean descent, and one Caucasian male. All three were found to have phenobarbital in their system. All three denied using the drug. Although testing has not been completed, it is likely that the phenobarbital found in the system of the three victims came from some type of drug delivery device."

"All three victims were found to have malaria, one victim died of complications battling the disease. Of the two survivors, one made a complete recovery; but, one has further complications, having landed on an ant colony after being drugged with phenobarbital. He survived the drugging and the malaria, and the ant attack, however, he has contracted diabetes as a result of being infected with a bacteria that produces the streptozotocin toxin."

"There is one other victim, deceased, Ann Opheles, found at Mission Bay, cause of death unknown, however, she was with the person of interest and four victims the night of the crime described above. David Bennett, the male victim with diabetes, further stated that he had met Ann Opheles earlier in the day, and that the two debated creation versus evolution on campus in an area called the Biomedical Quad, by the Paris Green, very close to the crime scene."

"The witness further told us that the person of interest, John London, dropped him and the three girls off in his yellow Hummer, previously described, near that location on campus that Friday night."

"The witness also described how the person of interest had a penchant for parasites, though I still don't understand his relation to the malaria."

"So all we really have on John London is that he was the last person to see all the victims except perhaps for for Ann Opheles, that a car like his was seen at the crime scene, and that there was a scuffle. For all we know, there may be at least one other party orchestrating this symphony. It could be that John London and this Peter Falciparum are not one and the same. They could be two different people. Their descriptions are similar; but, who knows. And we think that Michelle is still alive. Given that the three friends she left behind needed urgent medical attention, I would say that there are exigent circumstances, yes?" Sharon asked.

Lance thought about it for a moment and said, shaking his head in the affirmative with raised eyebrows, "Yeah, looks like that's what we have."

Sharon continued, "We know that it isn't like Michelle to not call her friends or family. Also, nothing of any value is missing. This looks like a kidnapping case, and everything else is incidental to the kidnapping. I think we should focus on the kidnapping; we could drive to John's last known address and see what we find there. I bet he isn't even there. But we might find out his actual location from anyone at the scene that may have heard of him or Peter."

"Agreed."

Sharon put thirty dollars on the bar near their plates and said, "We're good here, thanks."

"Oh, thanks so much, have a great day," said the female bartender from the distance.

"It's getting better by the minute," Sharon said out of range of the bartender, though Lance heard her.

As they walked out, they couldn't help but notice two mildly obese patrons, a man and a woman, just starting their lunch, each with a triple cheese burger, what seemed to be a pound of French fries, ketchup, coke, and a milk shake, vanilla for the guy, chocolate for her. One of them, the female, was dousing her separate plate full of fries with ketchup as Sharon said, "I wonder if they know it's the carbs doing all that harm."

"Probably not," Lance quickly replied.

There were no back-up police units when they arrived at the address given to them by Lisa. And the house was no mansion. It was in the old section of San Diego; mostly single story houses on small lots. Most were unkempt, and this particular house was sandwiched in the middle of the block, non-descript, save for some cactuses that didn't match the dirt-white siding.

"Should we wait for back-up?" Lance asked Sharon.

"We have guns, Lance," Sharon retorted. "Phenobarbital's no match for lead."

Lance smiled and said, "I'm unbuckling my holster just in case."

"Good idea. I'll do the same."

The two approached the door, both holding their standard issue, extremely reliable, Glock 22, forty-caliber, semi-automatic weapons in their holsters, their index fingers pressing down on the holster's lever allowing them to easily remove the gun if need be, with their finger ready to be where it needed to be, on the trigger guard, ready for firing. Lance rang the bell.

The door slowly opened. A little, elderly lady peered out from behind, prevented from fully opening it by the door chain.

"Good afternoon, ma'am," Sharon said. "We're detectives with the San Diego Police Department. We are looking for Peter Falciparum and John London. This is the address listed in their records. Have you seen either of these men?"

"Just a moment," she said, as she closed the door in order to remove the gold security chain. Sharon and Lance's badges were clearly visible on their belts; no doubt she opened the door because she saw the badges. Lance and Sharon looked at each other, still grasping their guns.

"Come on in."

Lance and Sharon were both relieved; they each took their hands off their weapons almost at the same time.

"Are you the only one here this afternoon, ma'am," Lance asked.

"Yes, just little old me," she replied in a quiet though friendly voice. As if asking them if they wanted some afternoon tea she added, "What do you think my boy's done now that you'll never be able to prove?"

Lance and Sharon looked at each other bewildered.

"Ma'am, first, which of those names is your son?" Sharon asked.

"Peter," the lady retorted nicely. "Peter Falciparum, though I think he's using another name because you people keep hounding him, making it too difficult for him to make a living using that name."

"So you're Mrs. Falciparum?" Lance asked.

"Yes. I'm a widower. My husband passed away a long time ago; I had to rely on my son Peter after a while. He's very smart you know."

"Mrs. Falciparum," began Lance, "we don't know if your son's in trouble or not, we just need to find him. It could be that he's contracted a disease, and like I said, we need to find him. Other people he came into contact with are very sick, and he and someone else are still missing. Do you know where he is?"

Before she could answer, Sharon asked, "Would you mind if we looked around inside, Mrs. Falciparum?"

"Not at all, go ahead. It's just me here; me and my memories."

There were framed pictures all over the walls in the small living room that they were in. It looked like a two bedroom, two bath house, with a living room, attached to another room, and a kitchen. Two bedrooms were in the back on the right most likely, one with its own bathroom, and another bathroom in the hall. There was a very small backyard that they could see through the window in the kitchen door.

"As you can see, there's no one else here."

"Please tell us where we can find your son," said Sharon, a little more sternly this time. "We can subpoena your phone records and look through your mail, but we'd prefer if you just tell us."

"You think my boy is sick or maybe he knows where the missing person is?"

"That's right," Lance said.

"Well, that's odd, not many people come to my door with their hands on their guns to tell me that my son is sick. Normally they do that when they want to arrest him for something he hasn't done. He's very smart you know."

Lance and Sharon again looked at each other.

"So, the police have been here before looking for your son?" Sharon asked.

"Oh, yes. In 2001, 2002, 2003, twice in 2004, and; well, my memory isn't as good now as it used to be. I'm not sure if they came again in 2005; but, I wouldn't rule it out."

"What did he do?" inquired Sharon.

"Nothing."

"Nothing?" asked Lance.

"That's right, nothing."

"Mrs. Falciparum, no disrespect intended, but how could he have been arrested all those years for doing nothing?" Sharon asked.

"Well, first, I realize you're both police; but, remember that little detail about being innocent until proven guilty in a court of law?"

"Oh, yeah, that," Sharon replied, less tense than she was a moment ago. She looked at Lance who was also calm.

"Well, my boy was never convicted of anything. They said he did this and that," Mrs. Falciparum stated as she used her hands to help express her thoughts, "that he sent spam to people and companies, and made a lot of money. Now, making money isn't a crime, is it?"

"No, making money's okay," Sharon answered calmy.

Mrs. Falciparum continued, honestly, confidently, and nicely, "I think the issue is that he did it with a computer, and the way he did it hadn't been invented yet, and after a time, they made new laws that declared using a computer to get people to send him their money was illegal. The problem is, although he was arrested many times, they never could prove what he did was illegal in a court of law. Probably because they didn't really understand what it was that he was doing. And I got a bunch of people that came to my door, just like you, with their hands on their guns. That's how I know you probably don't think my boy is missing or sick, you just want to arrest him for something, for something that you'll probably not be able to prove."

"Okay, Mrs. Falciparum," Sharon said, "we'll level with you. We think he kidnapped a girl, or maybe someone else kidnapped them both."

"My boy kidnapped a girl? C'mon now, you should see how all the girls go to him. They can't keep their hands of him. I can't believe Peter would do something like that. Just look at him!" She pointed to the pictures in the living room.

Although somewhat old, the pictures were of Peter at the beach, a community pool, other pools as well, and each picture was of a thin, buff, good-looking young man with a noticeably chisel-like face. In some of the pictures, Peter was wearing long beach shorts, known in old-school surfing circles as broad shorts. In others, a small, thin, Speedo®-type bathing suit.

"Okay, Mrs. Falciparum, I believe you," Sharon said, kind of believing her because she looked at some of the pictures on the wall.

"Mrs. Falciparum," Lance began, "here are the facts: we have a witness that saw a yellow Hummer at the scene where he was drugged and his friend went missing. It was the same yellow Hummer that he saw earlier in the night that he was in when he was dropped off on campus. Maybe it was your son, maybe it was someone else, but our witness places your son — or his look-alike — and the car at the scene where three people got sick. And one is still missing. That's the truth, and we, at a minimum, would like to find Peter and ask him some questions, see if he knows about any of that, and maybe even help him if he's sick. He owns a yellow Hummer, doesn't he?"

"Yes, he does. I keep telling him that he should get something that doesn't waste so much gas; but, it is fun to ride in," Mrs. Falciparum said with a little laughter in her voice. "Have you ever ridden in one?"

"No, I've never been in a Hummer," Lance said.

"Me neither," Sharon added.

"Well, you two seem like nice kids. Okay, I saw Peter just a couple weeks ago and helped him decorate his new place. He's in one of those work/live communities near the pier by the beach. I have the address in the kitchen."

The three of them walked into the kitchen where Mrs. Falciparum took off a sheet of paper held on the refrigerator by a banana shaped and colored magnet.

"Here you go," Mrs. Falciparum said as she handed the piece of paper to Lance.

"Thank you Mrs. Falciparum," Lance said.

"Please treat him nicely; and, remember, he's very smart. He's also all I've got, so please don't hurt him."

"We won't, Mrs. Falciparum," Sharon sincerely stated. "We just want to ask him some questions. If he's sick, we want him to get better. Either way, we'll let you know how it goes."

Just then, there was a knock at the door.

The three of them walked toward the door and opened it. Two officers — Lance and Sharon's back-up — were at the door.

"Please stay with Mrs. Falciparum and make sure she doesn't call her son or anyone else for that matter until we've secured the scene where we're going."

"Yes sir, detective," the younger officer at the door said as he entered.

"Goodbye Mrs. Falciparum. Nice to have met you. We'll be in touch," Lance said.

"Bye bye."

With that, Lance and Sharon quickly walked to their car; Sharon to the driver's side, and Lance, cell phone in hand, the passenger side.

The car took off just as Lance hit the send button.

"Good afternoon, sir," Lance said into the phone. "May I please speak with Judge Robertson.

"May I ask who's calling?" the voice said.

"This is Detective Lance Smith with San Diego Police Department with an urgent warrant request.

"Hold on just a second," the voice on the other end of the phone said.

A moment later, a female voice was heard over the phone say, "This is Judge Robertson."

"Good afternoon, Your Honor," Lance said. "This is Detective Lance Smith."

"Hi Lance; it's been a while. How can I help San Diego's finest this afternoon," Judge Robertson said.

"Your Honor, I have a request for a search warrant with exigent circumstances."

"Exigent circumstances? Let me get a pen and some paper. While I get those please place your right hand over your heart. Is the testimony you are about to provide the truth, the whole truth, and nothing but the truth?"

"Yes, Your Honor," Lance said, as he pulled his memo pad out of his pocket.

"The time is now 1:50 p.m., Pacific Standard Time, Friday..." Lance dropped the phone as Sharon took a tight turn, lights and siren blaring.

Lance picked up the phone quickly and heard the judge say, "Please tell me the facts of the case, in your own words."

"Thank you Your Honor," Lance said, momentarily exchanging glances with Sharon as if to say "phew."

Lance took a deep breath, and, reading from his memo pad, began his case, "On or about Midnight, Friday, twenty-one days ago, a witness, David Bennett, graduate student at the University of California, San Diego, identified a yellow Hummer near a crime scene, at the time of the crime, in an area on the UCSD campus where that sort of vehicle is rare."

"That crime scene is where one missing person, Michelle, presumed alive, was last seen after some sort of scuffle, as described by the witness, David. In addition, three unconscious but living victims were found Saturday morning, two females of Korean descent, and one Caucasian male, the witness. All three were found to have phenobarbital and alcohol in their system; they were all in a coma when they arrived at the hospital and for several days thereafter. When they awoke from their coma, two of the three denied using the drug. Although testing has not been completed, it is likely that the phenobarbital found in the system of the three victims came from a drug delivery device such as a dart."

"All three victims were found to have malaria; one of the female victims died of complications battling the disease before we could question her. Of the two survivors, one, the female, made a complete recovery; but, one has further complications, having landed on an ant colony. He survived the drugging and the malaria, and the ant attack, however, he has contracted diabetes as a result of being infected with a bacteria that produces a toxin that primarily causes diabetes."

Lance realized that after he said that part about getting diabetes from bacteria from an ant attack that he may have lost the judge. It wasn't quite believable to him either; but, that's what the evidence suggested.

He paused for just a couple of seconds, long enough to take it all in again for himself, took a deep breath, and continued, "There is one other victim, deceased, Ann Opheles, found at Mission Bay, cause of death unknown, however, she was with the person of interest and four victims the night of the crime described above. David Bennett, the male victim with diabetes, further stated that he had met Ann Opheles earlier in the day, and that the two exchanged words on campus in an area called the Paris Green, very close to the crime scene."

"The witness further told us that the person of interest, John London, dropped him and the three girls off in his yellow Hummer, previously described, near that location on campus that Friday night."

"The witness also described how the person of interest had a penchant for parasites, though we still don't understand his relation to the malaria."

"According to one of the victims that survived, Kimmy, Michelle and her friends had met the alleged perpetrator, John London, at a bar the week before but had no other contact with him. We know that it isn't like Michelle to not call her friends or family; also, nothing is missing in terms of money or anything of value. According to my experience as a detective, this looks like a kidnapping case, with exigent circumstances necessitating a search of John London's premises."

Lance was pleased at his summary for the judge, though a little pessimistic that she believed everything he said.

"Okay, Lance," Judge Robertson began, "I think I have everything I need to make a decision. You're saying one perpetrator, John London, likely kidnapped one victim, Michelle, and that it is most objectively reasonable that he alone is holding her at his location. Everything else can be sorted out later, and, if a complaint is lodged, it can be amended."

"Yes," Lance said relieved. "We, my partner and I, are requesting a search warrant for evidence of the kidnapping only, which would include the phenobarbital and its delivery device, which we reasonably believe is in the possession of one John London."

"Just one question, Lance," the judge said. "How did you find the location of the alleged perpetrator?"

Lance was ready with his answer, "The witness remembered that the alleged perpetrator was bit by a mosquito at the alleged perpetrator's rented house, where they had been the previous night. We brought a forensic team to that location about two weeks later to gather evidence. That evidence was analyzed by the San Diego Police Lab and was found to contain the DNA of one Peter Falciparum by way of a cold hit with the FBI's Combined DNA Index System. We pursued that lead and found Peter Falciparum's mother at the location specified on the DNA profile; she provided us with the address that we now seek to search and confirmed that her son lives there currently."

"How do you know that Peter and John are one and the same person?"

"We have a similar description from the witness," Lance said, "but we just received the news of a cold hit from the crime lab technician and just received the address from Peter Falciparum's mother."

"So you do not know with reasonable certainty that they are, in fact, one and the same person," the judge stated in a less positive and less supportive tone.

"Based on my experience, I'm reasonably certain that whether or not they are the same person, this Peter Falciparum can help locate John, who may be able to help find Michelle," Lance said, not sure if the judge bought it.

"Lance, I cannot provide a search warrant at this time," Judge Robertson said, "however, if you can confirm a connection between John London and Peter Falciparum, I would sign off on the warrant for phenobarbital, a drug delivery device, and the victim."

"Thank you for your time, Your Honor," Lance replied, "I'll get back to you shortly."

"Good luck, Lance," the judge said.

Lance turned off his cell phone and put it back into his pocket.

"So?" Sharon asked.

Replied Lance, "We need to get David."

- - - - - - - - - - - - - - - - - - -

"Two jaw fragments with three molars from a single individual and some non-associated teeth discovered in Kenya are all the is known of the *Orrorin tugenensis* skull and teeth," a professorial yet still red fissured and pin-holed David stated to his class, similarly distributed as three weeks before, with half zombies, an attentive quarter, and the other quarter tired from a mid-afternoon meal of snacks. David was teaching again, and, apart from the obvious small scars polka-dotting his entire body — though only the ones on his head, neck and arms showed — he looked and acted fine, albeit longing and muted.

Lance and Sharon got out of their car and began quickly walking up from the small parking lot in the back toward the sliding glass doors of the Biology Annex. As they got to the door, they couldn't help but to notice the statue "Standing" right in front of them. They looked at each other, and, instead of going through the sliding glass doors, walk up to the statue.

"A finger bone, a right arm bone shaft, a small thigh bone fragment, the upper two-thirds of two left thigh bones, one with and one without joint surfaces, and more recently an end finger bone represent the totality of *Orrorin tugenensis* skeletal fossils so far unearthed," David said confidently, though longing for something.

Lance was seen squatting at the edge of the Music Building, imagining the scene that David described: being bit by something, falling backwards, missing the brick wall, landing on a mound, and seeing the image of a yellow Hummer to his right — exactly where Lance and Sharon had just parked — before finally passing out. Yes, it was all possible Lance thought; of course, the ants were long exterminated.

Back to David. He was saying, "*Orrorin* means original man in the Tugen language. The species name *tugenensis* refers to the Tugen Hills where it was found. All *Orrorin* fossils are housed in the National Museums of Kenya, in Nairobi, Kenya." He was interrupted by a knock on the lecture room door.

David turned his head to the left and looked through the door's glass pane. There was Lance, with Sharon right behind him. He motioned for them to come in with an upward nod of his head and raised eyebrows.

David stopped his lecture and met them halfway into the room. All the students watched as their discussion section lecturer begain talking to what looked like two detectives.

"David, we need you to come with us," Lance said.

"Did you find Michelle?" David asked, the longing on his face changing to hopefulness.

"David, we may be able to find where she is; but, more importantly, we need you to come with us to ID someone. It's a long story, but we need you to come with us. We think we may have found her," Lance said, trying not taint the witness identification nor let the students hear him.

David turned to the students and said, "Class dismissed; see you next week." As the students got up, David added, "Just be sure to read the chapters as detailed in the workbook."

With that, Sharon, Lance and David, in that order, walked quickly out of the room and to the car, with happy students disbursing not far behind.

Not ten minutes later, Sharon, Lance and David arrived at the location that was written on the piece of paper that Mrs. Falciparum handed to Lance not an hour ago.

"I'll be right back," Lance said as he exited the car. He walked over to the trunk and opened it. David could hear him shuffling through it — he even felt the car move a little — then heard the trunk close. Lance re-entered the car with what looked like a large camera case and opened it up.

"David, we're going to go to the door and ring the bell. If we can get the person to come outside, you be sure to get a good look at him through these binoculars," Lance said, handing them to him.

Sharon said, "Here's my cell phone. I'll call you from Lance's phone. When you answer the phone, all you have to do is say the person's name."

The excited, reddish-brown polka-dotted David — he was mostly healed by now — responded, "I look at the person through these binoculars and when you call me, if I recognize the person, I say his name. Sounds like a plan,"

Lance and Sharon got out of the car and headed toward the front door. The industrial complex, covered in off-white siding, blocks from the ocean, was made up of several sections — from above they looked like aisles — each with several large, floor-to-ceiling, roll-up garage doors capable of fitting semi-tractor trailers. Behind each pairing of industrial-sized garage door and metal front door was the industrial space for tenants. Lance rang the bell.

"Who's there," said a man through the intercom.

"It's the police," Sharon said at the intercom without having to push any buttons.

"The police?" the man asked.

"Yes, the police," Sharon said. "Please open the door."

"Hold on," the man said. Lance and Sharon heard a chain being placed on the other side of the door. After a brief pause, the door partially opened the distance of the security chain, which was visible at eye level.

Lance, who was wearing a suit jacket, made sure his badge was visible; Sharon's badge was already visible on her belt. She normally wore pants and today was no different. Both were wearing their holsters and San Diego police-issued Glock semi-automatic hand guns, also visible.

The man stood in the doorway behind the chain. Lance and Sharon positioned themselves so that David could see the man in the doorway behind the chain.

"How can I help San Diego's finest today," the man said from behind the chain.

Lance said, "Sir, we are investigating the disappearance of a young woman from the University of California, San Diego, and we have reason to believe she is on the premises. In addition, we have reason to believe that she and, maybe you, are infected with a disease. We would like to see if she is here and if either of you are in need of medical attention."

"A disease?" the man asked. "No, I am not sick, and there's no one else here."

"We'd like to come in and take a look around," Sharon firmly stated.

"Do you have a search warrant?"

"We can easily get one," Sharon stated.

"Well, I assure you, there's no one else here, and I am not in need of a doctor."

"Can you please let us in to make sure everything's okay?" Lance asked.

"I'd be happy to...once you get a warrant."

Lance and Sharon looked at each other and, before they could respond, the door closed.

Lance handed Sharon his phone and she quickly dialed her own phone number on speaker before they walked back to the car. If David didn't get a good look they were ready to try something else.

David answered the phone before the end of the first ring and excitedly said, "Yes, that's him! That's the guy. That's John London, the guy with the yellow Hummer!"

"David, are you sure that you got a good look at him?"

"Yes!" David replied loudly. Sharon hung up the phone and handed it back to Lance. They walked back quickly to the car and got back in.

David was prepared. He had Sharon's cell phone in his right hand extended out to the front seat. Sharon grabbed it with her right as she entered the car, then turned around to sit forward and called for backup. Lance called the judge to tell her how David identified John London and Peter Falciparum as one and the same person.

Not five minutes passed; there were now three police cars in front, lights flashing. As the fourth car pulled up, a large police SUV, all the officers got out of their cars. As the four officers in the SUV got out, they walked to the back. Two of them walked out from the back of that SUV carrying semi-automatic rifles; the third and fourth men pulled out a three-foot long battering ram, placed it on the ground, closed the back door, picked the battering ram back up together and joined the team. Ten uniformed officers, all men, their guns and rifles drawn, save the two with the battering ram, and Sharon and Lance walked up to the door. Sharon knocked on the door.

"Police!" Sharon shouted. "Search warrant! Open this door or we will break it down."

There was no response.

"Police!" Sharon shouted again. "Search warrant! Open this door or we will break it down."

Still no response. She waited a few moments.

"We are breaking this door down; please step back from the door," Sharon stated loudly but with no emotion.

She gave a go-ahead signal to the two police officers who were now holding the battering ram. They walked calmly to the door, side by side, with the battering ram between them, each holding it with one arm. When they reached the door, they faced each other, each hand that held the battering ram became the hand at the rear, then each used their other hand to hold the front handle. They swung it backward, then forward, then backward again, then "BAM!" In one motion the door was crushed straight in, bent in the middle, and came completely off its hinges, with screw fragments flying in all directions inward.

The two officers let the battering ram fall to the floor and got out of the way. Guns drawn, safeties off, the police stormed in. The two officers that had battered the door down drew their guns and stood watch at the opening, securing the perimeter.

"Is there anyone else in here?" one of the officers yelled to the man sitting at a desk on the left-hand side.

The man, Peter Falciparum, also known as John London, didn't say a word.

One of the officers took out his handcuffs and said, "This is only for your and our protection. At this time you are not under arrest; but, we are going to secure this space and perform a search. Once it is secured we may take them off you." He put the handcuffs on John — Peter — from behind.

"Can I see the warrant?" John — Peter — inquired calmly.

Lance joined the officer handcuffing the person of interest and said, "We don't have to show it to you, Mr. Falciparum, however, we are looking for one Michelle Park, approximately twenty years old, phenobarbital, and anything resembling a phenobarbital delivery device. If you know where the girl or these items are you can save yourself some time by telling us."

The two officers securing the perimeter allowed David to enter the commercial space. As he walked in, he looked at the bare walls and the slew of unopened boxes which no doubt contained the various stuffed octopuses, dolphins, killer whales, crabs, snakes, tigers, lions, teddy bears, spaceships with legs, and fanged and non-fanged worms. The big giraffe was over in the right corner, wrapped in plastic, next to the stuffed — but very real-looking — dog named Zack, similarly wrapped. And there were generic looking desks and chairs throughout the space, most with papers, files, and semi-opened boxes on top.

In the middle of the room, a large, open area, there was a huge aquarium, with several fish and white crustacean-like animals in it. Yes, it was the same tank David had seen three weeks earlier at John's house. He walked over to it.

"Here they are!" David exclaimed. "See, here they are!"

Most walked over to him.

"Look," David said, pointing to the fish in the huge tank. Lance and Sharon flanked him on either side. David put an index finger into the water like a lure, immediately prompting a couple fish to propel toward it. One of the fish opened its mouth above the water line, and, just as David expected, one of those nasty little tongue monsters could be seen waving its arms and hissing.

Both Lance and Sharon gasped, each taking a step back.

"Jesus Christ," Sharon said in disgust.

"What the hell is that!?" one of the officers said.

Lance looked at John then back at David. "What in the world is that?"

John — Peter — said nothing.

"*Cymothea exigua*," David said to the Lance, Sharon and those officers gathered at the tank. "It's a crustacean, a female crustacean, a barnacle, a parasitic barnacle. It enters through a fish's gills then causes the degeneration of most of its tongue, then attaches to the remaining tongue stub and floor of the fish's mouth by hook like legs. It survives by drinking blood from an artery. Once the fish's tongue is gone, it attaches itself as a new tongue, and manipulates the fish's food and consumes the free food particles as the fish eats."

More fish came to the surface, showing off their wares.

"That's disgusting," one of the officers said.

"What, are you some kind of Frankenstein?" another officer asked of John.

John remained arrogantly silent.

"Got it!" an officer said from further back in the room.

The rest of the uniformed officers and Sharon walked toward him. Lance, his detainee and David stayed by the tank. The officer was standing in front of a huge Sub-Zero® refrigerator with double glass doors on the top and two freezer drawers on the bottom, exactly as David had seen in John's house three weeks earlier. There were stacks of medication several rows deep in unopened rectangular packaging that could be seen through the glass doors. "Phenobarbital" was clearly written on many of them; but, there were many other types of drugs. And, also in the refrigerator, were vials and Petri dishes with other unknown "things" inside, and on a shelving unit next to the refrigerator, and on the floor. There were still many more boxes with who knows what inside them throughout the back of the room.

"Someone call a Hazmat team," Sharon said. One of the officers could be seen and heard making that request on his shoulder-mounted radio.

And there were weapons too. On a desk toward the back were a couple small, easily concealable, semi-automatic handguns, two large scopes that could be attached to those handguns, an infrared targeting sight, a laserscope, cleaning tools and solutions, and two pairs of night-vision goggles. And leaning against the wall next to that desk was a black rectangular case about four feet long, maybe a foot wide and not much more than a few inches thick. It could have been a hard pool cue case for multiple cues. One of the officers picked it up, cleared some space, and placed it on the table.

As the uniformed officer opened the case, Sharon exclaimed, "That could be it!"

On top of and within thick, padded, form-fit inner liners, the "it" was a unique-looking rifle consisting of two very slender, black metal barrels going through a stock and all the way to the butt. At about the middle of the stock were the trigger and pistol grip on the bottom, scope on top, and a CO_2 cartridge sticking out in the middle parallel to the barrels. There were several back-up CO_2 cartridges and other supplies in the case with the expensive dart rifle.

Said the officer, "I've seen animal control use something like this before. The double barrel comes in handy when you don't know what dosing level you need until arriving at the location and seeing the situation. You get to pre-load the rifle with two differently dosed darts, one in each barrel, choose which dart to fire and shoot both rounds off quickly."

"And this must be the ammunition," he said as he pulled out one of the containers from the case, opened it, and emptied several small, unused syringe darts. Small, yes—about an inch long—but with enough capacity to drop a human.

Sharon added, "Yup, that's what we we're looking for."

And then they heard the sound of something hitting the floor in the back room. In the first second, aside from each of the officers looking at each other, they hardly moved. Then, nearly all the officers quickly reached for, grabbed hold of, raised and pointed their weapons toward the back. Without fear they all walked in the direction of that noise, sans David, Lance and Peter. Someone had to keep tabs on Peter. David stayed frozen with the thought that they would find Michelle in some late stage of torture.

Only one piece of music could do this scene justice.

"*Nessun Dorma*," Italian for "None Shall Sleep," is an aria from the final act of Giacomo Puccini's opera *Turandot*, and is one of the best-known tenor arias in all opera. It is sung by Calaf, the unknown prince, who falls in love at first sight with the beautiful but cold Princess Turandot. There's just one troubling detail: any man who wants to wed Turandot must first answer her three riddles. If he fails, he will be beheaded.

In the previous act, Calaf correctly answered the three riddles. Nonetheless, she recoils at the thought of marriage to him. Calaf offers her another chance by challenging her to guess his name by dawn. If she does so, she can execute him; but, if she does not, she must marry him. The princess then decrees that none of her subjects shall sleep that night until his name is discovered. If they fail, they will all be killed.

The final act opens at nighttime. Calaf is alone in the moonlit palace gardens. In the distance, he hears Turandot's heralds proclaiming her command. His aria begins with an echo of their cry and a reflection on Princess Turandot.

"Nessun dorma! (None shall sleep!)
Nessun dorma! (None shall sleep!)
Tu pure, o Principessa, (Even you, O Princess,)
nella tua fredda stanza, (in your cold bedroom,)
guardi le stelle (watch the stars)
che tremano d'amore, (that tremble with love,)
e di speranza! (and with hope!)"

"This is the police," an officer said. "Search warrant!" With that, he tried opening the door; it was locked.

"Ma il mio mistero è chiuso in me; (But my secret is hidden within me;)
il nome mio nessun saprà! (none will know my name!)
No, no! (No, no!)
Sulla tua bocca lo dirò quando (On your mouth I will say it when)
la luce splenderà! (the light shines!)"

One of the police officers ran to the front door, grabbed hold of the battering ram, and, although it was heavy, carried it as quickly as he could to the back where he started. He was greeted by another officer who grabbed hold of the battering ram with his left arm. Facing each other, they each grabbed the front with their other hands, then, in the same manner as the other pair did to the front door, these two officers brought the ram back, then front, back again, then "BAM!"

This door, much lighter than the front door, immediately gave way. Several police officers rushed in, guns drawn, safeties off.

"Ahhh!" screamed a girl in the distance. It could have been Michelle; it could have been anyone. There could have been more than one person in the room. Sharon entered. No gun shots were heard, only some unintelligible sounds emanated from within.

Outside the room, David still stood uneasily by the fish tank with Lance and the detainee.

"Ed il mio bacio scioglierà (And my kiss will dissolve)
il silenzio che ti fa mia! (the silence that makes you mine!)"

"Il nome suo nessun saprà (Chorus: No one will know his name)
E noi dovrem, ahimè, morir, morir! (and we must, alas, die, die!)"

Obviously, this is all taking place in an industrial park in San Diego; but, the opera is set in Peking, the customary name for Beijing in English, originating with the French missionaries four hundred years ago, corresponding to an older pronunciation of the Mandarin word. And the symbolism runs deep; Calaf doesn't want Turandot to marry him reluctantly; he wants to defeat her cold-hearted defensiveness and have her fall in love with him. That is, in fact, exactly what happens at the end of the opera, similar to what's about to take place in this musty, dark, industrial space.

David walked to the doorway. Not sure what would greet him there, he paused before turning completely to look inside, and closed his eyes. He took a deep breath, and, as he opened his eyes, he saw policemen surrounding Sharon, who, in turn, was standing next to, and talking to…Michelle. He gasped, frozen in place, absolutely unable to make a sound. A second passed, then two. When he was finally able to move and speak he shouted out, "Michelle!"

"Dilegua, o notte! (Vanish, o night!)
Tramontate, stelle! (Set, stars!)
Tramontate, stelle! (Set, stars!)
All'alba vincerò! (At dawn, I will win!)
Vincerò! Vincerò! (I will win! I will win!)"

Michelle ran to David; David ran to Michelle. They hugged immediately. Michelle kissed his face — his healed though still pock-marked face — all over as David kissed hers.

"Ni-nun nuh-duh chun-suk ha-dah," Michelle desperately said in Korean to David as she hugged and kissed him.

"Ni-nun nuh-duh chun-suk ha-dah," she said again.

David didn't understand a word she said and pulled her off him though still tightly grasping her arms, as she held him. They were looking directly at each other.

"I don't understand," David said, almost crying.

Michelle, tearing, unexpectedly said, "You Americans are so stupid; why don't you learn another language like me?!"

David, amused by that, laughing through his tears, said, "What did you say?! What did you say?!"

"I choose you, David. I choose *you*," she said through her tears, kissing his face, her arms wrapped tightly around him.

"I've missed you Michelle, are you okay?"

"I'm fine David, I'm fine," she whispered in his ear.

"Are *you* okay?" Michelle asked, finally noticing his healed wounds, touching his face.

"Yes, I'm fine."

"You look so skinny," Michelle said, as she kissed him and touched his face and squeezed him closer to her.

David smiled. "I'm fine, Michelle."

"Where's Kimmy? Where's Kimmy and Shirley?"

David, still looking in her eyes, opened his mouth as if to tell her everything; but, instead, said, "We have a lot to talk about Michelle." He hugged and kissed her again, and again, until they finally embraced in a long, longed for, loving kiss.

"You have the right to remain silent. Anything you say or do can and will be held against you in the court of law," said Lance to John—Peter—his voice loud enough to be heard by both David and Michelle. "You have the right to speak to an attorney. If you cannot afford an attorney, one will be appointed for you. Do you understand these rights as they have been read to you?"

"Yes, thank you detective," Peter said calmly.

Two police officers took hold of Peter, turned him around and escorted him to the door. From there they probably placed him in a squad car for transport to the Central Jail.

Michelle and David, still embraced, heard Sharon say to Lance, "We've got the victim, her testimony, the drugs, the delivery device, and the suspect. This one's a done deal."

A Done Deal

Three days later: Monday morning

"Case number CD312811, the People of the State of California, plaintiff, versus *P. Falciparum*, AKA J. London, defendant," the short, muffin-shaped, aged bailiff announced.

His name must have been Samuel Wojciehowicz; it was engraved on a gold, rectangular name plate on his left shirt pocket. He was bald save for a few strands of stiff, combed-back black hair and wore cheap, black, thick-framed and lensed, glasses. Technically in uniform, his wrinkled shirt, faded striped slacks and old, worn shoes spoke to his near retirement.

Bailiff Wojciehowicz continued, "One count Murder in the first degree, per California Penal Code sections 187, 188, and 189; one count murder in the second degree, per CPC sections 187, 188, and 189; one count kidnapping, section 207; one count abduction for..." he paused, looked at the defendant, raised his eyebrows in surprise as if thinking he'd heard it all until now, then continued, "...for marriage or defilement, section 265..."

Judge Richard Rosenstein—one could only notice from in front of the raised bench that he was old, with a roundish-face, thick black glasses, almost a full head of whirling gray hair and matching thick, unkempt eyebrows partially connected in the middle—was not really paying close attention; he started his response before the bailiff was done, "How do..."

Sam the bailiff looked at Judge Rosenstein as if he wasn't quite done, somewhat loudly cleared his throat and pointed to the paper in his hand. The judge looked back at him as if—save for the full head of gray hair—a mirror image alter ego insincerely and paternalistically begging forgiveness for the interruption. Sam could have been Richard had he studied; Richard could have been Sam had he not.

The bailiff continued, "Four counts administering stupefying drugs to assist in the commission of a felony, section 222; four counts battery, section 242; five counts assault with a deadly weapon or force likely to produce great bodily injury, section 245; two counts unlawful possession of sniperscopes, section 468; eight counts possession of restricted biological agents, section 11419 (b) (6) of the Hertzberg-Alarcon California Prevention of Terrorism Act; three counts possession of designated controlled substances, section 11350 of the Health and Safety Code, specifically Schedule Four Substances, per section 11057 of the Health and Safety Code."

After a moment of incredulous silence in the courtroom, the judge sarcastically asked of the bailiff, "Anything else?"

The bailiff looked back at the Complaint, then again to the judge and replied, "No, I think that's everything, Your Honor."

"Peter Falciparum, *pro se*, Your Honor," John said confidently yet humbly, the weight of the arm and leg shackles noticeably annoying him. "Waive reading."

He looked relatively at ease though distracted by the full-body, standard prison-issue orange jumpsuit. He had worn similar clothing in the past—it was like wearing yet another non-custom rented tuxedo for yet another yearly wedding ritual he attended for yet another friend—except this time it was one piece, and orange. "Waive reading," by the way, means that the defense requested that the details of the alleged crime not be read aloud in the courtroom. No need to hammer home what was allegedly done, thought Peter on advice of counsel.

"*Pro se*, huh," the judge replied. "Who is that standing with you?" Judge Rosenstein asked, referring to, well, the lady standing next to him.

"Mona Spryer, Your Honor," the neutrally dressed, tall, thin, conservative looking young lady in a gray flannel skirt, white shirt, pulled-back in a bun blond hair and thin black glasses said.

"The defendant has prepared motions including to proceed *pro se* and request for standby co-counsel; I am his standby co-counsel," Mona stated matter-of-factly.

"Very well," the judge said. "How does your client plead? I'm sorry. I mean, Mr. Falciparum, how do you plead?" The judge's insincerity and absent mindedness were more humorous than off-putting to John.

"The defendant pleads that he is not guilty of the offenses charged," John said confidently, professionally.

The judge came out of his insincere, absent-minded fog and asked with keen interest, and a little incredulity, as he looked directly at John, "The defendant pleads that he is not guilty of the offenses charged?"

"Yes, Your Honor, that is my pleading," John stated quietly, subtly, confidently.

The judge continued to look at John for a moment without a word, squinting a couple times, probably wondering why someone like this — clearly well educated — was standing before him in chains, accused of such a long list of serious charges.

"People on bail," the judge finally asked of the Assistant District Attorney, Susan Berman. Equally conservative as Mona, Susan was not as tall, pretty, confident, well-to-do, thin, curvy, or blond.

Susan pleaded, "Given the long list of charges — serious charges which include murder and kidnapping and special circumstances for each including lying in wait — the defendant's resources, and his penchant for breaking the law, we deem him to be a flight risk and thus seek remand Your Honor." She was confident and poised as she had won remand for defendants charged with lesser crimes and with less evidence.

"Your Honor, if I may," John, who was really, and will be referred to henceforth as Peter said.

"Go ahead Mr. Falciparum."

John continued, "I have never been convicted of one single crime in my life, notwithstanding miscellaneous parking and speeding tickets. Though it is true that I have been falsely arrested several times; in 2001, 2002, 2003, and 2004, for federal and state charges of identity theft, fraud, and, at the time of my last arrest, in 2005, the Federal Government's charge of violating the Can-Spam Act. None of these charges have ever been substantiated; yet, I can't seem to shake them, let alone defend myself from the egregious consequences said charges have wrought to my life. I have—and can provide the court all the documentation—I have had all my records, in all the courts that I've had a privilege to attend, expunged; yet, here I stand today with the prosecutor defaming and slandering me, my name, and my reputation by saying that I—what did she say?— that I have a penchant for breaking the law? Yet in my, my friends', my family's, my network's, and most importantly, in a court's—hopefully this court's—eyes, I have no such propensity. There is no evidence."

Peter thought for a moment then concluded passionately, "I object to this defamation of character, and ask the prosecutor for a formal apology."

The normal hustle and bustle of a large, packed courtroom came to a halt. No one in that courtroom had heard such eloquence emanating from the mouth of any defendant, let alone anyone wearing an orange jumpsuit accessorized by handcuffs and leg chains.

The judge, being surprised to hear such an impassioned plea from any defendant, looked at the prosecutor, who remained motionless, then back to Peter, and said, "Mr. Falciparum, this hearing is simply to determine bail." He turned to Mona and chided, "Ms. Spryer, please instruct your client to limit himself to the matter of bail."

"Yes Your Honor," Mona said. She looked to Peter, leaned over to him, as Peter also leaned toward Mona, and the two engaged in a brief, whisper-like conversation.

"Forgive me, Your Honor," Peter began again. "The fact is that all the evidence that the state in collusion with the federal government has against me is based upon an illegal search of my premises. As I was saying earlier, I do have arrests, but no convictions. And it is my understanding that the evidence obtained is a direct result of an illegal search of my mother's house at gunpoint, without exigent circumstances, most-likely based upon a search of the CODIS database, of which my DNA—and I don't know how they could have obtained my DNA from the crime scene as I wasn't there—showed a match."

"Now, *if* my DNA *is* in the CODIS database, the file is a relic of many past arrests, unconstitutionally stored and used by the government. You see, those records were supposed to have been expunged. Yes, I can produce original documents attesting to that expungement. And the expungement order specifically stated that those records were not just to be sealed; but, to be destroyed."

"Thus, the prosecution's evidence against me is thrice illegal: unlawful storage and access of my DNA, assault of my mother, and burglary of my premises. Furthermore, my very presence here before you today, Your Honor, is the culmination of the illegal actions of the San Diego police department, perhaps at the behest of the District Attorney's Office, validated by a sitting judge, equating to *de facto* vandalism, larceny, first degree burglary, first degree robbery, kidnapping, and false imprisonment, sections 584, 484, 458, 460, 211, 207 and 236 respectively of the California Penal Code, and I seek redress." He paused momentarily, continuing with, "Such redress will, at a minimum, be in the form of granting several motions that have bearing on this matter, Your Honor, including a motion to suppress illegally obtained evidence."

Mona Spryer handed him a piece of paper with the motions listed, and he began to read that list aloud. "In addition to that motion to suppress illegally obtained evidence and for hearing, I intend to submit a motion for preliminary examination, motion to proceed *pro se* at trial, defendant's request for standby counsel, motion to reduce bond, motion for discovery, motion to suppress tangible evidence, motion to quash—which I understand to be to suppress testing any of the evidence gathered at the scene..." as Peter said that the judge nodded his head as if to confirm this last point, "...motion to go beyond the face of the affidavit supporting the search warrant and challenge the truthfulness of statements made in the affidavit, motion to exclude DNA, motion to permit accused to appear in court at trial and other public hearings dressed in civilian clothes and without shackles or other restraints, motion for speedy trial, and, assuming my motion to suppress is granted, a motion to dismiss."

Nearly everyone in that courtroom was captivated listening to him deliver that plea, not least of all the bailiff, police officers, judge and prosecutor. Peter and Mona noticed the influence they had on their audience, and both quietly looked at each other and smiled in acknowledgement.

After a couple seconds of silence, the judge spoke. "Thank you for your impassioned *plaint*, Mr. Falciparum. You're saying that the only evidence against you was found as a result of an illegal search and seizure, yes?"

"Yes, Your Honor," Peter quickly, sincerely and respectfully responded.

"Does the prosecution have a response," Judge Rosenstein said directly at the Assistant District Attorney, Susan Bergman.

Susan, normally quick and light on her feet, began to shuffle some of the papers given to her by an assistant, and nervously said, "It is our understanding that the, uh, search was conducted legally, that we have a warrant signed by a judge, and that it was executed in good faith. We stand by our request for remand." As she finished those words she felt a little faint, as if she was just starting the downward plunge from the top of the world's fastest, highest rollercoaster. She was no longer confident in her case.

"Mr. Falciparum," Judge Rosenstein began, "as I stated earlier, the purpose of this hearing is strictly to obtain your pleading and to set bail. The prosecutor wants remand; yet, all I need to judge is if you will make it to the next court date. I cannot even in the rarest of circumstances dismiss a case because the accused challenges the evidence unless both parties agree; but, the evidence before me is that, as you stated, you were arrested, the FBI does in fact maintain a DNA database that includes that from previously arrested individuals, and, on its face, a validly signed and executed search warrant. So, it seems, all that's left for me to adjudicate is bail."

"Thank you for your candor, Your Honor," Peter stated. "In response, I took responsibility for my past alleged misgivings and attended all my previous court dates: in 2001, 2002, 2003, 2004, and 2005. I never missed an opportunity to defend myself, to dutifully serve my part of the social contract, and to learn more about the greatest legal system in the world. But I submit that the prosecution shouldn't be rewarded for their lack of admissible evidence, for keeping my DNA profile in their systems when they should have been expunged. No authority should be able to obtain any valuables from others by resorting to physical force. If not for their incompetence, at best, or, at the other end of the continuum, contrivance, I wouldn't have suffered the aforementioned and a hundred other hardships, and be standing before you today in this poor accoutrement. The law should be a shield and not a sword."

The judged opened his dreary and pessimistic eyes wide, again looked at the prosecutor, back to Peter, Mona, then paused briefly before saying, "Bail is set at a hundred thousand dollars cash or bond. Referred to Part B, Central Division. The judge there can settle these other issues including your numerous motions. How does a week from next Tuesday work for you, Mr. Falciparum?"

"That would be fine, Your Honor, assuming the prosecution provides me with the discovery I have motioned for and I am able to review it."

"Good. Next case," the judge said, returning to his prior dull, insincere, pessimistic, semi-conscious self.

The bailiff at that point should have called the next case; but, instead, the prosecutor walked over to the judge in a sidebar, whispered something, prompting the judge to, moments later, say, "The court will take a fifteen minute recess."

The prosecutor then went to the second row on the right-hand side of the court, as viewed from the gallery, to discuss the events that had just unfolded. Seated in that row, from the aisle to the end, were several middle-aged people from Korea, with Michelle and a thin David at the far end.

Shirley's mother had flown in to California to attend the hearing, flanked by two Korean Deputy Consulate Generals, Kimmy, her mother, Michelle's mother, Michelle, and David. The prosecutor lowered herself uncomfortably toward Shirley's mother, as the rest of the aisle, still seated, turned inward toward her to listen, and said:

"Again, we're very sorry for your loss, Mrs. Lee. We have the man responsible for your daughter's death in custody, and will do all we can to keep him behind bars. I won't lie to you however; it looks like we will have a fight on our hands. I'll have my entire office working on the case to make sure that he doesn't see the light of day again." Although she tried to convey confidence, the Korean delegate, perceptive in American affairs, couldn't help but be a little skeptical.

"Ms. Bergman," said the first consulate administrator, "we all have faith in your abilities and trust that you will work hard to prosecute this animal responsible for Mrs. Lee's daughter's death, the sickness of Ms. Kim, the abduction of Michelle, and David's unfortunate illness, however, we can't help but question what all those motions will come to." The entire aisle quietly showed their agreement with what he had just said.

"Well, it is somewhat complicated," Ms. Bergman began, "but I will keep you informed at every step. Right now, I have to prepare the case with my team. The next court date is in a couple weeks, as the judge said, and I'm confident that we will prevail. There is no precedent for what he is asking for, that is excluding his DNA evidence, but I do have to make sure that the warrant was in order. There's no point in worrying about it any more than you have already; so, for now, all I can say is that we will do the best we can and regroup next week." Ms. Bergman stopped, pleased with her response, paused, then looked at everyone seated in the aisle.

"How are you feeling Kimmy, Michelle, David?" Ms. Bergman said to each in turn.

Kimmy began to cry, but said through her tears, "I'm okay. I really miss Shirley."

"Me too," Michelle added. David just nodded his head as if to say "I'm okay."

The prosecutor looked once more at Mrs. Lee, reached over both Korean administrators to touch Mrs. Lee's hand, and touched her left hand as if to say everything will be all right. Mrs. Lee kept her head down until Ms. Bergman retracted her hand, then looked up, and in perfect English, said, "Thank you Ms. Bergman. We all wish you success and good luck."

At the same time, Peter was saying goodbye to Mona, two guards flanked him and brought him to the door on the left-hand side which led back to the prisoner holding area, and Mona began walking over to Ms. Bergman. She waited for Ms. Bergman to finish her consultation with the group. As Ms. Bergman stood up and turned, Mona Spryer simply said, "You'll have our motions on your desk first thing tomorrow morning." Neither Mona nor Susan gave the other a parting *ad hominem* remark, often added by adversaries. These two were professional in every way, albeit team Mona seemed to have more confidence.

A Done Deal II

Ten weeks and two continuances later: Thursday morning

William Pinski, Bailiff, was the name on the rectangular, gold badge of the man that said in a stern voice, "All rise." He must have came out of the same mold as the bailiff at the initial bail hearing, Peter and Mona thought. Short, fat, in a uniform that did and didn't meet standard: right pants, right shoes, right shirt, but wrinkled, worn, and faded all. Same hairstyle, same black, thick-rimmed, thick-lensed glasses. Same balding head interspersed with the same straight, black hair. Perhaps it was only the pock-marked face and lack of hair gel that set this Bailiff apart from the last.

He continued, "Hear ye, hear ye. The Central Branch, Superior Court of California, County of San Diego, Department 22, Part B, is now in session, the Honorable Judge Jane Whitehall is presiding."

Judge Whitehall, an experienced trial judge, known by colleagues, prosecutors and defense attorneys alike as being fair and no-nonsense, would be unrecognizable in laughter. Gray hair, prim and proper, austere — she wore no make-up or jewelry — thin, completely aware of and in charge of her courtroom, she put the machine in motion.

"Please call today's calendar," the judge said sincerely.

"Your Honor, today's case is the preliminary examination of the state of California versus Peter Falciparum, AKA John London."

"Is the prosecution ready to begin?"

"Assistant District Attorney Thomas Rath for the prosecution. Yes Your Honor, we're ready," Mr. Rath said as he stood from the right-hand side of the table on the judge's right.

Not a very affable man, or one with much of a personality, he was a true public servant, an idealist, always trying to make a difference. He was thin, tall, with black hair and no glasses. His face was dull, with sagging, dark half-circles under his eyes.

Susan Bergman, seated just to the left of Thomas Rath, stood and said, "Associate District Attorney Susan Bergman, Your Honor." Today she wore a conservative, though partially polyester, suit. Recall that she was slightly thick, but not fat, with dirty-blond hair very similar to that of the decedent from Utah, Ann Opheles, though Susan's hair was somewhat shorter. Although she lived in California, she had no tan, attesting to the fact that she worked hard to get through law school, and harder still keeping up with the workload given to her in the District Attorney's office, thus she had no time for fun in the sun.

"Is the defense ready this morning?" Judge Whitehall said, now looking at the table on her left.

"Peter Falciparum, *pro se*, Your Honor. Yes, I'm ready to proceed," he said standing, dressed in an impeccable, blue suit with white shirt, red and blue striped tie, and polished, laced, black shoes.

"*Pro se*," she mumbled to herself beneath her breath correspondingly raising her eyebrows. She seemed to weigh the value of his decision in her head for a moment. "You are aware of the dangers of representing yourself, Mr. Falciparum?"

"Yes, Your Honor. I'm aware. I've engaged the services of Ms. Mona Spryer here to serve as standby and co-counsel in the event the primary defense attorney stumbles."

The judge cracked a barely discernable smile on the left side of her face. She was amused, perhaps even a little aroused at his confidence, however, she would rarely show either emotions to her colleagues, and, by all accounts, probably didn't own them.

"May it please the court. Mona Spryer, standby counsel for Peter Falciparum in this action, present and ready to proceed," Ms. Spryer said standing to Peter's right. She too was confident, though much more conservative than Peter, and looked to Peter as if for his leadership.

"Good morning, Ms. Spryer," the judge said, in her quiet, subdued style.

"Good morning, Your Honor," Mona responded.

"Let's review," Judge Whitehall began, speaking to Peter. "Your motion to proceed *pro se* at trial was granted, as was your motion to permit accused to appear in court at trial and other public hearings dressed in civilian clothes and without shackles or other restraints. You've already posted your bail, and you're here, so I'm not inclined to grant your motion to reduce bail."

"Yes, Your Honor, I understand," Peter said, empathizing with the judge. He had a talent for tuning into the thoughts and actions of other people, perhaps even influencing them as well.

"Has the prosecution made good on your motion for discovery as previously granted?"

"Yes, Your Honor," Peter said sincerely.

"So…" the judge began again, "all that's left to adjudicate before trial and any motion for speedy trial, is your (1) motion to suppress illegally obtained evidence and for hearing, (2) motion to suppress — exclude — tangible evidence, (3) motion to go beyond the face of the affidavit supporting the search warrant and challenge the truthfulness of statements made in the affidavit, (4) motion to exclude DNA, (5) motion to quash, and if any or all of them are granted, your (6) motion to dismiss. Has anything changed since the last time we met, or are these the true and correct matters before the court today?"

"Thank you Your Honor," Peter said graciously. "Yes, I have been given discovery and have decided to withdraw my motion to go beyond the face of the affidavit supporting the search warrant and challenge the truthfulness of statements made in the affidavit. I'm satisfied that the detectives in this case acted in good faith, gave a true and valid representation of their case to the judge, who in turn acted judiciously in granting the warrant."

Both detectives were in the courtroom, and they were floored. As were the prosecutor and his staff, and the many unknown figures seated at their table. They all gasped in their own way. Both detectives—Lance and Sharon—felt a great weight lifted from them.

It took a startlingly long ten seconds for the Judge to allow everyone in that courtroom to digest what he had just said, when she replied to him incredulously with her own words, "You are satisfied that the detectives in this case acted in good faith, gave a true and valid representation of their case to the judge, who in turn acted judiciously in granting the warrant?"

"Yes, Your Honor," he said humbly, though confidently. "I feel that I have enough evidence coupled with the correct amount of motions to support dismissal of this case without the testimony of those fine San Diego detectives." Mona looked up to him like her hero, with more than just a subtle smile. Some people in the courtroom noticed that, and wondered about the true relationship between Peter and Mona. Had she slept with him? Had she not?

"Okay, then," the Judge Whitehall said after a brief pause, perked up a little from the defendant's preceding comments. She too was affected by Peter's sincerity, his ability to keep eye contact with her, and subtle but passionate gestures.

The judge continued, "We will be working on the following five motions today: your (1) motion to suppress illegally obtained evidence and for hearing, (2) motion to suppress—exclude—tangible evidence, (3) motion to exclude DNA, (4) motion to quash, and (5) your motion to dismiss. Since some of them are parallel and, perhaps, interchangeable with the others, I think we should proceed in that order, with the motion to dismiss last. Is that okay with both parties?" That question was probably a demand framed in the form of a question.

"Yes," responded Thomas Rath.

"Yes," Peter affirmed.

"Please proceed Mr. Falciparum," Judge Whitehall plainly stated.

"Thank you, Your Honor," Peter began. "I am a man who loves his life and does not sacrifice my love or my values for anyone or anything. I am here before you today because other men do not think as I. Other men do not love their lives as much as I; they willingly sacrifice their love or their values—if they had any—for the sake of public credit, money, or an adoring, sycophantic following, a false love." Mona cold not help but stare admiringly at Peter, as did most of the women in the courtroom except for the judge.

Peter continued, "Your Honor, I am proud of my own value and of the fact that I wish to live free. I am here before you, ultimately, because I sent e-mails. I created new programs too for web sites that, while they made great sums of money for my clients, always gave people—the target market of those websites, otherwise known as the users—the opportunity to click on the "no thank you" hyperlink, at which point in time the pop-up would disappear. Regarding the emails, if it became a nuisance for anyone, they could have downloaded a spam filter; at that time they were free."

"I am really here before you because I was arrested many times, fingerprinted and DNA'd, so to speak, forever to be in a system from which there is no escape, even for the innocent. 'We have a backlog,' the bureaucrats will say, ensuring such records never make it out of the system. It has become *de facto* compulsory for our citizenry to contribute their DNA into the system: the federal, state, and local CODIS database."

"Many things have been theorized as to what would or wouldn't make our founding fathers turn in their graves; forcing our fellow humans to submit their blood for testing and profile creation, and then having that subsequent profile available to the executive branch of the government to use at their leisure without a satisfactory oversight mechanism — something that would allow for a timely deletion of that profile — amounts to the *sin qua non* expression of illegality in search and seizure and cannot be denied to be at the top of the aforementioned list of in-the-grave-turning causes."

"I created. I started with ideas, then wrote thousands, perhaps millions of lines of code. I innovated. I created. I made things where no things existed before. I educated all sorts of people, from Wall Street to Madison Avenue executives, and nearly everything in between. I could make their products, their stores, their brands appear prominently on millions of computer screens across the country, across the world — anywhere there was a computer and a connection — and customers would be steered to their sites, where a percentage of them would choose to buy. I served as a matchmaker, bringing ready, willing, and able demanders to interested, ready, willing, and able suppliers. *I* did that; *I* created value. Those were my creations that influenced relationships. And people at every stage in the process from both sides of the aisle had the ability to decide their own destiny by simply deleting my creations with the touch of a mouse, a click in the upper right-hand box on a web browser, or, even simpler, by not even clicking on a hyperlink to begin with. That most didn't is a testament to my abilities, to the desirability of the suppliers' products, and the level of interest of independent users."

"Although I separated people from their money I caused no harm. A snake oil salesman I was not. I didn't promise a cure where no cure existed. I didn't surreptitiously nor with thunder falsely raise people's hope then fail to deliver. I didn't promise health benefits then proceed to kill. I didn't falsely claim a benefit, like the big pharmaceutical companies that have managed to cultivate a mass fear of one of the most important molecules in the body — cholesterol — and then manufacture, market, and sell drugs to rid the body of it, hyped with propaganda that only Hitler would envy, only to get wealthy watching the masses of people that took my drug lose their memory, strength, and money, taking my drug to no avail, like thinking that hard work will set them free, becoming emboldened, even self-actualized watching them not recover."

"I didn't manufacture or market a brand of cigarettes, nor did I glamorize smoking them, thus not building my wealth off of consumers that became addicted to smoking my brand, developing cancer with every puff they took."

"Nor did I manufacture and market sugar or any other processed or not carbohydrate in any form whatsoever — candy, bread, pasta, potato, rice, fruit — to the two-hundred million plus diabetics worldwide, nor did I buy then watch my stock in any pharmaceutical company that manufactures or markets insulin grow with time, as the diabetics themselves grew fat and died early of complications."

Peter paused to gauge his effectiveness. He happened to make eye contact with David, who, seemed to agree with him about his last comment. Everything in David's body wanted to see Peter burned-alive at the stake, however, Peter's words, delivery, poise, presentation, temperament and empathy seemed to recruit David's at least temporary, legitimate admiration.

Satisfied with his opening remarks, Peter made his way to the crux of his motion. "But I'm not here today to justify my behavior to you, as this argument most likely falls upon deaf ears; those accomplishments of mine, those creations, are far in the past, and you probably do not, will not, and cannot appreciate them. No, I have paid my price for being the fittest male in the pack, the fittest specimen, by being hunted time after time, caught, persecuted, prosecuted and condemned to jail by hyperparasites. Yes, if I'm a parasite, then what are the judges, prosecutors, police and special interest groups that have bought into their dogma over my creativity, innovation, and entrepreneurial talent but parasites of parasites. They publicize that they are working to rid the world of my kind, all the while needing me for their very existence. I will *not* do penance for my virtues or let them be used as the tools of my own destruction."

He paused again, pouring water from a cheap but clean glass pitcher provided on the defense table, into a simple, cheap glass. Peter raised the glass to his mouth and took one, two, three medium sized sips while staring at the opponents on the other side. As he finished, he put the glass down deliberately, confidently, and continued his defense.

"No, I'm here today because of the injustice — the absolute injustice — done to me on behalf of the people, by agents of a magistrate and prosecution, the cat's paws, if you will, who egregiously used information that, although garnered legally, was supposed to be destroyed. Destroyed because, in legal terms, accusations imposed upon me were legally dismissed — I was acquitted — having the effect and force on me of not having occurred in the first place."

"Everyone in this room will stipulate to the following point; that someone convicted of a specific crime can have that conviction used in court by the prosecution to show that he or she has a prior conviction in the specific case that a similar crime was committed by the same person. It can also be used by opposing counsel to challenge a convict's credibility. In short, a prior conviction *can* be used to prejudice jurors with knowledge of a prior bad act. Once expunged, however, that person does not have a conviction as it relates to a private job search — public office or law enforcement are exceptions — or being sentenced for a different crime. So a conviction, whether expunged or pardoned, can rightfully elicit certain negative bias in the courtroom. The operative word, of course, being 'conviction.' I do not have any convictions, and never have. Yet, I stand before you today as if I have had many prior convictions."

"With my cases dismissed, being acquitted of all charges, and all arrest records expunged, I was released from all penalties and disabilities resulting from each offense which I had been accused. Released from all penalties and disabilities means just that, and if the California legislature intended to say otherwise, they would have said so. I can lawfully state that I have not been convicted of a crime when asked on a job interview from any employer, private or public. The only exceptions where disclosure is required are only for those *convicted of a crime*, and are set out by statute."

Peter reached for an index card on the table and began reading from it, "...the order does not relieve him or her of the obligation to disclose the conviction in response to any direct question contained in any questionnaire or application for public office, for licensure by any state or local agency, or for contracting with the California State Lottery."

He put the index card back on the table and continued, "But again, I have never been convicted, only arrested. I have stood accused — several times and for nearly the same offense — but every time acquitted. A defendant? Yes, that I've been. A convict? No, never."

Mona Spryer, unable to contain herself, let out a brief, subtle, amorous sigh. Peter smiled, looked around the courtroom, making eye contact with the prosecution, some members of the gallery, and finally the judge.

After the pause, Peter said slowly, chidingly and with a scowl, "DNA extracted from a dead mosquito lying near the front door of my rented summer home." He paused.

"None of my DNA at the crime scene; no blood, saliva, hair, dead skin, fingerprints, footprints, or anything else placing me at the scene of the crime."

His tone changed to sarcasm, "Oh wait, there was a car that looked like mine parked in a parking lot near the scene."

He paused again, looked around the courtroom, then restated what he had chided the prosecution with the first time, "DNA extracted from a dead mosquito lying near the front door of my rented summer home. The prosecution's case rests upon a match of DNA found in a dead mosquito lying near the front door of my house with that of DNA records in CODIS, the Combined DNA Index System. But those records were expunged — should have been expunged — more than five years ago. Had things worked the way they were supposed to have worked, with even the most generous margin of error, I would not, should not, and could not be before you today. Let me remind you of the process."

Peter picked up a more than two-inch thick, blue, soft-cover book entitled *California Penal Code*, and, before opening it, said the following, "California Proposition 69, passed by the electorate on November 2, 2004, amended the California Penal Code. I have here the *California Penal Code of 2010*, in which Section 299 isn't substantially different from that in effect in 2005, when I expunged my arrest records."

Peter, now holding the thick book with his right hand, smoothly, in one motion, turned to the page with a plain white placeholder with his left, and stated, "The following comes from Chapter Six. DNA and Forensic Identification Data Base and Data Bank Act of 1998." Then Peter began reading from the book, "Article five. Expungement of Information. Section 299. Reversal, dismissal or acquittal; request for expungement of information; procedure; specimens from persons no longer considered suspects. (a) A person whose DNA profile has been included in the data bank pursuant to this chapter shall have his or her DNA specimen and sample destroyed and searchable database profile expunged from the data bank program pursuant to the procedures set forth in subdivision (b) if the person has no past or present offense or pending charge which qualifies that person for inclusion within the state's DNA and Forensic Identification Database and Data Bank Program and there otherwise is no legal basis for retaining the specimen or sample or searchable profile."

"(b) Pursuant to subdivision (a), a person who has no past or present qualifying offense, and for whom there otherwise is no legal basis for retaining the specimen or sample or searchable profile, may make a written request to have his or her specimen and sample destroyed and searchable database profile expunged from the data bank program if: (1) Following arrest, no accusatory pleading has been filed within the applicable period allowed by law charging the person with a qualifying offense as set forth in subdivision (a) of Section 296 or if the charges which served as the basis for including the DNA profile in the state's DNA Database and Data Bank Identification Program have been dismissed prior to adjudication by a trier of fact; (2) The underlying conviction or disposition serving as the basis for including the DNA profile has been reversed and the case dismissed; (3) The person has been found factually innocent of the underlying offense pursuant to Section 851.8, or Section 781.5 of the Welfare and Institutions Code; or (4) The defendant has been found not guilty or the defendant has been acquitted of the underlying offense."

"(c) (1) The person requesting the data bank entry to be expunged must send a copy of his or her request to the trial court of the county where the arrest occurred, or that entered the conviction or rendered disposition in the case, to the DNA Laboratory of the Department of Justice, and to the prosecuting attorney of the county in which he or she was arrested or, convicted, or adjudicated, with proof of service on all parties. The court has the discretion to grant or deny the request for expungement. The denial of a request for expungement is a non-appealable order and shall not be reviewed by petition for writ. (2) Except as provided below, the Department of Justice shall destroy a specimen and sample and expunge the searchable DNA database profile pertaining to the person who has no present or past qualifying offense of record upon receipt of a court order that verifies the applicant has made the necessary showing at a noticed hearing, and that includes all of the following: (A) The written request for expungement pursuant to this section. (B) A certified copy of the court order reversing and dismissing the conviction or case, or a letter from the district attorney certifying that no accusatory pleading has been filed or the charges which served as the basis for collecting a DNA specimen and sample have been dismissed prior to adjudication by a trier of fact, the defendant has been found factually innocent, the defendant has been found not guilty, the defendant has been acquitted of the underlying offense, or the underlying conviction has been reversed and the case dismissed. (C) Proof of written notice to the prosecuting attorney and the Department of Justice that expungement has been requested. (D) A court order verifying that no retrial or appeal of the case is pending, that it has been at least 180 days since the defendant or minor has notified the prosecuting attorney and the Department of Justice of the expungement request, and that the court has not received an objection from the Department of Justice or the prosecuting attorney.

"(d) Upon order from the court, the Department of Justice shall destroy any specimen or sample collected from the person and any searchable DNA database profile pertaining to the person, unless the department determines that the person is subject to the provisions of this chapter because of a past qualifying offense of record or is or has otherwise become obligated to submit a blood specimen or buccal swab sample as a result of a separate arrest, conviction, juvenile adjudication, or finding of guilty or not guilty by reason of insanity for an offense described in subdivision (a) of Section 296, or as a condition of a plea."

Peter gently placed the book back on the table and spoke again directly to the judge, "Your Honor, I followed the letter and spirit of the law. You have before you a copy of, and," he looked at the prosecutor, "you also have a copy of," then looked back at the judge and completed the sentence, "the original expungement order and certified copies of confirmation receipts from the various federal, state, and county entities as specified in the aforementioned section 299 of the California Penal Code."

"I should not be here, *we* should not be here today because, having met the requirements of, and having followed the process of, CPC 299, my records should have been expunged, ergo no cold hit of my DNA on CODIS should have come back matching the extract of a dead mosquito at my summer home, ergo the police would not have found the address listed on my profile, ergo they would not have accosted my mother at gunpoint to elicit my current address, ergo no evidence could have been planted there by a third party and illegally seized."

Peter was not completely finished, though he was pleased with his argument. He made eye contact with the judge as if signaling to her "let the prosecution respond," prompting the judge to look at the prosecutor, who looked like he was ready to proceed. Peter was hoping the prosecutor would inadvertently help his case by reciting for the court that part of section 299 that Peter had left out, enabling Peter to bring his argument home. He had placed the lure on the hook, now it was up to the prosecutor to bite.

The prosecutor was quick to stand up and chime in.

"Your Honor," Thomas Rath said confidently, "that's all well and good, however, I'd just like to make two points. First, whether or not Mr. Falciparum's DNA extracted from that mosquito that matched the DNA found in the CODIS database was expunged or not is a moot point. The police acted in good faith. In the United States versus Leon, the Supreme Court articulated the good faith exception to the exclusionary rule, holding that evidence obtained in violation of the Fourth Amendment is nonetheless admissible if the officer who conducted the search acted in good faith reliance on a search warrant. That an officer obtained a warrant is prima facie evidence of good faith. Mr. Falciparum himself at the very beginning of this preliminary examination stipulated that the officers acted in good faith." Mr. Rath was pleased at his argument, confident he would prevail.

He continued, "Furthermore, a defendant may rebut the prima facie evidence of good faith by presenting evidence to establish that: (1) the issuing judge wholly abandoned his judicial role and failed to perform his neutral and detached function, serving merely as a rubber stamp for the police; (2) the affidavit supporting the warrant was so lacking in indicia of probable cause as to render official belief in its existence entirely unreasonable; or (3) the issuing judge was misled by information in an affidavit that the affiant knew was false or would have known was false except for his reckless disregard of the truth. We have none of that here. Mr. Falciparum himself has provided no evidence rebutting the prima facie evidence of good faith. On the contrary, he testified in affirmation of the detectives' good faith."

Mr. Rath took a breath, pleased with his first argument, and then began again, "And second, Mr. Falciparum failed to completely recite Section 299 of Article 5, Expungement of Information." As Mr. Rath paused, ready to read aloud the missing verse, Peter humbly smiled to himself, knowing full well that he had purposefully left what the prosecutor was about to say, out. Thomas Rath had taken the bait.

The prosecutor then, reading from a similarly thick and blue-bound book, proudly proclaimed, "Any identification, warrant, probable cause to arrest, or arrest based upon a data bank or database match is not invalidated due to a failure to expunge or a delay in expunging records. In short, Your Honor, we have a good faith exception to the exclusionary rule and you should allow all evidence seized at the site into the trial, and convene such trial at the earliest possible date, as we agree with the defense in securing a speedy trial, are ready, willing and able for such a trial, and, in pursuit of justice for the People of the State of California, look forward to such a trial."

The prosecutor was clearly happy with his argument. He was composed and confident. The evidence against the defendant was significant. It would be a done deal. They had the phenobarbital found in the storage unit, guns, sightings, scopes, night vision goggles, the drug delivery device—a double-barreled tranquillizer gun replete with custom darts, biological specimens that had been analyzed by the lab, and, ultimately, they would have Michelle's testimony. She was ready, willing and able to testify that she was abducted and held against her will by none other than John London, whose real name turned out to be Peter Falciparum.

And then Peter Falciparum slowly, quietly and humbly rose to his feet. Palms facing upwards, he began his sincere plead for justice, "Aristotle spelled it out best more than twenty-three-hundred years ago in his Principle of Contradiction: X cannot be non-X. A thing cannot be, and not be, simultaneously. Nothing that is true can be self-contradictory or inconsistent with any other truth. That that is, is; that that is not, is not. All logic depends on this simple principle; rational thought and meaningful discourse demand it. To deny it is to deny all truth. You cannot be able to expunge something and not be able to expunge that same thing at the same time." Peter let his arms fall to his sides, bowed his head for a moment as he gathered his thoughts, and continued.

He raised his head, looked directly at the judge, and spoke humbly, "Section 299 of the *California Penal Code* is troubling. It teases applicants by explaining the requisites, requirements and process for expungement—the *de jure* law—and then, treating those applicants like donkeys chasing a carrot on a stick, never, or, at best, selectively, allowing them to reap the benefits of said expungement, because—*de facto*—the state has no responsibility to carry out such expungement. They may fail or delay or both."

"*Dilationes in lege sunt odiosae;* delays are odious to the law. Delay, by the way, means the act of postponing or slowing. It also means an instance at which something is postponed or slowed. For example, 'delay' as used in the sentence 'The delay in starting the trial made it difficult for all the witnesses to attend,' implies that the trial eventually took place after a short amount of time, and that some of the witnesses missed it and some didn't. Delay thus refers to the period during which something is postponed or slowed, which, in and of itself, indicates that said delay will come to an end and the thing delayed will be realized."

Peter picked up an index card from the table and continued, alternating between reading form the card and speaking directly to the judge, "Synonyms for delay include break, dalliance, dawdling, defer, deferment, deferral, dilly-dallying, drag your feet, drag your heels, filibuster, gap, hold up, impediment, intermission, interruption, inactivity, lag, lateness, moratorium, obstruction, pause, postponement, procrastination, prolongation, put on the back burner, putting off, setback, shilly-shally, slowness, stall, stay, suspension, tardiness, trifling, wait, and others." He put the card back on the table. "I don't believe it was the spirit of the law to allow paid bureaucrats to forever dilly-dally, thereby denying justice for applicants."

"If we were talking about a week, a month, perhaps even six months from the time custodians of my DNA records waited before destroying my file or files, I would probably not be wasting the court's time. But we aren't even talking about a year, which would still be repugnant. No, we're talking about more than five years from the date of my 2004 arrest, five full years from the time my expungement order was signed, sealed, delivered, and, by way of certified mail, receipt confirmed. Five full years of living a clean, sober, legal life, believing that my arrest with no conviction was behind me, that I had paid my non-debt to society, that I was a free man, free from government constraints, restraints, oversight, intrusion and intervention, an individual free from the arbitrary authority of a despot."

Peter's demeanor changed slightly after pausing for a moment. He became more humble, saying, "Five years. What does five years look like? How can we imagine five years? To a bureaucrat living in quiet desperation, every day of every year looks pretty much alike. But I am a man who loves his life."

Peter looked at Mona with widely opened eyes and raised eyebrows, subtly moving his head up and down once as if signaling "now." Mona, smiling back at him, moved her briefcase toward him as he leaned over the table and reached into it, pulling out, one by one, several white 2¾-inch by 1¾-inch by ¾-inch rectangular cardboard boxes, each with a ¼-inch thick red band on all five sides of the flap's back end, with indistinguishable black lettering on the front. Peter pulled out a total of twenty of those small boxes from Mona's briefcase; he placed them neatly, side by side, in five rows of four.

"Paper clips," Peter said, gracefully opening one of the packs and pulled out just one of the silver objects with his right hand. "Here's one, little, smooth-finished paper clip from a box of a hundred. Consider this one paper clip to be equal to one day in my life." Peter lobbed it underhand onto the table, and then grabbed a small handful of them from the same carton.

"In my hand now are about thirty paper clips; equivalent to a month of my life." Peter lobbed them on the dense, wood table; no sooner had his right arm recoiled to his side than all the thrown paper clips came to rest, unevenly distributed on the table. Peter then grabbed what was left in the first box and said, "And here's the remaining paper clips, amounting to, say, about seventy more." He lobbed them all onto the table.

"A hundred paper clips in all, equivalent to three months and ten days. That, Your Honor, is a representation of a delay. A postponement. A stall."

Peter grabbed another box, and, instead of reaching in to hold any, he just turned it upside down onto the table. As the contents came to a rest after being emptied onto the table, Peter added, "And there's another three months and ten days; six and two-thirds months total. I wouldn't argue that that wasn't still a break, dalliance, dawdling, deferment, lag, pause or trifling."

He grabbed another box of a hundred, emptied it too onto the table as he said, "And another hundred days," he said, as he reached for another box and did the same thing. "And another. That's now four-hundred paper clips; a full year and a month. That, Your Honor, is not a delay. That is a denial. But that's not how long I've waited." With that comment, Peter reached for another two boxes with his fingertips, slid them closer to him on the table through the mess of individual paper clips, picked them each up, opened them, and, holding a box in each hand, raised them over the table, turned them upside down, and watched as both boxes emptied onto the table.

"Six hundred days," he said, reaching for and opening two more boxes. Peter emptied those two boxes out onto the table with the same dramatic flare. "Eight-hundred days; two years, two months and a week."

He did it again, saying "One thousand days."

And again, "Twelve-hundred."

And again, "Fourteen-hundred."

And again, "Sixteen-hundred."

And yet again, "Eighteen-hundred," he said. Quite a pile of paper clips had accumulated on the table. Peter reached for one more box with his right hand, opened it with his left, grabbed about thirty of them with his right hand and said, "And just to round it to the nearest year, here are about thirty more." He slowly let go of the paper clips in his hand that he held from eye level and watched and listen to them, with everyone else in the courtroom, hit the table or bounce off of other paper clips. "That's five years in all, one or two leap years notwithstanding." He paused for a moment to let the demonstration sink in.

Peter looked around the courtroom, straightened his suit jacket, and began his close. "By all accounts I had been working to rebuild my life, paying my taxes, being responsible. But what was the government and its agents doing? Nothing, it turns out. While the agents tell their leaders, who tell the elected officials, who in turn tell their constituencies that they are building and maintaining a database, what they were doing was buying time, purposely evading a court order in order to keep their tabs, their paws, on me. For my troubles, I get more troubles. Five years is far too long to allow the state to be incompetent, and I ask this court to grant my motion to suppress, and, given that, subsequently, there is no evidence against me, to dismiss this case. I ask that you send a message to the state that it cannot, should not, nor will not benefit from either incompetence or contrivance. For more than five years I have lived with the assumption that here in the United States, even if not everywhere on Earth, a proper, human way of life is possible to me, and justice matters. *Justitia non est neeanda non differenda;* justice is neither to be denied nor delayed."

Most people in the gallery were obviously moved by his arguments; they coughed, adjusted their position in the pews, and whispered to each other as if in transition between movements in a Beethoven symphony or piano concerto. So too was the judge, her true feelings betrayed by her inability to maintain a poker face. A moment later, she simply glanced at the prosecutor, who rose to speak.

"It's clear to me the spirit of CPC 299 comes from CPC 295: '...to enable the state's DNA and Forensic Identification Database and Data Bank Program to become a more effective law enforcement tool.' Perhaps Mr. Falciparum is unhappy with it being effective in his case."

Judge Whitehall was somewhat shocked by Mr. Rath's comments and knew how Peter would respond.

Peter rose with a confident smile on his face and said, "I couldn't agree with the prosecution more, Your Honor. 'Effective,' however, is the operative word. Perhaps Mr. Rath is oblivious to the fact that I am not arguing effectiveness; on the contrary, I have argued that the state should not benefit from incompetence."

Peter continued, "Every state has a criminal DNA database. Only four states authorize DNA collection upon arrest: California, Louisiana, Texas, and Virginia. Only two — California and Louisiana — refuse to overturn a conviction based on DNA obtained by mistake. And only one of them — California — specifies that failure to follow its DNA database act does not invalidate a database match."

"My argument comes down to this: the Fourth Amendment applies to DNA sampling as it prohibits unreasonable searches and seizures and protects individuals from invasive government acts. Taking DNA is a seizure under the Fourth Amendment. Courts generally rule that convicts have a lowered expectation of privacy and find DNA collection is only a minimal intrusion. The key component in all these cases is that a court has convicted the individuals of a crime. Let me remind you once more that I have never been convicted of a crime."

Peter, still looking fresh, composed and confident, paused for a moment before wrapping it up, "A hypothetical example will serve as my conclusion. Police arrest a suspect on suspicion that he committed a crime, but lack probable cause. During booking his sample is taken and sent to a laboratory. At a hearing to determine the validity of the arrest, counsel for the accused succeeds in showing the arrest was unconstitutional. The court proceeds to dismiss the arrest and all evidence resulting from it. Meanwhile, back at the lab, the sample matches the suspect to DNA at the crime scene."

"Normally, the police could not use this identification; a court should exclude derivative evidence resulting from a constitutional violation, however, Section 297 of the California Penal Code states that a judge cannot dismiss any identification, warrant or arrest for failure to purge records. Thus, police can use the tainted identification to obtain a valid warrant to re-arrest the suspect, search for additional evidence, extract a new, legal sample of DNA, and successfully prosecute him. The primary purpose of the exclusionary rule is to deter violations of Fourth Amendment rights. Here it woefully failed. While a court can exclude the first sample, Proposition 69 prevents it from fully remedying the problem."

"The shift from sampling on conviction to sampling on arrest raises serious due process issues. The quick collection and forwarding of the DNA sample of an arrestee encourages abuse. It is possible to make questionable arrests to obtain genetic evidence because police collect the sample immediately. Together, California Penal Code Sections 297 and 299 prevent exclusion of wrongfully obtained DNA evidence. That prohibition unconstitutionally conflicts with the exclusionary rule."

"For almost eight-hundred years—that is, since the Magna Carta in 1215—there has been no clearer principle of English or American constitutional law than that, in criminal cases, it is not only the right and duty of judges to judge what are the facts, what is the law, and what was the moral intent of the accused; but that it is also their right, and their primary and paramount duty, to judge the justice of the law, and to hold all laws invalid, that are, in their opinion, unjust, oppressive, and all persons guiltless in violating or resisting the execution of such laws. The codes are unjust; I ask that you remedy this injustice by granting my motion to suppress. Justice delayed is justice denied; and, justice denied is…un-American."

Peter subtly tilted his head down and then back up, as if signifying his confidence in the righteousness of his arguments. The gallery had been, and still was, captivated by his presence, word choice, argument, and presentation. As he concluded, there was obvious movement and a little noise coming from people changing position, whispering to each other, and throat-clearing. Peter walked to his chair on the aisle side of the defendant's table, and sat down. Mona lightly touched his left arm with her right arm as she looked at him in admiration, although he did not look back at her.

"I've heard the arguments from the defense and the prosecution on this motion before me," Judge Whitehall stated, putting a fast end to the gallery chatter. She paused for a moment as she looked at the prosecutor, Mr. Rath, then the "second chair," Susan Bergman, then at the two seated at the defense table.

Judge Whitehall thought for a moment, scowled, and said, "This court will stand in recess for thirty minutes; I'll have my decision for you then on this motion, and we can move to the other matters before us." She looked at the people in her court one more time, then glanced over to the bailiff and nodded her head slightly as she stood.

"All rise," the bailiff said, commanding the attention of all those present in the courtroom. Everyone there stood up immediately. The judge left the courtroom accompanied by complete silence, all eyes upon her.

Forty-five minutes later, the chatter in the courtroom screeched to a halt as soon as the bailiff stood. When he stated loudly and firmly, "All rise," courtroom bodies became absolutely tight and straight, as the judge re-entered the courtroom directly to her leather chair without being distracted. She carried no files, no papers, no notes of any kind and sat down quietly, albeit not so gracefully, pulling the large leather-backed chair toward her, adjusting the chair to her liking, which made its slight, signature, squeaky-wheeled-bottom sound. She looked around the courtroom at the different people in the gallery, the prosecutor, and, finally, the accused.

"Mr. Rath," the judge said quietly, ending with a scowl on her face. That scowl disappeared as she took in a breath before beginning her decision. "I agree with you; the penal code does in fact state that any identification, warrant, probable cause to arrest, or arrest based upon a data bank or database match is not invalidated due to a failure to expunge or a delay in expunging records. This it states after carefully depicting how to expunge said records from the numerous databases."

"Mr. Falciparum," Judge Whitehall, looking directly at Peter, said, "I too believe that California Penal Code Section 299 is troubling. The dramatic changes brought by Proposition 69 to California's DNA database raise several concerns. The discretionary standard for removal hearings and the inability to appeal, along with the limitations on expungement, render hearings meaningless and ineffectual. The most troubling modifications are those restricting expungement. I agree with you that these restrictions are an unconstitutional abrogation of the exclusionary rule and may encourage police misconduct. The statute encourages investigative detentions because police can use a database match even when the initial arrest is invalid."

The judge, still looking at Peter, hesitated for a moment, thinking to herself. She continued, "You are an interesting creature. You have a gift for legal research and argumentation, you present your case logically and passionately, and are able keep your focus. You missed your calling Mr. Falciparum; you should have been an attorney."

"I can also see that if, as you said, if you are considered a parasite, then what am I, what are we…" she said, turning her head back and forth, and using her eyes and arms to draw the gallery's attention to the bailiff, defense attorney, and clerk, "but parasites of parasites. When it comes to lawyer-bashing, I've heard it all. They promote needless complexity; they're aggressive, hired guns; lawyers are self-serving rather than problem-solving; opportunistic, manipulative, greedy, money-driven monopolists who charge a tariff on matters of common right. They are parasites that produce nothing but future generations that tax similar hosts. They feed off productive members of society oftentimes aligned with the undeserving, the privileged, and the powerful."

"The parasite critique is that lawyers don't make anything; but then neither do managers, bankers, insurers, accountants, stock brokers, consultants, police, inspectors, etcetera, etcetera. That various individuals and groups have and continue to disparage attorneys because they don't make anything exposes deep apprehension about the meaning of productivity in our information age. Beneath this anxiety lies a legitimate question: do services, particularly those that are concerned with regulation and facilitation, contribute anything of value to society? I think so. Nevertheless, the value exchanged between an attorney and client oftentimes falls short of equitable. After being part of this system for decades now I've concluded that that inequity is due to people in the world having significantly differing skills, tools, knowledge and credentials, thus needs, which drives the demand for attorneys and the value exchanged. Perhaps part of growing up attorney is coming to terms with how much parasitization we can stomach."

"And here you stand, asking for my help, my remedy. Well, this attorney, this judge, this devoted citizen who cares deeply about the public good and is prepared to sacrifice my own well-being for it, has an answer for you."

"If a seizure violates the Federal Constitution, the judge must exclude the evidence. Even a state constitution cannot annul certain rights because the Federal Constitution guarantees a minimum level of protection. Exclusion of evidence is one of those guarantees. I believe that if I didn't dismiss the motion, it would be reversed on appeal. Thus, it is the decision of this court to grant your motion to suppress."

Shock raged through the right hand side of the gallery. Not surprisingly, only Mona and Peter were sitting on the left hand side at the front table, and they were both pleased.

Peter and Mona stood; Peter said, "Thank you, Your Honor," humbly. There was no celebrating or with Mona.

The judge looked at the people on her left—the right side of the gallery—and allowed the emotional set-back to run its course. Kimmy and Michelle were looking at David, and, though they didn't understand all the words that the judge used, they nevertheless fully understood what it meant based on Peter's reaction.

Peter spoke to the judge directly, no more or less confidently than previously, "Having granted my motion to suppress illegally obtained evidence, Your Honor, there then being no evidence with which the prosecution has against me to offer at trial, I simply ask that you grant my motion to dismiss, with prejudice."

The judge looked at Mr. Rath, who slowly, like a beaten-down wolf with his tail between his legs, rose to his feet.

"We do reserve the right to re-file if evidence becomes available," Mr. Rath stated.

"What evidence could that be, Your Honor?" Peter said confidently. "All the evidence that was planted in my storage space cannot now or in the future be used against me, as it is all now fruit from the poisonous tree. There is no witness testimony, nothing placing me at the scene of the crime, nothing tying me to the crime. If the prosecution does not have any evidence now, what is it that they think they will have in the future? The prosecution never argued inevitability. Maybe they think that because I have been arrested in the past that a future arrest is inevitable? The doctrine of inevitable discovery requires that lawful actions independent of the misconduct would have inevitably discovered the evidence. Speculative future actions cannot prove inevitability; the actions must be capable of verification. This doctrine requires historical facts a court can verify. I assure you, another arrest is not in the cards."

The prosecutor tried to say something; but, nothing came out of his mouth. If there was a model of quiet desperation, it would be at this moment him.

Judge Whitehall noticed this inaction; she took a good look at Mr. Rath, allowing him plenty of time to make a further argument. He did not. She then looked at Peter and said, "Motion to dismiss is granted. Case is dismissed with prejudice. Mr. Falciparum, you are free to go."

The gallery erupted in disbelief and shock; the prosecution team bowed their heads in defeat.

"Order in the court!" exclaimed the judge. It was an effective demand, albeit a cliché.

Thank you, Your Honor," Peter stated humbly, quietly, "however, there is one more item to consider."

The judge looked at him for a moment, and then simply asked, "What is it, Mr. Falciparum?"

Like the one spirited though still quite cautious male black widow spider out of a group of less daring male onlookers approaching the humungous female of the species — the term for a physical or behavioral difference between males and females of any particular species is "sexual dimorphism"; a larger female is explained by their having to bear the energetic cost of producing eggs, a much greater cost than that of males making sperm — Peter made the following request, "I respectfully ask that you order the state to expunge — to purge — all my previous DNA records from every jurisdiction — county, state and federal — as well as all the records from this most recent arrest, Your Honor." Unlike the male black widow spider that weakly fastens the female to her web with his own silken ties to mitigate his chances of being scathed, or worse, eaten in retreat after copulation, Peter was much more vulnerable to Judge Whitehall's possible fury.

Again, there was absolute silence in the courtroom as Judge Whitehall looked him over. She thought long and hard before responding, "As I've learned from this case, Mr. Falciparum, that will apparently not guarantee results, I'm sorry to say. You'll be best served by taking the issue up with the fine folks in Sacramento." She paused, and then added, "But I can and will approve the motion if you file the correct paperwork."

Thank you, Your Honor," Peter quite sincerely said, his vision of being eaten alive by a human-sized black widow — the judge leaping out and down from the bench, her two frightful rows of four poorly seeing eyes momentarily fixed on his two before piercing his mid-section with her large, sharp, curved fangs, envenomating him with toxin that quickly dissolves his innards, and then sucking him dry — yes, that whole dreadful vision come to a fast and thankful end. He was in good company as it turns out; male black widow spiders escape a similar fate more than eighty percent of the time. Mona embraced him, unaware that his enthusiastic reciprocity, his relief and thanks, wasn't motivated exactly by what she thought prompted it.

"This court is adjourned," Judge Whitehall said.

"All rise," Mr. Pinski billowed, as the gallery stood on their feet to watch the judge walk to her chambers.

Still standing, Kimmy, her right arm locked with Michelle's left, said with tears, "That wasn't real, was it?"

Michelle held Kimmy tighter, and replied, "We seem to have heard it."

David, his left arm locked with Michelle's right, looked at both the girls and added, "There was nothing we could do; we couldn't help it."

After a very brief pause, Kimmy, still looking forward, said, "We don't have to believe it, do we?"

"No," said David, quietly. "But it is horrible."

Kimmy replied, "It's immoral. It's one-sided, heartless, ruthless and immoral. It's the most vicious decision ever made." They stood there for a few moments in disbelief as others left the courtroom.

Epilogue

They had to park on the street because the driveway at 1859 Royal Blue Court was at capacity. On the right was the fully restored gray Pontiac Woodie, still with a bunch of stuff in the back. A late model, clean, black, four-door Mercedes sedan was parked in the middle and a nearly-new silver Volvo stood on the left.

David got out of the car from the backseat first, followed by Michelle from the passenger-side front, then Kimmy. David held his hand out for Michelle to grab as Kimmy made her way curb-side. The three of them walked up the driveway on the left side of the Volvo and stopped for a moment at the fountain, the now fully functional dolphin fountain.

"So pretty with water coming out," Kimmy said.

Michelle added, "I love dolphins."

David let go of Michelle's hand, walked up to the door and rang the doorbell, expecting the Westminster chimes in response. Instead, "Catch a Wave" by the Beach Boys started to play rather loudly on hidden outdoor speakers, and, probably inside as well.

"Catch a wave and you're sitting on top of the world..."

The three musketeers looked at each other, smiled and giggled. Michelle and Kimmy, holding hands still by the fountain, turned toward David and the front door when Donny White opened it.

"Well, hi there," Donny said with a big smile. "You must be David; I'm Donny White." He was wearing the same blue "tennies" — VANS® brand canvas, thick-soled, lace-up shoes — without any socks and faded Levi's® blue jeans that he had when we first met him weeks before. Instead of a t-shirt, however, he had on a California Reyn Spooner® Hawaiian shirt.

David smiled and responded, "Yes, I'm David. Nice to meet you Donny. The detectives told me a lot about you."

"And that must be Michelle and Kimmy," Donny said, motioning with his head to the two young women still hovering over the fountain.

"Yes, that's them," said David. He turned to the girls and said through a smile, "Hey pumpkin, Kimmy, this is Donny." They slowly walked over, somewhat still focused on the dolphins.

"Hi Donny, I'm Michelle," she said, extending her arm to him. Donny shook Michelle's hand and smiled.

"I'm Kimmy," she said, offering her hand as well.

"Hi Kimmy, I'm Donny White."

"The fountain looks so beautiful with the lights on and the water running," Kimmy said to Donny.

"Yeah, I always loved that fountain," Donny said. He paused, lowering his head in the process, then raising his head again added, "I can't tell you how sorry I am for everything you three have been through."

"It's been an education," Michelle said to Donny. David and Kimmy shook their heads in agreement, but smiled; the three musketeers looked at each other as if bonded from the events.

"Well, come on in," Donny said. Michelle and Kimmy nervously walked in, remembering who and what they had met there many weeks before. They were closely followed in by David, also a little tentative; he closed the door as he crossed the threshold.

Beyond the door loomed the familiar large landing with dark, solid wood floors; but, instead of the big, black and tan German Shepherd sitting on the floor, there was a stack of about ten surf boards of various colors, each little more than nine feet long, in front of several more boards fanned-out in the shape of a peacock's tail.

"Wow, nice surf boards Mr. White," Kimmy said.

"Thanks; but, please, please, just call me Donny," he said.

Kimmy blushed then shyly said, "Okay, Donny."

Although the furniture and wall decorations were different, the place was as the three musketeers remembered it. There was no table or chair on the right, though the coat hooks were still there. Beyond the surf boards, on either side descending alongside both stairways were numerous framed pictures. Many, many pictures of surfing scenes, some in color, some in black and white. As they walked down the right-side semi-circular stairway, still covered with durable, off-white, Berber carpeting leading down to the main floor, Donny White described some pictures pointed out by the three musketeers.

"Oh, who's that?!" Kimmy asked excitedly. It was a black and white picture of a man leaning backwards and standing at the very tip of a surf board, atop a wave, his left hand in the air as if being whiplashed while riding a bull.

"That's one of my favorite action shots, Kimmy," Donny said. "That's David Nuuhiwa's magical nose ride from 1996. David was just seventeen years old when that picture was taken at Huntington Beach Pier."

"Wow!" Michelle said.

"Yeah, wow," Kimmy added.

"It is sweet," Donny said. The four of them took just one more step down each when Donny started talking about the next picture without being asked.

"And this is Jack Haley at the first US surfing championship in 1959, at Huntington Beach Pier, almost forty years before David's picture." Kimmy, Michelle and David smiled, interested in hearing Donny describe it, but didn't say anything.

They reached the main level and immediately Donny walked over to the largest framed picture, still on the right-hand side, beside the ones he just described. It was enormous: about three feet by five feet.

"This is one of the finest surfers in the world then or now," Donny began, "and I have a bunch of different pictures of him. It was taken at Sunset Beach, in Hawaii, and it is my favorite surfer, Phil Edwards." The picture depicted a surfer riding a wall of water; the wave looked to be about four times the size the surfer.

"That is amazing, Donny," Kimmy said.

"Yes, amazing," Michelle added.

"It sure is, or was at the time," said Donny. "I don't remember exactly when that was taken, but I do have his autograph there," Donny said, pointing to the autograph on the lower right corner in thick, black marker.

"Say, are you guys hungry?" Donny inquired. "We've got a whole lot of chow in the kitchen; the professor is here as are a few other people you may know," Donny said looking at David.

"I thought I saw Professor Ross's car," David said. "Who else is here?"

"I don't remember his name, but as I understand it, he was your doctor," Donny stated. "His and the professor's wives are also here, as are the detectives."

"Lance and Sharon?" David asked with a smile.

"Yes, they're here," Donny replied.

"Nice," David said.

The group headed toward the kitchen, though they were still looking at the wall on the right side which had numerous pictures, a couple large plasma screen televisions, and, at the end by the huge floor-to-ceiling window overlooking the gorgeous San Diego Bay, was a completely covered aquarium-sized fish tank. David, Kimmy and Michelle tried not to focus on the tank, and, instead looked at the pictures.

On the right, far in front of the tank, were numerous, autographed, large pictures of various surfers that had found their waves: Butch Van Artsdalen, Greg Noll, Miki Dora and Mike Doyle to name just a few.

And on the left, adjoining the kitchen, in back of the huge, new and very comfortable-looking U-shaped, tan leather living-room suite—itself consisting of a generously long, four-person sofa abutting small square tables at both ends, spatially connected via an aisle to two three-person couches altogether surrounding a large, nearly solid neutral stone table—were numerous small advertisements from decades ago, when surfing was the "it" thing to do. There were advertisements of several John Severson movies including one that read "The Great Surfing Movie of 1963: *The Angry Sea*," right next to another for the movie *Big Wednesday* from 1961. Below that and to the left of a huge, framed color poster—to be discussed shortly—was an autographed black and white copy of the advertisement reading "Bud Browne presents *GUN HO*, the greatest surf film ever made."

And then in the middle, the aforementioned centerpiece, was a huge, wide-angle color shot from the beach of at least a hundred feet of shoreline and ocean, depicting several surfers "scratching for the horizon"—headed out to catch a wave—most oblivious to the scores of dolphins just ahead in the distance launching, twisting out of the waves. They were having the time of their lives, seemingly saying to the surfers approaching them "look at what we can do."

"Dolphins!" Kimmy said as she ran toward the picture.

"Oh, I love dolphins!" said Michelle. Donny and David joined them and shared their delight.

"Yeah, dolphins," Donny said, "I love that picture too; it reminds me that all the work we do isn't just to search for the next perfect wave."

"The work you do?" Kimmy innocently asked. "Does that mean that you're a surfer too? We were told you're the owner of a bunch of surf shops; but, not that you also surfed."

Donny replied, "I started out as a surfer, stayed a surfer, and still am primarily a waterman through and through. The mountains are always there; nothing too special about climbing one, other than the challenge, of course. If you catch a wave, however, it's yours. No lifts, no motors, just you and the ocean. I'll tell you, with enough time and enough money, I could spend the rest of my life following summer—surfing—around the world." Kimmy smiled.

Although the door to the kitchen was closed, they could hear other guests talking, though they couldn't make out exactly what those other guests were saying. They passed the last picture just to side of the kitchen, an old black and white advertisement for Duke Kahanamoku Surf Trunks by Kahala, with the caption "There are logical reasons for buying Kahala surf trunks, but who cares about logic?"

Donny opened the door to the kitchen and the four of them made their entrance ordered Donny, David, Michelle and Kimmy.

"David!" Professor Ross said uncharacteristically loud, already on his feet.

"Hi Professor Ross," sincerely replied David. "You remember Michelle, don't you?"

"Of course," Professor Ross said in his comforting tone.

"And this is Kimmy," David said.

Kimmy nearly melted when Professor Ross said, "Very nice to make your acquaintance, Kimmy. I'm Alphonse Laveran Ross, Professor of Evolutionary Biology at the University. You must take one of my classes soon. David is my star teaching assistant, and one day he'll teach the whole class."

Kimmy blushed; her first thought was to bow as is common in Korea when you meat an older or such a respected person such as Professor Ross. She was quite red and, instead, giggled through her response, "Very nice to meet you, sir."

Professor Ross gave a humble laugh. Behind him, walking over to the group was an angelic, short-haired woman in a light orange summer dress. She could have been the professor's daughter, or...

"And this is my wife," Professor Ross said, "Diana Ross."

Everyone in the room laughed.

"Diana Ross?" asked a wide-smiling Michelle.

"No," Mrs. Ross was able to say through her laughter. "No, not Diana Ross." She looked at her husband lovingly, then back to Michelle, Kimmy and David and added, "He says that often; nice to meet you, I'm Mrs. Ross, alright. Tia Ross. No middle name, just Tia Ross."

Through her giggling, Kimmy said, "Nice to meet you Mrs. Ross. I mean Tia."

"Yes, nice to meet you Tia," added Michelle.

"Tia also works for the University," Professor Ross said. "She's a manager in human resources."

"Yes," Tia said, "and if you stay here long enough, you too will work for the University." The girls laughed.

"Hi Tia," David said warmly.

"Hi David," Mrs. Ross said warmly as she hugged him tightly. "So great to see you again. I do hope you're okay; I'm so sorry for everything that's happened." She looked around to Michelle and Kimmy and added, "To all of you. I'm so sorry it all happened. Please let me know if I can do anything."

"We're all okay, Mrs. Ross," David said.

"Well almost everyone," Michelle added.

Kimmy looked at Michelle, who looked down at the ground, then to Mrs. Ross and said, "But there's really nothing you can do. We appreciate everything, especially your thoughts. Thank you for the cards; I received all of them. It's really great to finally meet you." They hugged for a time; as they disembraced, Mrs. Ross held both of Kimmy's shoulders and gave her a very comforting look before finally letting go.

Meanwhile, Dr. Salvatore Martino walked up to David and said, "Hi there David! Long time no see!"

"Dr. Martino!" David said, "Hey, how's it going?"

"Good, good, David. Tell, me, how are you?"

David replied, "I'm much better; in fact, aside from some of the scars I feel perfectly normal."

"That's all we can hope for," was all that Dr. Martino could say before Kimmy ran up and embraced him in a hug.

They were about the same height, though Kimmy was probably a hundred pounds lighter. While she held him tightly, she simply said, "Dr. Martino."

The good doctor hugged her while gently patting her back and said, "Kimmy. There, there. Hi Kimmy. Yes, it's great to see you're doing well. Are you going to go back to school next semester?"

Kimmy released her grasp, backed up a little and, still touching his left arm with her right hand said, "Yes, I start school again this spring semester. I missed—we missed—our first semester, but most of the courses are offered in the spring, so our first year is going to be a little backwards, taking the first semester courses in the second semester and then the second semester courses in the first semester of next school year."

"I see," Dr. Martino said. "And this must be Michelle."

"Hi Dr. Martino," Michelle said. "David and Kimmy told me a lot about you."

"Lies, all lies," Dr. Martino kiddingly said.

After a moment of laughter, Michelle sincerely said to Dr. Martino, "You're responsible for saving the lives of my two best friends. Thank you."

"Oh, well, that's uh, that's what they pay me for," Dr. Martino said jovially. Everyone laughed a little.

A pretty, thin woman with just a touch of make-up walked over to where Dr. Martino was standing as he said, "David, Michelle, Kimmy, this is my wife, Penny."

Wife? It could have been his daughter; an older daughter, anyway, David thought. No, none of the guests said that out loud.

"Hi Penny, nice to meet you," said Michelle, smiling.

"Yes, nice to meet you," Kimmy added.

"Hi Penny," David said smiling.

Dr. Martino looked at David, clearly noticing that he was thinking how young she looked, changed the subject quickly by saying sincerely, "It's good to see you both doing well, Kimmy and David." After a brief pause he added, "And you will have to tell us about your thesis, David, or shall I say Dr. Bennett."

"Dr. Bennett!" Michelle excitedly said looking at David.

"Yes, that does have a nice ring to it," David replied.

Professor Ross released a humble laugh—all eyes landed immediately and directly on him—and said, "In good time, David, in good time."

The momentary silence in deference to Professor Ross gave way to a couple other salutations.

From the back of the kitchen, up walked Lance Smith who warmly said, "Hi David."

"Lance!" David replied shaking Lance's outstretched hand, "Great to see you."

As they were shaking hands, Sharon walked up, tapped David on the shoulder and said with a smile, "What's up my brother from another mother." Everyone laughed.

"Hi there Sharon," David replied through his laughter, giving her a hug.

When the laughter subsided, Lance said, "If we had it all to do over again, David, I don't think that we would have done anything differently."

"We did everything we could have done, and all by the book," Sharon added.

David replied, "I know; I think you did great work." Michelle and Kimmy shook their heads in agreement as did everyone else.

Added David, "Sometimes we do the best we can and still lose."

Donny White stopped leaning on the kitchen island with the elegant, lighted faucet, walked over to David and the girls, and, looking at David, said, "Get up, dust yourself off, and move on with your life. That's all you can do, whether it's an unexpectedly large or too quickly breaking of a wave, a ruthless, hostile rival..."

"Or ants," Michelle said, interrupting, looking at David.

David burst into laughter, and seeing him laugh at Michelle's comment and what had happened to him, the others there were comfortable enough to laugh with him.

"Yes, or ants, Michelle," David said, still laughing.

"Dust yourself off and get back in the fight," Michelle repeated, not having heard that expression before.

"Yes, we must get back in the fight," Donny said. "A bend in the road is not the end of the road, unless we fail to make the turn." Michelle and the others thought about those wise words for a moment.

After the silence, Donny said, "Hey listen, let's grab some food and go into the other room, I have a few things to show you. What time is it?"

"About a quarter after," replied Mrs. Martino.

"Good, we have a little time," Donny said. "David, there's plenty of food for you, and, yes, I know, it's mostly protein. We have chicken, fish, and there's some steak I bought that came from a grass-fed ranch. And everything's broiled and basted with real, virgin coconut oil. For the carbohydrate lovers in the rest of us, there are lots of sides and some cake and other goodies for dessert. So everyone, grab some food, and I'll meet you in the other room."

Donny had already eaten a little bit, but still had a plate of food that he picked up off the countertop and carried into the other room. He sat down at the farthest spot on the three-person couch from the kitchen, placing his food down gently on the table. He was followed in time by Professor Alphonse Laveran and Tia "Diana" Ross who sat on the right-side end of the four-seat sofa, adjacent to Donny, then by the Martinos, who sat next to them on the same sofa, then Lance and Sharon that sat next to each other on the same three-person couch as Donny on his left. After a little more time passed, Michelle, Kimmy and David, in that order, sat adjacent to Penny Martino in the three-seat love seat close to the kitchen. They each placed their lunch on the large table in front of them. Thus, seated from Donny's left going around clockwise in the U-shaped living-room suite was Sharon, Lance, the professor, Tia, Sal, Penny, Michelle, Kimmy and David.

Penny couldn't help but notice that since she had sat down next to Kimmy exposing the left side of her neck, Kimmy was staring at the large, rounded, rectangular, bruised callous that was now clearly visible from Kimmy's vantage point. As soon as Kimmy realized that Penny noticed her staring at the bruise, Kimmy stopped staring and focused her attention on her lunch.

"It's okay," Penny said to Kimmy, "lots of people look at my scar and wonder how it happened." Sal patted Penny's right lower thigh a couple times with his left arm.

Kimmy kind of blushed, and said timidly, "What is it, Penny, are you okay?"

Dr. Martino started answering for his wife, "Penny is the first violinist in the San Diego Symphony Orchestra; that scar, or callous, is a common occurrence in violinists that constantly practice or play."

Penny amplified her husband's answer by saying, "Almost all professional fiddlers have a deep bruise on the left side, just where the violin chinrest tucks in beneath the jaw," she used her left arm and hand, neck and chin, to mime holding the violin, with her right arm miming how she would work the bow, showing everyone how it came to be. "Friction and irritation over hours of daily practicing, year after year, makes a nice...a nice hickey."

Kimmy burst out laughing, as did other guests.

"A hickey," Kimmy said still laughing. She looked at Michelle and both laughed some more.

When her laughter subsided, she turned to Donny and sincerely said, "Donny, you've really made your house look so much better than how I remember it."

Donny quickly replied, "Oh, thanks Kimmy. It's home now for me."

"Where were you before?" asked Penny.

"Well," Donny began, "I did live here before the summer, but just off and on. I've been travelling a lot, for almost as long as I can remember, going to and from all my stores to make sure business runs smoothly. I'm really quite tired from all that work and want to settle down. Learning about everything you three have been through," he said looking and nodding at the three musketeers, "as a result of me not being here helped too with my decision."

"Your decision, Donny?" Tia curiously asked.

"Funny you should ask," Donny said chuckling a bit. "It should be on about now," he said picking up the master remote control to the plasma screens on either wall. He turned it on, and suddenly different spots on the two walls came alive.

There were three plasma screens on each of the two walls, and they were all tuned to the same station. A sports channel at first, showing a baseball game, then, synchronized to Donny pressing a button on the remote, it changed to a local newscast. Donny turned up the volume.

"...And that should be taken up at the next city hall meeting, Linda," the male reporter said from on location.

"Thank you Mark. Hopefully we can get a follow up report when that happens," said the female news anchor, Linda. Both Mark and Linda were well-dressed, good looking — appealing to a wide, diverse audience — and thin.

"I will stay on the developing story and report the status to you after the next meeting," Mark said sincerely.

"Thanks again Mark," Linda said. "And in local business news, San Diego's own Donny White is..."

The collective volume on all the different plasma screens were momentarily drowned out by nine voices that gave some variation of a surprised "Oh!" and "Donny!" They quickly quieted down and listened to the report.

It was evident that Donny had TIVO® installed, and was adept at using it, because he paused the broadcast, went back to the beginning of the clip, and pressed "play."

"And in local business news, San Diego's own Donny White is calling it quits. Reports indicate that he has sold his small dynasty of ten surf shops to the largest surfboard, surfboard rental and lesson chain for a cool fifteen million dollars. Donny White agreed to an interview which will be broadcast later tonight on the five o'clock news."

Donny turned off the plasma screens to applause from his guests.

"Congratulations," Professor Ross was first to say.

"That must be a load off your back," said Sal.

"Thank you, thanks so much," Donny said to them both.

"Won't you miss it all, Donny?" asked Penny.

"Not really," replied Donny. "I can always go surfing; just now I won't also have the headache of minding the store or the people that run it for me."

"So, what will you do now?" was the appropriate question asked by Sharon.

"Good question," Donny replied. "Quite frankly, I haven't made up my mind. I have a lot of options, but I'm going to take some time off, think about it, and make a decision sometime later. For now, I'm going to try to enjoy myself, and maybe help out some friends." Everyone smiled.

Donny looked over to the covered tank, what at least Kimmy, Michelle and David thought would be a fish tank — one, hopefully without parasites that replace the tongue of any fish in there — prompting an observant Penny to ask, "Hey Donny, what do you have there?"

"Yeah, poker was never one of my strong suits," Donny replied.

"Just please don't tell us that you bought Peter Falciparum's old fish collection," said a half-joking, half-serious David. Kimmy and Michelle giggled nervously; Lance and Sharon got the joke and cracked a smile. Tia and Penny looked at Michelle, Kimmy and David as if they didn't understand.

Michelle looked at them each in turn and said, "That guy had a bunch of fish in a large tank like that one with these evil little things that ate their tongues and then served as its replacement. We saw them. No joke." Both being married to doctors weren't too shocked; they did, however, let out a nervous kind of giggle.

"I did plan to share it with you all, especially you Michelle, Kimmy and David. Now's as good a time as any." Donny got up, walked over to the large tank, and moved it a little toward the open end of the U-shaped lining-room suite, as it was on wheels, though clearly heavy. He moved it a couple of feet and then stood in front of it, facing the group.

Donny said, "David and Michelle, I heard from Professor Ross that you visited Birch Aquarium when you first met and that, although you liked just about all the sea creatures there..."

"The Martians," Michelle shouted.

Donny continued, "Ah, yes, the Martians. Although you liked just about all the Martians there, there was one that you liked best of all."

"Naw, you didn't," David said in disbelief.

"Yes, I did," replied Donny. And he began to unveil the enormous tank from right to the left. As the cover came off, David and everyone else there could see that it was a group of leafy sea dragons. Five near-adult specimens.

"No way!" Michelle shouted as she ran up to the tank. Kimmy and David followed her. Penny and Sal walked over from the left of the large, neutral colored table, Sharon led

Lance from the right, followed by the professor and Tia right behind them.

"They're so beautiful," Michelle said with a sense of wonderment. David looked at her and smiled.

"Yes, they are beautiful," Tia said.

"What are they?" Penny asked.

"Leafy Sea Dragons," stated an erudite Michelle.

"Oh," replied Penny. "Yes, they sure are beautiful."

Not a word was spoken for a few moments; everyone there just stood and stared. Michelle grabbed hold of David's hand, Tia hugged the professor around the waist as he put his arm around her shoulder, and Dr. Martino gave Penny a kiss.

At some point Donny made eye contact with Sharon and then Lance. Donny, suddenly feeling their presence there as police officers instead of friends or guests, said, "You're off-duty, right?" Donny stood up straight and, not knowing the answer to that question added, "I have the required import permits, and they all came from captive-bred stock."

Lance, keeping a straight face, said, "Do you have the 905V form?" Sharon couldn't contain her laughter, relieving Donny of his angst.

"What's a 905V form," a nervously smiling Donny asked.

Hesitating briefly, and still giggling a little, Sharon answered, "Vicious animal."

Donny laughed briefly, as did everyone else.

Once the laughter subsided, Lance said, "Police in California are really never off duty, they're either police or not police, though, perhaps, you can say that sometimes we're off watch. Nevertheless, there's no reason to think that you've done anything wrong Donny, and, besides, these sorts of things are the jurisdiction of the US Customs and Border Protection within the Department of Homeland Security and the US Fish and Wildlife Service, all federal agencies. Now, Sharon and I can detain you while we call some of our friends at those agencies if you want; but, we have no reason to believe that you've done anything wrong. And, contrary to popular belief, we get no bonus points for making arrests."

"No, I think I'll take a pass," Donny said with a smile laughing a little. Lance and Sharon returned the smile. It was all in good fun.

"So," Donny said, "I can't really take care of these fish; the other announcement I was going to make is that I will be donating all of them to Skripps. The folks there are quite well prepared to care for them and you'll be able to visit them anytime the aquarium is open.

"Nice!" Michelle enthusiastically said.

"Beautiful!" Kimmy added. They looked at each other and giggled.

"Yes, that's so nice of you Donny," Tia said.

Donny continued, "Thanks, Tia. Thanks Michelle and Kimmy. But before I donate them, there's just one thing. What would you like to name them?" He pointed to the one closest to the glass on the bottom left and asked, "How about that one?"

Michelle and Kimmy looked at each other. Their telepathy was working.

"Shirley," Michelle said with confidence. Kimmy nodded her head in agreement. Even though none of the other guests save David knew Shirley, they nonetheless knew who she was and what had happened to her. In those few moments of silence, a sense of respect and closure permeated the room.

"Good," Donny replied after the brief interlude. "How about that one?" he said, pointing to the next leafy sea dragon that joined the one just named.

Kimmy, staring at the fish, turned to Donny and said, "Shirley."

"Shirley?" Donny asked.

"Yes, Shirley," Kimmy said.

"Shirley it is," confirmed Donny.

"Uh, how about that one," Donny said pointing to the one on top."

Michelle didn't take much time before she confidently said, "Shirley."

"I think I see a pattern developing here," Donny said. Everyone was looking at the fish; Michelle and Kimmy especially. Donny let them alone for a moment.

"I think it's safe to assume what the last two will be named," Donny finally said.

"Shirley," Kimmy said, holding Michelle's hand. Donny smiled.

Everyone stood there and stared at the leafy sea dragons for a while. Without saying a word, Donny headed back to his seat; others joined him in time, everyone going back to their same seat to finish eating their lunch. The five Shirleys would be visible for all to see from the couches.

"There's plenty more food in the kitchen if anyone wants seconds; help yourselves," Donny stated warmly. "There's plenty to drink too including coffee." The guests smiled, though no one left for more.

"So Donny, have you really not decided what you're going to spend your time on now?" Professor Ross asked.

"I have some ideas," Donny replied. "Did you ever toy with doing something else, professor?"

"I got into this racket probably like everyone else," Professor Ross said, captivating everyone with his prose, style, and temperament. "When I was young, I loved nature and wanted to understand what was happening. As I found answers to one question, I kept coming up with more questions, and answers to those, until eventually, found that I could use what I've learned to share with other people, and, eventually, make a living at it. No, I don't suppose I ever wanted to do anything else."

"I took biology in high school," Donny began, "but it was so...pardon me professor; but, the teachers when I went to school weren't as, uh, didn't have the same ability as you. I too loved learning about nature — and I still do, especially about those animals in the sea — but, I just couldn't find a way to make it work."

"A common criticism," Professor Ross said.

"I still don't even understand evolution," Donny confessed. "I always agree with people when they say that life evolved and is continuing to evolve; but, I really don't understand what that means."

And so, Professor Ross found himself in his natural habitat: all eyes on him with expectations of instant clarity. He smiled, gave his trademarked brief humble laugh, and began to explain the facts of life to this intimate audience.

"The modern theory of evolution — the fact of evolution — is easy to grasp, even though it's really a bunch of different theories," Professor Ross began. "It can be summarized in a single sentence. Life on Earth evolved gradually beginning with one primitive species that lived more than three-and-a-half billion years ago; it then branched out over time, throwing off many new and diverse species; and the mechanism for most, but not all, of evolutionary change is natural selection."

Donny, and everyone else, smiled at the professor's elegant, pithy definition.

Professor Ross continued, "Darwin did bring more theories to the public's attention, such as sexual selection, artificial selection, pangenesis — which is not valid — effect of use and disuse, and character divergence. However, when later authors referred to Darwin's theory they invariably had a combination of some of the following five theories in mind: First, evolution proper; second, common descent; then gradualism, multiplication of species, and, finally, natural selection."

"Now, evolution as such is the theory that the world is neither constant nor perpetually cycling but rather is steadily changing, and that organisms are transforming in time."

"The case of the species of Galapagos mockingbirds provided Darwin with an important new insight. The three species had clearly descended from a single ancestral species on the South American continent. From here it was only a small step to postulate that all mockingbirds were derived from a common ancestor—indeed, that every group of organisms descended from an ancestral species. This is Darwin's theory of common descent."

"It is probably correct to say that no other of Darwin's theories had such enormous immediate explanatory powers as common descent; none of Darwin's theories was accepted as enthusiastically either." Professor Ross paused, smiled, and stated, "With one exception."

Michelle chimed in with a smile, "The inclusion of people into the line of descent. No one wants to believe that we come from apes."

"Nice!" David said.

"Yes, very good Michelle," Professor Ross said quite comfortingly.

Kimmy was a little shocked at first, evidenced by her open mouth; but, that quickly changed to a smile, happily knowing that her best friend was so smart.

"I'm going to change my major and study biology," Michelle said with a smile.

"Beautiful!" was all David could say.

"You've been bit by the biology bug, eh?" Professor Ross asked.

"I'm hooked," Michelle responded to everyone. Then she looked directly at Professor Ross, who graciously looked back at her as she said, "I've been thinking about Mary Anning ever since I met you professor." His smile grew, as did everyone else's, as she continued with the children's rhyme, "She sells seashells on the seashore. The shells she sells are seashells, I'm sure, so if she sells seashells on the seashore, then I'm sure she sells seashore shells."

Professor Ross humbly laughed while saying, "Very nice Michelle," while others clapped for her.

"Yes, very nice," said Mrs. Ross.

"I don't think I've ever really said that whole tongue-twister before," added Dr. Martino.

"Oh, that was perfect," said Mrs. Martino.

Kimmy and David simply smiled, though David reached over and gave her a hug. As he let go, she leaned back into him and they kissed briefly.

"Sweet," said Donny subtly.

After a brief pause, Donny got the conversation back on track, "So, Professor, what were those last three theories?"

"Oh yeah, those," Professor Ross kiddingly said.

"Well, I don't know how I can follow such a wonderful performance of 'She sells seashells,' however, I think I can get through them quickly," the professor said. Everyone there, as did all his students and anyone else who heard him speak could attest to by their behavior, hung on his every word.

"Okay, Darwin's third theory was that evolutionary transformation always proceeds gradually, never in jumps. That was quite radical in its day, as virtually everyone at the time was an essentialist, meaning that the occurrence of new species, documented by the fossil record, could take place only be new origins, that is, by saltations. Nevertheless, nothing is said in the theory of gradualism about the rate at which the change may occur. Darwin was well aware of the fact that evolution could sometimes progress quite rapidly, but it could also contain periods of complete stasis.

"Moving along, in the multiplication of species theory, Darwin dealt with the explanation of the origin of the enormous organic diversity. It is estimated that there are five to ten million species of animals, one or two million species of plants, and perhaps a million or more species of fungi. Even though in Darwin's day only a fraction of this number was known, the problem of why there are so many species and how they originated was already present. In short, and it's much more complex than this, speciation is comprised of geographic isolation — whether on a different size of tree branch, different level of water, different height, different local, national, or world area – in which an organism finds itself needing to adapt in order to survive. It is there that develop the particulars that prevent mating by outsiders, at least in the sexually reproductive species."

"And last, but certainly not least, Darwin's theory of natural selection was his most daring, most novel theory. It dealt with the mechanism of evolutionary change, and, more particularly, how this mechanism could account for the seeming harmony and adaptation of the organic world. It attempted to provide a natural explanation in place of the supernatural one of natural theology. In Darwin's own words, '…in the struggle for existence which everywhere goes on, favorable variations would tend to be preserved and unfavorable ones to be destroyed.'"

"Of course, the theory of natural selection was the most bitterly resisted of all of Darwin's theories. But now, this last theory, the theory that is usually meant by the modern biologist when speaking of Darwinism, is firmly accepted by nearly everyone. Rival theories are so thoroughly refuted that they are no longer seriously discussed."

Everyone there was astounded, typical when Professor Ross spoke.

After a moment of comfortable silence, Donny said, "Professor, as I said, I never really understood evolution before today, and now, as you explained it, I think it finally clicked."

Professor Ross let out his humble laugh and smiled. "Thanks Donny. That's just an overview; it takes years of study in the field and in the laboratory to really appreciate what's going on. You know, most of my Ph.D. students over the past, say, twenty years, did their theses on problems of behavior. It's all about living animals and their attributes. Variation, adaptation, speciation, and evolutionary change cannot be fully understood unless you mix work in the lab and the library with work in the field. I think David has a novel idea worth developing. David, tell us what your plans are."

"Oh," said a somewhat surprised David to the group. "Well, yes, I am working on something."

Mrs. Ross—Tia—interrupted both of them with a curious comment, "Tell him, Alfie," she said sort of under her breath, yet as a demand. They clearly had discussed something beforehand.

Professor Ross looked at his wife in agreement, though pained. He looked at David, and, grimacing once more, said, "David, I, uh..." Professor Ross looked straight down. David said nothing; Michelle looked at David and sort of shrugged.

Professor Ross tried again, humbly admitting, "David, I own Lek's."

David didn't seem to mind, yet he was still a little surprised. Michelle and Kimmy seemed a little shocked and opened their mouths a little.

"I own Lek's and Mung's. Owned them for some time. But you have to know how sorry I am for what happened to you and your friends, and, especially Shirley." The professor was clearly looking for David's forgiveness.

David didn't give it much thought at all and said, "Professor, quite frankly I couldn't think of anyone else that could own those bars, let alone name them that, than you."

The professor was clearly relieved. "Thank you David," he said. "Fact is, I was never really able to make a living teaching. Before I met Tia, I thought it a good idea to go in with a few successful friends on these bars. Yes, I came up with the concepts and names, and they put up most of the money, and; well, the rest is history as they say. You really do forgive me, David, yes?"

"Of course," David said, with similar confidence, humility and smile as the professor.

"Me too," said Michelle.

"And me," added Kimmy.

The professor just kept smiling while holding his wife's hand. She gave him a kiss on his left cheek.

To break the seriousness of the moment, Donny asked, "Would anyone like some coffee?"

"Sure," the Martinos said, almost at the same time.

"I'll have some too," Lance replied.

"Coffee sounds good," Sharon said.

"Well, I'll be right back," Donny said, as he headed to the kitchen.

Tia Ross, still holding her husband's hand, proud that he told his pupil the truth, returned to the original subject, "So, David, yes, please do tell us about your thesis." Both the professor and Mrs. Ross made a great university couple: critical but supportive of each other, encouraging and distinguished.

"I can hear you from in here," Donny said from the kitchen. "Go ahead, David."

"Well, when I started eating mostly protein and fat, nearly all of what I heard centered on cholesterol. 'Aren't you worried about high cholesterol?' different people would ask me, especially health providers. But, c'mon, cholesterol is one of the most important molecules in your body, indispensable for the building of your cells and for producing stress and sex hormones as well as vitamin D. The idea that cholesterol in the blood should kill us if its concentration is a little higher than normal, seemed to me just as silly as to claim that yellow fingers cause lung cancer."

Dr. Martino heartily laughed as Donny came into the room and placed a large pot of coffee and two sugar and cream caddies on the table.

"I'll grab some cups," Donny said.

David continued, "So I started doing the research. Human-like atherosclerotic lesions could be induced in pigeons, for instance, fed on corn and corn oil, and atherosclerotic lesions were observed occurring naturally in wild sea lions and seals, in pigs, cats, dogs, sheep, horses, reptiles, and rats, and even in baboons on diets that were almost exclusively vegetarian. None of the studies did much to implicate either animal fat or cholesterol."

"And by cholesterol, I mean the waxy steroid of fat that is manufactured by the liver or intestines if we don't get enough of it from animal sources. If we do get enough from outside sources, then we produce less of it ourselves."

Donny returned with two stacks of five medium sized, white coffee cups and placed them on the table. Everyone grabbed a cup, including Donny, though it was Sharon that grabbed the coffee pot first and poured some into her cup. She passed the large coffee pot to her left, which, in order clockwise remember, would be Lance, Professor Ross, Tia, Salvatore, Penny, Michelle, Kimmy and David, who was about to continue where he left off.

"Here, let me help the discussion with a visual," David said as he reached for and picked up one of the sugar and cream caddies off of the coffee table. He grabbed a packet each of the different brand of sweeteners and then placed the caddy back onto the table on his right. He then put each of the four packets onto the table in front of him: a non-branded, real white sugar packet, a yellow packet of Splenda®, a pink packet of Sweet 'N Low®, and a blue packet of Equal®.

David continued, "Pretend that each of these differently colored packets contains the same substance, cholesterol. Instead of different colors, pretend that each are a different size. Cholesterol is transported in the body via lipoproteins, and here are the four main ones: the pink one will represent intermediate-density lipoprotein, abbreviated IDL, the blue packet will represent low-density lipoprotein, abbreviated LDL, and the white packet will represent very low-density lipoprotein, abbreviated VLDL." David slid each of three packets on the table toward his coffee cup and then opened up the packets one by one and poured their contents into it.

"Cholesterol is then transported back to the liver to be recycled by high-density lipoprotein, abbreviated HDL; we'll let this yellow packet represent the HDL." David lifted the yellow packet with his right hand, touched it to the coffee cup, and then brought it back toward himself. He opened up one end and poured the contents into Michelle's cup.

"So, that's why they have been named either good or bad cholesterol. Bad when it's the lipoprotein carrying cholesterol to the rest of the body, and good when it's the lipoprotein carrying cholesterol back to the liver. But, in reality, there is only one cholesterol; the labels "good" and "bad" refer strictly to the carriers. But there's very little evidence that any of those carriers are either good or bad. And there's nothing evil about cholesterol itself. Without cholesterol, we'd still be plants."

"What I found is that people with high cholesterol live the longest. This statement seems so incredible that it takes a long time to clear one´s brainwashed mind to fully understand its importance. Yet the fact that people with high cholesterol live the longest emerges clearly from many scientific papers."

"High cholesterol protects against infection. For example, a team in the Netherlands injected purified endotoxin into normal mice, and into mice that had LDL-cholesterol four times higher than normal. Whereas all normal mice died, they had to inject eight times as much endotoxin to kill the mice with the high LDL-cholesterol. And in another experiment researchers injected live bacteria and found that twice as many mice with high LDL-cholesterol survived compared with normal mice."

"For many years scientists suspected that viruses and bacteria participate in the development of atherosclerosis. Research within this area exploded during the last couple of decades and now about a hundred reviews of the issue have been published in medical journals. Due to the widespread preoccupation with cholesterol and other lipids, there has been little general interest in the subject, however, and few doctors know much about it."

Dr. Martino agreed with David, "I've read about it, David; but, the guidelines that I have to follow in my practice are almost ironclad. If I try to be creative in treating patients, I could lose my job or get sued or both."

David answered, "Yes, that's what I hear from medical doctors. Nevertheless, the demonizing of high cholesterol is obviously in conflict with the idea that high cholesterol protects against infections. Both ideas cannot be true."

After a brief pause, David continued his discussion, "If high cholesterol were the most important cause of atherosclerosis, people with high cholesterol should be more atherosclerotic than people with low cholesterol. But this is very far from the truth."

"If high cholesterol were the most important cause of atherosclerosis, lowering of cholesterol should influence the atherosclerotic process in proportion to the degree of its lowering. But this does not happen."

"If high cholesterol were the most important cause of cardiovascular disease, it should be a risk factor in all populations, in both sexes, at all ages, in all disease categories, and for both heart disease and stroke. But this is not the case."

"High cholesterol is associated with longevity in old people. It is difficult to explain away the fact that during the period of life in which most cardiovascular disease occurs and from which most people die, high cholesterol occurs most often in people with the lowest mortality. How is it possible that high cholesterol is harmful to the artery walls and causes fatal coronary heart disease if those whose cholesterol is the highest live longer than those whose cholesterol is low? The answer, of course, is that it's all a myth."

"If cholesterol was going to be the subject of my thesis, I'd conclude that anything enabling the reproduction and growth of microbial parasites — carbohydrates, nicotine, mental stress, and low vitamin B, C and D levels; but, not protein, fat or cholesterol intake—are primary risk factors for cardiovascular disease. Cholesterol and its carriers are protective."

It was Professor Ross that was now absorbed on David's words. Both he and Tia were brimming with pride at their protégé. Michelle and Kimmy were proud too, but, for a different reason. Others were engaged, albeit skeptical.

Donny said, "David, none of my doctors have ever told me anything like that. They tell me to eat low-fat foods and check my cholesterol regularly, which they say is normal. I'm in my sixties and in the best shape of my life, and I hope to continue, for a little while anyway." Donny smiled, and it brought smiles and empathetic looks from most of the guests.

"But you're saying to 'fuggeddaboudit,'" Donny said imitating a popular expression, garnering laughs and more smiles from guests, "to stop having my cholesterol checked and just get on with my life. You're saying to stop eating carbs and eat more fat and protein. I really don't know how to make sense of that considering how healthy I am."

David asked him, "Is it really so hard to believe that parasites are to blame for heart disease?"

"Yes, it is."

"What do you suppose is the root cause of ulcers?"

"That's easy," Donny replied confidently. "Stress."

David remained silent for a moment as Sharon shook her head "no." She said, "It's bacteria, Donny. My mom had an ulcer, and the doctor said it was caused by bacteria."

"Yes, bacteria," Dr. Martino said. *Helicobacter pylori.*"

Donny looked at Sharon, then the doctor. He grinned, shaking his head in defeat.

Dr. Martino smiled, chuckling to himself, then, turning to David, said, "You're saying that you're *not* going to write your thesis on cholesterol. All that work and knowledge and that's not your thesis? That certainly begs the question, what are you going to work on? I can't wait to hear more." Everyone nodded their head in agreement.

David calmly and confidently smiled, eliciting the interest and open-mindedness in his audience that would allow him to convey the new information, and them to understand it.

"Dr. Martino, Donny, everyone, I think I have some answers," David began. "We, all of us, do much of the time, perhaps all of the time, construct our concepts in shifting sands. Even in the best of all possible biological worlds our knowledge must always be incomplete and we often do not even know what it is that's missing. Certainty eludes us and we should be humble rather than assertive."

"Here, Here," Dr. Martino said.

David continued, "Nothing in biology makes sense except in the light of evolution. Since becoming diabetic, I thought that the more relevant research is whether or not humans are relatively adapted to the carbohydrates we eat." By their facial expressions, Professor Ross and Dr. Martino seemed to agree that that was the relevant work.

"So first, let's define the word 'adaptation.' I'll try to keep it brief." Michelle hung on David's every word. So too did everyone else.

"Remember, the target of natural selection is the individual within a species. Adaptation, as measured by evolutionary success, consists of a greater ecological-physiological efficiency of an individual than is achieved by most other members of the population or at least by the average. Adaptation is achieved by the greater survival or higher reproductive success of certain individuals owing to the fact that they possess ecological-physiological traits not, or only partially, shared by other individuals of their population, traits that are useful in the struggle for existence."

David glanced at Professor Ross as if looking for confirmation; the professor simply nodded his head and smiled.

"I'll need a dictionary to proceed," David said. "Donny, you wouldn't happen to have one, do you?"

"Sure, I have a dictionary, hold on a sec." He got up, walked to the hallway by the semi-circular stairway on his right, and disappeared. The group of nine remained silent during his temporary absence. Michelle grabbed then squeezed David's hand; they looked at each other and smiled. David gathered his thoughts.

Donny returned with a huge, thick hard-bound book. "Here you go, David," he said, handing him the dictionary.

"Oh, great. That'll work, here," David handed the thick book back to Donny who accepted it. "Could you be so kind as to look up and tell us what the word 'psychosis' means?"

"Sure. Let's see..." he said turning through the pages. "Here it is. Psychosis: (1) abnormal condition of the mind. (2) A severe mental disorder, with or without organic damage, characterized by derangement of personality and loss of contact with reality causing deterioration of normal social functioning."

"Good," David said trying hard to be sincere and not patronizing. "Abnormal condition of the mind. Now tell us what the word 'psycho' means."

"Okay," Donny said, quickly finding the word. "Psycho: a slang word for a person who is psychotic."

"Yeah, that's what it is, a slang word for a person who is psychotic, thanks Donny," David said sincerely.

"No problem," Donny said, closing the book and putting it on the table.

"So, let me try to coherently tell you what I'm going to be working on," David said, finding it difficult to not look at the professor. Naturally, Professor Ross gave him the "you can do it" smile, enabling David's confidence, and he was on his way.

"For my thesis, I'm going to take the prefix 'glyco,' meaning sweetness or sugar, and add the letters 's,' 'i' and 's' to it, making the word 'glycosis.' Similar to psychosis, the word glycosis will be defined as the abnormal condition of sugar in the body. Of course, since it's the added sugar that I'm proposing to be the cause of the problems, I'll add that glycosis is a physical disorder comprised of too much glucose in the blood, abbreviated by the capital letters 'BG,' which stands for blood glucose. As some of you know, the good doctor especially, although low blood sugar is acutely more serious, high blood sugar can lead to complications such as extreme hunger and thirst, fat, muscle or bone loss, frequent urination, depression, dementia, agitation, lethargy, loss of vision, loss of sensation, immune suppression, renal failure, liver and cardiovascular disease, gangrene, coma and death."

Dr. Martino quickly responded, "It sounds like you're describing type one diabetes, David. I treat many, many people in my practice that have diabetes. What you're saying is that you have a new word to name it, glycosis."

"That's only part of it, Dr. Martino. Yes, glycosis can refer to diabetics when their blood sugar is high," David responded with a similar smile that Professor Ross made famous. "What I'm also proposing is an explanation for why some people stay slim and healthy throughout life and others develop a deranged metabolism given the same carbohydrate load."

"When doctors, no offense," he said looking at Dr. Martino, "don't understand the cause of metabolic condition, they oftentimes refer to it as genetics, when scientists can't pinpoint a reason for an animal's behavior, they sometimes resort to just calling it instinct. You all probably know a slim, healthy person that eats far more than their fair share of cereal with milk in the morning, sandwiches made of white bread with potato chips for lunch, ice cream for dessert, and a thousand more calories for dinner made up of those same carbohydrates and a variety more, plus some sort of sugary drink, and still manage to look good at the beach."

He looked around at Michelle, Kimmy, Dr. Martino and his wife, Professor Ross and his wife, Lance, Sharon and Donny White. They were all shaking their heads "yes." Some were even looking at Donny. Donny smiled, giggled even.

David continued, "Although I'm happy for all those people that can eat whatever they want and not gain an ounce — yes, it all sounds so delicious — it was at first a disappointment."

"At first?" Penny asked.

David smiled and answered, "Yeah, at first. But then, after thinking about it for a while, I was able to convert that disappointment into a novel theory. Now, I don't mean a theory similar to a hypothesis; no, I mean something that explains reality better than anything else. It's true that I will need to gather data in support of the theory, and I do plan to present it as part of my thesis to Professor Ross," Professor Ross smiled as David said this, "but, I think that the theory is already ripe with observable data."

"Recall how we defined adaptation. Adaptation, as measured by evolutionary success, consists of a greater ecological-physiological efficiency of an individual than is achieved by most other members of the population or at least by the average. Adaptation is achieved by the greater survival or higher reproductive success of certain individuals owing to the fact that they possess ecological-physiological traits not, or only partially, shared by other individuals of their population, traits that are useful in the struggle for existence."

"What I am going to be theorizing is that some people in the human population are better adapted than others at utilizing processed sugars. That best explains why there are some people that stay slim and healthy throughout life and others develop a deranged metabolism given the same carbohydrate load. It is because they are better adapted."

David was encouraged by the engaged look on the faces of everyone in the room. He could see that they were thinking about what he had said, that the machinery in their heads were cranking away, and that they were all getting it.

David continued, "So let me tie that adaptation to the word I created, and express my thesis in such a way as to be falsifiable or not, the hallmark of a good theory. I define glycosis as the quantifiable maladaptation to one or more specific carbohydrates in a given species. For example, if a species that uses glucose as its sole food source is fed a different carbohydrate, the survival rate would serve as the measure of adaptation or maladaptation to that carbohydrate, depending on whether the value was high or low. If a hundred percent of the population survives, then there is no adaptational benefit to any select few and the species as a whole is adapted. If they all die out, then clearly they are completely maladapted."

"Quantifying adaptation in humans is complex because sugars are not essential macronutrients..."

Kimmy interrupted him, "Wait, you mean we don't have to eat carbohydrates?"

"Well, Kimmy, no, *you* can eat all the carbohydrates you want apparently and still look great," David said as Kimmy giggled a little to him then Michelle. "But humans on the whole have no essential need to eat any carbohydrates. We need amino acids—protein—and some fat, especially DHA and EPA, types of fat that you can find in fish oil, for example, and vitamins; but, we never need to eat carbohydrates."

"And by carbohydrates," David said, "I'm referring to an organic compound consisting only of carbon, hydrogen, and oxygen. Carbohydrates are divided into four groupings. Oligosaccharides and polysaccharides are commonly referred to as complex carbohydrates and serve as fiber and storage of energy, like starch, and as structural components, like cellulose in plants. Most complex carbohydrates reduce to simple carbohydrates during digestion. Most, I say, because humans can't digest cellulose because we don't have cellulase, the enzyme necessary to break down cellulose. Herbivores, on the other hand, like cattle, house bacteria in one of four compartments in the stomach for the purpose of digesting cellulose. Or maybe it's the other way around: bacteria use herbivores as food delivery devices."

Professor Ross and Dr. Martino laughed as they glanced at each other and then back to David.

After pausing, David continued, "Monosaccharides and disaccharides are referred to as simple sugars, and often end in the suffix 'ose.' Blood sugar is the monosaccharide glucose and table sugar is the disaccharide sucrose. In food, sugar almost exclusively refers to sucrose, which primarily comes from sugar cane and sugar beet. Other sugars are used in industrial food preparation, but are usually known by more specific names like glucose, fructose or fruit sugar, high fructose corn syrup, etc."

"Again, we never need to eat carbohydrates. Without carbs in the diet, the brain and central nervous system will run on ketone bodies, converted from dietary fat and from the fatty acids released by the adipose tissue; on glycerol, also released from the fat tissue with the breakdown of triglycerides into free fatty acids; and on glucose, converted from the protein in the diet. Since a carbohydrate-restricted diet, unrestricted in calories, will, by definition, include considerable fat and protein, there will be no shortage of fuel for the brain."

Dr. Martino chimed in again, "All true, David, all true. I love your theory; but, don't you think that eliminating carbohydrates from the diet is impractical?"

"Good question, Dr. Martino," David began. "I would agree with you that it's not easy. But it is practical. For diabetics it's essential. And it's simple. And another hallmark of a good theory is that it is simple."

"The real benchmark to use is what we ate before the agricultural revolution of ten-thousand or so years ago. There are four lines of evidence that have been used to reconstruct the evolution of subsistence of human ancestry. They are the interpretation of anatomy by analogy with living primates and other mammals, the material artifacts at archeological sites, and, more recently, direct chemical analysis of the hominid remains themselves. We also know what present-day hunter-gatherer societies — humans are essentially hunter-gatherers — use as their diet. On average, they consume a diet of sixty-five percent animal food and thirty-five percent plant food."

"Now, contrast that with the fact that seventy-two percent of the total daily energy consumed by all people in the United States is made up of dairy products, cereals, refined sugars, refined vegetable oils, and alcohol, all items that didn't exist until about ten-thousand years ago. The word for the difference between what we evolved to eat and what we currently eat is called 'discordance,' and that discordance is due to the fact that our cultural evolution has paced faster than our biological evolution. Our ancient, genetically determined biology—for most of us as I'm proposing—has not caught up with the nutritional, cultural, and activity patterns of contemporary western populations, and thus, many of the so-called diseases of civilization have emerged. Of course, there are lots of nutritional problems with the current western diet, like the acid versus base loads of foods, the sodium versus potassium levels, and more; but, the number one problem is the glycemic load of our diets. You're all familiar with the glycemic index, right?"

Most of the guests shook their head "yes," but Michelle and Kimmy didn't look like they knew.

David smiled and continued, "The glycemic index is a relative comparison of the blood-glucose-raising potential of various foods or combination of foods based on equal amounts of carbohydrate in the food. Refined grain and sugar products nearly always maintain much higher glycemic loads than unprocessed fruits and vegetables. Unrefined wild-plant foods typically exhibit low glycemic indices."

"Within the past two decades, substantial information has accumulated showing that long-term consumption of high glycemic load carbohydrates can adversely affect metabolism and health. Specifically, chronic hyperglycemia and hyperinsulinemia, induced by high glycemic load carbohydrates may elicit a number of hormonal and physiological changes that promote insulin resistance. Diseases of insulin resistance are frequently referred to as 'diseases of civilization,' and include obesity, coronary heart disease, type two diabetes, hypertension, acne, gout, some cancers, and many others. Diseases of insulin resistance are rare or absent in hunter-gatherer and other less-westernized societies living and eating in their traditional manner."

"In addition to high glycemic load carbohydrates, other new foods may contribute to the insulin resistance underlying metabolic syndrome diseases. Milk, yogurt, and ice cream, despite having relatively low glycemic loads raise insulin levels similar to that of to white bread."

"Fructose is a major constituent in high fructose corn syrup and maintains a low glycemic index; but, paradoxically may worsen insulin sensitivity and promote insulin resistance. In fact, about forty percent of the total energy in the typical US diet is supplied by foods that may promote insulin resistance and these foods were rarely or never consumed by average citizens as little as two-hundred years ago."

Kimmy asked, "So, are you saying that some people can still eat those things or that we should all stop eating them?"

"Well, I don't know the answer to that question because I don't know what the actual glycosis level is. It could be that some people can indeed eat any kind of carbohydrate they want. If you're obese, diabetic, or have cancer, you probably shouldn't be eating most carbohydrates save green leafy vegetables. Alternatively, health consequences take varying time periods. For example, lack of oxygen is lethal in minutes, scurvy develops after months of inadequate vitamin C, and insufficient dietary calcium commonly takes decades to produce clinical osteoporosis. Deviation from our ancestral nutrition and exercise can produce ill effects during early life; but, many individuals appear outwardly healthy well into middle adulthood and even beyond. We can expect that, despite our adaptability, most of us will eventually have to pay the piper. The evolutionary hypothesis proposes that chronic degenerative diseases are the price."

David paused to gauge the interest of his listeners. Although silent, they had all been intensely following his every word. Now that he paused, Sal and Penny, Lance and Sharon, the professor and Tia, and Michelle, Kimmy and Donny looked at each other, and then at their new friends around the table, understanding David's enlightening discussion to this point and agreeing with various types and degrees of body language.

Donny said, "Would anyone care for some dessert?" Everyone laughed; no one took him up on his offer.

As the giggling subsided, David continued, "An analogy might help. While I was in the hospital I saw a show on TV that aired some old commercials. One of those commercials had a big impact on me and in the ensuing few weeks helped me to devise an analogy. The commercial was for 'Off!,' a name-brand mosquito repellent. In the ad, they showed two bare arms, each connected to a live human, being placed consecutively into a long, glass container full of hungry mosquitoes. The first arm, which can be thought of as the experimental arm, was sprayed with a generous amount of 'Off!,' and the second, which can be thought of as the control arm, wasn't sprayed with anything. Not surprisingly, the first arm, the one sprayed with 'Off!,' suffered fewer, if any, mosquito bites than that of the bare arm. This analogy can be related to diabetes in that the mosquito bites represent the complications and the 'Off!' represents the insulin. Carbohydrates are equivalent to the actual sticking of the arm into the mosquito-filled glass container."

David noticed that everyone was following his discussion, and paused momentarily before dropping the bomb, "Clearly it would be ideal to simply not be sticking your arm into a container full of hungry mosquitoes." That set off some laughter from his engaged audience.

David continued, "Yes, 'Off!' would come in handy if you're hiking in the woods; but, how often do you do that? Similarly, for diabetics, and for the obese too—because insulin is the only hormone that stores fat and carbohydrates are the only macronutrient that raises insulin—doesn't it make sense to, at a minimum, reduce your intake of carbohydrates?"

Dr. Martino, through his laughter, responded, "Okay, okay, David, you win. It's not easy, but it is supremely practical and simple. Just one more thing, though, what about the theory of the thrifty gene? Do you think that there's any truth that somehow obese people have an advantage over skinny people, allowing them to survive in periods of famine?"

"Another great question from the man that saved my life. I've read about it, and I do have an answer for you." David looked around at everyone there; they seemed to want to know the answer. He asked, "It may take a couple minutes explaining; is everyone okay with that?"

"Good here," Donny said.

"Go," said Kimmy.

"Green light!" added Michelle.

"Yes, please go ahead, David," Dr. Martino said.

"Knock yourself out," said Sharon.

Professor Ross, noticing heads nodding "yes," said, "Looks like it's unanimous David, you have the floor."

Confidently then, David began, "The genetic paradox that James Neel—the man responsible for the 'thrifty gene' hypothesis—sought to address was this: diabetes conferred a significant reproductive, and thus evolutionary, disadvantage to anyone who had it; yet the populations Neel studied had diabetes in such high frequencies that a genetic predisposition to develop diabetes seemed plausible. Neel sought to unravel the mystery of why genes that promote diabetes had not been naturally-selected out of the population's gene pool."

"Neel originally proposed that a genetic predisposition to develop diabetes was adaptive to the feast and famine cycles of

Paleolithic human existence, allowing humans to fatten rapidly and profoundly during times of feast in order that they might better survive during times of famine."

"While Neel considered the thrifty genotype notion worth further investigation, in the early sixties he also proposed a counter-hypothesis, namely that the frequency of obesity and diabetes is a relatively recent phenomenon in which case the question should be 'what changes in the environment are responsible for the increase?'"

"In the decades following the publication of his first paper on the thrifty genotype hypothesis, Neel investigated the frequency of diabetes and, increasingly, obesity in a number of other populations, and sought out observations that might disprove or discount his thrifty gene hypothesis."

"Neel's further investigations cast doubt on the thrifty genotype hypothesis. If a propensity to develop diabetes were an evolutionary adaptation, then diabetes would have been a long standing disease in those populations currently experiencing a high frequency of diabetes. However, Neel found no evidence of diabetes among these populations earlier in the century. And when he tested younger members of these populations for glucose intolerance—which might have indicated a predisposition for diabetes—he found none."

"Moreover, one of the most significant problems for the thrifty gene idea is that it predicts that modern hunter gatherers should get fat in the periods between famines. Yet data on the body mass index of hunter-gatherer and subsistence agriculturalists clearly show that between famines they do not deposit large fat stores."

"Again, Neel wrote that modern, very-high levels of obesity and diabetes among formerly native populations were a relatively recent phenomenon most likely caused by changes in diet. Given that some thrifty gene populations, like the Inuit, experienced a rise in obesity and diabetes in conjunction with a *reduction* of the proportion of fat and protein in their diets, Neel surmised that the dietary causes of obesity and diabetes lay in carbohydrate consumption, specifically the use of highly refined carbohydrates."

"Oh," said Penny.

"Oooo," added Tia. Sal was shaking his head in agreement and Professor Ross was still smiling, proud of his student that had come into his own.

As David finished that last sentence, he offered a humble smile, just as Professor Ross would do, signaling the end of the thrifty gene speech.

Professor Ross said, "Very nice David. I'd like to see your manuscript as soon as possible." David shook his head "okay."

"Me too, David," Dr. Martino added.

"Beautiful speech, David, just beautiful!" Penny said. "That will make a great thesis; and you're already able to defend it."

Kimmy and Michelle each had a big smile on their faces, quite impressed with his confidence and ability to verbally articulate his thoughts.

"You're going to make a great professor, David," Michelle said with Kimmy nodding her head in agreement.

"Yes, you will," Donny added.

Tia Ross looked at her husband, the professor, who looked back at her, each accurately understanding the other's thoughts. She thought David's speech and professorial potential was due to her husband's leadership. Professor Ross knew that his leadership derived from his wife's presence, love and support; in short, from her leadership.

"Thanks professor, thanks Dr. Martino, thanks Penny," David said as he looked at each of them in turn. "Thanks Michelle, Donny, Kimmy, Tia. I really appreciate it; but, my thesis still needs some work. I'm trying to delve deeper into one particular species, us, and, although there's a great deal of explanatory power in the theory, I'll need to gather some data."

"You need to add some flesh to the skeleton," Professor Ross stated humbly, with that subtle smile.

David, reproducing the professor's mannerisms, continued, "Recall that I define glycosis as the quantifiable maladaptation to one or more specific carbohydrates in a given species. If a species that uses glucose as its sole food source is fed a different carbohydrate, the survival rate would serve as the measure of adaptation or maladaptation to that carbohydrate, depending on whether the value was high or low. Quantifying it in humans is complex because sugars are not essential — we get all the glucose we need from our livers — but, human adaptation to carbohydrates as an *energy source* can theoretically be calculated."

"One idea is to calculate it by subtracting the sugar industry's net income from the total economic burden of associated afflictions, like obesity, diabetes, cancer, etcetera. That could be done on a local, regional, state, country, international, or even global basis. The trick is to find the data — consistent data — to include in the analysis. A negative number would indicate humans in the area studied are relatively adapted to the energy source. A positive value would imply maladaptation, which would mean that individuals in that group — and the group as a whole — are relatively glycotic."

"Absolutely fascinating," Dr. Martino said, his wife nodding her head in agreement. "Let me know if I can help in any way. I do have access to some medical libraries and other resources that may not be available at the University."

"Thanks so much Dr. Martino," David replied, "I sure will take you up on that offer. I think I'm on to something; but, it'll take some work, and, well, some time."

"Yes, I imagine it will," the doctor responded.

"I'll also be presenting evidence that shows sugar in an altogether different light." David had everyone's complete attention once again.

"It's a parasite, right David?" Michelle asked, though she knew the answer, as they had previously discussed it at length.

David let out a subtle laugh and smile in nearly the same style as the Professor, then replied, "Yes, that's right princess."

"Princess," Michelle said beaming; she looked at Kimmy and both giggled.

"Well, to be exact," David said, "I'm saying that sugar is the tool, the lure of the parasite. The actual parasite is any of a number of plants that produce sugar, like species of sugar cane and corn—which are grasses—and the sugar beet, a tuber. Corn is an annual; that is, it germinates, flowers and dies in one year or season. So too are domestic grains, wheat and rice. Sugar beets are biennial, taking two years to complete their lifecycle, and the sugar canes are all perennial, living for years."

"Now, some plants produce fruit or nectar that they use to entice animals—we can also think of it as a bribe—to take and spread their seeds or disseminate pollen. The actual mechanism is that, in the case of seeds, an animal eats the fruit and the seeds inside it; the seeds survive the digestive process of the animal, and, days later, are deposited when the animal, uh, goes to the bathroom. With nectar, while an animal dines, plants deposit their pollen—mobile, single-use sperm production and delivery devices—on them by means of a range of elegant, even outrageous devices. An animal in turn then brings that pollen to another plant in the process of seeking even more nectar. Pollinators may never know that they're being used as such; but, even if they did, nectar is such a prized delicacy that I don't think they would ever mind."

"In the relationship between sugar and humans, I'm saying that sugar cane, corn, and sugar beets, to name the most abundant sugar producing parasites, lure some of us to eat the sugar because it tastes so good, albeit we don't spread their seeds when we go to the bathroom nor do we simply serve as pollinators. No, much worse, members of our species have devised a complex division of labor to face the ever increasing sugar demand. Although there's some overlap, we've separated into consumers that may or may not be glycotic, and producers that do exponentially more work to produce sugar beets, corn and sugar cane than any bee, bat, butterfly, hummingbird or moth can or would do, some dedicating their whole existence to that task, in exchange for wealth."

"Parasites manipulate us, altering our behavior in such a way as to get us to spend our time reproducing them. As if increase of appetite had grown by what it fed on, we eat more and more sugar, nurture the plants that produce sugar more and more, harvest them more and more, and continue that cycle more and more. All the while pursuing those ends, they benefit, and our health — at least those folks that are maladapted to it — declines. We are symbionts — the sugar-producing plants and humans live together — only they benefit at our expense. They are influential external parasites and we by definition are their hosts, their addicted, deteriorating hosts."

"Think about how much of these organisms we produce each year. Worldwide, we humans produce two billion metric tons of sugar cane, a billion metric tons of corn and about a half a billion metric tons of sugar beets."

"Now, of course, not all of that converts directly to sugar. Both sugar beets and sugar cane have a high water content, about seventy-five percent of the total weight of the plants. The sugar content of sugar cane ranges from ten to fifteen percent of the total weight, while that of sugar beets is between thirteen and eighteen percent. So, assuming seven billion people worldwide, that's more than a quarter-pound of sugar produced per day per person. And that doesn't include the high fructose corn syrup which is now nearly equal to regular sugar consumption. Add in the billion metric tons of corn — of which, admittedly, a large portion goes to produce ethanol, an energy source — and a billion metric tons each of wheat and rice, and we rapidly approach the potential for one to two pounds of edible carbohydrate production per person per day. Although rice and wheat do provide some protein, the protein and fat content of both beets and cane sugar is nil, a big fat donut hole."

Surprisingly, it was Kimmy, remembering what John London — Peter Falciparum — had said weeks ago, who then said, "Parasites might be the ultimate life-form; innovative and strategic, making a living off the talents and energy of others."

Totally unexpected. Even the professor was stunned.

The momentary and slightly strange silence was broken by the professor's reply, "Yes, Kimmy, it's an effective and efficient way of life." She then understood first-hand what it was like to be on the receiving end of the distinguished professor's praise. Perhaps she too would now major in biology.

All eyes went back to David, still the center of attention. He shrugged, gave a look of real understanding to Kimmy, then to Michelle and said, "Yes, I too learned a lot from our assailant; he altered my behavior."

Just then, Dr. Martino, who had also been relatively quiet during the afternoon, added some insight, "This discussion reminds me a lot about the flu virus, influenza. If you close your eyes and say the word aloud, slowly, it sounds lovely: *in-flu-ennn-za.* It would make a good name for a pleasant, ancient Italian village. Unfortunately, in the early twentieth century, a particularly virulent outbreak of the flu killed something like fifty million people. Even in years without an epidemic, influenza takes a brutal toll. Each winter, about thirty-six thousand people die of the flu in the United States alone; somewhere between a quarter million and a half million people die worldwide. Yes, influenza may sound elegant, but the word itself is Italian for…influence."

The room became silent again for a moment, after which David continued, "Thank you Dr. Martino. We've established that parasites influence their hosts. Physical parasites, be they plant or animal, or human social parasite, as in one certain arrested, accused, though dismissed *fiend*, influence those members of a species that are maladapted in some way, and/or, perhaps, those maladapted are attracted to the parasite. After all, not every member of a given species gets infected by the same type of freeloader."

"Parasites alter the behavior of their hosts, getting them to serve their interests. For example, those that try to eat just a little sugar are usually surprised and discouraged when after a few moments they crave more. It's no coincidence that sugar is sweet; sweetness is the most effective and efficient form of bribe the world knows. Once ensnared in the taste, victims become addicted, demanding more and more, driving still other people to plant, grow, harvest and sell more and more sugar, at both their expense, to the benefit of the plants, which the consumers and suppliers conspired with each other to reproduce. It would be win-win if we were bees or hummingbirds that simply spread a plant's pollen with little investment or danger; but, we humans toil away at great cost in terms of our health, work, and time. We wind up favoring the plant's interests at the expense of our own. Besides, again, we don't even need it; our livers convert some of the protein we eat to glucose."

He paused before saying, "All the negative comments about parasites aside, they can also serve as a major stimulus for other life forms to intensify a given function or to completely change it: to evolve. In short, parasites can contribute to the increasing complexity of other life forms, while they themselves adapt."

"Thus," said David confidently, sensing that his audience was about to put it all together, "there is a solution, a way to beat them." He paused one last time, satisfied watching Michelle and Kimmy — and the others there too — change their expressions over time from one of pain and disappointment, to admiration, and, finally, to understanding.

David looked directly at Michelle who, as she thought about it for a moment, came upon a clear conclusion, as if suddenly telepathic lines of communication opened up between them. Her eyes filled a little with tears, and although she looked terribly pained, she was actually filled with hopefulness as she asked, "Love, David?"

David, looking at Michelle, smiled and calmly said, "Yes, Michelle, love." She reached out for David's right hand with her left at nearly the same time he was reaching for her left with his right. "And knowledge. Knowledge of what to stay away from, as much as what to eat instead."

Enlightenment filled the room. Professor Ross and Tia, Salvatore and Penny, to some extent Lance and Sharon, and even Kimmy and Donny in an innocent sort of way, either held hands, moved closer together, or simply made eye contact.

"So what do we eat?" asked Penny.

David had done the research and was ready with a response, however, he offered his reply as if improvising, "The simple answer is for us to eat natural foods made up of predominantly protein and fat. I think it makes sense that those of us maladapted to carbohydrates should probably do our best to avoid them or eat them sparingly..." Everyone smiled with near-perfect understanding; some giggled.

David smiled and giggled a little himself, continuing, "When you do eat carbs, choose mostly leafy green vegetative parts. Natural fruits should only serve as turbochargers, if you need the extra energy for running or cycling and the like. No processed sugar."

"For protein, consider beef from grass-fed cattle, goat, deer, etcetera. And by the way, saying 'grass-fed cattle' seems strange to me because that's what they're supposed to eat; the technical term is 'graminivore,' meaning a herbivorous animal that feeds primarily on true grasses. Feeding them anything else, like corn—which although is *from* a grass, is technically the fruit, and thus a different carbohydrate—might be the bane of the livestock's own glycosis, not to mention the cause of consequential damages that await those that feed on them."

He took a breath before continuing, "Back to protein, besides cattle, deer, goat, and others, any variety of wild fish cooked or as sashimi, pork, fowl, fermented soy, whey, and eggs would work just fine."

Professor Ross chimed in with, "David, that's a nice list; but, I think it's missing a very large and often dismissed group from which we humans could potentially derive a considerable amount of nutrition."

The room was silent for a few moments, save for the low, muted, constant hum of the aquarium's pump. The sound assured both humans and leafy sea dragons alike that the water was clean, that the pump was working to circulate the hundreds of gallons of water constantly through the filter.

"Insects," David said, shaking his head in the affirmative, understanding exactly what the professor had in mind.

"Yes, David, insects," replied Professor Ross. Penny and Tia cringed a little, but not Michelle or Kimmy. Donny was amused, as was Dr. Martino. Lance and Sharon were just taking it all in, and both didn't seem to think much of it, having been exposed to many cultures and practices in their work.

Professor Ross continued, "Insects have a much higher food conversion efficiency than do more traditional sources of meat like cattle. It's cheaper to feed, care and prepare them, pound for pound, not to mention their better reproductive output, rate and lifecycle. And it's already a big part of the diet in many other countries."

Kimmy happily added, "I had fried insects in Bangkok when I visited a couple years ago." Everyone smiled.

"Well, I *did* eat a grasshopper taco in San Francisco last summer," Penny admitted.

Her husband smiled as he shook his head in agreement. "Me too," Dr. Martino said.

"Never did try those," Donny said, "but I sure do love San Francisco." Everyone smiled once again.

Slowly, humbly and with a smile, Professor Ross said, "Insects are already eaten in a majority of countries; it seems that to get them readily available here in the states we'd have to overcome people's negative perceptions. I'm optimistic that we *can* change public opinion; but, pessimistic that we *will* anytime soon." They all shook their heads in agreement.

"Thanks Professor Ross," David said, taking the conversational reins back. "Again, for those of us maladapted to carbohydrates, it's protein, including insects," he said smiling and looking around at everyone, "some natural carbohydrates—no processed sugar; but green leafy vegetables are okay—and fat. Now, every fat is part saturated, part mono-unsaturated, and part poly-unsaturated. All saturated means is that every carbon has a hydrogen atom attached to it. And there's nothing wrong with eating it. Of course, it's the trans-fats that you have to watch out for. Fats that are mostly saturated include coconut and palm oils, real cheese, cream, tallow, butter, cocoa butter, and nutmeg butter; fats made of mostly mono-unsaturated fat are macadamia nut oil, olive oil, pecan oil, almond oil, avocado oil, sesame oil, chicken fat, duck fat, goose fat, turkey fat, peanut oil, and lard. Last, mostly poly-unsaturated oils to include in your diet in much smaller amounts include fish oil, especially cod liver oil, flaxseed oil, black currant oil, borage oil, primrose oil, krill oil, and walnut oil. I've been eating a lot of coconut oil lately and feel great."

"So now you're telling us to eat saturated fat?!" exclaimed Donny. "My own doctor would be having a heart attack right about now." Everyone laughed.

Dr. Martino responded, "It's true, there's no evidence to suggest that saturated fat is bad. I tell my patients to avoid it at all costs; but, there is no evidence to support me telling them that. I make those recommendations because I have to."

Donny looked at him as if saying, "that makes no sense to me," but he didn't say a word.

David added, "And all of the studies that concluded coconut and palm oils are bad for you were based on using hydrogenated oils. Natural, unrefined coconut oil is perfectly fine to cook with and eat."

Donny came to terms with this new information, as did everyone else. It was hard not to trust what David was saying; he was sincere, credible, and centered on service to others.

"Would you say that to anyone, David?" Sharon asked. Should all of us follow that diet?"

David was thankful for all the work that Sharon had done behind the scenes to find the man responsible for his downfall and sincerely replied, "Assuming no other issues, remember, if you're maladapted to carbohydrates in some way, obese, diabetic, etcetera, then eating refined carbohydrates should be out of the question. That's all humans, regardless of culture."

"No rice?" asked Kimmy.

"No rice," David calmly responded with a smile.

Sharon laughed briefly and said to everyone, "No rice, no potato chips, no hash browns, no potatoes—my personal favorite—no cereal, no pasta, no bread, no fruit. It sounds like no fun too…" She laughed, causing others to laugh with her.

"But," Sharon continued, "I see that David can do it, and my mom can do it, so I don't see any reason why we all can't at least limit the amount of carbs we eat." Sharon's comment was greeted with agreement.

"I can do that," Lance said, "with an occasional slice of birthday cake."

"Me too," said Kimmy, "but it will be difficult to stop eating rice completely."

"I'm not sure I can stop eating pasta," said Sal, "that's my favorite."

Said Penny to Sal loud enough for everyone to hear, "We can suffer with more filet mignon."

Sal laughed, adding, "Or some New York Strip."

"Sure, why not," Penny answered, also laughing.

Moments later, Professor Ross stated, "I think what David is saying is that if you are currently afflicted with, say, diabetes, obesity, cancer, gout, to name a few, or if you think you might become afflicted in the future—there could be a time lag before specific health consequences—then you probably should be limiting your consumption of non-nutritive carbohydrates. And that fits nicely into the overall scheme of nature. We are the offspring of history, and must establish our own paths in this diverse world, one indifferent to our own suffering, and therefore offering us maximal freedom to thrive, or to fail, in our own chosen way."

Professor Ross paused and then said, "David, your ideas are among the most insightful I've heard in my career, and can't wait to read your first draft. From what I've heard so far, your theory best explains that part of the natural world in which you are concerned and is in line with the ethic that I've tried to live within nearly my entire life. And that ethic, in short, is a belief in humankind, a feeling of solidarity with humankind, and a loyalty toward humankind. We are the result of millions of years of evolution, and our most basic ethical principle should be to do everything toward enhancing our future."

"Amen," Dr. Martino quietly stated.

"That was just amazing," Donny said after a few moments of aquarium pump hum enhanced silence. "Look. There's a small south swell running. It's a perfect two-foot low tide. I've already got the racks on my 4Runner®. I'll load the boards up. We can drive to Tourmaline Street and catch some afternoon glass, stay, catch a bite and watch a beautiful sunset. I'll have each of you riding your first wave in fifteen minutes."

They were all speechless; but, not very surprised.

"I've never tried surfing before, Donny," Sal admitted, "I couldn't possibly get up on a board at this point in my life."

Donny immediately answered, "Nonsense! I've gotten seventy-year-old retired ladies from Iowa up and riding in a few tries, there's no reason you can't do it."

"Surfing, eh?" Professor Ross stated. "It's been a while since I tried that. And by a while I mean like thirty years." He paused for a second. "Sounds like fun. What do you say Tia?"

Tia laughed. "Sure, honey," she said with a smile.

"Maybe we'll see dolphins," Michelle asked.

"Always a possibility, Michelle," Donny answered.

Sensing no further comments, Donny said, "So it's agreed, then. Like I said, I've got all the equipment in my 4Runner®. I'll load the boards up. You can all follow me in your own cars. That way, you can stay as long as you want.

"Let's go," Michelle said to David and Kimmy; both agreed. Lance and Sharon, Sal and Penny, and Professor Ross and Tia made their final decision quickly between themselves in their own way.

As everyone got up to make their way to one of the two spiral staircases, out the door, and into their cars, they each had a different musical work in mind. For Lance Smith, it was surprisingly "One Love," by Bob Marley & the Wailers from their 1977 album *Exodus*.

Sharon Bennett was thinking more along the lines of "Just the Two of Us," a song made famous by Bill Withers.

And the Professor? Oh, he was a softy for the Temptations and was following his wife to "My Girl."

The lovely Tia Ross couldn't get her husband's joke about her being Diana out of her mind ever since they first sat down. She rose and walked to the door along with the real Diana Ross's hit, "Ain't No Mountain High Enough."

Dr. Salvatore Martino, on the other hand, was more a big band and swing aficionado; he heard Billie Holiday, his favorite singer, accompany his walk to the door singing "All of Me."

Penny Martino, in her off-time from playing music, typically didn't even like to listen to music, however, people would be surprised to know that she liked Led Zeppelin. At this particular time, walking toward the door, she heard "Ramble On" playing in her head.

Kimmy and Michelle glanced at each other, telepathy on, and were probably lost in a norebang, with Kimmy, to Michelle's lead, singing along in their heads to "Kissing You," by the Wonder Girls.

Donny White, behind them all turning off the lights, was lost in old school surf music of Dick Dale, his hit "Swingin' and a Surfin'," made popular in 1963 in the movie *Beach Party*.

David heard Kimmy in the distance ask Donny, "Who's that girl?"

"Oh, that's Heather Clark," Donny replied. "She won the African championship something like seven times. And she's a goofy-footer."

David heard Michelle and Kimmy laughing. "Goofy-footer?" Kimmy asked.

"Yeah, goofy-footer," Donny replied in the distance. "Most surfers stand up on their boards with their left foot forward. Heather Clark here and David Nuuhiwa — the surfer in the picture over there getting up on the nose — surf with their right foot forward. It seemed goofy to someone at some point when they saw a guy surfing with his right foot forward; and, well, the name stuck."

"Goofy-footer," Kimmy said laughing as she handed Michelle her car keys. Kimmy and Donny walked past the stairways, down the hallway to the enter the garage. They would be driving to Tourmaline Street together in Donny's 4Runner® with the surfboards on top and gear in the back.

David, the last one left on the main floor, walked over to the tank and glanced once more at the leafy sea dragons. Michelle quietly walked back to David and his — their — five friends in the tank, and then, giggling a little, grabbed his right hand with her left, then also her right, and leaned on him. Together, they both meditated on the five leafy Martians where previously David envisioned them accompanied by Robert Schumann's "*Träumerei*."

Transfixed together once again on dragons, they heard Donny and Kimmy each grab a surfboard from the landing then carry them to Donny's sport-utility vehicle. This time David could have easily chosen something from Beethoven, Mozart, Bach or Rachmaninoff to accompany them. Or Handel,

Albinoni, Haydn, Schubert, Mendelssohn, Chopin, Schumann, Liszt, Verdi, Wagner, Brahms, Saint-Saëns, Tchaikovsky, Grieg, Rimsky-Korsakov, Puccini, Debussy, Ravel, Stravinsky or Gershwin. Perhaps something even older, from the works of Dufay, Palestrina, de Prez, Gesualdo, or Monteverdi.

He didn't decide on any of those or the scores of other composers in his head, double entendre intended. No, nothing would be better to end the brunch and head for the ocean than Queen's "You're My Best Friend." Yes, Queen, he thought.

"Okay, we're done loading truck," Donny said, "Let's go."

Michelle kissed David on the cheek, looked once more at the leafy sea Martians dedicated to their friend Shirley, soon to be donated to Skripps, and said, "Rrret's go."

Michelle leading, they walked hand in hand to the stairway on the left, the one that they had walked up months before only to become separated. Michelle paused before taking a step, turned to look at David who seemed to be thinking the same thing. They smiled at each other, pair-bonded, confident that this time they would make it to their planned destination together, and then walked up that left stairway to the landing and out the door.

The house now devoid of charismatic, bipedal vertebrates, a gorgeous San Diego Bay view and surf memorabilia notwithstanding, the five leafy sea dragons, propelled by their undulating pectoral fins, glided, hovered and slowly weaved in concert throughout their interim liquidness. Although perfectly camouflaged from any potential predator — none are known, though crab, rays and tuna dine on their seahorse relatives — they beckoned wonderment: beautifully mesmerizing, graceful, successful and real.

Cast of Characters

Chun Hei "Michelle" Park: Female protagonist
Sang Hee "Shirley" Lee: Friend of female protagonist
Eu-Ju "Kimmy" Kim: Friend of female protagonist
Peter Falciparum, AKA John London: Male antagonist
J. David Bennett: Male protagonist
Professor Alphonse Laveran Ross: Male protagonist's mentor
Ann Opheles: Female antagonist
Luis & Walter Alvarez: University contractors
Dr. Salvatore Martino: Medical Doctor
Sue Robesen: Diabetes Educator
Brenda Michaels: Nurse
Rolanda Evergreen: Nurse's aid
Sharon Bennett: Detective
Lance Smith: Detective
Donny White: Owner, 1859 Royal Blue Court
Judge Robertson: Magistrate, search warrant application
Mona Spryer: Defense Attorney
Judge Richard Rosenstein: Presiding judge, bail hearing
Judge Jane Whitehall: Presiding judge, preliminary examination
Thomas Rath: District Attorney
Susan Bergman: Assistant District Attorney
Samuel Wojciehowicz: Clerk of the Court, bail hearing
William Pinski: Clerk of the Court, preliminary examination
Tia Ross: Human Resources Manager, UCSD
Penny Martino: First Violinist, San Diego Symphony Orchestra
Dr. Sabeena Chandrasekhar: Cosmologist, Skripps Observatory
Denise & Bob: Local radio station disc jockeys
Linda & Mark: Local television news anchor and reporter
Extras: Students, restaurant/bar staff & patrons, aquarium staff &
patrons, hospital staff, police, courtroom staff & visitors, townspeople

Acknowledgements

Glycosis was constructed entirely on my own—the word and the story—but, many insights and ideas belong to other people. Even the design of that sentence is someone else's and I owe the credit to Matt Ridley. His works, including *The Origin of Virtue: Human Instincts and the Evolution of Cooperation* (1996), the book from which that first sentence is derived, are lucid, lively, accessible and inspirational. This section expresses my gratitude to the numerous people responsible for the words, insights and ideas from which I liberally re-purposed.

First, the antagonist's argument used in his motion to suppress in "A Done Deal II," came from the wonderfully eloquent article "A Step Too Far: Due Process and DNA Collection in California After Proposition 69," written by Robert Berlet in 2007. It is available for review free of charge online.

Also in that chapter, the antagonist abridged the following quote from *An Essay on Trial by Jury* (1852), by Lysander Spooner: "For more than six-hundred years—that is, since the Magna Carta in 1215—there has been no clearer principle of English or American constitutional law than that, in criminal cases, it is not only the right and duty of juries to judge what are the facts, what is the law, and what was the moral intent of the accused; but that it is also their right, and their primary and paramount duty, to judge the justice of the law, and to hold all laws invalid, that are, in their opinion, unjust, oppressive, and all persons guiltless in violating or resisting the execution of such laws."

The quote beginning "As for the Lucies and Robusts, if they prove to be a single lineage..." stated by the male protagonist in his lecture from the chapter "Second Date," comes from Jonathan Kingdon's enlightening book *Lowly Origin: Where, When, and Why Our Ancestors First Stood Up*

(2003). The next paragraph beginning "Is the obvious geographic variation in modern *Homo sapiens* a sign of incipient speciation?" comes from the book *Human Natures: Genes, Cultures, and the Human Prospect* (2000), by Paul R. Ehrlich.

I sourced the paragraph about Conrad Gesner, as Professor Ross described in the chapter "Creation," from Martin J. S. Rudwick, in his book *The Meaning of Fossils: Episodes in the History of Palaeontology* (1976). Too, I wouldn't have known about William Hunter, Georges Cuvier, Professor Richard Owen, and many other historic figures had it not been for the book *When Life Nearly Died: The Greatest Mass Extinction of All Time* (2008), by Michael J. Benton.

Also in the chapter "Creation," the male protagonist exclaims: "I would rather be descended from an ape than from your God, your parents, or you who prostitutes the gifts of culture and eloquence in the service of falsehood." I have to thank Professor Thomas Henry (T. H.) Huxley for this quote. Of course, he probably wouldn't mind the slight had I not credited him; he passed away in 1895.

The story behind how the quote was originally used goes thusly: at a meeting of the British Association at the Oxford University Museum on Saturday, October 30, 1860, Bishop Samuel Wilberforce crossed swords with Professor Huxley. The Bishop had a track record of being against the theory of evolution and knew nothing of the book *Origin of Species*, but was coached by Richard Owen the night before. On this day, he ridiculed Darwin and Huxley savagely, and then probably made-up the line, "I would like to ask Professor Huxley," he said, "as to his belief in being descended from an ape. Is it on his grandfather's side or on his grandmother's that the ape ancestry comes in?" Nothing of the kind had been alleged, of course, but Huxley rose to the bait. "I should feel it no shame to have risen from such an origin," Huxley declared, "but I should feel it a shame to have sprung from one who prostituted the gifts of culture and eloquence to the service of prejudice and falsehood." The effect was tremendous; at least one lady fainted and had to be carried out.

Another memorable quote from that same chapter, that of Professor Ross, comes from the book *The God Delusion* (2008), by Richard Dawkins, and bears repeating: "The God of the Old Testament is arguably the most unpleasant character in all fiction: jealous and proud of it; a petty, unjust, unforgiving control-freak; a vindictive, bloodthirsty ethnic cleanser; a misogynistic, homophobic, racist, infanticidal, genocidal, filicidal, pestilential, megalomaniacal, sadomasochistic, capriciously malevolent bully." What delightful prose.

On another note, it was Dr. Dawkins that prompted such focus on the leafy sea dragon, inspiration that came from reading *The Ancestor's Tale* (2004), his best work, at least in my humble opinion.

Just above that Richard Dawkins quote about God, is one from Sir David Frederick Attenborough. In a December, 2005, interview with Simon Mayo on BBC Radio Five Live, Attenborough stated that he considered himself an agnostic. When asked whether his observation of the natural world has given him faith in a creator, he said he generally responds with some version of this story, making reference to the Loa loa parasitic worm: "My response is that when creationists talk about God creating every individual species as a separate act, they always instance hummingbirds, or orchids, sunflowers and beautiful things. But I tend to think instead of a parasitic worm that is boring through the eye of a boy sitting on the bank of a river in West Africa, a worm that's going to make him blind. And I ask them, 'Are you telling me that the God you believe in, who you also say is an all-merciful God, who cares for each one of us individually, are you saying that God created this worm that can live in no other way than in an innocent child's eyeball? Because that doesn't seem to me to coincide with a God who's full of mercy.'"

That homosexual behavior is realized as sex, courtship, affection, pair bonding, or parenting among same sex animals, along with descriptions of such behavior that our hero briefly discussed in "Creation," comes from the compendious book *Biological Exuberance: Animal Homosexuality and Natural Diversity* (1999), by Bruce Bagemihl, Ph.D.

The pillars of Creationism, namely, that Evolution is a theory in crisis, that Evolution and religion are incompatible, that society should balance Evolution with Creationism in the classroom, and others, came from *Evolution vs. Creationism* (2009), by Eugenie C. Scott.

The lesson that a rattlesnake's rattle is a decoy, dramatized in the chapter "At the Aquarium," comes from the book *Adaptation and Natural Selection* (1966), by George C. Williams. In fact, Professor Williams was the inspiration for the character Professor Alphonse Laveran Ross, which came to me while reading Matt Ridley's *The Red Queen: Sex and the Evolution of Human Nature* (1993). The idea for the character's name, Alphonse Laveran Ross—as well as Peter Falciparum, Ann Opheles, and others—however, is another story.

Professor Ross did, in fact, read from E. O. Wilson's Pulitzer Prize winning book *The Ants* (1990) in "Our Hero Awakens," just need to add that it was co-written with Bert Hölldobler. The discussion pertaining to Lenski's discovery of *E. coli* thriving on citrate comes from *The Greatest Show on Earth: the Evidence for Evolution* (2009), by Richard Dawkins. And the material "Unlike humans who have uncoupled food intake from functional needs, animals that must flap their wings fifty times a second in order to feed have a hard time staying fat, nor do they develop diabetes, at least as we know it," comes from the free online article "Adipose Energy Stores, Physical Work, and the Metabolic Syndrome: Lessons from Hummingbirds," by James L. Hargrove.

The San Diego Police Department demographics in "The Investigation" came from the online article "San Diego's Cold

Cases Turning Hot," by Keegan Kyle, originally posted on *Voice of San Diego,* a nonprofit news organization focused on issues affecting the San Diego region, on August 26, 2010.

The hero's description of *Orrorin tugenensis* in the chapter "The Investigation II," comes from the book *The Last Human: A Guide to Twenty-Two Species of Extinct Humans* (2007), by a host of authors led by Esteban Sarmiento, featuring pictures of reconstructions of skeletons and full models of each of the species remarkably created by G.J. Sawyer, Victor Deak and Blaine Maley.

Professor Ross's speech in the Epilogue comes from two sources. The detailed part comes from Ernst Mayr's *Toward a New Philosophy of Biology: Observations of an Evolutionist* (1998), as does the definition of adaptation a little further on in David's proposed thesis. The single sentence summary of evolution is from *Why Evolution is True* (2009), by Jerry A Coyne.

Right after Professor Ross's discussion of evolution, our hero first talks about cholesterol. That information comes from the researches of Uffe Ravnskov, M.D., Ph.D., and is available free online. His latest books include *Fat and Cholesterol are Good for You* (2009), and *Ignore the Awkward: How the Cholesterol Myths are Kept Alive* (2010).

The paragraph "Human-like atherosclerotic lesions could be induced in pigeons, for instance, fed on corn and corn oil, and atherosclerotic lesions were observed occurring naturally in wild sea lions and seals, in pigs, cats, dogs, sheep, horses, reptiles, and rats, and even in baboons on diets that were almost exclusively vegetarian. None of the studies did much to implicate either animal fat or cholesterol," within the hero's cholesterol speech in the final scene, is from *Good Calories, Bad Calories: Fats, Carbs, and the Controversial Science of Diet and Health* (2008), by Gary Taubes. From the same book is the paragraph later in the chapter that begins: "Without carbohydrates in the diet, the brain and central nervous system will run on ketone bodies..."

James Neel's 1962 paper referred to by the hero, where he proposed the "thrifty genotype" hypothesis, is entitled "Diabetes Mellitus: A 'Thrifty' Genotype Rendered Detrimental by 'Progress'?"

"As if increase of appetite had grown by what it fed on," a line from Shakespeare's *Hamlet*, Act 1, Scene 2, appears in the hero's speech supporting his thesis in the Epilogue. My knowledge of Shakespeare is a little rusty, however, and I have to admit that I obtained the quote from the compendious work *The Variety of Life: A Survey and a Celebration of All the Creatures that Have Ever Lived* (2000), by Colin Tudge.

By the way, I didn't come up with the mnemonic "Campbell's ordinary soup does make Peter pale," stated by a young woman during the hero's lecture in the chapter entitled "Second Date." No, that "traditional and insipid" mnemonic comes from *Wonderful Life: the Burgess Shale and the Nature of History* (1989), by Stephen Jay Gould.

From *Kidnapped* (1886), by Robert Louis Stevenson, came the quote "...and a hundred other hardships, and be standing before you today in this poor accoutrement," that the antagonist said in "A Done Deal." And "One feels certain that somewhere on Earth—even if not anywhere in one's surroundings or within one's reach—a proper, human way of life is possible to human beings, and justice matters," stated by the antagonist in the chapter "A Done Deal II," is a quote from *The New Left: the Anti-Industrial Revolution* (1971), by Ayn Rand.

Also by Ayn Rand, and also stated by the antagonist in that chapter, are the lines "I am a man who loves his life and does not sacrifice my love or my values for anyone or anything," and "I am proud of my own value and of the fact that I wish to live," and "I will not do penance for my virtues or let them be used as the tools of my own destruction." So too are the lines "It wasn't real, was it," "We seem to have heard it." "We couldn't help it," "We don't have to believe it, do we," "It's horrible, "It's immoral," "It's selfish, heartless, ruthless," and

"It's the most vicious speech ever made," although these last few lines were abridged in the story. Quotes are all from *Atlas Shrugged* (1957), one of my favorite books.

The quote "Jane Crofut, from the Crofut Farm…" stated by the narrator in the chapter "Our Heroine," comes from Act I of *Our Town* (1938), by American playwright Thornton Niven Wilder. Yes, all people *are* connected.

It was Glenn Gould that said, "I couldn't imagine a life in which I was not surrounded by music. It shelters you from the world, protects you, and keeps you at a certain distance from the world." I'm not sure when exactly he said that, but the recording of him saying it was used as part of the introduction in the documentary film *Genius Within: the Inner Life of Glenn Gould* (2009), directed by Michèle Hozer and Peter Raymont, and it was said by the hero in the chapter "Our Hero."

The quote "A flea hath smaller fleas that on him prey; and these have smaller fleas to bite 'em, and so proceed *ad infinitum*," stated by the antagonist in "*His* House," is from the 1733 poem "On Poetry: a Rhapsody," by Jonathan Swift.

Credit for the summary and translation of "Nessun Dorma" goes to Mark D. Lew, from his article "Turandot: Commentary on Symbolism, Poetry, and Nessun Dorma," available free of charge online.

And speaking of lyrics, I honestly don't remember the origin of the lyrics of every song in the story, however, one thing is certain: they all came from YouTube.com. I'm grateful that such a bastion of recorded free speech is available on Earth.

From the classic surfing movie *The Endless Summer* (1966), directed by Bruce Brown, came the quotes "The mountains are always there. If you catch a wave, it's yours. No lifts, no motors, just you and the ocean," and, slightly abridged, "With enough time and enough money, you could spend the rest of your life following the summer around the world."

And I wouldn't have known about that movie, or really anything about watermen, had it not been for Mike Dodson.

Mike's experience and knowledge about surfing and San Diego enabled invaluable insight into what the character Donny White would or would not say or do or own, and I couldn't have written the part without his generous help.

Most authors thank their mother for one reason or another; my Mom actually reviewed various drafts of the manuscript, and provided scores of corrections, as well as enhancements to readability and tone. Thank you for everything Mom.

Many thanks to Yanni Kadar, Christine Newton and Eric Zubiller for their advice, to Professor Kyle Graham for steering me in the right direction, and to my friends at the University Café in Palo Alto, California, for their hospitality. Thanks goes as well to many Wikipedians for providing the ideal first stop for reference material. Free, civil, dynamic and neutral, Wikipedia is the best online encyclopedia.

I also have to thank Dr. Louis "Leib" Krut for the following quote used in the Epilogue: "We, all of us, do much of the time, perhaps all of the time, construct our concepts in shifting sands. Even in the best of all possible biological worlds our knowledge must always be incomplete and we often do not even know what it is that's missing. Certainty eludes us and we should be humble rather than assertive."

"Nothing in Biology Makes Sense Except in the Light of Evolution," is a 1973 essay by evolutionary biologist and Russian Orthodox Christian, Theodosius Dobzhansky, criticizing anti-evolution creationism and espousing theistic evolution, first published in *American Biology Teacher*.

Dobzhansky described the diversity of life on Earth, and that the diversity of species cannot be best explained by a creation myth because of the ecological interactions between them. The central issue of the essay was the need to teach biological evolution in the context of debate about creation and evolution in public education in the United States. The fact that evolution occurs explains the interrelatedness of the various facts of biology, and so makes biology make sense.

A couple articles provided the backdrop for the hero's benchmark of our ancestor's diet in the Epilogue. Although changed in the story, the original quote "We have three lines of evidence that have been used to reconstruct the evolution of subsistence over this vast time period. They are the interpretation of morphology by analogy with living primates and other mammals, the material artefactual remains and, more recently, direct chemical analysis of the hominid remains themselves," came from the article "A Brief Review of the Archaeological Evidence for Palaeolithic and Neolithic Subsistence," (2002), by M. P. Richards.

The source for the fact that "seventy-two percent of the total daily energy consumed by all people in the United States is made up of dairy products, cereals, refined sugars, refined vegetable oils, and alcohol, all items that didn't exist until about ten-thousand years ago," is "Implications of Plio-Pleistocene Hominin Diets for Modern Humans," by Loren Cordain, published in the book *Evolution of the Human Diet: the Known, the Unknown, and the Unknowable* (2007), edited by Peter S. Ungar. The word "discordance," the list of health problems and the entire glycemic index discussion are also from that article. And with very slight edits for fit, the quote beginning "Suboptimal circumstances take varying time periods…" was sourced from the article "Evolutionary Health Promotion: A Consideration of Common Counterarguments," published and available free of charge online in 2001, by S. Boyd Eaton, M.D., Loren Cordain, Ph.D., and Staffan Lindeberg M.D., Ph.D.

The lines beginning "If you close your eyes and say the word aloud, it sounds lovely…" that Dr. Martino delivered in the Epilogue, came from the book *A Planet of Viruses* (2011), by Carl Zimmer. And I would be remiss if I didn't mention being influenced by his other book, *Parasite Rex* (2000), as well. It was in that book that I learned about *Sacculina* and many other loathsome creatures that didn't make it into this story.

For those other ghastly creatures "unclouded by conscience, remorse, or delusions of morality" — as Ash explained to Ripley in *Alien* (1979) — that did make it into the story, *Leishmania*, for example, I referred to *Foundations of Parasitology* (2009), a textbook by Gerald D. Schmidt and Larry S. Roberts. Other ghastly creatures, that is, except the viruses. Those I learned most about from *Origin of Group Identity: Viruses, Addiction and Cooperation* (2009), by Luis P. Villarreal. And it was Richard Dawkins that introduced me to the T4 bacteriophage — the lunar-lander of viruses — in *The Greatest Show on Earth* (2009).

I'll end the Acknowledgements as I did the story. The actual lines, abridged in the Epilogue "We are the offspring of history, and must establish our own paths in this most diverse and interesting of conceivable universes — one indifferent to our own suffering, and therefore offering us maximal freedom to thrive, or to fail, in our own chosen way," were written by Stephen Jay Gould in his book *Wonderful Life* (1989).

And it was the ethics of "evolutionary humanism," as Julian Huxley described of evolutionary biologist Ernst Mayr's book *Toward a New Philosophy of Biology: Observations of an Evolutionist* (1998), that Professor Ross abridged: "It is a belief in mankind, a feeling of solidarity with mankind, and a loyalty toward mankind. Man is the result of millions of years of evolution, and our most basic ethical principle should be to do everything toward enhancing the future of mankind. All other ethical norms can be derived from this baseline."

To everyone stated herein, together with ancestors from our hominid line back to some bacteria that engulfed — but did not digest — a mitochondrial ancestor, also a bacteria, back to LUCA, the last common ancestor, and to all the viruses, the environment, and environmental catastrophes that shaped their development, many sincere thanks.

Music

Introduction
Louis Armstrong: What a Wonderful World

Our Heroine
Boston: Party
Kate Perry (Featuring Snoop Dogg): California Gurls [*sic*]
Inna: Amazing
Pitbull (Featuring T-Pain): Hey Baby (Drop It to the Floor)
Beyoncé: Single Ladies (Put a Ring on It)
Mohombi: Bumpy Ride
Flo Rida (Featuring David Guetta): Club Can't Handle Me
B.o.B.: Nothing on You
Juanes: Es Por Ti

Our Hero
Wolfgang Amadeus Mozart: Piano Sonata No. 15 in C Major, K. 545, Mov. I
Maurice Ravel: *Gaspard de la Nuit* (Devil of the Night)
Maurice Ravel: Piano Concerto for the Left Hand in D Major
Frédéric François Chopin: Nocturne in E-Flat Major, Op. 9, No. 2
György Sándor Ligeti: Etudes, Book 2, No. 13, *L'escalier du Diable* (Devil's Staircase)
Frédéric François Chopin: Etude 25, No. 11, "Winter Wind"
Jelly Roll Morton: Finger Buster
Edvard Grieg: Piano Concerto
Sergei Rachmaninoff: Rhapsody on a Theme of Paganini
Frédéric François Chopin: Scherzo No. 2, Op. 31
Johann Sebastian Bach: Toccata and Fugue in D Minor
Frédéric François Chopin: Fantasie-Impromptu, Op. 66
Johann Sebastian Bach: Goldberg Variations, 1-7
Sergei Rachmaninoff: Prelude in C Sharp Minor, Op. 3, No. 2
Pyotr Ilyich Tchaikovsky: Piano Concerto No. 1, in B-flat minor, Op. 23, Mov. III
Franz Liszt: Hungarian Rhapsody No. 2

Frédéric François Chopin: Ballade No. 1 in G Minor, Op. 23

Ludwig van Beethoven: Sonata No. 14 in C-Sharp Minor, Op. 27, No. 2, "Moonlight," Mov. III

At the Aquarium

Ludwig van Beethoven: String Quartet No. 15 in A Minor, Op. 132, Mov. III

Camille Saint-Saëns: *Le Carnaval des Animaux* (The Carnival of the Animals), VII, Aquarium

Ludwig van Beethoven: String Quartet No. 15 in A Minor, Op. 132, Mov. II

Jacques de la Presle: *Le Jardin Mouillé pour la Harpe* (The Wet Garden for Harp)

Ludwig van Beethoven: String Quartet No. 16 in F Major, Op. 135, Mov. III

Tomaso Albinoni (Remo Giazotto): Adagio in G Minor

Ludwig van Beethoven: Piano Sonata No. 1 in F minor, Op. 2, No. 1, Mov. II, Adagio

Ludwig van Beethoven: Piano Sonata No 8 in C Minor, Op 13, "Pathétique," Mov. II

Ludwig van Beethoven: Piano Concerto No. 5 in E-Flat Major, Op. 73, "Emperor," Mov. II, Adagio un Poco Moto–Attacca

Claude Debussy: Claire de Lune

Jules Massenet: *Méditation de Thaïs*

Wolfgang Amadeus Mozart: Violin Concerto No. 4 in D Major, K. 218, Mov. II, Andante cantabile

Wolfgang Amadeus Mozart: Violin Concerto No. 3 in G Major, K. 216, Mov. II, Adagio

Wolfgang Amadeus Mozart: Piano Concerto No. 21 in C Major, K. 467, Mov. II, Andante

Wolfgang Amadeus Mozart: Violin Concerto No. 5 in A Major, K. 219, "Turkish," Mov. II, Adagio

Camille Saint-Saëns: *Le Carnaval des Animaux* (The Carnival of the Animals): XIII *Le Cygne* (The Swan)

Johann Sebastian Bach : Aria from Orchestral Suite No. 3 in D Major, BMV 1068, "Air on the G String"

Delispice: Confession from *The Classic*

Delispice: I am Yours, You are Mine from *The Classic*

Robert Schumann: *Träumerei* (Dreaming)

Karaoke
George Gershwin: Piano Concerto in F
2NE1: I don't Care
Park Bom: You and I
Wonder Girls: So Hot
Wonder Girls: Kissing You
Girls' Generation (SNSD): Genie
Girls' Generation (SNSD): Oh
Girls' Generation (SNSD): Run Devil Run
Whitney Houston: Saving All My Love for You
2NE1: It Hurts
Wonder Girls: Nobody But You
Sir Mix-A-Lot: Baby Got Back
The Commodores: Three Times a Lady

Back to Lek's
Lynyrd Skynyrd: I Know A Little
Lynyrd Skynyrd: Call Me the Breeze
Jewel Kid: Musica
Flo Rida: Low
The Banger Bros.: Supermassive
La Roux: In for the Kill
Nelly: Hot in Herre [*sic*]
Rihanna: Only Girl (in the World)
Israel "IZ" Kamakawiwo'ole: Somewhere Over the Rainbow
Avril Lavigne: Girlfriend
The Violent Femmes: Eep Opp Ork Ah-Ah (Means I Love You)

***His* House**
Wolfgang Amadeus Mozart: Overture to *The Marriage of Figaro*
Wolfgang Amadeus Mozart: Piano Concerto No. 21 in C Major, K. 467,
Mov. II, Andante
No Doubt (Featuring Lady Saw): Underneath It All
Gwen Stefani: Cool
No Doubt: Just a Girl

Let's Call it a Night
Franz Peter Schubert: Ave Maria
Alejandro Fernandez: Ella

Paroxysms and More
Unknown: Missa Orbis Factor
Sergei Rachmaninoff: Vespers, No. 1, O Come and Worship
Léo Delibes: Flower Duet from *Lakmé*

The Investigation II
Giacomo Puccini: Nessun Dorma from *Turandot*

Epilogue
The Beach Boys: Catch a Wave
Bob Marley & The Wailers: One Love/People Get Ready
Bill Withers: Just the Two of Us
The Temptations: My Girl
Diana Ross: Ain't No Mountain High Enough
Billie Holiday: All of Me
Led Zeppelin: Ramble On
Wonder Girls: Kissing You
Dick Dale: Swingin' and a Surfin'
Queen: You're My Best Friend

Made in the USA
Lexington, KY
29 October 2011